THE
GIRLS

Sunny Alexander

Book design by Maureen Cutajar
www.gopublished.com

ISBN: 9780984689958

LCCN: 2012950181

Twenty percent of the author's gross receipts from the sale of the book
The Girls will be donated to organizations supporting marriage
equality.

bashert

destiny
promises
to roam
with
precision
in our
lives

do we
pay
attention
or will we
bypass
the
very
essence
of
our soul's
direction?

Prologue

Tulare, CA
1939

Harry Scott and Ethel Smith met at Forester's Pharmacy and Ice Cream Parlor where Harry worked as a soda jerk, and Ethel worked at getting Harry to fall in love with her.

Ethel freely admitted she always was a sucker for a uniform, and even though Harry's was a white button-down shirt, white pants, black shoes and belt, and a traditional soda jerk hat, it was still a uniform. The fact that Harry had bright blue eyes and a lopsided grin only added to the attraction.

Forester's was the hangout for the teens in Tulare—an agricultural city in Central California. Ethel and her best friend, Marian Glock, saved up their babysitting money and on Fridays after school went to Forester's for a burger in a basket, served with French fries and a Coke, played the jukebox, and tried out the latest jitterbug steps in the back corner of the store.

This particular Friday, Ethel and Marian sat at the soda fountain's oval counter, coquettishly twirling from side to side on the chrome barstools, waiting for their order. Ethel smoothed her plaid skirt, straightened the puffed sleeves of her white cotton blouse, and used a napkin to shine her black penny loafers.

"I hate my ugly Oxfords," said Marian, displaying her brown-laced shoes. "I'm saving up for a pair of saddle shoes—I think beige and white, they're all the rage. And, I've got to do something about this outfit." She swept her hand in distaste across the blue and orange print blouse and beige jumper.

Ethel leaned toward her best friend. "I want a sweater, exactly like Lana Turner wore in *They Won't Forget*. If our fathers knew we sneaked in to see that movie...why, Marian, we'd both get a paddling."

Ethel giggled, and both girls, heads bobbing, spoke their favorite phrase: "What they don't know won't hurt them."

Harry brought them their burgers in a basket, leaned over to gaze into Ethel's periwinkle eyes, and impulsively allowed his hand to touch hers. "Ethel, I have a break in twenty minutes—catch a quick dance?"

"Well, Harry, if you just happen to mosey over to the back of the store you might find me there and if you're lucky..." She batted her eyelashes and smiled until her dimples showed.

"See ya then." Harry winked before he turned to make a milkshake.

Ethel's eyes sparkled. "Isn't he the cutest, Marian? I'm going to marry Harry Scott and live happily ever after."

"He is cute," Marian allowed, "but not nearly as dreamy as Sammy Grant. Sammy kissed me, smack on my lips."

"Marian Glock! Your mother would kill you if she knew."

Marian giggled. "I know! And I told him no more kisses until we're engaged."

Ethel slathered a French fry with ketchup and said, "As soon as we're done eating let's look at the movie magazines and see what new songs are in the jukebox. I can't wait for the school's spring dance."

Marian nodded. "Don't you just love Fridays? No school for two days and we get to spend the afternoon at Forester's."

Ethel put a nickel in the Wurlitzer jukebox, pushed the button for song A12, and watched as the record dropped into place and began to play the King of Swing—Benny Goodman's rollicking rendition of "Roll 'Em."

Ethel held out her hand to Marian and pulled her out onto the floor. "Let's practice the cuddle step. We'll be way ahead of the other girls at the dance." Once they were in the corner, she confided to her friend in an urgent whisper, "Marian, after I marry Harry, I'm going to have fun and dance my whole life!"

The girls joined hands and danced like there was no tomorrow, Ethel taking the lead.

"I believe you, Ethel!" said Marian breathlessly as they twirled, cuddled up, and twirled again.

Ethel smiled because she was seventeen, in love, and knew how to jitterbug.

Marian and Ethel thought about having a double wedding but decided they didn't want to share the spotlight. Marian and Sam got married on October 23, 1940, and Ethel and Harry on December 7, 1940.

Sunday, December 7, 1941

Harry never really understood what love meant until he married Ethel. He wanted their first anniversary to be special in every way. He smiled and thought about how fortunate he was. Ethel was everything he had ever dreamed about; her eyes danced when she looked at him, her body danced when she jitterbugged, and all of her danced when they made love. Life was good, and he knew he was the luckiest man on earth.

Harry woke up at his usual time, five a.m. It was Sunday, Harry's day off from working at Forsythe's Dairy Farm. He didn't mind mucking the stalls and milking the cows. It was worth it because he knew Ethel would be waiting for him when he came home.

Ethel was sleeping with her arms and legs wound tightly around him. He was excited about beginning his anniversary surprise and wanted to disentangle without waking her. He chuckled as she kept grabbing him until finally she rolled over on her side and fell fast asleep.

Harry slid quietly out of bed. He had planned this day for a year.

The *Tulare County Enquirer* was waiting on the back porch steps along with a package of freshly baked blueberry muffins, delivered by his mother, and a quart of milk and a pound of butter, delivered by Forsythe's Dairy Farms.

The owner, Abe Forsythe, was a kindly man in his sixties who lived by the motto, "Cows give milk seven days a week, and by golly, it'll get delivered seven days a week." Everyone in the community knew him and liked him, and they tolerated his aphorisms.

Harry wasn't very good in the kitchen, but he knew how to make coffee and juice, and with his mother's blueberry muffins his surprise should be just about perfect. He took out the silver tray, a wedding gift from his Aunt Bernice and Uncle Gerson, and began to fill the tray with breakfast. A milk-white plate for the muffins and a single red rose went on first. Then, the napkins; he couldn't forget them. The black and white sugar bowl and creamer in the shape of Holstein cows went on next.

He squeezed the oranges on their hand-held juicer and fished out the few seeds that had slipped through the strainer. He inspected the tray and was pleased at what he saw. He took the small box from Larson's Jewelry Store out of his tool chest and placed it on the tray. Inside the box was a gold bracelet with a single heart-shaped charm engraved with *I love you, Harry.* The other side was engraved with the date of their first anniversary: *12/7/1941.*

Harry had bought the bracelet the week after they were married and put it on layaway, seventy-five cents a week, and it was his in time for this momentous date.

Before pouring their coffee he opened the newspaper, clucking at the headline:

TENSIONS WITH GERMANY AND JAPAN
SPIRALING OUT OF CONTROL

He decided not to put the newspaper on the tray; Ethel would only worry. All the fellas knew war was coming, and he and Sam had talked about signing up with the Marines.

As he poured the coffee, a sobering thought chilled him: *What if this is the only anniversary we have?*

Ethel cried when she opened her gift, cooing, "I'm so lucky to have you, Harry." Their lovemaking was completely unrestrained and unusually passionate, as if somewhere deep inside they knew what their future would hold.

They stayed in bed, lost in pillow talk, until the phone's strident blaring broke the romantic mood.

"Let it ring, Harry," Ethel pleaded, stroking his chest.

He kissed her briefly. "I'll be right back," he said, throwing on his boxers.

Ethel could hear Harry's tense, angry words followed by the slamming of the phone into its cradle. She got out of bed, put on her new pink and white chenille bathrobe, and slid her feet into her pink scuff slippers.

Harry was in the living room, fiddling with the dial of their Philco radio-phonograph console, a wedding gift from his parents. He looked at Ethel, his face ashen. "Japan attacked Pearl Harbor. It means war, Ethel."

On December 8, Harry Scott and Sam Grant rose at five a.m., but instead of beginning their workday at Forsythe's Dairy, they joined the queue at the Tulare County Marine Recruitment Office. They took their place at the end of the line that snaked around the block, smiling and waving at familiar faces: high school friends, neighbors, and workers from the dairy farm. It seemed that half the town was there to help win the war one way or another. Those who were not there to join up were handing out enlistment forms or serving donuts and coffee. It was an excited group eager to get into the fight, certain it would be over in a matter of months.

"I told you we should have gotten in line last night," Sam groused. "Now, we're going to be here all day."

Harry shrugged his shoulders. "I didn't want to leave Ethel—she's really upset. She wants me to take the agricultural deferment."

"Yeah, Marian, too. You know, Harry, you have to show these girls who is boss."

Harry broke out in his lopsided smile. "With a girl like Ethel—Sam, she's a spitfire." He shook his head. "Nah, I wouldn't think of bossing her around. She's everything I could have hoped for, and then some." He grinned, remembering their frantic lovemaking before he left the house this morning.

Sam clapped his friend warmly on the back. "Well, I guess to each his own, but Marian knows who wears the pants in this family."

Ethel had dinner waiting for Harry when he came home. She had made one of his favorites: breaded pork chops, mashed potatoes, and peas. She didn't greet him as she usually did, she didn't smile and she didn't dance.

"I know you have to do what's right. It doesn't mean I have to like it." She began to cry. "Danny wants to enlist, too."

Harry held Ethel in his arms. "Your brother can't join, he's only sixteen. By the time he's old enough to enlist, the war will be over. I'll make sure of it."

Ethel looked up at him. Through her tears she saw his adorable crooked grin, the shock of reddish-blond hair, the broad shoulders.

She saw the face and figure of the man she loved; her lover, her protector, her friend. She knew his braggadocio was just for her benefit, but she wanted—she *needed*—to believe it.

"Ethel, I have to report to Camp Pendleton in San Diego on December 27. I want these next few weeks to be the best days of our lives."

She leaned against him, nodding between sobs.

The once sleepy train station teemed with families saying goodbye. A sense of excitement mingled with fear hovered over all; men certain of their call to duty stood tall, and women, also with a sense of duty, would not allow their tears to flow.

Harry held Ethel tightly, and kissed her longingly. "I'll remember the way you dance, Ethel," he whispered, "in every way."

Ethel blushed. "Come back to me, Harry. I'll be here, waiting. I'll write to you every day, every day, and I'll think of you every minute."

Sam and Harry boarded the train that would take them to Camp Pendleton, committed to winning the war. Certain of a quick and decisive victory, they waved and called out from the train, "Don't worry, we'll be home in six months."

Their prophesy of a six-month victory turned into a four-year separation.

Ethel and Marian went to work at the Forsythe's Dairy, milking the cows and mucking the stalls.

Abe Forsythe said, "Women have been working hard on farms since the beginning of time. Cows give milk every day, and by golly, they need to be milked every day."

Harry wrote when he could—brief letters to let Ethel know he was okay and that he loved her. Letters that would not tell her where he was, but small spatters of mud—which Ethel, in her mind, perceived as flecks of blood—on the paper told her more than she wanted to know.

Ethel never forgot her promise to write to Harry every day and to think of him every minute.

Harry and Sam fought in the Solomon Islands, where the heat and humidity ate away at their letters and their hearts, and the combat shattered their souls.

When the end of the war was announced, Harry and Sam patted each other on the back and hugged, but they never cried, not even when nightmares stole their sleep or the memories of what they had seen and done haunted them at unexpected moments.

They returned to the States on the aircraft carrier USS *Saratoga*. They had time to sit in the sun, play cards, and think about where life would take them. They knew they wanted a change from the small town of Tulare and thought about Los Angeles, a growing metropolis filled with opportunities. They were lounging on deck listening to the music blaring over the loudspeaker system when Bing Crosby's rendition of "San Fernando Valley" began.

They looked at each other, smiled and nodded when they heard the lyrics, *never more to roam*. Sam turned to Harry and said in a voice brimful of youthful idealism, "I hear it's a booming area with great opportunities for a coupla up-and-comers like you and me. Plus, it's a hop, skip, and a jump to Los Angeles. Let's make the San Fernando Valley our home."

Harry laughed. "Well, hell, why not? As soon as we're discharged we'll send for our brides."

Four long years of unspeakable bloodshed and carnage behind them, they tried to leave their dark memories of the ravages of war behind on the *Saratoga*. They would never speak of their experiences during the war, not between themselves or to their wives.

∞

The San Fernando Valley, a verdant paradise known for its farms and orchards, gradually changed as returning veterans clamored for inexpensive housing.

Five-gallon magnolia trees lined the wide streets leading to the Sunrise Homestead Estates in Van Nuys, a district within the Valley. Stucco houses on flat, cramped lots, 80 by 120 feet, lined up as neatly as troops during review. Each house had a living room, three 10 by 10 bedrooms, one bathroom with a separate tub and shower tiled in black and green, and a large kitchen with an eating area. One thousand square feet of dreams and hopes for the future: more than most of the returning vets ever thought possible.

The exteriors were all the same—little white boxes with three steps leading to a small covered front porch, asphalt-shingled roofs in dark gray, and trim painted in their choice of colors: red, green, gray, or white. After years of being pressed like sardines into drab barracks with a dozen other khaki-clad dogfaces or fighting in jungles and mud-filled foxholes, any choice at all felt like a miracle.

Harry and Sam lived two blocks from each other, working the same shift at the nearby General Motors auto plant, building Chevrolets. They had fought for freedom, returned as heroes, and now reaped the rewards of safe neighborhoods, good schools, and a guaranteed retirement package.

It was only natural for Sam and Harry's wives, Marian and Ethel, to remain the best of friends. They played mahjong every Thursday, exchanged recipes, had Tupperware parties, and attended the Evangelical Church of Faith and Light every Sunday, where Pastor Jeremiah Lockner regularly delivered his sermons on obedience to the Bible.

Marian and Ethel never talked about the dark changes that had crept in, like a ghost in the night: changes in their husbands and in themselves. Marian would sometimes have a strange-looking bruise on her arm; she said she was clumsy and fell a lot. Ethel's younger brother, Danny, barely nineteen, had died on D-Day—June 6, 1944—on a beach somewhere in Normandy, France. The spark that had once filled fun-loving Ethel was blown out and replaced with bitterness. No one talked about their losses; instead they focused on their homes and families and buried their pain as deeply as the bodies lying in faraway graves. The men went to work Monday through Friday, and mowed the lawns on Saturday. The women sewed kitchen curtains and made the newest Betty Crocker casserole recipes. Life moved on.

Marian and Ethel watched as their bellies grew in size, gave each other baby showers, and beamed when Marian had a boy, and Ethel, a girl.

Mitchell Samuel Grant and Emily Elizabeth Scott were born three days apart.

Ethel never spoke about her disappointment at having a girl. She had secretly wished for a boy—a boy like her brother Danny, with blond hair and deep blue eyes that sparkled. She held Emily in her arms and for a moment remembered that day at Forester's Pharmacy and Ice Cream Parlor when she was so sure of what lay ahead and told Marian: *After I marry Harry, I'm going to have fun and dance my whole life.*

The foolish sentiments of a stupid child, she now thought. Life is not about fun and dancing; it's about pain and disappointment.

Ethel looked at Emily with her dark tight curls and brown eyes. *She doesn't look anything like Harry or me. Is she really ours?*

Chapter 1

Thursday, October 1, 2020
Studio City, CA

The Girls—Em, Les, Max, Frankie, and Bobbie—gathered in the den at One Peppertree Lane, Studio City, their eyes riveted on the fifty-four inch OLED screen hanging on the wall.

The Girls, friends for more than forty years, and Maggie, Em's daughter, waited impatiently for the United States Senate session to begin.

Max relaxed back into the couch, studying the ginormous touch screen. "I think the set needs to be calibrated for color temperature and saturation. These organic light-emitting diode TVs are great, but they can be finicky. See how the red looks too orangey?"

Frankie ran her hand through her close-cropped, salt and pepper hair. "Orangey? For Christ's sake, Max, don't mess with the TV *now.*"

"Relax, Frankie. It's just a tweak." Max used the remote control to adjust the color. "Looks better, huh?"

Les said, "Max is buying a fully autonomous pod." Les and Max exchanged looks, their eyes glistening.

Max grinned, enamored as always by Les and anything high-tech. She brushed her gray bangs away from her eyes. "Yep, driving is a thing of the past. You program your destination, sit back and relax or," she continued after locking eyes with Les, "we can always neck."

"Jesus, you two. Get over yourselves," said Bobbie as she rolled her eyes.

Max ignored Bobbie's comment and continued examining the touch remote. "Hey, Em...did you know your remote is also an iPhone?"

Em spoke crisply. "The less I know, the happier I am. You know if it was up to me..."

Maggie sat on the arm of Em's chair, leaned over and kissed the top of her mother's head. "Mom's tubes finally blew. The TV was a birthday surprise."

Em bantered playfully. "Just don't mention which one, dear."

"Birthday or tubes, Mom?"

Em gently squeezed Maggie's hand. "Either."

The Girls, as if they were one unit, beamed at Maggie.

"*Shhh!*" Frankie shushed them. "They're getting ready to vote. This is it, girls."

Les sat next to Max, sinking into the couch's soft cushions, their hands intertwined. They gazed at each other, years of an uncertain future hidden beneath a veneer of calm. Les, still as tall and slender as when she was young, rested against Max, her long blond hair cascading across Max's shoulder. She whispered, "Darling, I wanted to marry you the first day we met. Let's hope we get our chance."

"I love you, Les—no matter what," Max said huskily. "No one can take that away from us."

The cameras focused on the Senate floor as the bill to legalize same-gender marriages was presented for the final vote. It was a watershed moment in history, and the world was watching. The votes would be tallied by roll call and tabulated one by one on a large computer screen. As the Senate clerk called their names, each senator walked to the rostrum to cast their vote by saying, "yea" or "nay." As each vote was cast, the Girls groaned or cried out excitedly.

Only one more "yea" was needed. The TV cameras turned toward California's Senator Iris Bentonfield, the author of the bill, as she was given the honor of casting the final vote. Iris stood up, squaring her shoulders and holding her head high, before striding purposefully to the rostrum. She stood waiting until a hush fell over the Senate. She held up her right hand and gave a thumbs up, while leaning into the microphone and saying the one word that would change history: "Yea!"

Iris remained standing, unflinching, as the Senate chambers boomed with loud applause, followed by boos from opposing senators, their faces twisted in rage and disbelief. She looked directly at the camera, smiled, and raised one eyebrow, a signal to the rest of the Girls that she had done her job.

Frankie quipped, "It's amazing she can lift that brow at all."

"That girl has been plasticized from bumper to bumper," Bobbie joined in. "But damn, she looks good!"

As if to illustrate, Iris grinned and turned full-face to the camera.

"This is a watershed moment in civil rights history for the United States and a model for the rest of the world," intoned the CNN commentator. "The Freedom to Marry Act has passed and will now be sent to President Julia Moorhead to be signed into law. This is Richard Moby reporting from Washington, DC."

The Girls hugged. They kissed. They cried. They shouted: *"Way to go, Iris."*

Maggie opened the bottle of 1996 Dom Pérignon, smiling as the cork popped, and poured the champagne into waiting crystal glasses. The Girls held the fluted stemware and turned to face the painting hanging on the den wall.

An ornate frame in gold leaf complemented the portrait of a woman sitting in a cafe, her head covered by a mauve floppy hat with a bright pink rose on one side, a fox stole with two heads and tails draped around her shoulders, hands placed under her chin, fingers bedecked with garish rings, while a whimsical expression filled with mystery and secrets played across her face.

They raised their glasses toward the painting and toasted the only Girl who had died: "To Char."

Em said, a catch in her voice, "If only she were here."

Maggie put her arms around her mother. "I know how much you miss her."

Les cleared her throat and wiped a tear from her eyes. "Em, you've kept things going exactly the way Char would have wanted—continuing to have the gatherings of the Girls here at One Peppertree Lane—even keeping her office the way she left it." A chuckle replaced Les's tears. "God, remember the way she would redecorate her office?"

Max bobbed her head in agreement. "She'd go to a seminar, and bam—she'd adopt a new psychological theory, which meant another change to the office."

"Char was one of a kind, wasn't she?" said Em in a faraway voice.

Bobbie leaned on her burl wood cane, gazing at the portrait. "Hey, you guys, remember that day? Char's fiftieth."

"Who could forget?" Frankie put in. "Char was the first one to hit the big five-oh. Putting that outfit together for her sitting and then cancelling her party the next day to do one of our rescues. 1986...we were in our forties. God, were *we* hot. Did you ever think life would betray us like this?" She held out her hands to show small red blotches on crinkled, paper-thin skin.

Bobbie tapped Frankie playfully with her cane. "Oh, fuck it. We still have *it*. Only *it* is inside, not outside."

"Come on, Bobbie, admit you're pissed off at getting old," said Frankie.

Bobbie moved closer. "Sweetheart, as long as we can ride our Harleys and tussle in the sheets, I'm not going to complain."

Em picked up the remote and turned off the sound. "I do know how to turn off the sound," she added defensively. "We're already half-deaf. Why kill off the other half?"

Captions now bannered across the screen. The TV cameras began to dart around the country. Cities, small towns, rural areas: a montage of elation as inaudible music played and happy, same-gendered couples danced.

A tornado of swirling rage showed in the background. Signs supported by sharpened stakes, held up high, depicted hell. Red and yellow flames contrasted against the poster board's plain white background, while figures, drawn with mouths agape, bodies contorted in pain, walked into the flames. One by one, the signs were ripped off from their support posts, leaving the pointed stakes to be used as taunting, threatening weapons. Out of control mobs overwhelmed the police and began to turn over cars and start fires.

"There goes a 2012 Lexus GS 350," sighed Max. "Crap, that was one great automobile." If nothing else, Max, the mechanic, knew her cars.

Les beamed, her eyes glistening at the sound of Max's voice. Les and Max looked at each other, exchanging a longing gaze that said: *I can't wait to get you home and into bed.*

The cameras moved to Times Square in New York. The reporter's face betrayed his excitement, news was breaking, ratings were climbing. The captions flashed across the screen, unemotional letters replacing the intensity of the announcer's voice:

This is something we haven't seen for fifteen years. A bus with the American flag painted on the side is pulling up behind the police barriers. The windows are blackened to shield the occupants from view. The door is opening...there they are ...the Defenders of Family Values. Folks, they are making their presence known after years of working underground to thwart the legalization of gay marriage.

The bus doors opened, allowing the cameras to focus on figures wearing the Defenders uniform: a white T-shirt with black Lego-style figures of a man and a woman pushing a baby carriage, underneath were scripted letters stating their slogan: *A Straight Way is God's Way.* Baseball caps sat firmly on their heads, with an American Flag on the background with *Save Our Families* written underneath. They stepped out precisely fifteen seconds apart to form an orderly line. No signs of protest...no sounds of disagreement...their outfits said it all.

The captions read:

The Defenders of Family Values are making their first appearance in over fifteen years. They're lining up, facing the police barriers with arms crossed over their chests. They're not moving; they're not making any attempt at confrontation.

The Girls, now in their seventies and early eighties, were frozen in horror and struck into silence, but their eyes were bright and on fire; they knew their mission was not over.

A persistent ring from the rewired 1959 Princess phone, resplendent in pink, interrupted the quiet that had fallen over the room. Em thought, *Hooey to technology.* It was Char's phone, and no matter what anyone else said, it was staying.

"Christ, Em. Shut off that damn phone, it's been jangling all day," said Bobbie, waving her cell phone that could bend without breaking. You need to join the *real* world and get one of these." Bobbie sat down on one of the dusty brown corduroy chairs and rubbed her knees. Les, ever the physician and caregiver, lifted Bobbie's feet onto the matching ottoman.

Bobbie flashed a smile of thanks toward Les. "You know it's just another damn reporter wanting to talk to *you,* Em."

Em—Emily Elizabeth Scott—was the author of *The Girls*, a series of seven books, set in the 1970s and '80s, about a group of women vigilantes. When society failed to protect the abused, the Girls stepped in.

The phone transferred to voice mail and began to ring again. Maggie rolled her eyes. "Last one, Mom. Enough is enough. I'm erasing the messages and turning off the ringer. We're done."

She strode purposefully through the office door toward the kitchen. The Girls could hear a murmured conversation that seemed to be going on too long. Maggie, looking contrite, peeked her head around the swinging door. "Mommy, a woman from the *Times* is asking for an interview."

"Again? You know my policy—no interviews. Weren't you turning the ringer off?"

Maggie looked at her mother, her dark brown eyes widening until she looked like a little girl of seven. "This one sounds different, Mommy."

The Girls tittered; they had seen this scenario enacted many times before. When Maggie called Em "Mommy," she was going to get her way.

"She sounds desperate and it's her fifth call," Maggie insisted. "The *Times* wants to publish a special magazine edition about *The Girls*. Mommy, it's a feature story. I really think you should do it."

Em stood firm. "I don't do interviews. It'll ruin my image as the reclusive lesbian writer."

Max stopped adjusting the TV set and looked at Em. "That's the first time you've declared."

"Oh, Max, as if you all didn't know everything about me. *Including* my abhorrence of new technology." Em turned toward Maggie. "Darling, you're probably getting suckered by a sociopath, but tell her we'll get back to her."

The Girls exchanged looks and chuckled in a loving way. None of them could deny Maggie. She was their shared daughter.

Maggie sat on the arm of her mother's chair. "I have to go, Mommy. Charlene gets out of school"—she glanced at her watch—"in fifteen minutes, and I have to get back to the clinic."

Em said, "Do you want Charlene to stay with us? We haven't seen our granddaughter for—"

"Two days? Not today, Mom. She's going to help in the office. This afternoon is the clinic's turn for low-fee vaccinations, and I suspect we'll be mobbed."

"Another vet in the family?" Em asked proudly.

"Maybe, but right now she's fourteen and way too boy crazy to be thinking of a career. Now, girls, don't be disappointed that it's boys she likes."

Maggie smiled as she planted another kiss on Em's head, and made the rounds hugging and kissing each girl goodbye.

"Well, we can hope, can't we?" Bobbie said, hugging Maggie tightly.

Em glanced around the room. Time had not passed the Girls over, but there was a fierceness that showed in their eyes that said, *Don't fuck with the Girls*. Only one was gone...only one.

Em held the phone message left by Maggie.

Treat Mason
(784) 555-7864
Please call.

"What do you think?" she asked.

"This might be our last hurrah," Les offered. "Em, you're the one who should tell our story. It was because of you that we became the Girls. And I think right now, our cause could use a boost." She glanced back at the TV. "Maybe we can still do some good."

"There wouldn't be a story if it weren't for all of you, and Char. Perhaps, after all these years, it's time. Although I'm not sure anyone will believe us. If we go forward it's no holds barred. Are you willing to give me carte blanche?"

The Girls glanced at each other and nodded.

Les said, "I'll call Iris today. If she agrees it's unanimous."

A slight tremor showed in Em's hands as she looked at the message. "Her name is Treat...Treat Mason. Hmm, unusual..."

Max said, "With a name like that, it shouldn't be too hard to check her out." She stood, motioning to Les. "Let's go, honey—this engine is fired up and ready for action."

Em moved smoothly from room to room, welcoming the mundane chores that greeted her. She rinsed the dirty coffee cups and dishes and started the dishwasher. She returned to the den, once Char's home office, fluffed the pillows on the couch, and looked briefly at the room, satisfied that everything was in its proper place. She stood for a moment gazing at the painting of Char, took a deep breath through her nose and let it out through her mouth, exactly the way she had been taught in her grief group more than twenty years ago.

It was Char's mysterious smile that continued to grab at Em's heart. The smile filled with secrets—funny secrets meant to surprise, sad secrets about a past hurt, unresolved secrets known only after her death.

Always a secret, always a secret, she thought as unexpected tears welled up. She stifled a sob and wondered *does it ever go away?* Now, years later, Em followed her nightly ritual. She kissed her finger and touched the portrait, gathering strength from the woman who gave her friendship when she was friendless, hope when she felt hopeless, and love when she thought love didn't exist.

Chapter 2

It was past midnight before Em opened her half-closed bedroom door. She felt the small aches that reminded her that she really was seventy-four. She stripped the queen-size bed and shook out the new linens, watching as they billowed before falling gently onto the bed. She grunted as she lifted the mattress and tucked in the cream-colored linens, made of Egyptian cotton, 1500 thread, exactly the way her mother had taught her more than sixty-five years ago. She was usually not that extravagant—in fact, tended to be frugal— but this night she needed to feel something sweet and special against her body.

Em decided to sleep naked. After all, no one was here to see her. *Christ, I'm seventy-four, and if I croak during the night, who the hell would care what I looked like?* She showered, letting her hair dry into natural, frizzy curls. She had always yearned for long, straight black hair, like Maggie's, instead of the mousy brown—now mixed equally with gray stiff strands— that seemed to be a mass of cowlicks looking for a home. She could hear her mother's voice echoing from deep within, "Don't complain about your hair. Other women your age don't have any."

Char had been the first to love the way her curls mingled and separated, each finally going in its own direction. But then, Char loved everything about her.

She slid under the covers and sighed at the feeling of soft cotton against her body and thought, *Sheets like these should be shared with someone.* Then, *A person's life story could be told through the sheets they've slept on, made love on, had babies on and died on.*

She remembered going with her mother to FEDCO, one of the first big box discount stores in California. Her mother was looking for the cheapest linens she could find. *How old was she? Four, almost five? It's strange,* she thought, *how certain experiences become the most resilient of memories, sometimes slipping away for years, only to return, uninvited.*

"Emily, stay close to me and pay attention," her mother admonished. Emily couldn't help but daydream, there were so many beautiful things to look at, to touch. She felt the velvety texture of a deep red party dress trimmed in white lace, started to pick up a package of day-of-the-week panties, when she was sharply pulled out of her reverie by a familiar tug on her hair.

"Put down the panties and hold my hand," her mother said, as roughly as the cheap sheets that chafed her four-year-old back and made her wiggle at night.

FEDCO was torn down many years ago, just like the General Motors auto plant where her father had worked building Chevrolets. They'd been replaced by shopping centers that had since been demolished and rebuilt with larger and more up-to-date complexes. *It's what we do in this country: build, tear down, rebuild. The only thing that lasts is our memories.*

Sleep was hard to come by this night. She kept thinking of sheets: coarse sheets, sheets that hung on the clothesline in the backyard of her parents' house, running through them as they fluttered in the late morning breeze. Burying her face, she breathed deeply, wanting to take in and hold onto the fresh air smell. The fragrance of the sheets after she and Char made love for the first time, their scents mingling and burrowing into the fabric. The day Char died, fresh linens put on the bed. Em had cried that night; where was she, where was Char? Her imprint removed from the bed, so easily erased through newly laundered sheets.

Her mother had bought her a Snow White bed set to match the theme of her fifth birthday party. *That was a loving thing for her to do,* she thought. There were so few tender things to remember. She tried to count them, but never got past the fingers on her left hand.

Em sighed, a long sigh intended to clear away the day's residue. Thoughts and memories came randomly, as if life really didn't have any continuity; not a smooth flow, as she would expect, but a sea of memories pounding against an ever-changing shore.

Emily Elizabeth Scott would start kindergarten in September and Mommy had begun to sew her school dresses, one for every day of the school week and a special dress for church on Sunday. On Saturdays, she could wear play clothes, but Mommy wasn't happy when she got dirty. "Little girls should play like little girls with their dollies, not like dirty little boys. Stop climbing trees, Emily, or you'll get a spank."

Emily knew what that meant. A single spank with the paddle Mommy and Daddy had named Mr. Smarty. Why couldn't girls climb trees the same as boys?

Emily tried to understand the difference between boys and girls. Well, boys had short hair, she knew that, but then she saw a couple of girls at FEDCO with short hair. Mommy said they were on the swim team and couldn't wear their hair long. There must be other differences. Daddy had a mustache, but so did their next-door neighbor, Mrs. Thompson. Mommy had breasts—she wasn't supposed to say the word—but so did Mr. Thompson. Were Mr. and Mrs. Thompson part boy and part girl?

Sunday was her favorite day of the week. Her Sunday school teacher, Mrs. Stone, would have the children sit on the carpeted floor in a circle. She would tell exciting stories about how God made the world in six days and took a nap on Sunday, and stories about how Jesus had died on the cross for them. Emily felt sad; she would never want anyone to die because of her.

They had pictures of Jesus to color, a different one every week. She liked the first one best, Baby Jesus in the manger. The next week was Jesus as a little boy taking care of the lambs. Last week was Jesus, as a grown-up, sitting on a rock having story time, just like at the library, she thought. Emily didn't especially like that picture, because she already knew how the story of Jesus would end.

Emily had trouble staying inside the lines and thought if she colored everything in yellow, no one would know. Mommy took away her yellow crayon and told her to stop being a baby and use all the colors. She cried; if she didn't have yellow, how could she color the sun?

Four little girls from her Sunday school class were invited to her birthday party: Mary, Marsha, Lisa, and Jacqueline. After she said her prayers at night—"Matthew, Mark, Luke, and John, bless this bed that I lay on"—she would silently say a secret prayer: "Mary, Marsha, Lisa, and Jacqueline, P.L.E.A.S.E. come to my party."

If Mommy had caught her praying for something for herself, she would have called her "sinful child" and pulled her hair or pinched her hard under her arm for being a bad girl, or even worse, have Daddy give her a spank with Mr. Smarty. She tried to understand all the rules, but if Mrs. Stone said, "God is a God of love," why wouldn't He want her to ask for something that would make her happy?

She wondered where the four little girls were now. She hadn't seen them since twelfth grade. Were they still alive? Were they crippled with arthritis or worse...living with a child who didn't want them?

Mommy ironed her birthday dress and gave her a bath before her party. Mommy washed her hair and Emily felt the warm water slosh over her legs and around her privates. She did something very, very naughty; she made pee-pee in the bathtub. She couldn't help it and once it started, it felt so good she didn't want to stop.

Mommy yanked her hair. "Emily Elizabeth Scott, God made toilets for little girls to use, not to be a baby and go potty in the tub!" Emily hung her head and cried, but her tears soon stopped because suddenly, it all made sense. *If God made potties then Heaven must be filled with pee-pee and poo-poo. So, that's where it goes.*

She said proudly to Mommy, "Heaven is filled with pee-pee and poo-poo."

Mommy got mad, oh so mad. She pulled Emily's hair and pinched her hard under her arm. "No, *Em-i-lee.* Poo-poo and pee-pee are in hell, and that's where you're headed."

At the mention of hell, Emily turned toward her mother with eyes wide as saucers.

Mommy held onto her hair; her voice was tight and mean. "Tell God you're sorry."

Emily put her head down and cried, "I'm sorry, God," just before the shampoo rolled down her forehead and leaked into her eyes.

They went to see *Snow White and the Seven Dwarfs* at the Rialto downtown, sitting in the balcony's plush seats with a perfect view of the screen, framed by a beautiful vermilion curtain whose folds undulated regally down to the stage. Her eyes still stung from the shampoo and she had to blink a lot. The witch scared her, but she liked it when the prince kissed Snow White.

Mommy baked Emily's favorite cake, chocolate on chocolate, and topped it with six pink candles. Emily closed her eyes, made a wish, took a giant breath and blew out the candles. Everyone sang "Happy Birthday" and Emily knew her wish had to come true.

She *loved* her presents. Marsha gave her a Tiny Tears doll that came with her very own baby bottle and a pipe that blew bubbles. She got a Snow White pop-up book, new coloring books with crayons—even yellow—and Monday through Sunday panties.

That night she lay in bed holding Tiny close and shivering, even though it was August and the Valley heat seeped through the stucco walls and entered the open windows.

The desert breeze from the east moved the branches of the avocado tree against the house, creating a soft scratching sound of claw-like hands creeping up the stucco wall toward the open window. She lay in bed with her blanket around her neck as if it were the coldest night in January and clutched Tiny Tears next to her heart. "Don't be scared," she whispered to Tiny. "We won't eat any apples." She whimpered because she was sure the witch was about to sneak into her room and get her. She gave Tiny a bottle, pressed her tummy and watched as Tiny's tears rolled down her cheeks.

She wanted to go into Mommy and Daddy's bed, but Mommy would be mad. Maybe, Mommy would turn over and make a small space, but she wouldn't hold Emily and make her feel all better. She didn't think Daddy would care; he was mostly quiet, and didn't smile much or get mad, but Mommy could get M.A.D! If Mommy got mad then Daddy would take out Mr. Smarty and Emily would get a spank. She didn't like Mr. Smarty or the spank. One on her butt, then she would say, "I'm sorry," and Daddy would say he forgave her. But, she always felt so bad after the spank. She tried to understand how a spank on her butt could move to her heart.

She held onto Tiny Tears; she was her absolutely favorite doll, even if she was more hard than soft. Emily thought about when the prince had kissed Snow White gently on her lips and woke her from her spell. She wondered who would kiss her and take her to a faraway castle to live happily ever after. It had to be true because she wished it, and when she opened her gift from Mommy and Daddy, there was a Snow White bed set and Mommy whispered, "Someday your prince will come..."

Chapter 3

Emily wore her only Sunday dress—a bright yellow floral print, with fluttery sleeves and a matching belt. She held out her feet, admiring her brand new, glossy black patent leather shoes, turning them one way then the other, trying to catch the light that peeked through the living room curtains.

Mommy sat next to Emily on the gold and brown tweed couch, a book nestled in her lap. Her legs were drawn as tightly together as a nun's, as was her custom, and her mouth was set in a prim line.

"Emily, you are ten years old and becoming a young lady." Mommy cleared her throat. "Now, girls' bodies begin to change when they are about to become a woman. Soon, you will"— Mommy blushed—"blossom."

Emily's eyes goggled. *At last, Mommy was about to reveal the secret of becoming a woman*, Emily thought, *just in time.*

Last week during lunch, Jacqueline and Mary told Emily about sexual intercourse. "And, that's how babies are made," Mary had concluded with a very smug look on her face after describing a process that sounded to Emily utterly ludicrous—and repulsive.

Emily's mouth dropped opened and she yelled, "Liars, liars!"

They had laughed at her and called her, "Baby, baby, baby," until she cried and ran into the bathroom to throw up.

"Now this book," Mommy said, handing Emily *God's Plan for Young Ladies,* "was recommended by Pastor Lockner. It will explain how your body will change in the next few years. There is something called menstruation, which is God's gift to women because it means we can become wives and mothers."

Emily felt her mouth creeping open as her mother added sternly, "It's time, Emily, for you to put aside some of your childish habits. Playing in the street with the boys, climbing trees, always wanting to wear jeans—those are masculine activities, unsuitable for the fairer, *ahem,* sex. Today, we will have a ladies' day out and you'll see how wonderful it is to become a woman."

Emily held the book in her hand. "Thank you, Mommy."

Emily couldn't wait to read *God's Plan for Young Ladies.* The secrets of life were about to be revealed, and on Monday she could tell Jacqueline and Mary that they were both wrong and she had the evidence to prove it.

Mommy said, "Pastor Lockner wants all the girls your age to read this book before Sunday. Mrs. Lockner is going to have a special class to talk about the meaning of the book. She will answer any questions you have."

Emily could hardly wait for Sunday. Her very first question would be, "What is sexual intercourse?"

They had lunch at Lady Margaret's Tea Parlor, where they dined on tiny crust-less sandwiches filled with cream cheese and cucumbers. She ate them because Mommy said the sandwiches were what princesses and queens ate, but Emily thought she'd rather have a hamburger. This becoming a woman didn't really seem like a whole bunch of fun.

They went to the movies and saw Jennifer Jones in *Good Morning,*

Miss Dove. Miss Dove was a teacher who understood all her students and helped them to feel special.

Afterward, Mommy took Emily to Barker's Ice Cream Parlor. They sat at one of the round, marble-topped ice cream tables. Mommy ordered orange sherbet and Emily ordered her very favorite, a scoop of pistachio with a cherry on top.

Mommy asked, "Did you like the movie, Emily?"

Emily nodded, wiping her mouth with a napkin. "Mommy, can I be a teacher when I grow up...just like Miss Dove?"

Mommy smiled. "Daddy and I were talking the other day, and we thought you would be a wonderful teacher. Now, Emily, if that's what you want to do, you have to get good grades in school and always remember you are a lady. Then you will be like Miss Dove."

Mitchell Samuel Grant discovered his path as well. On May 5, 1961, astronaut Alan Shepard became the first American to travel into outer space. He squeezed into a small capsule called *Freedom 7* and was launched into space for fifteen minutes and twenty-eight seconds and soared 116 miles above the earth's surface. Mitchell thought of how that must have felt, to slip the surly bonds of earth, as the poet had said—to soar above it all and be free. He knew his own destiny was to become an aerospace engineer.

Emily and Mitchell had celebrated their seventeenth birthdays, were seniors at Van Nuys High School, and on August 28, 1963, listened on the radio as Martin Luther King delivered his "I Have a Dream" speech on the steps of the Lincoln Memorial. They were stirred by the eloquent and charismatic black man's words, and wondered what personal meaning they might have for them in the future.

∞

Van Nuys High School was a stark, box-like structure built in 1914 whose only adornment was decorative Doric columns that stood like silent sentinels across the front of the main building. The agricultural fields and orange groves that surrounded Van Nuys High gradually disappeared as the school expanded decade by decade to accommodate the baby boomers.

By 1963, the orange groves were a dim memory and the hallways of Van Nuys High, once nearly empty, teemed with pupils hurrying to get to their next class.

The students dreamed about following in the steps of their famous alumni. Girls fantasized about becoming another Marilyn Monroe or Natalie Wood, and boys, of seeing their names alongside Robert Redford or Bob Waterfield—L.A. Rams NFL Hall of Famer.

Gray metal lockers screeched opened, complaining about years of misuse. Books became scuffed and battered as they were shoved inside or thrown on the floor while boys and girls frantically looked for a forgotten homework assignment, praying they had remembered to complete it, to bring it to school. The metal doors sang out as they were slammed shut, discordant music reflecting teenage angst. Some, less concerned about classes or homework, leaned casually against the light green, high-gloss painted walls. Girls, with hair fashionably cut in a chin bob, decorated their lips with the latest shade of lipstick, a transparent red. Their popularity rating rose or fell according to the number of cashmere sweaters they owned. Boys, dressed in slacks and white T-shirts covered by button-down or Hawaiian shirts, hoped to get a quick touch or a secret kiss from their latest girlfriend.

Emily saw Mitchell walking toward her. He stood out from the rest of the students not because he was particularly handsome or outgoing but because he was so much taller than the other boys. Mitchell threaded his way through the crowd, carefully avoiding getting bumped. His steps were exact, as if he were following an invisible line. His straight, medium brown hair was cut evenly, precisely one half-inch above the collar of his white shirt. Emily wondered if his mother trimmed it every morning—it never seemed to grow. It was shaped just as neatly around the outline of his ears.

His face was closely shaven, which only called attention to his eyebrows, two unruly brown caterpillars of hair, which seemed to be the one thing in Mitchell Samuel Grant's life that his father could not control.

The staid shirt couldn't wholly disguise a bony physique. *How would Mitchell look without his shirt on?* Emily mused. She smiled an inscrutable Mona Lisa smile, undetectable to anyone passing by. Remembering the body types learned in her physiology class, she thought, *Definitely ectomorphic.* She imagined he could be used as a model in their class for the human skeleton. *More fun than a chart,* she thought rather wickedly.

Mitchell smiled broadly. He had his braces removed last week and liked to show off his perfectly straight teeth. "Hi, Emily. My mom wanted me to tell you she's making tuna casserole for dinner, just for you."

Emily smiled back; her braces had been removed a month ago. "Mmm, that's my favorite. Your mom is so sweet to remember."

Mitchell looked longingly at Emily. She thought he was in love with her, and she liked it when he opened the doors and walked on the outside of the sidewalk. Mommy and Daddy said Mitchell would make a good husband; in their estimation he was raised right and was always a perfect gentleman.

Sometimes, in class, she would practice writing her married name: Emily Elizabeth Grant, Mrs. Mitchell Grant. She wasn't sure if she loved Mitchell, but she liked the way her name looked on paper.

Mitchell and Emily had studied together every Tuesday since their freshman year of high school. They trudged home, ignoring the other kids going into one of the many restaurants that now lined Van Nuys Boulevard.

The tantalizing smells from fast food restaurants and pizzerias mingled and called out to the hungry teens. Students stood in line waiting for a table, flirting, trying out their latest one-liners, happy to be set free from the prison they called school.

Mitchell and Emily were expected home by 3:20. No excuses and no stopping for a soda. They had given up sneaking envious glances at the other kids; their longings to join in were held tightly below the surface, bubbling upwards, threatening to erupt.

Mitchell said, "Tomorrow night is cruise night on Van Nuys Boulevard." He kicked a small branch that had fallen from one of the eighteen-year-old magnolia trees lining the streets to Sunrise Homestead Estates. "You know, we're the only kids in the whole school who can't go to cruise night," he lamented.

He sighed, his eyes cast down on the cracked sidewalks scarred by chewing gum. "It's not fair. Cruise night is..." he looked around to make sure no one else was in earshot, "it's bitchin'! All those cool cars and the kids hanging out, having fun, being *free*. A 1949 Ford convertible, that's my dream car. Can't you see us cruising up and down Van Nuys Boulevard? I'd be driving and you'd be waving. Gee, Emily, I'm so tired of being treated like a baby."

Emily's eyes widened. "Your dad will kill you if he hears you swearing. My dad says they're a bunch of sex maniacs and drug addicts."

Mitchell shrugged. "Oh, what's the use; you're on *their* side. Don't you want to have fun? Take some risks?"

Emily took his arm, a gesture that felt awkward but she thought it was expected. "Don't be mad at me, Mitchell. I wish I could dress like the other kids and listen to rock and roll, but my parents are still back in the fifties—they call it the devil's music. And you know how I love the folk singers—Joan Baez and Bob Dylan are two of my very favorites. My dad calls them all subversive *and* communists, *and* my mother won't even let me wear jeans unless I'm at home."

Emily looked down at her white blouse with its lace trim Peter Pan collar and her below-the-knee, navy-blue pleated skirt. "And no sleeveless dresses or blouses, *ever*."

Her lips quivered. "Don't you think I'd like at least one cashmere sweater? Mommy calls it frivolous spending, and she won't let me babysit so I can earn my own money. And the other girls—oh, Mitchell, the school lets the seniors wear hose on Fridays, and Mommy makes me wear knee socks. She says no hose until the senior prom. And...and...Mitchell, I don't even know *how* to dance."

"Me neither. We'll be the clumsiest kids there. That's what I mean. We may as well be on Devil's Island."

They entered the cement walkway leading to the Grants' kitchen door, just as they had done every Tuesday for the past two years.

Marian Grant stood at the sink, wearing a blue and white ruffled floral housedress with her house key safely tucked inside its wide pocket, sensible black shoes, and a white half-apron with red trim. It had been almost twenty-five years since she and Ethel sat at Forester's making plans for the spring dance, jitterbugging, and thinking about marriage. Life had not treated Marian gently. Sam had always needed to "wear the pants" in the family, but after the war... She thought of how he had changed, from needing to wear the pants to launching into out-of-control fits of rage.

Her forlorn expression changed to a soft smile when she saw Mitchell and Emily. Emily hugged Mrs. Grant, resting her head on her shoulder. Emily liked the way Mrs. Grant felt; she was heavier than Mommy and softer. *If Mrs. Grant were my mother,* she thought, *I bet she would have let me crawl into bed when I was little.*

Mrs. Grant said, "I've made fresh lemonade for you...after you drink your milk. And Mitchell, I baked the cookies you like."

Mitchell said indifferently, "Thank you, Mom."

Freshly baked cookies filled with softened pieces of bittersweet chocolate and tall glasses of milk waited on the kitchen table. Mitchell and Emily settled in, spreading out their books and papers on the tabletop, enjoying the taste of chocolate as it connected with ice-cold milk.

Trigonometry seemed like Greek to Emily, but she liked it when Mitchell became excited and his hazel eyes brightened as he explained how the sides and angles of a triangle were related. He made this dull and obscure subject—she was fairly certain it would never come in handy in "real life"—sound downright sexy.

After studying, Emily would help Mrs. Grant fix dinner and at eight p.m. Mitchell would walk her home—two blocks away. One evening he slipped his hand in hers and spoke seriously: "I'd like you to be my steady girlfriend, Emily."

Emily didn't like the feel of Mitchell's hands. They felt rough and his nails were bitten down to the quick. She didn't respond, either by moving her hand away or by tightening her fingers around his.

Mitchell said, "I mean, someday after college I'd like us to get married. You know, if you're a teacher and I'm an aerospace engineer, we can have a good life; take some vacations, go camping. Buy our own house." He squeezed her hand. "Even have kids."

"I'd like that," she said.

"Then you'll be my steady?"

She looked up at him with a subdued smile. "Okay, Mitchell. I'll be your steady."

His face broke into a wide grin and his eyes lit up. Before they got to her house he pulled her close and kissed her for the first time. Emily was hoping that Mitchell would be her prince, but he pushed his mouth hard against hers and his tongue moved deeply inside her mouth. She didn't like the way he felt. *This wasn't the way it happened in the movies. Maybe, after all, Snow White was only a fairy tale.*

Mitchell and Emily belonged to the Evangelical Church of Faith and Light Youth Group. They, along with the rest of the teenagers, were going to pledge, in front of their parents and congregation, to remain sexually abstinent until marriage.

Ethel Scott smiled as Emily stood in front of the full-length mirror, trying on the white dress her mother had sewed for the occasion. "I'm proud of you, Emily," she said. "You were such a tomboy as a little girl, but now, I can see you're growing up to be a respectable Christian woman."

Emily felt her chest tighten as tears filled her eyes. Had she ever heard her mother tell her she was proud of anything she did? "Thank you, Mommy," she said, gazing into the mirror and thinking of another white dress she would wear, sometime in the future: a white wedding dress symbolizing her purity.

The Evangelical Church of Faith and Light was located in an older neighborhood of Van Nuys, called "The Stew" by the locals. Originally part of a two-hundred-acre farm owned by the Heller family, the boxlike farmhouse, with its wide porch and pitched roof, was the lone reminder of the Stew's agricultural beginnings. Developed before zoning laws, the neighborhood was a hodgepodge of rundown homes and assorted businesses ranging from auto shops to beauty parlors to small grocery stores and sidewalk vegetable stands.

Pastor Lockner purchased the Heller farmhouse, vacant and in disrepair, two years after he returned from fighting in Europe.

While huddled in a foxhole, surrounded by bursting shells and the screams of the wounded and dying, he promised to dedicate his life to God's work if he should be spared. To his dying day, he would tell how he became surrounded by an intense light, heard ethereal music and felt God's presence. While others died around him, he survived, unscathed. He was certain God had answered his prayers, and he had been chosen to spread the teachings of Jesus Christ. A person of his word, he began his ministry in the living room of his one-bedroom apartment in Van Nuys. Two years later, Pastor Lockner had gathered a small but dedicated flock and was ready to preach the truth to the world.

"I don't know, Pastor," said the realtor and member of the church. "The Heller house has been vacant and neglected for several years. The lot is large, but the house is close to falling down."

Pastor Jeremiah Lockner stood in what had been the parlor, while a beam of sunlight shone through a crack in the roof, bathing him for the second time in light from above. Filled with faith, he said, "The Lord has led me here to do His work."

Fifteen years later, the first floor—originally designed with nine tiny rooms the size of cupboards, one bathroom, and the kitchen—had become the church proper; the second floor was home to Pastor Lockner and his family. The congregation had donated their time and money to knock down walls and build a sanctuary large enough to seat one hundred members. On most Sundays and all holidays, the church was filled to capacity with congregates who had faith in God and in Pastor Jeremiah Lockner.

Benevolent smiles radiated across the faces of the faithful as eight teenagers stood on the platform next to the lectern, where a beaming Pastor Lockner began to speak.

"This is, indeed, an auspicious moment in the lives of these eight young men and women." He turned to address them by name: "Mary, Marsha, Lisa, Jacqueline, Emily, Mitchell, and let us not forget my twin sons, John and Joshua."

His wide smile encompassed all eight, but it mostly shone with unalloyed pride for his two boys. "You are setting an example by pledging to remain chaste until marriage. We, as your parents and congregation, do not take this pledge lightly. Over the past six months, we have had open discussions on the meaning of chastity, the temptations and the benefits."

Pastor Lockner opened his timeworn Bible. "First Thessalonians 4:3-4 says: 'God wants you to be holy, so you should be kept clear of all sexual sin. Then each of you will control your body and live in holiness and honor.'"

He turned to the eight teenagers. "As I present you with this purity ring and place it on the ring finger of your left hand, it will become a reminder of the pledge you have made before God, your parents, and congregation on this joyous day."

Emily's mother and father beamed as the ceremony closed with Pastor Lockner's reading from Joshua 1:9: "'Have not I commanded thee? Be strong and of a good courage; be not afraid, neither be thou dismayed: for the Lord thy God is with thee whithersoever thou goest.'"

Ethel hugged Emily, impressing a demure kiss on her cheek. Harry took a small jewelry box out of his jacket pocket. "For you, Emily. Your mother and I are proud of you."

Her eyes grew wide when she opened the box and saw the gold necklace with a cross. She threw her arms around her parents and gushed, "Thank you, Daddy. Thank you, Mommy."

Harry fastened the necklace around Emily's neck, and for a moment, remembered his first anniversary when he bought Ethel a gold bracelet. A tear trickled down his cheek. So many years had passed. Were they ever that young and in love?

As a vote of confidence, Mitchell and Emily's parents gave them permission to have a Saturday night date at the movies because they were seventeen, in twelfth grade, and had promised in church before their families, congregation, and God to remain pure until marriage.

Sam Grant's heart never softened after the war, and he ran his home like the sergeant he had once been. Sam pre-approved the movie using the Recommended Movie List provided by the Evangelical Church of Faith and Light, checked the movie schedule, the mileage on the car, and handed Mitchell the keys to the family's new 1963 four-door Oldsmobile 98 luxury sedan. Painted in a willow-mist green, with modern air conditioning and an AM radio, it was Sam Grant's pride and joy.

He barked out the itinerary in a gruff staccato voice, a top sergeant addressing his troop of one: "Ten minutes to drive to the theater, ninety minutes for the movie, and ten minutes to drive home. No sitting in the car—you walk Emily to the door and say goodnight. And remember, you're driving a *new* car."

Mitchell stood at attention, a lone marine on the parade field during inspection. "Yes, sir," he said, his chin tucked in and his eyes staring straight ahead.

After Mitchell returned home, his father grilled him on the content of the movie, checked the mileage on his car, and demanded the ticket stubs.

Harry and Ethel Scott waited in the living room until Emily came home. Ethel would be knitting or darning, while Harry read the newspaper and shared his thoughts on how the world was going to hell in a hand basket.

"Can you believe it, Ethel? Minimum wage is up to one dollar. Women's lib and civil rights...bunch of damn commie-hipsters taking over the country. And the neighborhood...did you see who moved in two doors down? *Colored people.* There goes the damn neighborhood. I'm telling you, Ethel, it's not going to be safe living here. Is this what we fought for?"

Ethel spoke tersely as she stopped her darning to peer over her magnifying glasses. "Their kids with *our* Emily. Why, there's no telling what—what could happen." Ethel pursed her lips and returned to repairing the hole in Sam's socks.

When Emily came home, her father would glance up, look at his watch, and go back to his reading. Her mother scanned her clothing, looking for a wrinkle that wasn't there before, a blouse that might not be buttoned correctly; nothing escaped Ethel Scott's prying X-ray eyes.

Colorful cotton pedal pushers along with sleeveless blouses became the casual weekend wear for girls. The hemline on dresses was gradually getting shorter and boys' hair longer. Emily's skirts remained below the knee and Mitchell's hair, it seemed, didn't dare to grow at all.

Mitchell and Emily's Saturday night dates became their lone avenue of rebellion.

They bought tickets to see *Flipper*—the approved movie about a boy and a dolphin—and were sitting in the aisle seats in the furthest back row.

"Can you believe our parents would make us watch a little kid's movie?"

"I know, Mitchell. They're in the dark ages."

The lights dimmed and the previews began.

Mitchell looked around, didn't see any ushers, and whispered, "Okay, Emily, let's go."

Mitchell bent his knees to hide his height; Emily, a petite five foot two inches, barely had to hunch over as they sneaked out of *Flipper* and dashed into Theater Number Two, to see *Tom Jones*.

Tom Jones was number one on the prohibited movie list provided by the Evangelical Church of Faith and Light. They were sitting in the last row of the theater watching the lascivious banquet scene between Tom Jones and Mrs. Waters. Albert Finney as Tom was certainly ruggedly handsome, but Joyce Redman, the red-haired actress, was equally fetching. Mitchell's arm was around Emily's shoulder, his hand slowly sliding down to touch her breasts. No one had ever touched her breasts before, and she waited for the forbidden sensations. *Where was it,* she wondered?

During the lunch hour at school, Jacqueline and Marsha talked about going to second, even third base. Had they forgotten about the promise they made in church? They spoke about it as if it were something wonderful and exciting. Was there something wrong with her?

Mitchell and Emily strolled back to the car, each filled with visceral memories of the lustful scenes in *Tom Jones*.

Emily said, "I thought the movie was sensuous." She liked the way her lips moved when she said the word. She wondered if it gave her a pouty look, like Marilyn Monroe, who had tragically died last year, in 1962—her drugged body found in the nude, a fact her parents had called "an abomination against God" at the time.

Mitchell said gloomily, "We're in prison, Emily."

"We'll be out soon—it's only a couple of months before graduation."

"I don't know. My dad's going to choose my college classes. He's afraid I'll get corrupted and you know...I want to be free and experience life, like Tom Jones."

"I thought you wanted to get married."

"I do...to you. You're *my* girl." He stopped and pulled Emily into the shadows of a darkened building. His hand roamed under her skirt and she could feel his erection pressing against her body.

Emily pulled away. "No, Mitchell. We promised in church, remember?"

"I want you so bad. We can be careful." He reached in his pocket. "See, I have a condom."

"Mitchell, where did you get *that?*"

"John Lockner."

Astonished, she said, "You're kidding! The pastor's son?" She shook her head. "It's not right."

"Everyone's doing it...even the pastor's son."

"With Jacqueline?"

"Yes, with Jacqueline." He pulled her closer and whispered, "In the church basement. John brought down an air mattress. Please," he begged. "I'm going to die if we don't. I'll join the Marines and go to Vietnam and get killed. My dad says we're headed for a big war. At least I'll die a hero, not some kind of do-nothing coward."

"Oh, Mitchell, don't do that," she pleaded. "I don't want you to die."

"Then listen to me. I've thought it all out. Next Saturday, I'll ride my bike to the theater and buy the tickets early. I've saved the money for a motel room. We'll have an hour...a whole hour to be adults, to experience life like Tom Jones. Just think, the two of us, alone. Please say yes."

Emily remembered the Sunday school picture of Jesus dying on the cross for her. She didn't want Mitchell to die in Vietnam; it would be her fault.

She whispered, "Okay, Mitchell, next week."

The main fixture in Mitchell's sparsely furnished bedroom was a twin bed covered with a brown corduroy spread. A three-drawer oak dresser with an attached mirror held everything that Mitchell owned, except for the clothes hanging in the closet.

A drafting table, last year's Christmas gift from his parents completed the limited world of Mitchell Samuel Grant.

He sat hunched over the drafting table, his eyes fixed on a road map, glancing up from time to time to look at the framed poster of Alan Shepard in the *Freedom 7*. *Some day*, he thought, *I will be designing spaceships.*

He used his drafting tools to plot the route to the motel, studying the map as if he was plotting a mission to Mars. An intense feeling of power surged through his body when he discovered a way to hide the extra mileage from Sergeant Sam Grant.

Mitchell glanced at a dog-eared Marvel comic on his dresser, depicting a green-skinned monster fending off an assault by the US military. He smiled, imagining himself as Bruce Banner transforming into the Hulk, and finally being able to destroy his "evil" father.

Feeling triumphant, he went to the bookcase and opened his copper bank in the shape of Abraham Lincoln's bust and carefully fished out the dollar bills with his Barlow knife. He counted them methodically, smoothing them one at a time, and then placed them carefully in his wallet.

That Saturday night he drove to Emily's house, more self-assured, his wallet filled with carefully saved dollar bills and his lone Ramses condom, fresh in its wrapper and begging to be put to good use.

He knocked on the door and shook Mr. Scott's hand.

"Good evening, sir."

"Good evening, Mitchell."

Ethel said, "Emily, it's chilly out tonight. Take your heavier jacket."

"Yes, Mommy."

"Have a good time, kids," said Harry as he settled into his chair and reached for his newspaper.

They crisscrossed side streets and avoided traffic lights, finally arriving at an area near a private airport located in Van Nuys—three miles from the movie theater.

Langford Motor Inn was a one-story, U-shaped stucco building of connecting rooms with entry doors facing a dimly lit parking lot. Built in the 1940s, and at one time occupied by respectable travelers, it had fallen into disrepute as modern hotels sprung up along Van Nuys Boulevard. It was now mainly a haven for prostitutes and their johns, cheating husbands and their mistresses—and the occasional teenage couple that had tired of clumsy groping in the backseats of cars and wanted to consummate their passion, if not in style, at least in private.

Buzzing neon lights cast their candy-colored light onto a rust-filled metal sign:

LANGFORD MOTOR INN
ROOMS FOR RENT
WEEKLY, DAILY, HOURLY RATES

Mitchell said, "Wait here, Emily. I'll just be a few minutes." He leaned over and kissed her gently on her lips.

Maybe she was wrong about Mitchell. This kiss was sweeter, much more the way a prince would kiss a princess.

Mitchell was shaking as he entered the motor inn's office. Not because of what he was about to do, but due to the fear of getting caught. For a panicky moment he thought, *Oh, God, what if my father finds out?*

The clerk behind the counter had a gray scruffy beard and smelled of stale beer and cigarettes. "ID," he said, without looking up.

Mitchell thought about his driver's license that would show he was underage. He tried to deepen his voice but it rose an octave as he squeaked out, "No ID."

Beady eyes looked up and scanned the Olds parked outside. "No ID...costs you double."

"B-b-but—"

"No buts, kid. You want to fuck that little girl in the car? One hour, thirty bucks—otherwise, get the hell out."

Mitchell reached in his wallet to take out a year's worth of savings, thirty-five dollars. He counted one bill at a time and laid them on the counter.

The clerk dangled a key. "Room 103. One of our nicer rooms." A smirk crossed his face as he licked his lips and ceremoniously dropped the key into Mitchell's outstretched hand.

Emily was in a foreign land where the darkness was unfamiliar and became a cover for forbidden sins. She hugged her jacket as Mitchell opened the warped, weathered door and turned on the light in the room.

A single low-wattage lamp on a rickety nightstand hid the gray smudges on the once white walls. Fusty odors permeated the brown and green patterned bedspread and worn tweed-brown carpeting. Mitchell opened the dresser drawer, caught a glimpse of a Gideon Bible, quickly dropped his wallet, keys, and promise ring inside and pushed the drawer shut.

Emily covered her face with her hands and began to sob. "Mitchell, I'm scared. I don't think we should do this. I want to go home. I want to go home."

Mitchell put his arm around her shoulder. "Emily, it'll be okay, you'll see. An hour together like grown-ups, not like kids, being told don't do this, don't do that." Mitchell imitated his father and Emily couldn't help but laugh.

"You'll see, it'll be fine. It's just that the room is cold. I'll get the heat going." The gas heater sputtered, complaining about being turned on and off with every passing hour.

Mitchell folded the threadbare spread, first in half then in half again—exactly the way he had been taught. "At least the sheets look clean," he said, smiling.

Emily thought, *Mitchell is being funny and sweet; maybe he is the one.*

Emily returned his smile and went into the bathroom. She had tucked her special nightgown inside her purse, the one she wore to sleepovers. She undressed and slipped on the soft pink-floral flannel gown, trimmed with eyelet lace at the neckline. It was the nicest one she had. She looked at her image in the black-spotted mirror. She wished she had eyes like Audrey Hepburn in *Charade*—cat eyes that shined with excitement and passion. She liked that her eyes were large and dark brown, but she could see the dullness in her reflection. Maybe, like Snow White, they hadn't woken up yet.

Mommy had told Emily that good girls always slept with their panties on. She hesitated remembering the time, after the purity ceremony, when Mommy and Daddy had said they were proud of her. The necklace they had given her suddenly felt like a crown of thorns. With a sigh, she unfastened the clasp and removed the necklace. She took off her panties and promise ring, gathered the fragmented pieces of her existence, and placed them safely in her purse.

∞

It was not what she had dreamed of. She had looked at the clock on the nightstand: 8:05 p.m. She wanted to remember the time because she knew it would be wonderful and romantic. Mitchell had trouble getting the condom on, and had pushed inside her until she cried and bled. He gasped, then fell on top of her. She looked at the clock again: 8:12 p.m.

She felt something wet between her legs. "I'm bleeding!" she cried. They watched in fascinated horror as bright red blood flowed upon the hotel sheet, forming a dark Rorschach blot. Mitchell rushed to the bathroom and brought her a hand towel.

"I'm sorry, Emily. I didn't mean to hurt you," he said sadly, his face now drained of all color. "John Lockner said all girls bleed the first time."

Emily put the towel between her legs. "The hell with John Lockner! Close your eyes, Mitchell," she demanded angrily.

He cast his shame-filled eyes downward as she moved from the bed to the bathroom. She turned on the faucet; a slow stream of cold, rusty water came out of vibrating pipes. She found a wrapped hotel-size bar of soap, and did the best she could to wash herself clean. *Could she ever feel clean again?*

Emily sniffled all the way home. She wanted it to be the way it was in the movies, where there was a happy ending and true love lasted for eternity. Emily glanced at Mitchell, his face a mask of concentration as he watched the mileage on the car and drove his pre-planned route home.

Reality struck Emily. Mitchell wasn't her prince, and he wasn't even the perfect gentleman that Mommy and Daddy thought. At her house she bolted from the car and turned to Mitchell. "I don't want to see you again," she said harshly.

He looked at her with eyes deprived of feelings, as if she had just told him the day of the week. "Okay," he said, pulling away from the curb in his father's willow-green Olds.

Daddy was waiting up, his face buried in the newspaper. He glanced at Emily and then at his watch. "Your mother went to bed early...one of her headaches. Did you have a nice time?"

She nodded before kissing him goodnight on top of his balding head.

Chapter 4

1963

Emily wanted to forget that Saturday night in April. Had it really happened? Maybe it was only a bad dream. She hadn't seen Mitchell for more than a month, except for an occasional glance in the school hallways. She told Mommy and Daddy that she was concentrating on school and stayed in her room on the weekends, studying. She checked off each remaining day on her school calendar. Only four more weeks until graduation then she would be F.R.E.E. She thought about everything she had missed: all the folk singers she loved so much, cruise night down Van Nuys Boulevard, even the drive-in movies. All the things that normal kids got to do. Mommy and Daddy had taken her once to the Starlight Drive-In to see *The Swiss Family Robinson*, a sugary-safe flick from the Walt Disney Company. Mommy didn't like it. She said the kids were wild and the popcorn rancid.

There was a May heat wave that made the headlines in the local newspaper, the *Van Nuys Herald*:

ONE HUNDRED TEN DEGREES AND CLIMBING

Below the headline was a list of things to do to stay cool: *Drink more water. Stay indoors in an air-conditioned building, if possible. Wear lightweight clothing...* The list went on and on.

She thought, rather disgustedly, *The least they could do is say, "Eat lots of ice cream," as one of the things.* She didn't understand it, but all she had wanted for the past couple of weeks was soft comfort foods: pudding, ice cream, *and* snow cones.

The heat was bothering her; she had lost her appetite for solid food and her mother commented on her paleness. "Emily, you have to eat more."

No matter how high the thermometer rose, Thursday night was still Thursday night. Liver and onions, fifty-one nights a year; the only exception was Thanksgiving. Her mother piled her plate extra high, along with the advice that it was good for anemia.

Emily hated liver—its gamy flavor and the texture when she chewed—but she had been taught to eat everything on her plate.

"Eat it warm or eat it cold, but eat it you will," was her mother's mantra.

She had learned not to taste: chew, chew, and swallow. Chew, chew, and swallow.

Emily felt a sudden rush of bile rising in her throat and ran from the table to the bathroom. She leaned over the toilet and began to vomit. She retched until there was nothing left but painful dry heaving. She rested her head against the cool porcelain of the nearby bathtub and wondered what was wrong. Her Aunt Jenny had died from stomach cancer—could she have it?

She felt woozy, but stood to splash cold water on her face. She was reaching for her toothbrush when she saw her mother's angry reflection in the mirror. Her mother spun her around and commanded, "Take off your dress."

Emily didn't understand. Had she vomited on her dress? She hadn't been feeling well for a couple of weeks now. Queasy. She thought it was the flu; now she was convinced it was stomach cancer.

Her mother's voice stung as it echoed through the black and green tiled bathroom. "Emily, take off your dress or I'll rip it off!" She grabbed Emily by the arm, her voice rising to a shrill pitch. "Did you hear me? I said: Take. Off. Your. *Dress!*"

Emily unbuttoned her shirtwaist dress, letting it slide onto the floor where it rested, a blue heap encircling her feet. She stood in her bra and slip, confused, her eyes focused on the tile floor.

Her mother stared at her body, moving closer as her eyes widened. "Slut!" she screamed, her hand rising and hitting Emily across the face. "Jezebel!" she roared.

Emily began to cry. "Mommy?" she questioned.

Her mother stood back, anger changing to astonishment. "Stupid girl, so stupid. You don't even know, do you? You're pregnant. It was that Mitchell, wasn't it?"

"Mommy?"

A look of revulsion crossed Ethel Scott's face as she walked out of the bathroom, locking the door behind her.

Emily had been locked inside the bathroom for over an hour, slumped on the floor of the green and black tiled room. How could this have happened? It wasn't even fun; she didn't even like it. Four weeks before graduation and her life was ruined. She was still in her bra and slip when her father unlocked the door, looking at her with vacant eyes. "Get dressed, the Grants are here."

Sam Grant and Harry Scott had gone through a war together, had expectations for a lifetime of friendship, and now sat in the Scotts' living room as opponents. The inevitable blame game rocked the very foundation of their relationship.

Harry sat glaring, his jaw muscles working. "Your son took advantage of an innocent child," he looked at Emily, "a stupid, unworldly child, but innocent nevertheless."

Sam scowled. "Mitchell will be punished, you can believe that. But, it takes two to tango."

Harry's work-hardened hand roved over the couch's brown and gold tweed fabric. He picked on a loose thread, pulling it until there was a small hole. *Ethel will be furious,* he thought, as his fingers dug deeper and deeper into the fabric.

Ethel Scott and Marian Grant cried, reaching from time to time for tissues placed conveniently by their sides. Mitchell and Emily didn't dare to look at each other; their eyes remained firmly fixed on the floor.

Emily sat on the end of the couch, rocking back and forth. Maybe this was a bad dream, a nightmare. She pinched her arm. *Ouch!* This was a nightmare, but she wasn't sleeping. She wouldn't be surprised if they stoned her or excommunicated her. Or burned her at the stake like Joan of Arc.

How could she face her friends? What would happen to her dream of becoming a teacher? What would she do with a baby?

Pastor Jeremiah Lockner stood on the porch of the Scotts' home, a lean figure bending to the sudden gusts of the Santa Ana winds blowing from the high desert. He hated the feel of the gale-like force, as if he and the world were out of control. His large ears kept his glasses tightly fixed on his face; even the strongest currents of air could not budge them. Thick lenses magnified his faded blue eyes, giving him the appearance of a goldfish under water.

Pastor Lockner heard the sounds of shouting and crying through the door, through the wind. He shifted his Bible to one hand, smoothing his worn black suit and straightening his gray tie with the other. He was overcome with grief. Mitchell and Emily had been model children; raised right by parents who followed the principle of spare the rod and spoil the child. They attended Sunday school religiously, were leaders of the teen group, and had made a promise to stay pure. He puzzled, *What could have gone wrong?* He bowed his head and said a quick prayer, asking for guidance to lead these children from the darkness and back into the light.

Emily had never seen her mother cry. Another stone to be thrown at her: She had made her mother cry. She heard the knock on the front door. *Oh, God,* she thought, *Pastor Lockner. Who else could it be?* She turned red and stinging tears leaked down her cheeks. *Lord, let me have a seizure. Maybe if I have a seizure, they would care.*

She looked at Mitchell, his head in his hands, his thin frame folding into itself. *Why isn't he saying something? Why doesn't he tell his father he's going to enlist and get killed in Vietnam?*

Pastor Lockner entered the room, his head bent humbly, but in control.

Harry Scott rose, shook Pastor Lockner's hand, and thanked him for coming so quickly in their hour of need.

Ethel Scott, an avid reader and firm believer in Emily Post's advice on proper etiquette, stood and offered Pastor Lockner some refreshments. "A glass of ice tea, Pastor?" she asked, her voice quivering. He shook his head, motioned for her to sit down, and said with compassion in his voice, "Perhaps a little later."

Pastor Lockner asked everyone to bow their head as he recited the 23rd Psalm: "'Our Father who art in Heaven...'" He was certain that prayer would bring a sense of calmness to the room.

Sam Grant's eyes hardened as his words spat out like venom. "I won't be shamed in front of our community and our church. These two," he jabbed an accusatory finger at Emily and Mitchell, "have sinned against God and nature."

Pastor Lockner said, "This is not a time for casting blame. We all need to take a deep breath and realize the Lord works in mysterious ways—"

"Baloney!" Sam cut him off. "Forgive me, Pastor, but there's no mystery to this one."

Harry, a pragmatic man by nature, put in, "We can't change what has happened. The deed is done. As I see it, there's only one option." He turned to Emily and Mitchell. "Emily, we tried to keep you on the right path, and Mitchell, we treated you like a son. You have betrayed the trust given to you by God, your parents, and your church. I am sorely disappointed in both of you. You are bringing a child into this world, and there is only one solution. You need to get married."

Mitchell came alive. "Married?" His voice cracked on the formidable word. He turned to his father. "But Dad, what about my career as an aerospace engineer?"

His father looked at him, darkening eyes devoid of every feeling but rage. "Well, boy, you put your finger in a boiling kettle, and now you're surprised it's burned." He leaned over and grabbed Mitchell's hand and squeezed. "Understand?"

Emily could see the pain in Mitchell's eyes, followed by tears and a barely audible, utterly defeated, "Yes, sir."

"Then it's settled," said Pastor Lockner, relieved that a solution had been reached so quickly. "A quiet wedding in my chambers in two weeks. You'll see, this will blow over in time." He looked at both sets of parents. "They're both under eighteen. Will you give your consent for these wayward lambs to wed?" There were nods all around. "Very well. You'll have to go to the county to get a marriage license and blood tests. After that, your fate will be in God's hands."

Chapter 5

E m shuffled into the kitchen wearing her favorite pink and white chenille robe and bright pink scuff slippers. She followed her morning routine by inserting a single-serving packet of coffee into the brewer and removing the cat food from the pantry shelf. She read the label, "Mother's Organic-Vegan Cat Food," the only food her spoiled darling would eat. She never knew that a cat could gallop, but when the kibble hit the bowl, she heard the frantic scampering of four white paws on the tile hallway. There was clearly nothing wrong with Boots's hearing, but then he was still young and had a lot of kitten in him.

She knelt, rubbing Boots's black and white head. "You tuxedo cats are so snobby." He looked at her as if to say, "And regal, too," before rubbing up against her leg and turning to his hoity-toity cat food.

Em picked up the faded mug from the brewer and smiled, as she did every morning, at the two female stick figures wearing dresses, leaning forward to kiss. She continued with her morning routine by turning on her computer and checking her inbox. She moved through the e-mails at a fast pace, deleting the daily avalanche of junk by looking at the sender and the subject. The one from Max caught her attention. Max had done her homework, and Em couldn't help but imagine what else Max and Les had accomplished. Feeling a pang of envy, she inhaled her coffee's fragrance, and thought there are so few pleasures left at this age.

She wondered how Max and Les had managed to hold onto their attraction after fifty years. Their backgrounds were so different. Les, born into a prestigious Californian family of physicians and attorneys; Max, with motor oil running through her veins. She had never seen them argue, perhaps their disagreements only came out when they were alone. But, the glow that came over their faces when they looked at each other—that was something that couldn't be made up. A mechanic and a physician...hmm, she'd have to think about writing a short story on that unlikely combination.

On the other hand, there was Frankie and Bobbie. She knew their love ran deep, but oh, my God, the way those two bickered!

She thought about the love she had shared with Char, and the unspoken thread that still bound them together, a tightly woven secret that went from this world and into the next.

She opened Max's e-mail and downloaded the JPEG attachment: Treat Mason, twenty-eight years old, attended Chapman's School for Girls in New York State, graduated *egregia cum laude*— with outstanding honor—from Latham University in 2016 with a double master's in English Literature and Women's Studies. Spent two years traveling through Europe. Has worked for the *Times* for two years.

She had included information on the car Treat drove, her credit score, and her dating (more or less) history. Max included a playful comment: *She plays on the other team.*

Em had to laugh at that one. Max didn't miss a beat. She looked at the photo taken of Treat Mason getting out of a cab. Em studied her face. Thin, angular. Straight auburn hair pulled back in a pony-tail. Beautifully arched eyebrows, but a brow that was so furrowed it was difficult to see the shape and size of her eyes, only that they were light brown, bordering on the color of honey. She looked stressed, troubled.

Em glanced at yesterday's message from Treat Mason. She picked up the phone to call.

Chapter 6

October 2, 2020
New York

Treat liked being in control, and she liked being on top.

Jack knew what would drive her crazy. He raised his head to gently flick her nipples with his tongue. Her soft moans changed, intensifying to a throaty groan.

Touching her, listening to her, drove him crazy too, but like Treat, he liked being in control and on top. He tried to move away from his feelings and back into his head. He glimpsed at her half-closed eyes with their faraway, unfocused look, an expression of determination embedded on her face. Her long auburn hair swayed; a thin layer of dampness glistened across her body as she kept up an unshakeable rhythm.

Christ, she's beautiful, he thought. He closed his eyes, letting his physical needs win, as primal grunts escaped, and his body shuddered. It was a game they played, and he always lost. It was only afterward that Treat's expression would become softer, and she would let herself enter the space where she could join him; after all, she had already won the game.

Treat moaned again, finally letting go and collapsing against Jack. She panted, "Oh God, Jack. That was wonderful." She relaxed against him as Jack wrapped his arms around her.

Treat liked the way he held her and kissed her, whispering how much she meant to him. She felt safe, in those few moments, but the feeling didn't last; she shifted her body, disconnecting physically and emotionally.

Before he released her he murmured, "Marry me, Treat."

She smiled as she reached for her bra and panties. "How many times is this, Jack?" she asked playfully.

"Twenty-nine, but who's counting?" He sat up, leaning on his elbows, watching the way she moved when she hooked her bra and slid her panties on, all in one smooth movement, always methodical and in control. "I'm still waiting for my 'yes' or at least my 'I'll think about it.'"

"Okay. Answer number twenty-nine is coming up." She continued to dress, and he could tell her thoughts were moving away from the bedroom to the outside world.

"We both want to be in control, and not only in the bedroom. The reason this works for us," she put on her navy-blue sweater and beige slacks, "is because it's confined to this room and an occasional dinner out. We can play our game, enjoy each other's company, and move on." She slipped on her beige pumps, leaned over and kissed Jack on the cheek. "Don't forget, birthday boy, tomorrow night at seven thirty at De Luca's."

With her hand on the door, she turned to Jack and smiled. "Answer number twenty-nine is 'no.'"

Treat lived alone, and always had. No roommates shared her space...ever. Friends were few and kept safely in their respective niches. She met with colleagues from work on Fridays for a weekending drink at their favorite bar, Sammy's. She saw alumni from Langford University at reunions and stayed in touch with a few through chatty e-mails. Most of them had settled into life, were married, had or were having children.

She was a loner, partly from choice and partly because she seemed to be missing that subtle ability to connect on a deep level. She had once seen a therapist—actually, three times. Dr. Wilson was pleasant enough, but Treat became bored—didn't seem to feel the connection others felt toward their therapist—and decided to let her life be what it was.

Once Treat got the job at the *Times,* she began the dreaded chore of finding an apartment. Someone at the office told her about a rumor that was flying around: a one-bedroom on Bedford Street in Greenwich Village going for an under-market price. She left work, got a cab, and during the ride dug around in her leather satchel for her checkbook. She arrived shortly before nightfall.

"You're lucky to be here before dark, miss," the driver commented. "Ma Nature's putting on quite a show right about now."

The black lampposts with their curved mast arms and teardrop luminaries cast their light on the pink flowering Okame Cherry trees. Petals, lifted on the evening breeze, drifted upward before wafting gracefully to the ground.

"It'll be a carpet of petals by morning," said the cabbie appreciatively.

"It is beautiful," Treat replied as she leaned over and paid the fare.

I've got to get this apartment, she thought, sprinting to take the stairs two at a time.

The leasing agent, a middle-aged man with thinning hair and black-rimmed glasses, was sitting at a folding table, handing out flyers. A few couples milled around the apartment, appraising, debating.

It took her less than a minute to scan the apartment and return to the agent. "I'll take it," she said, as she steadied her hand before writing a check for six months' rent: $14,400. She knew that would ace anyone else out of the bidding war, and she couldn't pass up an apartment in the Village offered at that bargain fee. *Net worth,* she thought, *under two hundred dollars.* She would deal with that later.

Her apartment in the Village was her sanctuary and her single greatest expense. She liked the hardwood floors and the high ceilings and the expansive windows that gave her a view of the street with its brownstone buildings and parkway trees—an illusion of neighborhood and intimacy. She felt safe in her home. The super lived in the basement apartment, and she chuckled out loud when she thought of Thomas, whom she considered her super-super. The leasing agent had told her that Thomas had a mild brain injury, and advised to be sure she spoke to him slowly and distinctly. It was odd, but she seemed to be able to connect to Thomas.

"Please don't call me Tommy," he had said on the day she moved in. That was the only thing he had ever asked of her, and perhaps that was why she felt a connection. He asked nothing and she asked nothing—except if there was a serious issue with the apartment. *Only one,* she thought. *The time the shower drain backed up and flooded the bathroom.* It was a quick fix and except for hellos and goodbyes when they saw each other their relationship remained casual. It seemed to suit them both.

Her bedroom was large enough for a queen-size bed, but she chose to sleep on a twin and thought of the room as a gym with a bed. It was far more spacious than she had grown up with, and no man had ever been invited to her home, let alone been asked to share her bed.

One third of her salary went for rent, but she was clever at purchasing labeled clothing at closeout prices, and except for a few dinners out, she ate at home and had trained herself to be the proverbial frugal gourmet.

The arrangement with Jack suited her fine. He seemed to enjoy their sparring in his bed and the occasional dinner out. She enjoyed those things, too, and found him an entertainingly witty conversationalist, adept at engaging her in discussions on new books, favorite films, and the challenges of climbing the corporate ladder. She liked the way his mind worked, and the excitement that showed on his face when he told her about winning his latest case as a defense attorney.

If she were selecting a mate or father to sire children, Jack would be perfect: handsome, bright, and not bad in bed. *Not bad at all,* she thought.

She knew their relationship was doomed; she knew it as soon as they met. It wasn't only Jack; it was the same with every relationship. Men fell in love with her, or at least thought they had. Perhaps it was because of the game. She set the boundaries, and she never changed them. She didn't say the words, but the message was clear: Take it or leave it.

She turned on the television to CNN, wanting to catch up on the latest turmoil around the Freedom to Marry Act. Senators stood on the steps of the Capitol building facing a bank of reporters, while threatening lawsuits against this "latest abomination." She would change the channels as she followed her nightly exercise routine, trying to keep in mind that her goal as a journalist was to stay neutral. She reminded herself to "gain perspective on everyone's point of view," a phrase she had heard from Miss Lily and Miss Violet, whenever there was a squabble among the girls at Chapman's.

Treat set the treadmill for the five-mile ARMY Protocol program. She thrived on goals and set the speed at 6 mph with a plan to work up to 7.76 mph.

She liked to feel her body respond to the challenge, and she liked to push herself to the edge. She did that with everything in her life. Afterward, she downed a bottle of Evian and moved to the Bowflex Xtreme—another bargain picked up through a small "for sale" card posted at the local coffee shop. She had to laugh when she saw it: coats and sweaters stacked on the seat, like most home-gym equipment it was barely used. She would use it. She had her routine and so far it paid off—a lean body with 15 percent fat. She knew that eventually the years would take their toll on her body; not from having babies—no kids for her—but just from the natural progression from birth to death. She would spar with time just as she did with everything and anyone who wanted to enter her life. An hour later, she was ready to peel off her sweat-soaked shorts and tee, get clean, and have dinner.

It was the bathroom, with its black and white checkerboard tile floor seeming straight out of a 1930s Hollywood musical, that convinced her to sign the lease, even though the apartment was more than she could afford. The shower, with two clear-glass walls, provided a view of silhouetted tree branches brushing against the transom window. The octagonal tub and sink complemented the art deco style, but with up-to-date conveniences.

She debated: shower or tub? She needed the shower to wash off the day's residue, and she needed the tub to soak out the knots from exercising. Treat decided, as she did almost every day, to shower first and then soak. She turned on the water and blessed the instant water heater as the room quickly filled with steam. Everything she needed was arranged in order on the shower shelf. She followed her routine, first shampooing and conditioning her hair. Then she squeezed two pumps of body cleanser in her hands and worked downward from her neck and shoulders. She was thorough, she was methodical, and she didn't dally. Turning to face the spray she let the water cascade until the last remnants of the hair conditioner and body cleanser were erased. She rested her head against the shower's black marble wall and let the pulsating water beat full force on her back. She lingered for a few minutes, letting the hot water penetrate her muscles, until she began to feel guilty about wasting time. She could hear Miss Violet lecturing the students at Chapman's School for Girls in her condescending singsong voice: "Time is finite, a gift not to be wasted."

Treat put on her terrycloth robe and brushed her teeth as the air-jet whirlpool tub filled with water. She sprinkled one cup of Epsom salts before choosing an essential oil. Rosemary, lavender, chamomile, citrus scents—they all served a different purpose. She reached for the lavender oil, known to calm nerves, muscles, and mind, held the bottle over the tub, and counted out twenty drops. Treat took off her robe, pleased at her reflection in the mirror. She had strived for and achieved a lean athletic figure. No flab, no jiggle when she looked at her triceps. *It's all worth it,* she thought. One goal achieved, but she had others. Ambitious ones. She wanted that interview with Emily Elizabeth Scott, and she wanted that corner office at the *Times.*

She eased into the tub, positioning the jets against her back, and soaked until the tight spots were dissolved.

Treat opened the door to the walk-in closet, where seven pairs of gray sweatpants and seven T-shirts in various colors were folded and stacked neatly on a shelf. She didn't bother picking a color; the azure-blue shirt on top would do.

She made her usual dinner of salad, steamed broccoli, and cauliflower, Southern Gold potatoes, and four ounces of organic chicken breast. It was only after she had eaten, rinsed her dishes, and put them in the dishwasher, that she began to respond to her voice mails. She moved through them rapidly, listening to a few words before hitting the delete button, but one caught her off guard. She was surprised to hear herself gasp. She played it again, feeling her heart begin to beat faster.

"Treat Mason, this is Emily Elizabeth Scott. You called about an interview. Please call tomorrow morning between eight and ten, California time."

With the Freedom to Marry Act now signed into law, piercing the mystery around the Girls could be her ticket to that corner office and a future with a major network. She listened to the message again; no goodbye from Ms. Scott, just a slight crack in the door that Treat intended to push all the way open.

De Luca's was Jack's favorite restaurant. *Know what a man likes to eat and you know the man,* thought Treat. Tucked away in a corner in the Village, De Luca's was northern Italian cuisine at its finest. It was deceiving from the street: a simple red-brick building with a black double door and an engraved brass plaque:

WELCOME TO DE LUCA'S
RESERVATIONS REQUIRED

Jack held Treat's hand as they took the curved tiled staircase to De Luca's lower level, a remodeled basement from the early 1900s. Guests looked up at the striking couple coming down the stairs. The gentleman was indeed natty in a double-breasted Ralph Lauren suit, but it was the woman—wearing a strapless red chiffon gown that floated and moved with her every step—that held them transfixed.

Jack leaned over and whispered, "Every man here wants to take off your dress, and every woman won't eat another bite of food."

"That was my intention," Treat replied, smiling at her admiring and envious audience.

They were shown to a black leather booth at the far corner of the restaurant. Jack slid in first; they liked to sit side by side, and he knew Treat always wanted the aisle seat. *A quick escape,* he thought. He knew so little about her. Only a clinical résumé of personal information: Her parents divorced when she was seven, and she was sent to a boarding school in the Adirondacks when she was eight. "Raised there," she had told him. "Let's just say, my parents weren't involved in my life."

He wondered how he could feel so in love with someone he

barely knew. Maybe that was part of it; he was infatuated with the mystery and took pleasure in the chase.

"I love this restaurant," said Jack.

Treat smiled. "Besides the food, Jack?"

Jack raised Treat's hand to his lips and kissed it gently. "Look at the walls. Parts of New York are right here: reclaimed bricks from the streets and historic buildings. Can you imagine the stories they could tell, the secrets they hold?" He became thoughtful, a sad look crossed his face. "It's about valuing, not discarding."

Treat said softly, "It was the right choice, then."

Treat had preordered their dinner. She knew what Jack liked; she had an instinct to observe, to analyze, and then to create a mental dossier on everyone she came into contact with. At Chapman's her teachers called it a gift, at times, she thought of it as a curse.

The wine steward poured the white wine, a bottle of 2015 Sine Qua Non Body & Soul, followed by their first course, salmon *carpaccio*: thin slices of marinated salmon fillet garnished with citrus fruit.

They ate in a companionable silence, savoring the delicacy of the cuisine, the flavor of the full-bodied dry wine.

Treat leaned over, kissed Jack on the cheek, and handed him an envelope. "Happy Birthday, Jack," she said, smiling.

Jack's gaze remained fixed on his name on the envelope. Treat had crayoned "Jack" in large letters, a different color for each. *Not unlike a child,* he thought. Maybe that was a clue about the child hiding inside this serious, driven woman.

He expected a funny card, hoped for a romantic one, and was surprised to find a card with a generic sentiment suitable for "just friends." The handwritten invitation inside, however, calligraphed in red ink, suggested a more provocative message: *Jack...tonight is your treat.*

"Really?" he smiled.

"Yes, really."

"Anything I desire?"

He could see her lips begin to form into a "yes," but quickly changed to, "Within reason."

Treat raised her glass. "To Jack and tonight," she toasted.

Jack smiled and gestured to the wine label, Body & Soul. "This is the perfect wine for making my wish come true."

"Tell me, Jack, what is your wish?"

"Do you really want to know or do you want to wait to find out?"

"Tell me now," she whispered seductively.

He was enjoying this new game: cat and mouse. "Close your eyes," he said.

His hand moved to the zipper of her dress, moving it down an inch. He whispered, "Your dress has been driving me crazy. I want to undress you. I want my hands to move slowly down your body, touching you as if I'm discovering you for the first time, and I want you to undress me in the same way."

He saw the beginning of a small smile. "Then what?"

"Then, I want you to lie on the bed next to me and let me hold you...for the night. I want us to talk about who we are. I want to kiss your tears away if you cry and hold you against my chest. I want to wake up in the morning and watch you sleep. Then I want to make love to you; not fuck you. Make love to you, exactly as the label says, body and soul. That's what I want."

She put her wine glass down, a deep furrow forming across her brow. "I can't do that, Jack. I'm really sorry. I thought you understood the parameters of our relationship."

Jack looked at Treat, his eyes reflecting caring and sadness. "Parameters? Treat, did something happen to you?"

Jack wasn't the first to ask her that question. "Do you mean, was I molested?" She shook her head. "No, nothing like that. Right now, it's about my career. Remember that interview I was telling you about?" she added, not so subtly changing the direction of the conversation.

"Hey, you got it?"

She nodded. "I got it."

He held her hand. "I'm happy for you, Treat."

"It can make my career if I play it right. It could mean the corner office and then, who knows?" Treat looked down. "I think I need to make this an early night. I need to get ready for the interview, prepare questions, and—pack."

She leaned over and kissed him, a sweet, lingering kiss. She knew that's what he wanted: a kiss that promised more. For Treat, it was a kiss that said goodbye.

Chapter 7

Monday, October 5, 2020
Studio City, CA

The Girls had given Em a surprise gag gift party for her sixty-fifth birthday. They laughed, they roared, as she opened each gift: black lace panties and bra, a box of sex toys labeled, *Open at your own risk if you are sixty-five*, chocolate handcuffs, and foot fetish lollipops. Bobbie and Frankie had presented her with a DVD, *Yoga for the Active Senior*. Everyone tittered, but Em had always thrived on routine, and on Mondays, Wednesdays, and Fridays, her day began with yoga. On those days she struggled into her yoga pants. Were they tighter? Had she gained weight or was it just senior citizen bloat?

One day, sixty-four—not senior—the next day, sixty-five—very senior. Now she was fully entitled to the benefits of seniorhood. Discounts at the movies and restaurants, Medicare insurance—what else? She couldn't remember. Oh, a senior moment! She was entitled to that, too.

She thought about all the euphemisms people showered on those getting long in the tooth—God, what an ugly expression! *Oh my, isn't she growing old gracefully?* Graceful? You've got to be kidding. *You're only as old as you feel.* The idiot who coined that one is probably under forty. Watch out, you'll feel differently about it when *you* turn sixty-five. And her favorite: *Doesn't she look good for her age?* Why can't people simply say, *She is really looking old and decrepit.* Why is it so hard to say, *She's had to say goodbye to so many dear friends, and there won't be many hellos from now on.*

Em had spoken with Treat Mason, a brief conversation that lasted only long enough to give her directions to One Peppertree Lane and a time of arrival: 10:00 a.m. That would give Em barely enough time to shower, dress, and have breakfast.

The bell, mounted in the brick wall at the entrance to the gated courtyard, announced Treat Mason's arrival. Em pushed the automatic gate opener and walked from the kitchen to the front door. She peered through the speakeasy door grill as Treat Mason strode across the courtyard, her eyes fixed straight ahead. *Hmm, that's a little odd,* thought Em. Usually, when someone visited for the first time, they stopped to admire the three-tier fountain and the white bougainvilleas that climbed toward the red-tiled roof.

Em was surprised at how young Treat Mason looked, younger than her photo. Perhaps it was because her troubled expression and furrowed brow were gone. She looked calm, but determined: a woman on a mission.

Em waited for the knock on the front door. She extended her hand, smiled, and said, "Ms. Mason, welcome to One Peppertree Lane."

Two hands, touching for the first time: one youthful and un-lined, smooth and firm as alabaster; the other nearly translucent, its prominent blue-green veins mapping the river of life.

Em showed Treat to the den. "Please," she said, motioning to the couch. Em eased into the cacao-colored leather recliner opposite the couch, placing her half-full mug of coffee on the marble end table.

An angry meow was heard, followed by a black and white face peeking out from behind the recliner, glaring at the stranger sitting on *his* couch. Quick as a ninja, the handsome tom jumped gracefully onto Em's lap.

Em said, "I think we may have disturbed Boots's morning nap." She petted his head and put her face close to his. "Forgive me, darling." She glanced at her guest and said, "I'm sorry, I didn't introduce you. Ms. Mason, this is Boots—actually Puss 'n Boots."

As if to illustrate his name, Boots began to groom the white paws trimming his muscular black legs.

"He's quite young, entering adolescence, and very particular about his naps. He's my second kitty." Em wiped a tear away. "It's always difficult to lose anyone, person or animal. My first cat lived to be almost twenty years old. That would be equivalent to ninety-seven in human years."

Treat had witnessed people's overindulgence of their pets before and knew it was best to humor them. "He certainly is a handsome fellow," she said as pleasantly as she could manage.

Em chuckled lightly. "Boots really owns the house. I hope you're okay with cats. No allergies or fear of fur on your clothing?"

Treat said solemnly, "No, Ms. Scott, I was raised around animals."

"Good, one less hurdle to deal with. How was your flight, Ms. Mason?"

Treat nodded. "Fine, thank you. It's always more pleasant when it's not too crowded. Ms. Scott, I want to thank you so much for allowing me this interview. It's such a privilege to meet you."

Em nodded. *A privilege? Time will tell.*

Treat looked around the room, her eyes widening. "Is this where you do your writing?"

"Yes, I do most of my writing here. And sometimes late at night in bed, if I can't sleep."

Treat opened her briefcase and began to take out her laptop.

Em said tersely, "Not so fast. Before we begin, a few rules."

Boots jumped off Em's lap and sauntered into the kitchen.

"As with most cats, Boots hates rules. You know, cats really do control their owners."

Treat raised an eyebrow infinitesimally. "I'm sure."

Em caught the subtle dig in Treat's tone and handed her a yellow legal tablet and two pens. A look of puzzlement crossed Treat's face.

"You *do* know how to write?" Em said with a sarcastic edge.

"Yes, of course."

"So many of the young people today don't know cursive, it's thought to be a useless artifact from the past. What society has failed to recognize is how it helps to form the brain."

"Not to worry, Ms. Scott," Treat replied. "I went to a school that emphasized penmanship: an hour a day spent copying passages from the classics."

"Excellent—from your hand to your brain. You need to know I'm a firm believer in rules and boundaries. The world cannot exist without order."

Em closed her eyes for a moment. Treat wondered if she had dozed off. Em's eyes bolted open and she chuckled. "A bad habit of mine, closing my eyes to think. This is how many of my stories begin: my eyes shut, a character pops up, and we're off and running. Let's see, where were we?"

"Rules," prompted Treat.

"Yes. Three rules...I think that should do it. Rule one: no computers, no recorders, and no cameras. When you're done writing for the day you'll transcribe your notes at night, return them in the morning, and I'll okay them, one day at a time."

Treat thought, *And they say* I'm *a control freak? Everything I've read about her said she's eccentric. They weren't kidding.*

"Rule two: Don't call me Ms. Scott. It's Emily, or if you're feeling extra friendly, Em. And if you don't object, I'll call you Treat. There is something unnatural about being formal when we are here to discuss a very intimate topic."

Treat smiled and nodded. "I'd like that, Emily."

"Rule three: hours. You'll come at 10:00 a.m.—sharp. We'll work for two hours, then break for lunch. We can sit out by the pool, weather permitting, of course. Did you bring a suit?"

Treat shook her head, mouthing the word "no."

"Don't worry, we have dozens; one will fit. I try to swim every afternoon, rain or shine, for a half hour. The two-hour lunch break is for relaxing, getting to know each other. Oh, and I prefer that you don't take any notes during that time. Note-taking can get in the way of our relationship. We'll start again at 2:00 p.m. and work for another two hours."

Treat thought, *Relationship?* "Ms. Scott, umm, *Emily*, I was only given two days for the interview. I flew in early this morning, and I'm scheduled to leave tomorrow night on the red-eye."

Em said, not unkindly, "If your paper wants the interview you'll go by my rules. There's no way the story behind *The Girls* is going to fit into a two-day interview. I suggest you call them and tell them you need more time. Figure on four to seven days, not a day less."

"I'll make it happen."

"It'll be worth your while. Now, Treat, how do you take your coffee?"

"Black, please."

Em reached for the carafe and handed Treat a mug. "I see you're gazing at the portrait, *Woman of Mystery*."

Indeed Treat was. "The outfit...and her expression," she said, mesmerized. "Her eyes look as if she is holding onto a secret, and the slight smile—so mysterious. It's quite captivating. Who is she?"

"Char. She was one of the major players in forming the Girls."

Treat sipped her coffee. "Char? A nickname?"

Em seemed not to hear Treat's question. She closed her eyelids and leaned her head against the back of the chair. "Hmm, I almost forgot," she said, opening her eyes. "You're going to need this." She handed Treat a three by five filing card. "This card is critical to— let's say, our adventure."

Treat held the card, looking quizzically at the two columns.

"On the left side are the given names of the Girls," Em explained. "On the right side are the fictionalized names used in the novels. You see, when the Girls agreed to do this interview, we decided no holds barred, and it will be easier for me to use their actual names—first names only, for now."

Treat held onto the card as if she had just won the lottery. *First names, for now, with a hint of more to come.*

Em's voice softened. "You were asking me about the portrait. So many years have passed, a lifetime ago. Everyone called her Char. Look at the card now. You see, column left is Char; column right is Sarah. Easy, huh?"

"As falling in love."

Em had to smile. "I think I might take a shine to you after all. Well, about the portrait. It was her fiftieth birthday, thirty-four years ago. Char would be eighty-four had she lived. We were lovers for almost twenty years." Em's lips trembled. "Such a loss to everyone who knew and loved her." She looked around the den. "Char was a psychologist and this room was her home office."

Em shook her head and smiled. "Almost everything that Char wore had the flavor of a costume. She certainly had her own style. The Girls put that one together for her birthday portrait. It was our surprise gift to her. What a time we had, shopping at antique shops, flea markets. We even went to the Pasadena Rose Bowl swap meet."

Treat looked puzzled. "Swap meet at the Rose Bowl?"

"You've heard of the Rose Bowl?"

"Yes, of course—the New Year's Day football game."

"Right. Well, once a month a giant swap meet is held there. What an excursion that was. We found the floppy hat and most of the jewelry. You see the bracelet with the devil's head?"

Treat began to stand up. "May I look closer?"

Em nodded.

Treat examined the bracelet and commented, "It's most unusual."

"Char's mother always told her she was full of the devil. When we saw that, we thought, perfect! But the coup was finding the fox stole." She lowered her voice to a whisper. "I found that in Char's own closet. She had talked about her mother having a fox stole, and while she was working, I sneaked into her storage closet. I struck the mother lode!"

Em grinned, the thrill of hitting pay dirt written all over her face, but just as quickly became pensive. "Hmm...perhaps we're getting ahead of ourselves."

Treat said, "I did prepare some questions, but they're on my computer."

Em thought, *Two minutes and already pushing the boundaries.* She smiled. "Why don't we see what pops up without prompts from your gadget."

Treat returned the smile. "There were seven volumes in your series, *The Girls*. Each volume is about how the characters, seven women, aided victims of domestic abuse in the 1970s and '80s. When society failed to protect them, the Girls stepped in. For years fans have speculated on how much of the stories were based on real life."

Em nodded approvingly. "Nice bit of exposition there, Treat. Quite a bit actually. Of course details were altered, not only to protect the privacy of the rescued, but to keep the Girls safe as well.

"Almost all of our rescues were women and children, although we did have one case that dealt with a man. I believe that was *The Girls: Number Five*. People tend to forget that abuse is about power and control, not gender."

A look of defiance crossed Em's face. "It's one thing to pass a law; it's another to enforce it and protect the victim. It's been an uphill battle. If you get nothing else out of this interview, Treat, remember that each generation stands on the shoulders of the previous generation."

Treat hunched over the legal-sized paper, the pen held tightly in her hand, her hair falling around her face as she focused on capturing as many facts as possible. She had bragged about her penmanship courses but the truth was, she found writing by hand a miserable chore that her generation scorned.

Treat looked up. "Emily, I'm curious. How did you and the other girls meet and become friends?"

Em's eyes danced. "Now, that's an excellent question and the perfect place to begin. To understand the Girls, you have to understand seven individuals who came from very diverse backgrounds and yet melded into the closest of friends—family, really."

Em looked directly at Treat, their eyes connecting. "I believe that certain people are destined to be in each other's lives. We may begin thousands of miles away or on different continents, but we're drawn toward each other by an energy force. I like to think of it as an invisible thread. At some point we cross paths, and if we allow the connection, we are following our destiny."

"There's a Chinese legend about the invisible thread that connects us to those we are destined to meet," Treat offered, intrigued by the theory.

"Exactly! My belief was born many years ago when I began to look at my life and wondered why it took the twists and turns that it did. Perhaps now you can understand why this interview can't be done in two days."

"Emily, I'm committed to be here for as long as it takes."

Em chuckled. "A wise decision, Treat. Perhaps you have just changed the course of your life. Many years ago, when I was very young and naive, I chose a path that altered my life. Painful? Yes. But, I've come to believe that I needed to take that road to eventually reach my destiny.

"Char had a Yiddish word for it. She called it *bashert*. You know the word?"

Treat shook her head. "Can't say that I do."

Em smiled beatifically. "It means preordained."

Chapter 8

1963–1969

Emily's wedding was not the church wedding she had dreamed of. It wasn't supposed to be this way—not at all.

During sleepovers the five teens, Mary, Marsha, Lisa, Jacqueline and Emily—now seventeen and with their braces off—would munch on popcorn while thumbing through bridal magazines, choosing their wedding gowns, sighing at the photos of church weddings with long processions of bridesmaids, groomsmen, and flower girls. Fantasies sprung to life as a choir wearing navy-blue robes, their faces a mixture of holiness and smiles, sang the wedding hymn, "Give Me Joy in My Heart." What an occasion!

After the girls went to bed, the chattering slowed and then stopped as they fell asleep, one by one.

Emily burrowed deep into her flowered sleeping bag until only the top of her head showed. After she closed her eyes she would have visions of her very own wedding.

The church would be filled with friends and family. In the background the choir would begin to sing the love song "Because." Emily's mother had played the Perry Como record over and over again, and Emily knew it would make Mommy proud of her—something that rarely happened. *Twice,* she thought. The time they went out for lunch and the time she stood in front of the church congregation and received her promise ring.

Her bridesmaids, Mary, Marsha, Lisa, and Jacqueline, would wear dresses made of silky pink chiffon with dyed-to-match shoes, long-sleeved gloves, and pearls. She thought about adding pillbox hats, similar to the ones Jackie Kennedy made fashionable. It would be a Camelot wedding!

Emily would wear the gown she saw in a recent issue of *Modern Bride* magazine. She was sure Mommy could make it: a sheath of white organza, covered in Chantilly lace with a bustled cathedral train. Her bridal bouquet would be a spray of white cymbidium orchids, and her veil—her fantasy would begin to spin out of control—would be shimmering white lace floating beneath her waist. A comb would make sure that the veil wouldn't stray, and, best of all, it would hide the tight curls that no one ever seemed to like.

Her father would walk her down the aisle and Mitchell, now an aerospace engineer, dashing in a white tuxedo, would wait a little impatiently, a broad grin shining across his face, as he held out his hand to his bride. Daddy would kiss her, tell her how much he loved her, and Mommy would beam, as thoughts of grandchildren danced in her head.

Emily's actual "storybook wedding" might well have been penned by the Brothers Grimm.

Emily and Mitchell stood in front of Pastor Lockner, their parents the lone guests and witnesses to a wedding founded on disgrace rather than joy. The pastor's office was a reflection of his austere beliefs: a simple oak desk, two well-worn leather chairs, and a single bookcase holding his collection of books on the Christian philosophy of child rearing; several versions of the King James Bible (including the 1611 version), books on the Dead Sea Scrolls, and tour guides on his hidden desire: to travel to Israel and walk in the footsteps of Jesus.

Marian Grant, the only person to show Emily any kindness, kissed her on the cheek and pinned a white gardenia corsage on her now snug, navy-blue Sunday dress. Ethel Scott looked away, overcome with shame and anger, not with the pride that Emily had once dreamed about.

The bright yellow building and red neon sign welcomed the Scotts and the Grants to the Valley Ranch Steakhouse, a familiar Van Nuys icon where families came on special occasions to dine on steak and lobster. The bar was overflowing with young men and women celebrating the end of the workweek and the beginning of the weekend. Country Western music played loudly in the background, drowning out any possibility of conversation. Emily heard Patsy Cline's soaring falsetto rise above the general clatter on "I Fall to Pieces."

Emily choked back her tears. She was falling to pieces, but not in the way the lyrics told the story. She would never know the thrill of being in love or even the pain that came from love...lost.

The Scotts and the Grants, now bound together through a marriage based on the most sinful of life's vicissitudes—a baby conceived out of wedlock—waited in line to be seated, each fading into their own world of broken dreams. Somber faces made them appear as if they had just returned from a funeral instead of a wedding.

The hostess, a wide welcoming smile pasted on her face, wore the restaurant's uniform of a red cowgirl shirt with a black yoke, a short black-fringed skirt, and a bright red Stetson tilted to one side of her head.

"Special occasion, honey?" she asked, seeing Emily's corsage. The hostess's eyes wandered away from the corsage and drifted downward to Emily's tightly fitting navy-blue dress.

"I just got married," Emily whispered.

"Congratulations, honey," the hostess said, shooting Emily a quick, confidential wink that said she knew the score as she motioned for the dinner party of six to follow her.

As they were seated, Emily overheard the hostess whisper to the waiter, "Comp that table for desserts."

Mitchell ordered the porterhouse steak and lobster combo, with a baked potato soaked in butter and topped with sour cream. Emily watched as Mitchell rearranged the food on his plate, methodically carving one piece of steak, chewing it like a cow with its cud, and then digging out one morsel of lobster tail, chewing it, and repeating the whole process like a damned machine. Had she never noticed the way he ate before? Would she be watching this for the next fifty years? *Oh, God, what if they lived to be one hundred?*

Emily toyed with a bowl of over-salted clam chowder and excused herself to use the restroom; she needed to get away, to escape from the caged-in feeling. Maybe this was as far as she could go right now; not like Joan Baez, who could travel the world, singing about freedom—meeting fascinating people, making a difference, leaving her mark in this vale of dross and tears.

The bathroom was empty except for the hostess, who was putting on fresh lipstick. She saw Emily's reflection in the mirror and impulsively went over and gave her a gentle hug. "Honey, it happened to me, too. You'll get through it. It's not perfect but it's the way life works."

When they finished eating, Emily's father handed them a card with a crisp one hundred dollar bill safely tucked inside. "Mitchell and Emily, I'm not going to pretend that your beginning is ideal, but a good marriage is determined by how you overcome the difficulties. Let this beginning be seen as God's way." He raised his glass. "To Mitchell and Emily: happiness and a long life together."

They spent their wedding night at one of the newer glass-fronted hotels on Van Nuys Boulevard. The elevator swept them to the top story of the hotel. "Tenth floor," the bellhop announced. "This is the tallest building in Van Nuys. Featuring the latest in conveniences, and you'll have a sweetheart of a view from here." He showed them where the light switches were and pulled back the drapes so they could enjoy the view of the city lights. He held his palm up for a tip. "Congratulations, Mr. and Mrs. Grant," he said, tipping his cap smartly, after Mitchell put two dollars in his outstretched hand.

Emily said, "It was nice of your parents to pay for this room. Do you think they've forgiven us?"

Mitchell said seriously, "Your dad said it all, Emily. It's up to us now."

Mitchell opened the complimentary bottle of sparkling Concord grape juice and poured it into the waiting wine glasses. "To us, Emily," he said as he reached for her.

This time, Mitchell didn't have to say anything about the sheets being clean. This time, she didn't care about her nightgown, and this time, she didn't have to look at the clock.

∞

Her mother made an appointment with Dr. Otis Shelby, the obstetrician who had delivered Emily. The waiting room was crowded with women, none as young as Emily, with bellies of differing sizes: some barely showing, others looking as if they would burst, like a balloon, at any moment.

The lone man in the room sat next to a woman whose tummy looked uncomfortably large. He kept his face nervously buried in an ancient copy of *Parents* magazine. *Field and Stream, Outdoor Life, Car and Driver*—manly man mags were verboten in this bastion of femininity. Occasionally he would look up and scan the room with an anguished look that said, "What am I doing *here*!"

Emily, her mouth slightly open, stared when the woman stood, her abdomen protruding and drooping. She looked like she was going to give birth to a hippo. The soon-to-be mother looked at Emily. "Twins," she said proudly as her skittish husband leapt to his feet and dutifully began to rub her back.

Emily smiled wanly as terror raced through her mind and body. *How will she get them... How will I...get this...out!*

Mother and daughter, strangers at best, sat next to each other on two of the hard black Naugahyde chairs with chrome arms. From time to time, Emily would stare at the oak wood-framed pastoral print hanging on the wall. She became engrossed in the scenery of sheep grazing in a dark green meadow, encircled by weeping love grass. She closed her eyes, imagining the fresh, early summer air, basking in the warmth of the sun, wishing, praying, that she could lie down in the meadow and fall asleep, forever.

The nurse opened the door to the back office, holding a brown medical file in her hands. "Emily Grant?" she called out.

Startled out of her reverie, Emily looked at her mother. Ethel shook her head. "I'll wait here."

The nurse had her undress and put on a worn blue cotton gown. She took Emily's temperature and blood pressure and told her the doctor would be right in. Emily wished her mother had come into the exam room with her. She wondered if Mommy would ever forgive her.

She didn't know what Dr. Shelby meant when he told her to put her feet in the stirrups. She cried because he hurt her; she cried because she was alone; she cried because she was just a little girl.

Emily and Mitchell's apartment was located in a seedy part of downtown Van Nuys. The weathered brick building, built in the

1920s, held Carter's Supermarket, Gracey's Bakery, and Barney's Hardware Store on the first floor. A glass and wood framed door led from the street to the apartments above.

Their one-bedroom apartment was furnished with a couch donated by Pastor Lockner, a ten-inch black and white tabletop television set with rabbit ears, a chipped laminated kitchen table, and twin beds with a shared nightstand.

Emily spent most of her days crying and trying to stay cool from the early summer heat. When they went to bed, Mitchell wanted to "make love," but she didn't know where the love was.

Her mother refused to let Emily attend her high school graduation ceremony, even if her budding bump could be safely hidden underneath the crimson and silver graduation gown. "You will not parade this...this *stigma*," her mother said, pointing to Emily's belly. "Isn't it enough that you shamed us and everyone knows what you did?"

Mitchell returned from graduation sunburned from sitting in the Valley sun for two hours. He waived his diploma, grinned, and told her all about graduation.

"Boy, Emily, the kids were out of control. Some of them wore shorts under their gowns, and when they took their gowns off, one girl was wearing a bathing suit. I thought my father was going to have a stroke." Mitchell grinned and laughed out loud.

Emily stifled her envy and said, "Mitchell, was my name called?"

"I'm sorry Emily. Your mother thought it best—you know, given the circumstances."

"I'm a *persona non grata*," she said, wiping her tears away with the back of her hand.

"Huh? You know I didn't take Latin."

"Never mind, it doesn't matter."

The first and only time Mommy came to visit, she sat Emily down and explained how important a routine was for a successful marriage. "Make lists of things you have to do, Emily. It will give you purpose."

Emily took Mommy's advice to heart and discovered she liked keeping lists.

Number one on her list was to clean the apartment and plan dinner. She bought what she needed at Carter's and saved the receipt for Mitchell.

Number two was to eat her lunch while watching the soap opera *Days of Our Lives*. The characters were becoming more real to her than her own life. She thought about one of the actresses, Susan Flannery, who played a physician. *A woman doctor*, she thought as a lump in her throat made it impossible to finish her bologna sandwich. Number three was to take the stairs to the compact metal mailbox where their name was scribbled on a small piece of cardboard: *Grant.* It wasn't much to look forward to; they got a few bills and lots of advertisements, but she followed her list and checked the box every day except Sunday and holidays, when there was no mail delivery at all.

One day, more than a month after graduation, she found a brown envelope stuffed into the mailbox. Emily saw the return address: Van Nuys High School. She waited to open it until she was back in the apartment and sitting on the worn tweed sofa. She slid her finger under the flap and carefully pulled out the contents: her diploma, along with a letter congratulating her on her 3.9 grade point average. She rested her head on the arm of the sofa, crying, until she fell asleep. When she woke she took the diploma and the letter and put them in the bottom of the lone dresser drawer that belonged to her.

Her friends stopped calling. Mary, Marsha, Lisa, and Jacqueline moved on with their lives. Mary and Lisa went to college seeking their MRS degrees—slang for attending a university with the sole purpose of getting a husband and never graduating. Lisa joined the

Peace Corps, against her parents' wishes, and Jacqueline married the Pastor's son, John.

Mitchell got a job with the post office delivering mail. He came home after the interview, his face flushed with excitement. "I got 99 percent on the exam *and* I got the job. I have a career, Emily, a career with a future!"

Now, instead of talking about trig and college, their conversations were filled with the nuances of how the mail was sorted and delivered, a subject Emily, the dutiful wife, pretended to find endlessly fascinating.

One day, when the summer heat was at its fiercest, Emily lay on her bed, a wet washcloth across her forehead, hoping to fall asleep. Suddenly, from somewhere deep inside, she felt a flutter of butterfly wings. She put her hand over her abdomen and felt it again. The doctor's office had given her a booklet: *Becoming a Mother: Stages of Pregnancy*. She sat up and flipped to the page on feeling your baby move. She lay on the bed, making small circles on her belly with her fingertip. She felt the flutter again. She thought, *A person is growing inside me. My baby. I will use words, only words. Never a paddle, never. I've got to learn the right words.* And with a newly discovered sense of determination, she opened the door and left the apartment.

Emily walked the two blocks to the thrift shops that lined the nearby streets. The accumulation of litter on the streets and sidewalks was overwhelming; the stench of stale urine, overpowering. She tried not to look at the source of the odors. Homeless men, lingering outside the thrift shops with hollow cheeks and vacant eyes, stared at Emily as she walked by, hope blooming for a moment on their dirty faces as they thrust out paper cups. Emily put her hand inside the pocket of her maternity top and felt the coins left over from her three-dollar a week allowance. Was she being selfish not to drop it into someone's cup? But which one? There were so many. Emily thought about how hard Mitchell worked so that they would have a home and not live on the street. She made a mental note to be kinder to him, to try to make dinners that he would enjoy, and to not freeze up when he wanted to make love. She skittered past the derelicts, whose cups went down, whose eyes lost their fleeting hope.

Emily entered the Old Time Thrift Shop, relieved to escape the summer heat and the guilt that came from feeling the weight of the coins in her pocket. She felt a sense of comfort at the familiar wave from the cashier, Monica, and the movement from the ceiling fans as their breeze caressed her face. Usually, Emily would be looking for baby clothes or a maternity top, but today she wandered over to the used books with their musty smells that tickled her nose and made her sneeze.

Sometimes, she would use her allowance to buy something sweet, but this time she used her last thirty-five cents to purchase a soiled and scuffed dictionary. Its binding was loose; it was obviously well used, and Emily liked the fact that somebody before her had gotten as much service from it as she intended to do.

She carried the tattered book back to the apartment. She thought she would start with the "A's" and work her way through. That would be number four on her list of "Things to Do." Every day after watching *Days of Our Lives*, she would lie on the couch, the dictionary resting on her belly. As her belly grew, she liked to think she could feel the baby's foot or hand trying to reach out to her. *I will never hit my baby or pull its hair or pinch its back. I will rock this baby and love this baby.* She thought it because she knew how it felt not to be loved.

The dictionary became her window to a world of words. Words that could express her feelings and make her ponder. *Ponder*: to think about something before you act.

What an inspiring, hopeful word. She decided that was her favorite word for the day.

Chapter 9

Treat looked up from her note-taking. "I'm so sorry, Emily. I can't imagine being seventeen and pregnant. And to feel so alone."

"There's a saying: What doesn't kill you makes you stronger. Do you believe that, Treat?"

"The quote is from *The Twilight of the Idols* by Friedrich Nietzsche. The original quote is, 'Out of life's school of war: What does not destroy me, makes me stronger.'"

Em clapped her hands softly. "I'm impressed. You're well-educated, I'll give you that. But from a *feeling* level, do you believe it?"

Treat thought about how difficult it was for her to identify any of her feelings. "I'm not sure. I'm just not sure."

Emily spoke softly, a catch in her voice. "Well, I believe it; from my experience, it's true. I was so very young—just a child unprepared for the world—for becoming a mother; so very naive. I became depressed sitting alone in that dismal apartment, day after day." She shook her head to dispel the cobwebs of bitterness. "I had to fight my way out, but eventually I found my strength through words. A battered thirty-five-cent dictionary lit a spark that was waiting to be ignited. What if someone had thrown the book away instead of donating it? Would my life have been completely altered?"

Treat, noticing a grumbling in her stomach, said, "It's food for thought."

Em looked at her watch. "Speaking of food, I've forgotten about the time difference—it's three p.m. for you. I'll bet you're hungry."

Treat said shyly, "I am, Emily. Actually, I'm starving."

"Let's raid the refrigerator!" Em crowed. "There'll be plenty of leftovers. I gave up cooking when I found Madeline, a wonderful chef trained at the Cordon Bleu in Paris. I think my cooking genes wore out, like a battery; having Madeline has been a godsend.

"As with most relationships, we had to get used to each other at first. When I insisted on no salt or sugar and low-fat meals...well, let's say it was a bit of a challenge, but she rose to the occasion."

"You're lucky to have her."

"I don't know what I'd do without her, and that's the truth," Em concurred. "Now, when the Girls gather, we follow Char's tradition of deli food. The rest is up to Madeline. She does my lunches and dinners and takes care of all the holiday meals. The fridge is always loaded with healthy food and..." a mischievous smile lit Em's face, "*if* I look really carefully, I can find something I shouldn't be eating.

"Let's make this day a 'we can eat anything we damn well please' day and put aside any diets or restrictions. You see, Treat, everything we do in life can be an adventure."

She looked at Treat's lean, muscular body; she could tell this was a woman with discipline. *But she needs to loosen up a bit*, thought Em.

Em said, "We'll swim after lunch. I discovered you really don't have to wait an hour after eating before swimming, *and* I have just the right swimsuit for you."

Treat dreaded the prospect of wearing a community-shared bathing suit. "Uh, that's okay—if you don't mind I'll pass on the swimming."

"This one is new. I bought it for my granddaughter for her birthday. It'll fit you, and it's still in the package. I'll get her another one next week."

Treat blushed. "Am I that readable?"

"I thought I saw you flinch, but it's understandable. Wearing someone else's suit is rather intimate, don't you think?" Em asked rhetorically. "And, while we're eating, I want to hear about the school you went to that taught you cursive—an hour a day copying the classics." Em laughed. "I don't know, frankly it sounds a bit torturous."

Em turned on the overhead fans in the den. "It's getting a bit stuffy. This room gets the afternoon sun."

Treat said, "Thanks for lunch, Emily. I haven't had peanut butter and jelly sandwiches for years. I've never had it before with potato chips in the middle."

"A delicacy I invented years ago. Now confess, aren't you glad you went swimming?"

"Yes, I am. It helped with the jet lag."

"The suit was perfect for you."

"I usually wear black."

"*Agh*, you're too young for black. My suit is black, with a skirted bottom. It's for old ladies. And don't try to tell me I'm not old."

"I won't, Emily. But, you can still kick butt in the water."

They laughed. Em thought, *She's starting to loosen up; peanut butter and jelly sandwiches, with chips, will do it every time.*

Treat picked up her pad of paper and flipped through its note-filled pages. "I'm running out of paper," she said, frowning.

"Don't worry, Treat, I'm sure I have everything you'll need."

Chapter 10

1963–1969

On November 22, 1963, President John F. Kennedy was assassinated in Dallas, Texas.

On January 15, 1964, Christopher John Grant was born.

At ten months, Chris was a sun-shining baby, with blond hair, lively blue eyes, and a wide, captivating smile. On Sundays after church, Emily and Mitchell would take turns having lunch at their parents' homes. Perhaps it was Chris's personality that softened the hearts of his grandparents, but whatever shame and anger they had felt, or still felt, toward Mitchell and Emily was not transferred to Chris. He was held and played with, and once, Emily saw her mother feeding and rocking Chris while she softly sang "Danny Boy." Unaware of being watched, Ethel Scott had wept as she brushed Chris's hair away from his eyes and kissed his dimpled hands. This unexpected vignette melted Emily's heart, and she couldn't help but wonder if her grim mother had ever loved her so unconditionally.

∞

The 1964 World Series between the New York Yankees and the St. Louis Cardinals was being televised on NBC. The sale of larger television sets was booming and a twenty-three inch Zenith, set in a French provincial cabinet—and guaranteed to have been made in the USA—sat in all its glory in the Scotts' living room.

Sam, fit to bust with pride, bragged, "Look at that color picture! Clear as a bell. I picked out the brand and size and Ethel—"

"—and *I* got to pick out the cabinet." Ethel rubbed her hand over the cherry wood credenza. "It is beautiful, isn't it?"

Emily nodded. "What happened to your old television?" she said, thinking about their pitiful little ten-inch set waiting at home.

"Donated to the church, of course."

Figures, Emily's mind screamed.

Ethel held out her arms, eager for the transfer of Chris from his mother to her. "Let me have that grandson of mine!" She held Chris close and smiled. "Ooo, I think he's gained at least five pounds since I saw him." When Chris reached up and playfully squeezed his grandma's cheek, she kissed his little hands, perfect as a doll's. "Well, little man, how about if you watch the game with Grandpa and Daddy while Grandma and Mommy fix dinner?"

She lowered Chris into the waiting portable crib. He grinned when Emily laid him on his back and handed him his bottle. Holding it with both hands, he kicked his plump legs, sometimes taking the bottle out to observe, to listen, or to say, "Ba-ba." His eyelids fluttered as he fought the need to sleep. Gradually, as the Sandman won out, the nipple slipped from his mouth, the bottle fell from his grasp, his eyes closed, and he fell into a deep slumber.

Emily said, "He's becoming so independent. Sometimes I miss the way he would let me hold him for every bottle. Well...I guess he's just growing up. He'll sleep now, it's way past his nap time." She leaned over to cover Chris with a light blanket.

∞

NBC was broadcasting game four of the Fall Classic on Los Angeles Channel 4.

Sixth inning score: Yankee 3, Cardinals 0.

Sam and Mitchell, their voices hushed and expectant at first, crept to the edge of their seats, shouting encouragement, as the Cardinals loaded the bases. When Cardinals' third baseman Ken Boyer hit a grand slam home run, the men leapt from their seats, pumping the air with their fists and hollering as if they had done the deed. The Cardinals went on to win the game 4–3, tying the series at two games apiece. As dyed-in-the-wool Cards fans, Sam and Mitchell couldn't have been happier.

Ethel shook her head and clucked her tongue. "Men and their sports! They'll wake the baby."

Emily said, "I like sports too, Momma."

"You always were a tomboy," said Ethel dryly, shooting her daughter an accusatory look.

Manly exultations from the living room continued to float into the kitchen as the aroma of baked ham and candied yams answered back. Emily knew she would be given a care package to take home and thought, *Thank God, I won't have to cook tomorrow.*

It was Emily's job to shell the peas. And ever since she was a little girl, she liked to guess how many little peas would be in each shell. She felt good when there were at least three, and sad when she only found one, or sometimes an empty shell—the way she felt so much of the time. As much as Emily loved Chris, she couldn't seem to shake the shroud of sadness that had blanketed her since his birth. She had no females to confide in, only her mother. With the idyllic picture of Ethel and Chris in her head, Emily felt emboldened to test her mother's mellowness.

"Momma, I'm feeling sad all the time," she said, tears streaming down her cheeks. "Since Chris was born...it's been so hard."

Ethel Scott stood next to the sink, mashing the potatoes while she slowly added warm whole milk and a quarter pound of melted butter. She looked at her daughter, disappointment hanging in her eyes.

"Momma, won't you ever forgive me?" Emily pleaded.

"Does Mitchell hit you?" her mother asked dryly. *Mash, mash, mash.*

Emily shook her head. "No, Momma."

"Does he go to work?" *Whip, whip, whip.*

Emily whispered, "Yes."

"Then be grateful for what you have." Her mother scooped the potatoes into a Pyrex casserole dish.

"Momma, why do you hate me so?" She hung her head and gave vent to several small, tearless gasps, like a cried-out child.

Unmoved, her mother opened the oven door, found a space for the bowl, and slid the potatoes inside. She rubbed her back as she stood up straight. "I don't hate you, Emily. You were a girl who didn't act the way a little girl should act—a tomboy who got herself into trouble. If truth was told, Emily, you were not what I expected."

Mitchell and Emily were the proud owners of a used 1959 Chevy Impala station wagon. It boasted an all steel body, a fading blue and tan two-tone paint job, and a removable back seat. The wagon fairly screamed "old married man," but Mitchell liked the peppy 238 V8 automatic transmission and tried to convince himself the car's rear fins gave it a certain stylishness, while Emily liked its roominess— plenty of space for baby items, groceries, and her thrift store finds. They drove the short distance home from their parents in silence. They had so little in common, except that they were married and had a child together.

Mitchell seemed unusually optimistic. "That was one heck of a game. Maybe soon, we can afford a new TV. Not fancy like your mom and dad's, but a little bit bigger than what we have. We're starting to move up, Emily. We've got a car now, and we can manage the payments, if we're extra careful."

Emily wondered how she could be more careful. The last movie they had seen was *Tom Jones*, and that was almost two years ago. They never ate out and relied on their crummy ten-inch black and white television for entertainment.

Mitchell continued, "I was talking with your dad."

Emily listened attentively. It was so unusual for Mitchell to talk about anything except work.

"Emily, I came up with an idea. You know, things are really hard financially. It might be a good idea for you to work part-time. Maybe four hours a day."

"What could I do? I'm not trained for anything. And Chris takes up so much of the day."

Mitchell grinned like the cat that ate the canary. "I've been offered the night shift...midnight to eight. It pays more and eventually, I'll get a shot at being a supervisor. I don't want us to be stuck in an apartment for the rest of our lives. Old man Carter is looking for help at the market. You know, bagging and checking. Chris is an easy baby—I could watch him while you're working, and Carter's is right downstairs."

Emily felt a sudden sense of hope. "I like that idea, Mitchell. I'll talk to Mr. Carter tomorrow."

The customers called him Stan, his wife called him Dear, but to Emily he was always just plain Mr. Carter. He was an affable man who looked to Emily like an older and much fatter version of Dick Van Dyke, and she liked him immensely. Carter's Supermarket had a service meat department, with Mr. Carter as the chief butcher. A large pickle jar and wheels of cheddar and Swiss cheese sat on the glistening porcelain and glass meat counter, and Mr. Carter was quick to give samples to his customers with a winning smile.

"Giving the customer a little taste is good for sales," declared Mr. Carter, stabbing the air with his finger, which was as big as a sausage. "If they like it they'll buy more, and even if they don't, they'll remember Carter's." He lowered his voice. "You see, Emily, the chains can't do that. We can."

He gave Emily a tour of the store and took her into the meat refrigerator, where carcasses were hanging from metal meat hooks. Emily instantly felt her gorge rise.

"Emily, this is where your meat comes from. In the morning, I take down what I think we'll need for the day and break it down." He poked a steer quarter with his hand; the meat spun grotesquely on its hook. "You'll get steaks and tender roasts from this."

His chest puffed out as he described the complexities of his profession. "People think it's easy to be a butcher, but it's a real skill. You have to know when to use a knife, and when to use your hands. I learned how to butcher back in the old days, as an apprentice. Now, you go to some of the big stores and everything is precut."

Emily did her best to pretend interest but thought she would never eat meat again.

He led her out of the refrigerator and back into the store.

"It's important for everything to be kept spotless. I empty the cases every night, and on Sundays, when the store is closed, I scrub them clean. No one has ever gotten sick from meat sold at Carter's Supermarket," he added proudly.

"Now, Emily, you'll start out bagging groceries. And *if* you don't break too many eggs, you'll learn to be a checker."

"Thank you, Mr. Carter. I'd like that, and I'll try to never break an egg."

Mr. Carter smiled. "I can tell we'll get along fine, Emily, just fine."

Emily made $1.25 an hour bagging groceries and, true to her word, never broke an egg. Mr. Carter reminded her, "Smile at the customers, Emily. It'll make them *and* you happy. And, it's okay to talk to them, too. Remember, this is a family-friendly business, and all our advertising is word of mouth."

Emily discovered that chatting with the customers made her life more interesting, and Mr. Carter was right, smiling with them made her happy.

Peeking out from under her veil of sadness was an Emily who had a sense of humor and could connect with the customers, especially the children.

Mr. Carter smiled and said, "The customers really like you, Emily. Keep up the good work." When Emily got her first paycheck, Mr. Carter wrapped two steaks in butcher paper and told her she was one of his best employees.

On the days she wasn't working, she walked with Chris to the thrift shops, looking for children's clothing, and oh, how she loved to find a good book! She adored Muriel Spark's *The Prime of Miss Jean Brodie*—about a remarkable Scottish teacher's mentorship of six girls—and found Lillian Hellman's play *The Children's Hour*—about the headmistresses of a boarding school accused of having a lesbian affair—oddly fascinating. Her mother would have a heart attack if she had known she was reading such "smut." Life was not the dream she had wished for, but she took her mother's advice, as sparse as it was, and tried to be grateful for everything she had.

Their home life was routine. They went to work, had an early dinner with their parents on Sundays, and on Mitchell's nights off, would take their showers and wait for Chris to fall asleep. Emily would move into Mitchell's bed, hoping that tonight would be different.

Mitchell would kiss her twice—long, sloppy kisses that she never enjoyed—and then lift her nightgown to briefly run his hands over her breasts. She tried to pay attention, hoping she would feel something. Lists kept springing up in her mind: grocery lists, lists of things to do...good books to read.

She could hear the condom opening and would make her legs relax, not because of the pleasure that would follow, but because she knew in three or four minutes it would be over. Mitchell would release her and turn on his side, away from her. They didn't hug; they didn't talk. Emily would say good night and move to her bed, content with her 39-by-75-inch sanctuary—she knew its dimensions because, curiously, she had measured them herself and derived comfort in having some personal space, however paltry—and fall asleep.

Chris was in preschool and would be starting kindergarten in the fall. Emily loved that he was smart and verbal. "Big boy school," he called kindergarten. Chris was beginning to read, picking out familiar words from library books. Whenever she thought of Chris, a warm sensation wrapped around her heart, and although it was unfamiliar, she knew it was love.

Mr. Carter promoted Emily to checker, and she was working more hours. Working and taking care of Chris and keeping the apartment clean left her with little energy to spare.

The vomiting started at work; she barely made it to the bathroom. Mr. Carter looked worried and sent her home with a fresh chicken and the commandment: "Make chicken soup, Emily. It will cure anything."

She dragged her feet up the stairs, the wrapped chicken in one hand, her other firmly fixed to the stair rail. Mitchell would be picking Chris up from school, and she needed to lie down. *Five minutes,* she thought. *I'll shut my eyes for five minutes.* She curled up in a small ball on the couch and fell into a deep sleep.

Mitchell shook her. "Emily, wake up. I've got to go to work. Overtime shift. Extra money, you know. I'll grab a hamburger on the way."

She sat up, half-awake, and held her arms out to Chris, taking in his little-boy smell that told her he had played hard in the sun, had peanut butter and jelly left on his hands from lunch, and a lingering baby scent—so sweet, so clean, so pure—that seemed to fade a little more every day.

"Mommy, Mommy, see my art work!"

Chris held up a finger painting of a square building, with three stick figures standing on the sidewalk, and a large sun, more egg-shaped than round, that took up most of the paper.

"Put on fridrator, Mommy?"

She gave him a quick kiss. "In a minute, sweetie. Mommy has to go potty." She rushed into the bathroom and began to throw up. She sat on the floor and cupped her face. *Sweet Jesus,* she thought. *When was my last period?*

Chapter 11

1969–1970

Emily was surprised but not unhappy to discover that Dr. Otis Shelby had retired. She was startled at the changes when she opened the door to Dr. Lesley Walker's office. Comfortable uphol-stered couches in beige, and wing chairs in pastel colors, had replaced the hard Naugahyde furniture. Photos of Hawaiian waterfalls and or-chids hung on the walls. It was the yellow and white orchids that caught Emily's attention: the brightest yellow—like the sun drawn by Chris—and the purest white, like the wedding dress she had once dreamed about. The only thing she missed was the print of the sheep grazing in the meadow that used to hang on the waiting room wall. She sighed, longing for a place to escape to, even if it was only in her mind.

This time, there were more men in the waiting room, some holding hands openly and unashamedly with their wives. One leaned over, smiling, as his hand made small circles on his wife's belly. She knew Mitchell would never sit next to her and rub her belly. He loved Chris in his way, but his focus was on work and managing their money.

The receptionist, Donna, smiled and handed Emily new patient forms to complete. Emily was caught off-balance at the section that asked about herself: *How do you spend your days? Do you work outside the home? What hobbies do you have?*

She wasn't sure how to answer. Should she say, *I spend my day cooking and cleaning and taking care of my son, Chris. I work as a cashier at a grocery store, and my hobby is making lists of things to do.* She decided honesty was the best policy and put down exactly those words, wondering if they would sound as dull and pathetic to the doctor and his staff as they did to herself.

Afterward, she was shown to an office, paneled in white oak and lined with matching bookshelves filled not just with medical books, but also with leather-bound novels that made her feel as if she were in the library of an English mansion.

A woman with long, blond hair, swept into a ponytail, and wearing pink and blue teddy bear scrubs, sat behind the desk. She looked up and smiled, her deep blue eyes sparkling as if she had just heard an amusing story. "Hi, Emily. I'm Dr. Lesley."

Emily looked surprised.

"Whoops, did I catch you off guard?" she said, coming around from the desk to shake hands. "It happens a lot. People automatically assume I'm a man—but whom better to give obstetric advice to a woman than another woman? We women are making strides in the medical field but there's still a lot of work to do. The name doesn't help, either. Lesley is actually androgynous; it means garden of hollies. My parents didn't want to bother thinking about two names, so I'm just plain old Lesley Walker, MD."

Dr. Lesley motioned to a velvet chair facing her desk. She spoke softly. "Are you okay with a woman physician, Emily?"

Emily thought about Dr. Laura Horton on *Days of Our Lives*, nodded, and suddenly felt like crying. She croaked, "You're so young."

"Yeah, but don't hold that against me," she said cheerfully. "It's what happens when you graduate high school at fourteen—it pushes everything forward. You know, there are more and more women fighting their way into male-dominated professions. I just happen to be one of them."

Emily's eyes widened. "You have so many books."

Dr. Lesley followed Emily's gaze and turned back to the girl, smiling. "What kind of books do you like, Emily?" she said, leaning against the desk.

"Fiction. And I like dictionaries. I like words."

Dr. Lesley went over to her bookcase. "Here, Emily, a thesaurus for you to borrow. I want you to come in with a new word at every appointment. Deal?"

Emily smiled. "Deal!"

This time she knew what Dr. Lesley meant when she told her to scoot down. Afterward, Dr. Lesley asked her to sit up. "I'm going to run some blood tests, but everything looks really good. I'd say you're about ten weeks pregnant. You had a vaginal delivery with Chris. I would expect the same this time. How was it?"

"How was what?" Emily said, confused by the question.

"Your experience during delivery."

No one had ever asked her that question.

Dr. Lesley waited.

"I'm not sure..."

"I mean, what was it like for you during labor and delivery?"

Emily began to cry. "I'm sorry. They drugged me and left me alone. I was so scared."

"Things are changing, Emily. Women weren't meant to be alone during childbirth. Having a baby is, well, let's say it's a group effort. You have to do most of the work, but we're your support team. The way I practice is different. I have privileges at Brown Memorial Hospital. That's where you'll be admitted. And your husband can stay with you; he can even go into the delivery room."

Emily shook her head. "Mitchell won't want to."

"What about family, friends...?"

"Not really."

Dr. Lesley held her hand and looked directly into her eyes. "You won't be alone, I promise you that. I'll be there or one of my midwife nurses will be with you the entire time. Donna is going to make your next appointment. I'd like to see you in two weeks."

"So soon?"

"Just a chat in the office."

"Mitchell will ask why. He worries about money—a lot."

Lesley suspected something was wrong, even if Emily didn't. "You'll have a single fee no matter how many appointments you need. Tell him I'm watching your blood pressure. And don't forget, bring in a new word."

"Blood pressure?"

"No extra charge, Mitchell. She's just being careful."

In a moment of unexpected tenderness Mitchell said, "I'm sorry you have to go through this again. I don't understand how it happened. I've used a condom every time."

Emily was touched, but she heard the unspoken declaration. Her husband didn't want any more children. Did she?

Mitchell rubbed his forehead as if lost in deliberation. "I've been thinking, there's a lot of overtime at the post office and if we're careful, you can stop working. I hear a lot of people talking, and women are going back to school in droves. You always wanted to be a teacher. Why not go back to school? By the time the baby is five, you'll be able to work full-time. You'll make so much more as a teacher than working part-time as a checker. We'll need a two-bedroom apartment for now, but I think we should have a goal of buying a house. Emily, it'll be our five-year plan. Wouldn't you like that?"

She whispered, "Yes, Mitchell."

It was rare for him to pour his heart out. Mitchell had turned into a *Days of Our Lives* character before her eyes. She felt her heart warm with fondness, but the feeling would be short-lived.

"I know I haven't been much of a...husband. I'd like to at least give you this. There's only one thing I ask." His face turned red, a mixture of shame and anger. "I'm a man and I have certain needs. I don't want to be refused."

Emily looked down. "I'm sorry, Mitchell. I know it's my fault."

Mitchell nodded. "As long as we understand each other." His voice became terse. "That's our agreement. Keep it."

Emily became a fixture in Dr. Lesley's office. She didn't understand why she needed to be seen so often. Dr. Lesley would take her blood pressure and say, "Everything looks good," then sit in the chair opposite Emily and demand with a grin: "Got my word?"

Emily would smile and try to remember the hardest word she could think of. Dr. Lesley would almost always get them right. When she was wrong she would laughingly concede that Emily had won the game. Emily worked hard at trying to find the most diffi-cult word. Trying to stump Dr. Lesley became a new "thing to do" on her list.

"Laconic," said Emily on one visit.

Dr. Lesley scratched her head while Emily held her breath. "You win!" Dr. Lesley laughingly replied.

Emily thought she had the most beautiful laugh. "Dr. Lesley, it means using fewer words."

"That's a great word, Emily, and I'll have to remember that when I'm doing crossword puzzles. Now, tell me about your week."

Emily liked that Dr. Lesley was interested in what she did but couldn't help but wonder: *Is this a new form of doctoring?*

"Mitchell thinks it would be a good idea if I returned to school and became a teacher."

"And what about you?"

"It was always my dream. I'm excited and worried at the same time. I've done some research, and I qualify to get into the teaching program at California State University at Northridge. They have a three-day a week program, but it means putting the baby in daycare and getting home to fix dinner before Mitchell leaves for work. And then there's Chris. I can't let him feel neglected—you know, sibling rivalry and Mom not being home as much."

She paused and added shyly, "I really want to go, Dr. Lesley. I missed my high school graduation, and I want to learn."

"It sounds hard but doable. I think it's a wonderful idea. We'll talk more about how you can juggle everything. Your check-up appointment is next week. Does Mitchell want to come in?"

"No. That just isn't Mitchell."

"Have you talked to him about being in the delivery room?"

"Yes. He thinks the idea is—his word—sissy."

Dr. Lesley bit her lip.

"He asked if you would call him after the baby is born, in case he's at work," Emily continued. "Mitchell won't miss work, not even for our baby girl."

"A girl, huh? You're sure?"

"Yes, and her name is Maggie."

This time, she was awake and not alone. Dr. Lesley and Cheryl, her nurse midwife, coached Emily through the labor and delivery.

Dr. Lesley said, "You were right, Emily! You have a daughter, and what a beauty she is! Head full of black hair and dark brown eyes that are wide open and shining with wisdom. Welcome to the world, Maggie."

Cheryl placed Maggie on Emily's abdomen. "You did a wonderful job, Emily, and so did Maggie."

Emily touched Maggie and began to cry. "She's so soft and beautiful. Thank you, Dr. Lesley and Cheryl. Dr. Lesley, you'll remember to call Mitchell?"

Lesley felt a stirring of anger but spoke softly. "As soon as we're done here. Right now my focus is on you and Maggie. I want your thoughts on your baby girl and nothing else right now. Okay?"

"Okay, Dr. Lesley."

"Okay! Take some deep cleansing breaths and let's get your placenta delivered."

Dr. Lesley stood at Emily's bedside, beaming. "That was a textbook delivery. You check out and so does Maggie. Her Apgar score is a perfect ten! You should be proud. Are you ready to feed her?"

Emily nodded, and for the first time, put Maggie to her breast. The babe looked up, her eyes locking with her mother's. "Maggie's my lovely girl and hungry, too," Emily gushed. "She's really latching on! I'm so glad you encouraged me to breastfeed."

Dr. Lesley never tired of seeing this picture of mother and child. "Wonderful, Emily. You'll be here for a couple of days. The lactation nurse will be checking in with you and so will I. Remember now, for the first week or so, Maggie is going to want to be at your breast, well, let's say constantly. That's nature's way to bring the milk in and stretch your nipples so they can reach Maggie's palate."

Emily nodded but kept her eyes on Maggie.

"I can see you're a natural and so is Maggie. Your nipples may get sore, but hang in there, don't give up."

Emily looked at Dr. Lesley, her eyes moistening. "I promise I won't—I won't give up."

Maggie was six weeks old when Emily had her final examination.

Dr. Lesley admired Maggie, who was sleeping in the infant carrier. "You make beautiful babies," she said, smiling. "How's the breastfeeding going?"

"I wouldn't do it any other way. I was discouraged when I had

Chris; maybe that's why I felt so sad all the time. I don't feel that way this time, Dr. Lesley. Maggie weighs almost ten pounds—she's really plumped out!"

"I'll say! But she's a real beauty, especially with her double chins," quipped Dr. Lesley. She handed Emily a box covered in Noah's Ark gift-wrap. "For you and Maggie."

"No doctor has ever given me a present before," Emily said shyly, as she unwrapped the package. "A breast pump! Thank you. I was worried about how I would supplement while Maggie's in daycare."

"Every working mother needs one of these." The doctor smiled. "And school *is* work. Now, I want to spend some time talking about birth control. What are your plans?"

"I—I hadn't thought about it."

"You have choices, Emily. Perhaps something that will let you feel in control. Let's talk about your options."

Dr. Lesley fitted her with a diaphragm. "Don't forget to use the spermicide," she said, a small smile crossing her face.

Maggie was just months old and in daycare, three days a week. Emily arranged her class schedule, pumped her breasts, and couldn't wait to pick Maggie up from daycare. She would drive to a secluded spot, park under a shady tree, and put Maggie to her breast. Maggie suckled like there was no tomorrow whether she was hungry or not. Emily would put her face close to Maggie, taking in her scent, making soft soothing sounds that brought comfort to mommy and baby.

Emily saw Dr. Lesley for her six-month check-up and brought in photos of Chris and Maggie—and a new word.

Dr. Lesley said, "The kids are beautiful and you are looking very happy."

Emily smiled. "Very tired, but very happy. Dr. Lesley, I haven't forgotten about your new word."

"Okay, let's have it."

Emily folded her arms and enunciated precisely: "Inchoate."

Lesley scratched her head and looked puzzled. "Inchoate...okay, you win!"

Emily laughed. "It's me, Dr. Lesley. Just beginning and not fully formed or developed."

Chapter 12

Em stood to close the den blinds from the waning afternoon sun. Returning to her chair, she spoke in a yearning tone. "Sometimes, it is tiring to dredge up these memories."

"I know this must be difficult for you, Emily."

"It's necessary, Treat, if you are to get the full story of the Girls." Em continued her story. "I was twenty-four, a freshman in college with two children, and a husband to care for. Lesley was the first person who really listened to me, encouraged me. And as I discovered, years later, she was one of Char's close friends. You see, Treat, when I talked earlier about the thread that connects us—it's beginning to form. And one by one, you'll see how we became the Girls."

Em looked at her watch. "The day has flown by, and we do need to stop."

Treat opened her briefcase and tucked in the sheaf of handwritten notes. "Thank you, Emily, for sharing so much with me. I'll see you tomorrow morning at ten."

Em nodded curtly. "Have a good evening, Treat."

The four o'clock traffic news warned Treat of a gridlocked freeway and suggested an alternate route: Cahuenga Pass, the pre-freeway connection from the San Fernando Valley to Hollywood.

Renting the Audi had been a good choice, she thought. It was the same model as her own car and gave her a sense of familiarity and control. She became invigorated as she drove the twists and turns of the mountain pass, shifting gears and feeling the car responding to her touch.

The drive provided stark views of hillsides dotted with concrete and stucco houses. Modest, single-story homes, built in the 1950s and '60s, rested precariously on stilts, where recent rains had threatened to wash away their underpinnings. Sheets of plastic had been laid on the denuded hillsides, an optimistic but slim protection against further erosion.

Being with Emily Elizabeth Scott was proving to be more of a challenge than she had expected. Treat had thought: two days, in and out. Write the article on the flight home, and that was that. Now she was caught in a web of emotionally charged stories, and she had more than twenty pages of notes to transcribe.

She was aware of being thrown off balance by Ms. Scott—Emily—Em. She thought, *That woman seems to notice my every move, to read my every thought.*

After this assignment was completed she would need to regenerate, to restore her defenses. When she got home she would arrange a few vacation days at Chapman's. It had been almost two years since she had seen the headmistresses, Miss Violet and Miss Lily. She knew they would welcome her, and she could stay in the cabin farthest away from the students and teachers, the one that was reserved for guests.

She longed to take the road to Chapman's, nestled so safely in the Adirondacks; a winding road with a vista of white pines, hickories, and elms—so many species to comfort her.

And the meadows...

She first saw the meadows when she was eight years old. She sat in the backseat of Miss Violet and Miss Lily's car, trying not to cry. It was springtime and the meadows were ablaze with wildflowers: purple trillium, white flowering Canada violet, and the one she came to love the best, the downy yellow violet whose cheery face peeked through scattered rocks and boulders. There was something soothing about the way the flowers moved in the gentle breeze, as if they were dancing with invisible fairies. She fell asleep and when she woke, they had arrived at Chapman's.

Treat wondered if Emily's purging of her memories were triggering something inside her. Memories that she had hoped had been laid to rest, but now seemed to be surfacing once again.

Her thoughts drifted away to the times the students would have a summer campout. "You can learn to survive in any environment," Miss Violet would say as she showed them how to identify edible plants and herbs.

For two weeks every year, New York City became their playground. They rode the subway system, went to art galleries and museums, shopped at Barney's or Sax Fifth Avenue, and were taught proper etiquette for dining at the finest restaurants.

"This is a different environment, but you must be prepared to survive here as well," Miss Lily would say.

Now, she was in a foreign territory with Emily Elizabeth Scott. She was aware of how quickly Emily had thrown her off balance and eroded her underpinnings by taking away her iPad and computer. She was beginning to feel as fragile as the houses hanging precariously from the barren hillsides of Cahuenga Pass.

She exited at Hollywood Boulevard and came to an immediate stop as the street became crowded with late afternoon tourists hoping to connect with their favorite celebrity, even if it was only through a cement hand and footprint in front of Grauman's Chinese Theater.

She turned onto Crescent Center Drive, a dismal part of the city, one without the sparkle and glamour that drew the tourists to Hollywood. She entered the parking lot of the Moon and Stars Hotel, a three-story concrete and glass building, built more than sixty years ago, and now in desperate need of refurbishing or better yet, she thought, a candidate for demolition. The lobby was shabby, but the desk clerk was friendly and gave her directions to the local market. She thought that had to count for something.

Treat dumped the grocery bag holding a container from the local market's skimpy salad bar on the desk. Wilted lettuce, pale, tasteless tomatoes, and not-so-fresh vegetables would be her dinner, apples and pears her dessert.

She thought her boss, Evan Perket, would have at least ponied up for a three-star hotel, after all she did work for the *Times*. A smirk had crossed his face as he handed her the travel voucher. She looked at it and knew it was payback for her rebuking his sexual advances. She wanted to wipe that smirk off his face—her black belt in taekwondo gave her the power—and for a moment she let her fantasies run free. She wanted to see him on his knees, begging for his life, as she delivered the final blow, standing with one foot on top of his lifeless body. Except, when she allowed that fantasy to come to life, she saw herself as a little girl, not as the woman she was today.

Evan had said, "You know I don't approve of this wild goose chase. Anything above this voucher and you're on your own. And I don't have to tell you if you screw up on this—"

"No, Evan. You don't have to tell me shit." Her anger had slipped out of her control and into Evan's hands.

She was still fretting over that mistake as she covered the bed with the sheet she had brought from home; she didn't trust any hotel, but this one in particular. Plus, damn it, there wasn't a workout room.

Now she had to make a two-day trip last up to a week. And she had to transcribe handwritten notes. She lifted the bundle of notes, removed the rubber band, and with an angry "Fuck it!" threw them across the room, watching as they floated and then drifted into a carpet of scattered reminiscences.

Chapter 13

Tuesday, October 6, 2020
Studio City

"We're dressed alike," Em said, commenting on the red T-shirts and jeans she and Treat were wearing.

"I was hoping you wouldn't mind if I dressed casually. I didn't pack for five days."

"Not at all, although someone might take us for twins."

Treat glanced at the portrait of Char Owens before she sat on the den couch.

Em leaned over, handing Treat a mug of coffee. "Where are you staying?" she asked casually.

"The Moon and Stars Hotel."

"What? That dump in Hollywood? I guess that says a lot about the value of the Girls."

Treat's face flushed and her hands became clammy. "My boss wasn't on board. I had to beg and he finally gave in, but with a very small voucher."

"He sounds like an asshole."

Treat was taken aback by Emily's choice of words. She relaxed and chuckled, "You've met him?"

Em laughed. "No, but others like him."

Em passed Treat a plate of chocolate and apricot delcos. "You should try these, they are wonderful with a cup of coffee."

Treat waved the plate of cookies away. "No thank you, I don't eat sweets."

Em insisted. "You should try one, Treat. These are made with wholesome organic ingredients. We're meant to have something sweet once in a while. That is why we have been given all our taste buds. Taste buds are like feelings, they come with a full complement; none should be denied."

Treat thought, *I don't dare kill the goose that might lay the golden egg, but God, she's relentless. What a controlling, pushy woman.* Reaching for a delco, she hesitated before taking a small bite that unleashed an immediate rush of euphoria.

"Here's my transcript from yesterday," Treat said, wiping away the crumbs from her mouth. "Emily, these are really outstanding. What are they, again?"

"They're called delcos. Char got me hooked on them. My, how she loved them—the sinful taste, of course, and how they evoked the childhood memory of going to the Jewish deli and bakery on a Sunday with her daddy. I knew you would like them. You just needed to get pushed into trying something different." Em chuckled. "Not unlike myself when I was your age."

Treat's eyes wandered to the plate of delcos. Em smiled and passed the cookies. "Another one won't hurt you, I promise."

This time Treat didn't hesitate to take two. She sat back, her cup of coffee in one hand, a cookie in the other. She remembered how the students at Chapman's were lectured on proper nutrition.

She was only eight, but Miss Violet's words still echoed in her mind: "You are given one body, and *only one*, to care for. Serve it well and *it* will serve you well." Miss Lily and Miss Violet were kind and gentle, but everything was so regimented. She felt a lump rising in her throat. Suddenly the years at Chapman's did not seem as halcyon as she wanted to believe.

"Are you okay, Treat?"

"Yes, Emily. I had forgotten how enjoyable sweets could be."

"Life should be sweet, in every way."

I wonder if I should write that pearl of wisdom down, Treat thought sarcastically.

Em said, "Do you remember where we ended yesterday?"

"Maggie was born, you had returned to school, and it sounds as if you and Mitchell made—shall I call it an arrangement?"

"Politely put. School opened up my world, but put even more of a distance, if that was possible, between Mitchell and me. I had Chris and Maggie." Em shook her head. "They were my blessings. I never realized how much I could love or be loved.

"I remembered my mother telling me to be grateful for what I had, and that's what I tried to do. I tried to accept that there would always be one part of my life that would remain unfulfilled."

Em became pensive. "I think a good place for us to pick up the story of the Girls, is with the beginning of my relationship with Char. We might call this the prelude."

Chapter 14

1975

Emily Elizabeth Grant sat in the next to the last row of the over-crowded Johnson Auditorium at California State University at Northridge. It was standing room only as teachers, therapists, and social workers scrambled, at the last minute, to get their required Continuing Education Units (CEUs). It had sprinkled during lunch break, and someone had equated a light sprinkle with cold and turned the heat on in the auditorium. Damp jackets and wool sweaters cooked in the high temperature, creating an unpleasant mildewy smell throughout the closed room.

Emily had parked eight blocks away and had forgotten her lunch and thermos. Now, she was trapped in a boring lecture on Applied Psychology, listening to her stomach grumble as the lecturer droned on about sub-fields and job opportunities. Students were beginning to nod off, caught between a lack of oxygen and disinterest. Her yellow lined tablet meant for taking notes was filled with orderly numbered *Things to Do*. She was up to fifty.

She stifled her own yawn and looked at the wall clock—two more hours to go. She thought, *I'm not going to make it.* Now, to add to her discomfort, her legs began to twitch and she began to shift in her seat.

Her head was beginning to nod, her eyes rolling back in her head. *God, I hope I don't fall asleep. God, I hope I don't snore if I do fall asleep.*

"*Psst! Psst!*"

Emily turned to see a woman in her mid-thirties sitting behind her with heavily lidded hazel eyes and shaggy, layered auburn hair.

"Can I borrow a pen?" she whispered.

Emily held out three.

"Thanks. I only need one." She held out her hand. "I'm Char Owens. Is this a boring lecture or what?"

They shook hands and exchanged smiles. "I'm Emily Grant and it's deadly."

"Are you taking it for CEUs?"

"Yes, I'm a teacher, and it was recommended by my school's principal."

Char pointed to a steel door behind the last row. "There's the escape hatch. We can get a cup of coffee and come back before the lecture's over. We'll still get our CEUs."

It never would have occurred to Emily to sneak out of a lecture, but she jumped at the opportunity. "I'd love that."

"Leave your books on the seat. I'll leave first, you follow in about a minute. I have a way to guarantee our return," Char whispered as she took out a roll of Scotch tape.

"What are you going to do with *that*?"

"It's a technique I use—push the door latch in, then tape it. When we sneak back in, I'll take the tape off. Don't worry, it works every time."

They met outside the exit door. Emily said, "I feel as if I've just committed a bank robbery."

Char laughed, her eyes twinkling. "You're just an accessory. I think you'll get a suspended sentence."

Emily stared at Char's long-sleeved chambray shirt. "That's a beautiful job of embroidery. Did you do it?"

"Yeah, it's my lazing-around denim shirt. I embroidered all of it, every flower, every rainbow. Most of it done during boring lectures."

"That sounds like fun. I make lists of things to do."

Char frowned. "That definitely doesn't sound like fun."

"I know. I usually end up forgetting all about them. Embroidery sounds like a better idea."

As they walked toward the school cafeteria, the scattered rain-filled clouds began to drift closer, hiding the sun, creating a foreboding atmosphere. An unexpected cold wind caused Char and Emily to hug their jackets and dodge the slippery leaves that had fallen from the surrounding jacaranda trees.

Char said, "Do you know the fable about the wind and the sun?"

"Aesop's Fables, one of my favorites. I use it in my class, to demonstrate that kindness wins over harshness. You know how the sun and the wind are arguing over who can make the traveler take off his cloak?"

"You mean jacket?" Char laughed as she tightened her hold on her red ski jacket.

Emily smiled. "Exactly. The students' assignment is to do an act of kindness when they go home. The next day they have to give an oral report on what they did, everyone's reactions, and how it felt to them. One little boy set the dinner table and his mother cried. He thought he had hurt her feelings, so we talked about tears of sadness and tears of joy. His self-esteem jumped about one hundred points."

Char stuffed her hands into the pockets of her jacket. "I wish you were my teacher. I'll bet you get some funny reports."

"Funny *and* sweet...and sometimes sad. It tells me a lot about their lives and their families."

Char and Emily waited in line at the Troubadour Dining Hall's self-service counter. Saturday customers, trying to find some comfort from the unexpected fall chill or a boring seminar, quickly depleted the barebones selection of food.

"I guess we aren't the only ones sneaking out of a lecture," said Char, surveying the dwindling choices. "I hope the coffee's good."

"I wouldn't count on it," Emily sighed. "My study group used to meet here once a week. I think sludge might aptly describe it, but we were desperate for caffeine. Maybe it's improved."

"As long as it's hot, I'll suffer through. Do you want to share a piece of chocolate cake?"

Emily said, "I have to confess, I'm not good at *sharing* chocolate cake."

"Then it's two coffees and two pieces of chocolate cake. Let's grab that table in the corner." Char pointed to a square table with a heavily chipped brown laminated top and two green plastic stacking chairs.

Emily wiped the top of the table with a napkin and settled into one of the chairs. "Same table, same chairs, and probably the same coffee." She smiled.

Char put cream and sugar in her coffee, stirring it carefully with the wooden swizzle stick. "Not too bad," she said, shuddering as she took a sip. Her eyes met Emily's over the top of the cup. "I saw you sitting toward the back and thought you might want company."

Emily nodded, her mouth filled with cake. "Thanks, I needed rescuing. I left my lunch in the car. I can't believe how hungry I am."

"My problem is, I would never forget my lunch, and I would still eat the chocolate cake. That's how I earned these extra fifteen. You'll have to tell me your secret to staying so slender."

"Metabolism, I think. Plus, I forget to eat some of the time."

Char chuckled. "That'll do it. I spotted a cheese sandwich in the case. It may still be there. Can I get it for you?"

Emily shook her head. "Thanks, I'll stick with the cake. I have a horrible sweet tooth."

"Umm...me, too. This cake isn't bad. And I won't comment on the coffee. So, Emily, where do you teach?"

"Marvin Elementary in West Hills...third grade. My first year as a full-time teacher," she said shyly.

"Congratulations. We always need good teachers. Do you have kids of your own?"

"Two." Emily searched in her purse and took out a photo folder. "Chris is eleven—and Maggie's five. I'm a bit of a photo addict, at least when it comes to the kids."

Char took her time, focusing on each photo. The boy was so fair: blond hair and blue eyes and a very mischievous smile. The girl had the most beautiful black hair and looked quiet and introspective. "Maggie's an old soul—it's written all over her," she said, hoping Emily would take it as a compliment. She handed the photos back to Emily. "They're both beautiful."

"Thanks. What about you? What do you do?"

"I'm a psychologist." Char dug in her backpack and handed Emily her card.

Char Owens, Ph.D.
Individual and Couple Therapy
By Appointment
Studio City, CA
(213) 555-7864

Emily said, "Kids, husband lurking somewhere?"

"Divorced. One son, Lawrence, fourteen. He lives with his father in New York. Wait, I have a photo here someplace." Char rummaged through her backpack. "I can never keep this thing organized. Aha, here it is." She handed a photo to Emily. "It's Lawrence's bar mitzvah picture."

"He looks very grown-up and serious," Emily commented. "It must be difficult for you. I don't think I could manage the separation."

"Wait until they're in their teens, you might change your mind."

Emily chuckled, and then, casting her eyes down, became solemn. "This probably happens to you all the time, as a psychologist. People asking—"

"Ask away."

"Maggie started kindergarten in January." Emily wiped unexpected tears from her eyes. "I'm sorry. I can't think about it without crying. I got a call from her teacher the other day. She's concerned because Maggie's not interacting 'normally.'" Emily made quote signs in the air.

Char smiled empathetically and nodded for her to go on.

"She plays with the other children, but spends most of her free time sitting in a corner talking to the stuffed animals. I'm so worried that something's wrong, or that Maggie will get labeled. I know this is a lot to ask—you don't even know me—but could you...would you come to our home and meet Maggie?"

Char patted Emily's hand. "I don't usually work with children, but if you're asking me over as a friend, I'd like that."

Sunland Gardens Estates was located at the west end of the San Fernando Valley in an area called Woodland Hills. Gentle rolling hills where sheep once roamed were chewed down by massive bulldozers, the material moved to create two-hundred-level lots on sloping streets. Built on pool-sized lots, they offered up to four bedrooms, three bathrooms, and a family room with a wood-burning fireplace. Sunland Gardens helped to make the New American Dream of "bigger is better" a reality. The surrounding farmland that had supplied fruits and vegetables to southern California now provided neighborhood shopping centers to families seeking a suburban "everything-within-easy-driving distance" atmosphere.

Women, once stay-at-home moms, were returning to work in droves. Children were coming home after school to empty houses, and the modern latchkey generation was born. Strip malls, that seemed to spring up on every corner and all boasting an eclectic array of eateries, provided a welcome relief from cooking. Except for a quick breakfast or holiday dinner, the houses' large kitchens seldom rang with the happy voices of families.

The world, ever in a state of flux, rocked as the family structure changed.

Emily had pulled her hair back into a short curly ponytail and was wearing her favorite weekend outfit of soft blue jeans, a blue and white striped seersucker shirt, and white tennis shoes.

She heard the doorbell and smiled as she looked through her kitchen window to see Char standing on the porch.

They hugged briefly. Emily said, "I'm so glad you could come. Don't mind the mess—we moved in a month ago, and I'm still putting things away, or trying to."

Char glanced at the array of boxes and toys cluttering the family room. She chuckled and shook her head. "Where children live, clutter follows. It's a healthy sign."

"I've never quite thought of it that way. I just want everything to be...perfect...sort of." She added shyly, "It's our first house."

"It's really quite lovely out this way, and I like the open floor plan," Char commented. "You can be in the kitchen and still keep an eye on the kids."

Emily said apologetically, "We don't have much furniture. In fact, most of the rooms are pretty empty. My parents bought Chris and Maggie their bedroom sets. The rest will have to come a little bit at a time."

"That can be fun, too. Eventually, you'll get it just the way you want it."

Char handed Emily two bottles of wine. "I wasn't sure what you were serving so I covered all bases: Pinot Noir and Chardonnay."

"They're perfect," Emily said, looking at the winery label. "Andy and Stephan's Winery. I like the label, especially the small rainbow. It looks so cheerful."

Char held in her giggles. *She's such a sweet soul, but oh my God! Am I going to be having dinner with Pollyanna?* "It's from a small winery outside Santa Barbara. I went there with some friends on a wine tasting excursion."

"It sounds like fun," Emily said, motioning Char to follow her outside. "Come meet Chris and Mitchell. They're getting the barbeque going. I hope hamburgers and hot dogs are okay. I didn't think to ask if you're a vegetarian."

"I've tried being a vegan, but I like meat too much. It sounds perfect."

They walked through the kitchen and out to the backyard.

Emily said, "It seems there's so much to be done. Mitchell works overtime and..." she lowered her voice, "being a handyman is not one of his talents. He tried to hammer in a screw, and I thought, boy, we're in trouble! I'm learning to be the handyperson. I bought a bunch of how-to books at a garage sale and a few basic tools. I've started a vege-table garden, too. It's exciting to see the seeds blossoming into seed-lings, and I'm hoping it'll encourage the kids to eat more vegetables."

Char was impressed with Pollyanna's gumption. "A woman of many talents. Houses are a lot like people: a work in progress and never completely finished."

"I'm finding that out." Emily waved to Mitchell and Chris. "Chris, stand back when Daddy lights the fire."

"Mom, I'm eleven!" the towheaded boy groused. "I learned all about fire safety in the Webelos and the Boy Scouts."

Char whispered, "What's a Webelo?"

Emily whispered back, "It's the rank between a Cub Scout and a Boy Scout."

Mitchell waved hello to Char, then turned to Chris. "I don't want to tell you again. Don't talk back to your mother. Next time you'll lose your privileges for a week."

Chris looked down. "Yes, sir," he said dejectedly.

Emily spoke slowly, "I'm sorry you saw that. Mitchell tends to be overly strict, especially with Chris. Why don't we go inside? I've made ice tea. Is that okay?"

Char said, "It sounds perfect."

Maggie came into the kitchen, sniffling and carrying a life-size gray and white plush squirrel with a bushy tail that looked as if he had been played with, slept with, and taken a bath or two with.

Maggie looked at the woman sitting at the kitchen table, drinking ice tea, and ran to Emily, wrapping her arms tightly around her legs. Emily lifted Maggie onto her lap. "What is it, pumpkin?"

"Squirrely has a tummy ache," she said, looking at the stranger out of the corner of her eyes.

"Do you think Squirrely is hungry?"

Maggie nodded.

Emily gave Maggie an apple. "Can you share this with Squirrely?"

"He likes apples."

"And so does my little girl," Emily smiled as she kissed the top of Maggie's head.

"Maggie, I'd like you to meet Dr. Char."

Maggie's eyes grew wide, tears formed in her dark brown eyes and rolled down her cheeks. "No shots, no shots, Mommy!"

"Maggie had to have a vaccination last week," she explained. "No more shots, darling. Dr. Char doesn't ever give shots. Dr. Char talks to people."

She stroked the top of Maggie's head. "Maybe after dinner you'll show Dr. Char all your animals."

"Even Mr. Gorilla?"

"Yes, even Mr. Gorilla."

∞

Chez Bouguerau was located on Ventura Boulevard midway between Char's home and Emily's school. Once part of the six-hundred-mile trail used to connect the Spanish missions built throughout California, it was now home to dry cleaners, bakeries, and corner grocery stores catering to the after work group that needed to run a quick errand before heading home. Art galleries, bookstores, and restaurants filled to capacity on the weekends as the workweek faded from memory and Monday was in the distant future.

Emily saw Char sitting at one of the outdoor tables and waved. "I'm sorry, I'm a little late. I had to drop off Chris and Maggie at my parents."

"You're lucky to have parents who are willing to babysit."

"It's funny. They were so strict with me and now…they're softer with Chris and Maggie."

"It's amazing how that happens. It was the same with Lawrence and my mother. They adored each other."

Emily gazed at the dining area filled with blue umbrellas, round Carrara marble tables, and beige rattan bistro chairs. White and purple sweet alyssum struggled through the cracks in the flagstone flooring, creating a random pattern of color.

"This is lovely," said Emily, leaning forward. "I want to thank you for spending time with Maggie."

"It was really my pleasure. The kids are great, and you're quite wonderful with Chris and Maggie."

Char looked down, her fingers moving up and down the stem of her empty wine glass. "Emily…you know I don't work with children."

"Are you about to give me bad news? I've been worried sick all week."

The waiter came over with menus. "We'll need a few minutes," said Char. "No, not bad news at all. Maggie interacted with me for over an hour. She told me a story about each animal and what was going on inside of them. She very bright, and I do mean *very*." Char shook her head. "We're learning more and more about the way the human mind works, but we still know so little. I don't think anything is wrong with Maggie. On the contrary, I think she has found a way to express her worries through her stuffed animals."

Char paused for a long moment. "Emily, is it okay if I call you Em?"

"No one has before." She smiled her inscrutable smile.

"You're smiling..."

"Just a little. I was remembering, when I was around four, I taught myself how to print my name. I knew all my letters and I sounded it out. M. Lee: capital M, capital L, lower case e, e." She smiled again, this time she didn't try to hide it. "I like the way Em sounds."

"You were bright and imaginative. I think Maggie takes after you. Squirrely has a tummy ache and Maggie's hungry. Mr. Gorilla yells a lot." Char looked at Em. "Would that be Mitchell?"

Em spoke softly. "Yes. Mitchell and I would have never married, except—"

"Chris?"

"I was seventeen."

"I think Maggie's sensitive to the tension in the family, and she's acting it out through her stuffed animals. That's quite adaptive. I don't suppose you and Mitchell would consider marriage counseling."

"I would, but Mitchell? Never. He's not that way. Char, tell me what to do to help Maggie." She added purposefully, "It's up to me."

"My opinion, for what it's worth?"

"Please."

Char sat forward in her chair, her hand resting next to Em's. "Children like Maggie see the world in a different way. They simply don't fit into our 'one size fits all' educational system. Maggie needs to be in an environment that will help her work through her conflicts and honor her creativity, not destroy it."

Em looked down and shook her head. "I know what you're saying. I struggle with it as a teacher, but we can't afford a private school. Mitchell would never agree to it."

"I want you to visit this school." Char handed her a brochure. "Friends of mine own it, and there are all kinds of private scholarships. Check it out, okay?"

Em looked at the brochure. "Valley Farm School. I'll call tomorrow."

"Good. Let's order. I'm starving, and I'd love a glass of wine."

"Make that two."

"Chez Bouguerau is known for their *bouillabaisse*."

Em smiled, relaxing back in her chair. "I haven't eaten it before, but I'm up for a new adventure."

They played phone tag, each busy with their lives, their careers—quick messages, hurriedly picked up between classes or patients, that gradually took on a certain guarded intimacy and comfortableness.

*

Hi, Char. It's Em. I took Maggie to visit the Valley Farm School. It was made for her! There's so much space and the teachers were wonderful. You should have seen her eyes bugging out when she saw all the animals. She may not want to come home at all.

She starts next week. I'm going to volunteer by tutoring four hours a week and some weekends. With my volunteering and a scholarship, we won't have any out of pocket expenses. I can't thank you enough. Can I take you out to lunch?

*

Em, you won't regret it. I'd love to have lunch with you...when?

*

Hi, Em. It's Char. Are you busy next Saturday? I thought the kids might enjoy going to Griffith Park. There's Travel Town that has all kinds of old trucks and a miniature train set that will make Chris's eyes

132

bug out. And there are pony rides close by for Maggie. Afterward, I thought we could swing over to one of the parks for a picnic.

*

Hi, Char. It's me. Chris has a Boy Scout campout, but Maggie and I would love to go.

*

Em, hi. I'll pick you up at, say, tennish. Don't worry about food; I'll pack the lunch. Will that work?

"It's so beautiful here," said Em as they exited the freeway toward the entrance to Griffith Park and the pony rides. Em turned to Maggie, who was busy in the backseat having a conversation with Mr. Squirrely: "Don't be scared, Mr. Squirrely. We'll find a slow pony."

"Maggie, is Mr. Squirrely getting a little frightened?" Em asked.

"He's afraid of falling off."

"You'll get to meet all the ponies, Maggie," Char assured her. "We'll find one that makes you *and* Mr. Squirrely feel safe."

The road curved away from the freeway and changed from an off ramp to a country lane surrounded by riding trails and shaded by California oaks. Groups of riders, out for a Saturday adventure, followed the guide as they meandered into the surrounding hillsides for a view of the valley below.

Char whispered, "Is that Maggie or Mr. Squirrely snoring in the back?"

Em chuckled. "It's definitely Maggie. I should have warned you she falls asleep in the car."

Char said playfully, "So do I, hopefully not while I'm driving." After a pause, she asked, "Have you been to the park before, Emily?"

"Years ago, to the old zoo. We had a school trip in second grade.

133

My parents weren't big on doing things. I think they were grateful and content, after the war, to have a home and stay put."

"Your father fought in the war?"

"In the Pacific Theater, Solomon Islands. He won't talk about it. Says it's best to let sleeping dogs lie. I was born after he returned. *Soon* after he returned." Em laughed. "The hospitals started getting *real* busy nine months after the vets began to come home. It's as if they decided what they had been fighting for was..." she cupped a hand over her mouth and whispered, "*sex.*"

What an ingénue, Char thought, but she privately found her friend's modesty, in this anything goes age, oddly charming.

"What about your father?" Em asked.

Char wasn't ready to talk about her childhood wartime memories. She shook her head. "My parents didn't talk much about it, and I was pretty little when it started. My dad was 4-F—something about having flat feet. I remember when it ended. The air raid sirens blew, all the businesses closed and everyone got drunk." She laughed. "Now that's a childhood memory! Then, my family started to get information about the concentration camps. Our relatives in Germany were all wiped out. I was still little, around nine, but I remember my grandparents," her voice faded to a soft murmur, "praying and crying...praying and crying."

"I'm so sorry."

Char nodded, wiping a tear away. "I'm going to not so artfully change the subject. This is such a great park. There's so much to do here, one of the many hidden jewels in Los Angeles—something for everyone. Some call it the Central Park of Los Angeles. I think it's even better. There are tons of hiking and riding trails all around and a great summer camp for kids, too." Char stopped self-consciously. "God, I'm starting to sound like a damn brochure, aren't I?"

Em smiled. "I don't mind. Go on."

"Riding stables, not too far from here, where you can rent horses. They have a great evening ride up into the hills, a picnic dinner, and then watching the sunset. And let us not forget the observatory.

I'll bet Chris would like that."

"He'd love it, I'm sure."

"Any chance you could get Mitchell to take you and the kids to see the stars?"

Em shook her head and spoke softly. "Mitchell works nights and takes on as much overtime as he can get. He's not a bad man. He tries his best but he just focuses on work and finances. It's all he knows."

Char looked directly at Em. "It kinda makes you a single mom, doesn't it?"

"I've never thought of it that way, but I guess you're right."

"You know, the Hollywood Bowl is close by. I'll never forget seeing the Beatles there in 1965, screaming my fool head off."

"You saw the Beatles?" Em exclaimed. "Wow."

"Sure. Haven't you ever been there?"

Em shook her head. "No. I wasn't even allowed to listen to rock music. I must seem like such a dud to you."

"Not at all. You've been busy doing one part of your life, that's all. The Bowl is quite amazing. It started out as an empty field surrounded by hills. Someone recognized the natural acoustics and was reminded of the amphitheaters of ancient Rome and Greece. I went to see the Beatles with friends, but my parents used to take me there as a kid. Listening to classical music under the stars. Falling asleep with my head on my mother's lap."

"It sounds like such a sweet memory. You were lucky."

A sad expression crossed over Char. "Not always. You know, sometimes mothers and daughters...well, let's just say we weren't always a great match."

"I know that one all too well."

"I have a box at the Bowl—had it for years—seats four. They have children's concerts. Do you think you'd like to go sometime?"

"I would, but how do you get the kids to sit still for classical music?"

"It's magic at its finest. They show Tom and Jerry cartoons set to classical music. Then they end with fireworks. It's guaranteed to get any child interested in Mozart or Beethoven. Are you sure you can't get Mitchell to change his mind?"

Em's eyes filled with tears and she shook her head. "Mitchell won't change."

Char said, "Maybe the four of us, then?"

"I'd like that," Em whispered. "I'd like that a lot."

Maggie fell in love with a white pony named Sparkles. At first, Em walked around the large ring with her. "Okay now, Maggie girl?"

Maggie nodded. "Not afraid, Mommy."

Em and Char stood at the railing surrounding the pony track. Em reached in her purse. "I brought my camera—this is a Kodak moment if ever I saw one." She relaxed, taking photo after photo of Maggie bouncing up and down, sometimes serious, sometimes smiling, but definitely not scared.

The sun was out, the temperature was drifting into the mid-seventies and gentle breezes kept the smog at bay.

Em said, "This is one of those picture-perfect Southern California days. I can't remember every feeling so at ease, so relaxed."

"I'm glad." Char leaned against the fence, one foot on the rail. "Maggie seems to be quite a rider. You know what her next question will be?"

Em became pensive. "Oh, God, she'll want a pony! I hadn't thought that far in advance."

Char laughed. "They're going to be taking Maggie off Sparkles in a couple of minutes. Can I borrow your camera and take a photo of the two of you?"

"I'd love that." Em reached in her purse and handed the camera to Char. "This is one of the best days I've ever had. Thanks for thinking of it."

"My pleasure. Oops, we'd better hurry over there, we don't want to miss this Kodak moment."

∞

They drove the short distance to the children's park. Families, taking advantage of the weekend's mild weather, filled the surrounding area with colorful blankets, camp chairs, coolers, and picnic baskets. Some parents were engaged in intense conversations, while some lay on the lawn snoozing while their children played in the large sandbox filled with play equipment.

Em pointed to the nineteen-foot tall robot structure, an all-steel triple-decker tube slide, in the center of the sandbox area. "What's that?"

"That's called the Giganta Robot," Char replied. "Guaranteed to give any child a triple thrill." Em's face paled at the imposing automaton. "Don't worry, Em," Char added, "it's completely safe."

"I know I worry too much, but it looks really dangerous."

"No one has to go all the way up. Plus, there's other play equipment: monkey bars, sand boxes, and swings. And a garden variety slide for the less adventurous."

Char glanced around. "It's pretty crowded. I guess we aren't the only ones with this idea." She pointed to a spot near the play area. "There's a place on the grass."

"That's perfect," said Em. "I can keep an eye on Maggie and still relax." She cast another dubious eye at the gigantic metal structure. "Or *try* to relax."

"I'll help you keep watch. Two sets of eyes are always better than one."

They carried the cooler and wicker basket to the grassy area. Char and Em laughed as they each held onto two corners of the blanket, watching it puff up from the breeze before settling onto the ground.

Char said, "I hope everyone worked up an appetite. Maggie, just watching you bouncing up and down on the pony rides made me hungry."

"Sparkles went *really* fast. And I didn't fall off once!" Maggie turned to Em. "Mommy, can I have a pony for Christmas?"

"Wiggle out of this one," Char whispered.

"Change the subject for me, will you?" Em whispered back.

"Watch this technique."

Char opened the wicker basket and began to take out striped paper plates, bags of fresh fruit, and mysterious packages wrapped in foil. "Maggie, how do you like your new school?"

Maggie took a grape, popped it in her mouth and chewed. "Mmm, grapes are good. We sit in a big circle and talk."

"What about?"

"How high is the sky. Feelings...happy..." Maggie smiled and giggled, "or sad." She pouted and pretended to cry. "Or angry," she said, furrowing her brow and making *grrr* sounds while shaking her head. She stopped and became thoughtful. "Dr. Char, *Richard* has two mommies."

"Two mommies?"

Maggie nodded, turning to Em, but kept her eyes on Char. "Mommy, can I have two mommies?"

Em shook her head briskly. "Richard has two mommies, and your friend Krista has two daddies, and Maggie has a mommy and a daddy."

"Can't have two mommies?"

"No, darling."

"May I have some chips, please?"

"Yes, chips you may have." Em thought, *That's a good tradeoff, chips for two mommies.*

"I'm famished," said Em.

Char said, "Chicken salad on rye bread for us and peanut butter and jelly on wheat bread *and* chips for Maggie."

"PB&J! That's my best. Mommy, can I play on the monkey bars and the merry-go-round?"

"After you eat your sandwich and drink your milk."

Maggie dug in, taking large bites of the PB&J and messy gulps of milk. She rubbed her tummy. "All full, Mommy."

"Okay."

Maggie stood up. "Bye, Dr. Char. Bye, Dr. Mommy."

"Oh, my God," Char roared with laughter. "Well, she took care of that problem. She can't have two mommies but she can have two doctors."

"Out of the mouth of babes. She's blossoming and the school... Char, I'm just so grateful."

"Your kids are wonderful."

"Sometimes I worry about Chris. Mitchell's so hard on him."

"Your gentleness can mitigate that."

"I try, but I'm not sure I'm always successful. Sometimes I see a sharpness in him—I don't want him to grow up..."

"Angry?"

"Angry and bitter. Mitchell wasn't always this way. I try to re-member what he had to give up...his dreams of becoming an aero-space engineer. We were both so very young...and stupid." Em looked forlorn. "We've done so little. I've gone almost nowhere, and when I hear you talk about places to go, things to do, I feel sad at having missed out on so much."

"I don't want you to think of yourself as stupid. You were just a kid, only a few years older than Chris. You know, the judgment just isn't there at that tender age. It's never too late to make a change, to put fun in your life."

Em nodded and leaned back on her elbows, watching Maggie as she joined the other children on the merry-go-round. She sighed. "It's so pleasant here. Relaxing, away from the pressure." She paused. "Char...there's something I want to ask you. Well, it really isn't any of my business..."

Char put down her drink. "But, you're curious..."

"Yes. I don't know that much about you. I know you're divorced, but I don't know why, and I don't know why you don't see Lawrence."

Char looked down. "Em, you know I like you. We've become good friends, and I don't want to lose our friendship."

"You won't, unless you tell me you're an axe murderer."

Char became thoughtful. "No, but some might see it that way. I had an affair when Lawrence was three. My husband found out, sued for divorce and custody." She paused, wiping tears from her eyes. "He won. I was *granted—*" she spat out the word, "the usual visitation, every other weekend and some holidays. Then my ex moved to the east coast. I tried to stop it, but again, I lost. Lawrence used to come here for a month during the summer. When Lawrence was thirteen he had his bar mitzvah."

Em nodded. "Believe it or not, I've been to two, actually. Children of teachers I work with."

"Then you know it's a rite of passage into adulthood. I flew to New York, the pariah in the family who 'gave' her child away. During the ceremony he made his first speech as a man. All about values, honesty, the importance of family and friends. He thanked his father and stepmother for helping him to become a man, and lastly, he thanked me for giving him life."

Char picked some leaves of grass from the lawn. "Afterward he said he wanted to speak to me privately. I thought he wanted to reconnect, have a relationship. Instead he told me he never wanted to see me again. He blamed me for everything, and on some level I can understand. My heart won over my head, and I've paid the price. I'm giving him the space he wants. I send him cards on his birthday, holidays. I'm trying to be part of his life, even if it's only through the mail."

Char wiped her eyes. "I don't know how many times I have to be punished for making an unwise decision. I hold onto the hope that maybe one day he'll understand and his heart will soften."

"I'm so sorry," said Em softly, painfully aware of the word's inadequacy.

Char put her head down. When she looked up, tears were streaming down her face. "Em, my affair was with another woman."

Em looked shocked. "You're...?"

Char looked directly at Em. "Hard to say it, isn't it? A lesbian. That's the word. Look, if you want to leave now, I'll understand."

Em shook her head. "Char, give me a minute. The Valley Farm School has gay and lesbian parents. It's just that I've never really had a friend who's..."

"A lesbian? It's not a dirty word, you know."

"That's not it. I'm just surprised." Em spoke hesitantly. "I want us to stay friends. I've never had a good friend before."

"I'd like that. I'd like that a lot."

*

Hi, Em. I've got the tickets for the Hollywood Bowl, Tom and Jerry night. Are we still on?

*

Hi, Char. Yes, yes, yes! We're all excited, even Chris. What should I bring?

*

Just yourselves. I'll order picnic dinners; we can eat in the box. Make sure you dress warm. The evenings are quite cold at the Bowl.

"Excited, kids?" Char asked, opening the car doors.

Chris said, "Mom made us read about the history of the Holly-wood Bowl. I thought it was pretty boring."

Char saw Em cringe. "Reading about it can seem boring, but wait until you actually see it. Think of it starting out as a dirt field and a hillside. Can you imagine people trudging for blocks over a narrow pathway to listen to music?"

"Like Woodstock?"

"Well, kinda. You can think of it as the Woodstock of 1921."

"That sounds pretty cool."

Em mouthed a "thank you" before buckling her seatbelt and sinking into the front passenger seat.

Char said, "The traffic can get pretty gnarly getting in and out of the Bowl. I thought we could get there early, take a tour, and then have dinner in our box. Did you bring your camera, Em?"

Em patted her purse. "Right here."

"Great, I think we'll find a Kodak moment or two."

Artist George Stanley's *Muse of Music, Dance, Drama,* the sprawling monument that serves as the gateway to the Hollywood Bowl, loomed before them in all its Art Deco splendor. The group stood in front of the twenty-foot-high fountain, crowned by a fifteen-foot kneeling sculpture of the muse of music playing a harp; smaller figures, representing the muses of dance and drama, decorated niches on either side of the fountain. Anxious not to sound again like a walking brochure, Char resisted the urge to describe the monument's origins as a Works Progress Administration project at the tail end of the Depression. The monument represented "Old Hollywood" at its screwy, ballyhooey zenith and had been a favorite backdrop for photo ops for decades.

Char said, "Em, let me have your camera. I'll get one of you and the kids."

A woman standing nearby said, "Would you like me to take one of the four of you?"

Char hesitated. Em said, "Please, I'd like that very much."

It was 10:30 before the concert ended and they found their car in the packed parking lot. Em carried a sleepy Maggie to the car and buckled her into the back seat. Chris yawned, barely able to keep his eyes open. Char buckled Chris in and covered Chris and Maggie with blankets. They were both sleeping before they exited the parking lot.

Em said, "I can't thank you enough. We all had a wonderful time."

"Chris's comment was pretty funny."

"Which one? I think he was on a roll."

"When I asked him how he liked the performance."

Em laughed. "I couldn't believe that one."

"Hmm...let's see if I've got it right: 'I really liked the cartoons and the fireworks. It would have been perfect except for the music.' So much for introducing him to the classics!"

"I know Chris—he's a boy's boy and would never admit to liking anything remotely 'sissy,' but I think he probably got something out of the music, and he'll be talking about this night all week." She paused and mildly scolded, "But Char, you shouldn't have taken them into the gift store."

"I thought I was pretty well behaved. I set a dollar limit."

"Yes, that was brilliant, but I don't want them to get spoiled."

"Okay, I promise to be better next time."

The "next times" seemed to come naturally.

*

Hi, Char. It's Em. It's open house at the Valley Farm School. Maggie's class is having a school play, Dr. Doolittle. *Guess who has the starring role? Mitchell can't come and I was wondering if you could make it. It would mean a lot to Maggie.*

*

Hi, Em. I'll be there with flowers in hand.

*

Hi, Em. I'm having a holiday party. Can you and your family come? If it's warm, have the kids bring their bathing suits. You know we almost always have a heat wave in December, and I'll have the pool heated and lifeguards on duty. We'll start around one o'clock. Address is One Peppertree Lane.

143

Chapter 15

Studio City
1975

Peppertree Lane was aptly named after the California peppertrees that lined either side of the road. Lore had it that the Franciscans had brought the evergreen to their remote missions to provide much-needed shade, thus giving the peppertree a foothold in the state. Ferny, bright green leaves and weeping branches still provided that service, creating a canopy suggesting safety and protection from the elements, while the trunks, with their gnarled gray bark, tapered down to aggressive roots that snaked above the surface.

Once inhabited by chicken ranches, the ranches—and chickens—gradually disappeared as houses, built in the 1930s, '40s and '50s, were constructed on one- to five-acre parcels. Spanish style haciendas, sprawling ranch houses, and an occasional Southern-styled plantation house—with its wide veranda and grandiose pillars— now dotted the neighborhood. Never citified with sidewalks, the rustic enclave became a mecca for Hollywood studio executives and their families. A quick ride over nearby Cahuenga Pass connected the area—renamed Studio City—to nearby film studios.

"Dad, there it is, there it is!" cried Chris, fairly bouncing off the back seat of the station wagon. "Look, Dad, look at the old truck in the driveway. It's what I want when I turn sixteen."

Mitchell's eyes drifted to the black 1949 Ford pickup truck with red fenders. His throat tightened when he remembered being seventeen and dreaming of owning a 1949 Ford convertible, a failed dream he had shared with Emily so many years ago.

"Simmer down, Chris," Mitchell said, not unkindly. "Maybe you'll find out who owns it." His voice became sterner. "I don't want you annoying anyone, and I want you to remember your manners."

Emily said, "Do we have the right address, Mitchell? This house is so big."

"One Peppertree Lane—that's it, the Spanish house with the red tile roof. It looks like you've got a rich friend, Emily."

Emily said nervously, "I hope I'm dressed all right." She glanced down at her white linen pantsuit and purple sleeveless T-shirt. White pumps with a two-inch heel and pointed toes completed her outfit. *At least,* she thought, *my shoes are in style.*

Mitchell said, "Of course you're fine. This isn't the Academy Awards, you know."

They parked a block away next to a split-rail fence that surrounded a pasture where three horses and a goat were grazing.

Maggie hiked up her blue jean shorts and pulled on Emily's hand. "Mommy, do you think Santa can bring me a pony or a goat?"

"Oh, sweetheart, I don't think either one will fit into Santa's sleigh."

Chris, excited to see the truck, set the pace with Maggie skipping to keep up. Thoughts of ponies and goats, for the moment, faded into the background as the coolly styled pickup with its bulbous fenders and face-like grill—looking to Maggie like a giant toy— also captured the little girl's imagination.

"You've got to stop filling their heads with hopes and dreams that won't come true." Mitchell stumbled over one of the peppertrees' wayward roots. "Crap!" he blurted out as he caught his balance. "She can't have a pony or a goat because we can't afford it, and we don't have the property," he spat out the words, "like your rich friend has."

"It's just she's so little and her interests change so quickly. I thought maybe we could talk about getting the kids a dog from the shelter for Christmas. We've got a yard now, and it would teach them to take care of something besides themselves."

"Christ, Emily, no pony, no goat, and no damn dog! Did you stop to think about the cost of feeding it? And what about vet fees? They've got to learn that life doesn't work if it's filled with nonsense."

"I'm sorry, Mitchell," she said apologetically.

Maggie came running back as they approached the house. "Look, Mommy, there's a giant bell. Can I ring it?"

"Yes, but wait for Mommy and Daddy."

A forged iron gate and high stucco walls surrounded a Spanish-style courtyard. Sounds of a burbling water fountain, and classical piano music playing in the background, drifted to the walkway.

Chris said, "Mom, that's one of the songs they played at the Hollywood Bowl. It's the Lone Ranger song. Remember?"

"I'm glad you haven't forgotten. It's called *The William Tell Overture* by Rossini." Emily hoped she would have a chance to tell Char that the music at the Bowl had not been wasted on Chris.

Maggie stepped high on her tiptoes and pulled hard on the rope hanging from the bronze bell. She clamped hands over her ears as the clapper struck against the sound-bow.

"Hey," said Char as she opened the iron gate. The dolman sleeves of her rose silk caftan floated in the air as she held out her arms. "My favorite family. Welcome!"

They stood for a moment taking in the beauty of the courtyard. Mexican pavers covered the floor while white bougainvillea climbed the post supports, reaching for the red-tiled overhang. An open carved double door, complete with a speakeasy door grill, led to the entryway with its sixteen-foot-high coved ceiling.

"Dr. Char," asked Chris breathlessly, "whose truck is that?"

"I thought that would catch your eye. Love cars, do you, Chris?"

"I do, Dr. Char. Cars *and* trucks."

"You'll have to meet my friend, Maxine. It belongs to her. If you ask nicely, she might take you for a spin."

Chris's eyes lit up, a broad grin crossed his face.

She turned to Em. "Did you bring your bathing suits?"

"The kids did." She browsed her mental dictionary, searching for just the right word. "Your house is...breathtaking."

"I can't really take credit for it. It was my parents'; they were the first to build on this street. After they died, I inherited it. I grew up in this house, surrounded by chicken ranches and horses."

Char turned to Maggie. "Guess what, Maggie, I still have chickens. In a bit, I'll give you a basket and show you how to collect the eggs. You can take them home with you. There's nothing like fresh eggs."

The entryway connected to a wide hallway that passed through the center of the house. Some guests were in the living room, sitting or standing in small groups, involved in intense conversations.

Char said, "The intellectual group gathers in the living room every year. They're solving the world's problems—again. They won't move until it's time to leave. They'll say goodbye and won't see each other for another year, and then, at next year's party, they'll pick it up without missing a beat."

"They certainly are into it," Em said, admiring the passionate group, whose words were becoming louder and louder.

"I know. Sometimes I'm afraid they'll scare the other guests away."

"This is the perfect setting for a lively debate," Em observed, scanning the color-washed peach-beige room.

Unstained log beams contrasted with the walnut-stained, wide-planked wood flooring, while an atmosphere of intimacy was created through a series of conversation areas, anchored by muted-tone rugs and furnished with loveseats and armchairs topped with brightly colored throw pillows.

Two armless club chairs, covered in a bright red floral pattern, were placed in front of the riverstone fireplace: light enough to be turned to face the fire on a cold day, far enough apart for a tea table, and close enough to reach out and touch the one sitting next to you.

The open doors leading to the courtyard allowed the warm December breeze and sounds from the fountain to enter the room and mingle with the light tones coming from the mahogany baby grand piano placed in a faraway corner. A distinguished looking man in his fifties with gray temples and a cleft chin sat on the bench with a faraway look, his fingers dancing fluidly over the ivory keys.

"Char, who's the pianist?"

"That's Harold Levin." Char lowered her voice. "He was a child prodigy but his parents forced him to become a doctor. It's his big chance to perform."

They continued through the hallway to a rec room with a pool table and bar staffed by a bartender. "Drinks are here, and if anyone wants to play pool, the cues are on the table." Char turned to Mitchell and asked, "Do you play pool?"

"No, never had the time."

"Well, maybe you and Chris can learn together."

Chris looked up hopefully. "Dad?"

"We'll see, Chris, we'll see."

Char saw how quickly Chris's expression changed from hopeful to despair.

French doors led to the backyard where guests were gathered in small groups, some talking, some eating, and some cooling off in the kidney-shaped pool. Two lifeguards, dressed in red boxer swim trunks, blew a whistle, heralding the beginning of a new Marco Polo game.

Char said, "That's Teddy and Stanley. I think they have more fun than the kids. Em, I'm going to steal your husband away for a few minutes, I'll be right back.

"Mitchell, there's someone I want you to meet, Ray Kaminski. I think he may have served with your dad."

Char took Mitchell by the elbow and steered him in the direction of a well-muscled man in his early fifties. As they left, Emily was surprised to see Dr. Lesley standing with four other women.

Maggie said, "Mommy, can I go swimming?"

Emily bent down, kissing Maggie on top of her head. "I want us to say hello to some people first."

"Emily, you're looking wonderful," said Lesley as they hugged.

"I was surprised to see you here, Dr. Lesley."

"I guess we have a mutual friend. Emily, this is Maxine, Roberta, Francis, and Iris." They said hello, smiled, and shook hands.

Lesley said, "This young man must be Chris, and this very grown-up girl must be Maggie."

Maggie held out her hand. "Pleased to meetcha, Dr. Lesley."

The group all laughed as Maggie gave Dr. Lesley's hand two firm pumps. She did the same to the other ladies, holding out her chubby little hand and saying: "Pleased to meetcha, Dr. Iris... Dr. Francis... Dr. Roberta... Dr. Maxine." Every hand got two shakes: no more, no less.

Maggie looked up at Emily. "Dr. Mommy, Dr. Char has bunny rabbits, and Mommy," she added excitedly, "a rooster! Can I go see?"

Emily nodded.

They all smiled and waved goodbye as Maggie ran toward the other children gathered around Char's personal petting zoo.

Lesley said, "Where did she learn to do that?"

Emily said, "Chris taught her to shake hands and thought it was funny if she said, 'pleased to meetcha.' She added the rest on her own. Every woman she likes becomes a doctor. Char is Dr. Char and I'm now Dr. Mommy."

Lesley said, "Chris, what else do you do besides teaching your sister tricks?"

"I'm a Boy Scout, and I *lovvvve* cars and trucks." He looked up at Maxine longingly.

Maxine put her hand on his shoulder and broke out into a wide grin. "A fellow car lover! Come on, kid, you can sit in the truck. I'll even show you how to start it. It's a flathead 221-CID V8, generating 85 horsepower. If your folks say it's okay, I'll take you for a spin around the block."

Chris said pleadingly, "Mom?"

Emily nodded. "There'll be no living with him now."

Lesley sighed, "Car lovers! A different breed. How do you know Char, Emily?"

"She's a friend. We met at a seminar. And you?"

"Char and I have known each other since our college days."

"Yes," said Iris, rather slyly. "Didn't you room together for a while?"

Lesley didn't skip a beat. "For a very short time. You know how it is with dorms. Kids are always switching rooms."

Char came over. "I see you've all met. Em, Maggie's playing with the kids and trying to collect eggs. She'll be fine there. Come, I'll take you on a tour of the rest of the house."

After they left, Iris said, "Em? Hmm..."

Char took Em by the arm. "We can start in the back, if it won't confuse you. She opened a French door off the patio. "This is my home office."

"I didn't realize you worked out of your house."

"Well, I got inspired one year after I went to Vienna and saw Sigmund Freud's home office. I figured if it was good enough for Freud, it was good enough for me. It's worked out well. It's quiet and private, and most importantly, patients seem to like it."

Em said, "I've never been in a therapist's office before." She saw baskets of stuffed animals and children's books on a shelf. "I thought you didn't work with children."

"I don't." Char leaned against her oak desk. "Years ago, when I was first licensed, I followed a traditional path. I guess you could say I was pretty Freudian. Then, over the years, as I attended different seminars, I realized that treatment should be tailored to the patient, not the other way around."

She picked up one of the stuffed animals. "These, and the books, are used to reach the inner child. Sometimes you have to go deep into the past to get to the pain. But, no matter what the presenting problem, I work with patients to help them find meaning in their lives. Without meaning, what do we have?" Char went over to the bookcase, selecting a book from the shelf.

A sudden chill ran through Em and the room began to swirl. She felt her heart beat faster and perspiration dampen her face.

Char said, "I know you like to read. This is by Victor Frankle. *Man's Search for Meaning*." Char turned around and touched Em's arm. "Are you okay? You look like you're going to pass out."

"I think I'm a little hungry."

Char guided her to a chair. "Here, sit down and put your head down." Char went to a small refrigerator in the corner of the room and returned with a carton of orange juice.

"Some hostess I am, letting her guest starve while I'm gabbing away. You're probably having a sugar drop."

Em's hands shook as she drank the juice.

"Feeling better?"

Em nodded. "I don't know what hit me. It came on so suddenly."

Char said as she handed Em the book, "That's the strange thing about sugar drops; they come from out of nowhere. Now, let's get you something to eat."

Emily and Mitchell sat silently in the front bench seat of their worn-out station wagon, with as much space between them as possible. Chris and Maggie, exhausted from swimming, playing pool, and collecting eggs, were sleeping soundly in the back.

"Did you have a good time, Mitchell?" Emily asked.

"It was okay."

"The kids had a great time. Maxine took Chris for a ride in her truck and Maggie was in heaven with all the animals. I saw you talking to Ray. Does he know your dad?"

"Yeah—tough marine, served in Guadalcanal with the old man. He works as a private investigator for one of Char's friends. Iris...I think that's her name. The tall one. Some big shot attorney."

"I'm glad you had someone to talk to. And thanks for coming. I know it's not your thing."

"Is it *your* thing Emily?" he said brusquely.

"What do you mean?"

"You know, you think you're so smart, but in a lot of ways you can't see two feet in front of your own nose."

"Mitchell, I don't understand."

"We'll talk after the kids are in bed." A grim look crossed Mitchell's face as he switched on the radio to listen to the late news.

Chapter 16

Ray Kaminski unlocked the door to his apartment. He was relieved to be back in his own surroundings. He never was one for socializing, but he had to admit he always enjoyed Char Owens's holiday parties.

Ray took pride of the meaning of his surname: "stone or rock." Like his name, he was hard, inflexible. It's what gave him the backbone to be a marine, a lifer.

Raised in Southwest Chicago by Polish immigrant parents, he had gone through life with his dukes up. First, on the streets of Chicago, then as an amateur Golden Glove boxer, finally as a marine.

Funny that he should end up working for a woman, Iris Bentonfield. He was her process server and her bodyguard, although she would never admit to needing his protection. She fondly called him her intimidator. He didn't mind the word, and he liked his work. He was the shaker; for once in his life he felt like the good guy.

He looked around his apartment. No doubt it was a man's home. Sparse. Spartan-like. The living room held two chairs, a television, and a weight bench. He never bothered with a dining table; he ate his meals on a metal folding tray in front of the television, watching the news.

No one came up to his place except for Annabelle; once a week, like clockwork. He liked not having to answer questions or trying to relate. She gave him what *he* wanted, and he gave her what *she* wanted: fifty dollars, cash.

He began his mornings by doing one hundred sit-ups, one hundred push-ups—no more, no less. He made the same breakfast every day, 365 days a year, year after year: three eggs, six ounces of steak, and two pieces of white bread, lightly toasted. He didn't give a shit what they were saying about vegetables; he had the heart and body of a man twenty years younger.

He rubbed the wide scar covering his forearm. Nearly lost that arm in Korea. The doc looked him in the eye and said, "Son, looks like you and that arm are real attached; you're not going to lose it." He came close, six surgeries, but the docs never gave up on him.

He thought about today's holiday party at Char's. He almost laughed out loud thinking about her highfalutin ways, but she sure could throw one hell of a party. He really liked her...too bad she wasn't straight. But that Mitchell Grant...reminded him way too much of his dad, Sergeant Sam Grant—Old Guts 'n' Glory Grant, the guys had called him behind his back. It wasn't anything Mitchell had said, it was his eyes: a slight vacant look that didn't light up when he talked about his wife and kids. He felt bad for him having Sergeant Grant for a father. Christ, like being in boot camp your entire life.

Ray reached for the bottle of aspirin and swallowed two for the pain, a constant reminder of a war he couldn't leave behind.

His fax machine alerted him to a waiting message. He knew it would be from Iris; the law firm of Bentonfield and Associates exclusively used that phone line. Iris was the only one among her lesbian buddies to have a real name. The rest all had girls' names that had turned into boys' names. He shook his head. Strange group, if anyone asked him. No one did.

He looked at the brief note sent earlier in the day. Iris was not one to waste words.

My office: Monday, 2:00 p.m.
Court Summons needs to be served in Malibu.
Iris

Probably one of her movie clients. He shrugged his shoulders. No matter, it was all the same to Ray. A job to be done was a job to be done, and he would do it.

He tore the fax into small pieces, put them in a pie pan, struck a match, and watched as the thin, chemical-infused paper erupted into flames, then slowly turned to ashes.

Char was happy with the way the party went. Everyone had a good time, she told herself. And the Girls seemed to like Em and the kids, although Bobbie had told her that Iris had made a snide remark about her nickname, Em. Oh well, that was Iris.

The caterers and cleaning crew had finished taking down the tent canopy, removed the tables and chairs, washed down the patio, and cleaned the house; everything was back to its pre-party state.

The Girls were getting out of their clothes and putting on the terrycloth robes Char had bought them for Christmas. All the same color, white, but with their initials monogrammed on the right lapel. One size fits all, she was told. But Iris's would be a bit on the short side, hers a little too long, and Les's too wide.

There was nothing like a dip in the hot tub for a party postmortem. It was the frosting on the cake, the cherry on the hot fudge sundae.

Bobbie and Frankie eased in first. Bobbie complained it was too hot; Frankie complained it was too cold.

Iris brought out the wine and glasses and waited for everyone to settle into their usual spots before handing them their glass of wine. Iris was always the last one in; a grand entrance was a grand entrance, no matter where.

Char turned on the hydrotherapy massager. The Girls fiddled

with their individual jets until everyone, satisfied, relaxed with a glass of wine safely held in their hands.

Max said, "Great party, Char."

Bobbie and Frankie, a beat apart said, "Wonderful food."

Les was silent.

Iris said to Char, "About *Em*...not like you to go for a straight woman, especially with her husband peering out of the corner of his eye the whole time."

Les said angrily, "Why don't you be a little more direct, Iris?"

Iris was undeterred. "Clam up, Les. And what's your relationship with that sweet little lamb being led to the slaughter, Char?" she said sarcastically.

Another party postmortem with her five best friends, thought Char.

"Okay, let's stop it right here," she said. "There's no lamb and there's no slaughter. For Christ's sake, can't someone have a friend outside the group?"

Max, having been raised with four sisters, knew the value of changing the subject. "Hey, did you guys see Marilyn making out with the lifeguard?

"Marilyn Harper from down the street?" Les offered.

Max nodded and everyone laughed.

Iris cocked a disdainful eyebrow. "Isn't that the uptight neighbor who hates everyone who isn't made of Wonder Bread?"

"That's the one," said Char. "I guess she doesn't know that Stanley is biracial *and* bisexual."

They laughed. The tension was gone, and now they were into the down and dirty gossip that made the party postmortems so successful.

Emily used Pond's cold cream, the same as her mother. The familiar fragrance brought back memories, not unpleasant ones, of her mother's bedtime routine. She sighed when she thought of how few pleasant memories she had of her childhood. She tried so hard to build sweet memories for Chris and Maggie. She hoped today would be one; she knew it was for her.

Emily thought about Char, the way she dressed, the way she seemed so free. Maybe she could do something about her wardrobe, sew something a little more stylish, and buy a pair of bellbottom jeans.

She didn't want to tell Char, but she had almost fainted in her office. She glanced at the book, *Man's Search for Meaning.* She had meaning in her life—Chris and Maggie, her teaching. But something was missing. There had to be something greater; perhaps the book would help her to find the answers. Despite the pious examples of her parents and Pastor Lockner—or perhaps because of it—she had never sought succor in the Bible since her unceremonious introduction to adulthood.

She wiped the cold cream off her face with a tissue. What could be bothering Mitchell? It looked as if he was having a pleasant time with Ray. Well, she guessed it was progress; at least he said he wanted to talk about it.

Mitchell was sitting on his bed, taking off his shoes. An angry scowl crossed his face as he worked to untangle the shoelace knot.

"Mitchell, please tell me what's upsetting you."

"Emily, short and to the point. You are to stop having anything to do with Dr. Char Owens." He sounded as if he was Sergeant Sam Grant and Emily was *his* troop of one.

"Why?" She was amazed.

"Why? Because she and her friends are a bunch of goddamn dykes, that's why." The thud of his shoe hitting the wall punctuated his remark.

"Dykes...you mean lesbians?"

"Dykes, lesbians, homosexuals, what difference does it make?" he snarled as he threw his other shoe against the wall. "How can you stand to think about it? Two women or two men *together.* It's sick."

"I don't think about it. Mitchell, she's my friend and she's never done anything or said anything to me that was inappropriate."

"I'm saying it for the last time, Emily. You're done. No more lunches, phone calls, or having her over. I don't want her near you or *my* kids. End of conversation, get it?"

"N-no, M-Mitchell," she stammered. "You can't treat me as if I were a child."

She saw his face turn a bright red; saw his eyes change color from a soft hazel like his mother's, to a hard steel-gray like his father's.

What she didn't see was his hand coming.

The next morning she covered the bruises on her face with makeup. She hoped the children wouldn't notice.

Char, it's Em. Could we meet for coffee? Somewhere quiet?

Em, the quietest place is my house. Any time between noon and three. I have a break, then patients for the rest of the day.

*

Char, hi. I'll be there at one.

*

I'll leave the gate unlatched.

Char opened the front door and smiled. "Hi, Em." Her smile faded when she saw the red blotches on Em's face. "He's hit you."

Em turned away and mumbled, "It's not that bad, really."

Char showed Em to the living room, guiding her to one of the taupe couches. She sat on an ottoman, facing her, purposely sitting lower—hoping it would give Em a sense of control.

"What happened?"

Em looked down, wiping away the tears that were streaming down her face. "Mitchell put it together yesterday at the party about you and your friends'..." she scoured her mental dictionary, "orientation. Then at home he told me I couldn't see you again... I said I didn't want to stop and that's when...that's when..."

Char said, "Em, you should think about leaving Mitchell. Once an abuser crosses the line, anything can set him off. You and the kids are at risk."

Em's lips trembled. "I can't leave him, and I don't want to stop seeing you. Shit, Char, why can't I have a friend?"

"You can," Char said wryly, "apparently just not a lesbian."

"I was surprised. Lesley—I didn't know about her."

"There are six of us who hang out together. We've known each other for years, and we call our group the Girls. Les and Max are in a long-term relationship. Frankie and Bobbie own a high-end furniture delivery company, mostly antique furniture. And Iris is my attorney. They're good people.

"Listen to me, Em. You know how much I care about you and the kids. Your friendship means a lot to me, but maybe we should stop seeing each other. I've worked with women who have been abused, and it almost always escalates. I don't want to be the excuse for you getting hit."

"I don't believe Mitchell will do it again. I upset him by arguing with him. He's an old-fashioned man—he wears the pants, thinks he's got the right to do all the talking."

"Whatever you said or did, you didn't deserve to get hit."

Char reached for Em's hands, holding them gently, touching her for the first time. "I think you know how much I like you, but I can't put you in any kind of danger. My gut is working overtime, and I think you should leave him. I've seen this escalate, too many times. Look at me, Em."

Char put her hand on Em's face. Em shook her head. "I can't."

Char's voice became firmer, more insistent. "Yes, you can. I have to know you are hearing me."

Em lifted her tear-filled eyes until they met with Char's. "You're crying, " she whimpered.

"Of course I am! You don't think I want to stop seeing you, do you? You know what happened to me. If we sneak around, in any way, you might lose Chris and Maggie. I don't want that to happen to you. If you decide to stay—I know this is hard for you to hear, and it's hard for me to say...we can't see each other again."

Char reached up with a tissue and wiped the tears from Em's face. "No more tears, now."

"Can we...at least write to each other?"

"Pen pals? I'd like that. Once a month, just to keep up? I'll mail it to the school. Let me know how you're doing and how the kids are, okay?"

Em sobbed. "I'm sorry, I can't stop. It's just that I'm going to miss you. What do I tell the kids? You know how Maggie has connected us...she calls me Dr. Mom all the time now."

"Tell them I love them. Tell them..." Char wiped the tears from her own cheeks as she slowly let go of Em's hands. "You better leave now...it's time for you to go."

April 16, 1976
Dear Char:

Happy Passover (and Easter)!
I know you celebrate both holidays.
Here are the kids' school pictures. Chris turned twelve and is growing like a weed. He's tall and lanky like Mitchell, but is a sponge when it comes to learning. I guess he takes after me in

that way.

Maggie had her sixth birthday and has put most of her stuffed animals up on the shelves in her room. She has joined the Cloverbud 4-H Club (that would be like the Brownies) and switched to real animals—cows, horses, pigs. Maggie is in her glory.

Char, I found out where Maggie's scholarship came from. How can I ever thank you? You saved her life. I can never re-pay you for your friendship.

Miss you.

  Em

Except for the monthly letters, Emily became compliant, not un-like Mitchell's mother, Mrs. Grant, who seemed to be clumsy and fall a lot.

Chapter 17

Tuesday, October 6, 2020

"I made a choice, that day, to stay with Mitchell," Em said to Treat. "I've asked 'why' over and over again. Perhaps it was denial or fear of facing the world on my own. I've come to the conclusion that, at that time, it was all I was capable of doing." Em shrugged her shoulders. "Keep in mind, it was the 1970s. Spousal abuse and abuse in general was only beginning to get recognized—there were very few laws in place and even so, it didn't mean they would be enforced."

"I've read about that period of history, but it feels so different when I'm listening to your story. It seems that you and Char ended so abruptly. Didn't you have feelings about her not supporting you?"

"Well, I missed her terribly, but I knew she was suffering because of losing her son. She never quite recovered from that. Nothing she would have said would have convinced me to leave Mitchell."

"You and Char did get back together," said Treat, stretching after the long interview. She felt an odd sensation in her fingers. *Wow,* she mused, *writer's cramp!*

Em nodded. "Yes, but not for quite a while and not under the best of circumstances. But that's another story."

She looked at the clock. "My, but the time does seem to fly...it's noon. We're going to pass on the pool today. I'm taking you out to lunch to a sweet French cafe, only a few minutes away. Afterward we'll go to your hotel."

"My hotel? Why?"

"I can't have you staying at that fleabag when I've got spare rooms right here. I've just added a new rule: You're staying with me."

Em and Treat sat in the living room, the two red floral chairs turned to face the riverstone fireplace, a tea table between them, mugs of brandy-laced coffee held in their hands.

"A change in scene will be good for us. I don't want us to get locked into the den. I'll never forget the first time I saw this room," Em said, stooping to light the gas logs. "It was the day of Char's holiday party. The house overflowed with her friends—my, how she loved having a party! The windows and doors were wide open, a summer's day in December. Harold Levin gave the baby grand a good workout then; now it sits and collects dust, but that's life, isn't it? Sometimes, I'll come in this room, and I swear I can hear the music. Char and I would sit here when it rained, and believe me it does rain in Los Angeles. She loved to hear the wood crackling and the rain splashing against the windows. Now, we have gas logs—not quite the same."

Em looked at Treat. "Those pajamas are perfect for you. Admit it, wasn't our shopping excursion fun?"

"Yes, thank you. You're fun to be with, Emily. I don't think I've ever felt so taken care of."

Treat looked down at her one-piece red flannel pajamas. "I love the PJs, but I'm not sure about the feet."

Em laughed. "At least they don't have a drop seat. You'd be surprised how drafty this house gets in the morning. And just think, you'll be ready for Santa. You do believe in Santa?"

Treat looked down. "Not since I was seven."

"Don't tell my daughter, Maggie, or my grandchildren. They believe he swoops down from the North Pole on Christmas Eve. I think Maggie is still waiting for her pony."

Treat wondered what it would be like to believe in Santa...in *something*. "I think you said Maggie's a vet."

"Hmm, no surprise to any of us. She married David, an attorney who works for animals' rights. They have one daughter, Charlene."

"Named after Char?"

Em nodded.

"Char's name was Charlene, then?"

"No, Charlotte. Your hand is shaking a bit, Treat. Best to hold that cup with both hands. These old mugs must weigh a pound."

Treat obeyed. *The old broad doesn't miss a trick.*

"We missed our afternoon session—shall we pick it up now?" Em continued.

"Isn't that breaking your rules?" *Your self-imposed rules, Ms. Emily.*

"I know I'm breaking my own rule about stopping at four, but I'd like to finish telling you about how Char and I reconnected. You know, the best thing about being the rule maker is you can also be the rule breaker." Em laughed at her own joke, adding, "It's all about learning to be flexible."

"Did you want to get a pad of paper and take notes? They're in the den, stacked on the bookcase, under the portrait."

Treat nodded. "I'd like to take notes. It helps me to remember, to focus."

"You are a note-taker, aren't you?" Em said when Treat returned with two ruled tablets.

"I don't want to miss a word."

"I know you have a job to do, but I have found that writing is not so much about capturing the words, but capturing the feelings, the essence of the story."

Treat thought, *Damn, this woman needs to make up her friggin' mind. One minute she asks me if I want to take notes, the next she's scolding me for taking notes. Flexibility? Fuck! More like insane.*

Em closed her eyes for a moment. "I didn't realize how volatile Mitchell could be," she said at length. "I thought if I didn't set him off, I'd be safe. I learned to be careful, to try do everything right. I really believed if I got it right, it wouldn't happen again. And it worked for a while. As long as I didn't challenge him.

"I focused on the kids, trying to make life better for them, and I waited for Char's letters. How I treasured them! I've kept them all these years, and she kept mine as well. Now, they are tied together with a pink satin ribbon. She always said we would be connected through eternity, one way or the other."

Chapter 18

1977

Emily cradled the worn dictionary in her hands, remembering when she was seventeen and entered a thrift shop with only thirty-five cents in her pocket. A familiar friend, whose pages had turned a yellowish-brown and become brittle with age; pages, once held firmly together and bound to a rigid cover, had loosened over the years, threatening to separate and fall singly to the ground.

She thought of the double meaning of the word "tear." Tear: to rip apart. Tear: a teardrop. The bruises on her face had faded with time, but the tear in her heart remained, and the tears came unexpectedly late at night. Quiet tears, followed by carefully muffled sobs.

Her days seemed empty without a phone call from Char, a few words quietly spoken, a shared comment that made them laugh. With only memories to sustain her, life became like the fall leaves that drifted to the ground, crumbling and scattering in the wind.

The months flew by as she watched the kids growing up; sometimes too quickly, she thought. Since his "spin" with Maxine, all Chris could talk about was becoming an automotive engineer.

One Saturday in early spring, she navigated the freeways with Chris in tow, driving the twisting mountain road leading to the Griffith Park Observatory.

They stood in the central rotunda staring at artist Hugo Ballin's celebrated ceiling mural depicting icons of classical celestial mythology: pastel images of Atlas, the four winds, the planets as gods, and the twelve constellations of the zodiac.

Chris whispered, "Mom, this is really boring."

Emily was determined. "Look around, Chris," she demanded, sweeping her hand across Ballin's eight rectangular wall murals, each dedicated to a particular branch of science. "Let your eyes move to the walls and tell me what you see."

"A bunch of dumb pictures," Chris muttered.

"Chris, the murals on the wall portray the advancement of science. It's your dream—that's why I brought you here."

"I know, Mom." Chris rubbed his eyes with the sleeve of his shirt. "I read the pamphlet. Dad won't let me have my dream. He told me as soon as I'm eighteen I'm on my own, and I'll need to get a job."

Emily thought angrily, *No Mitchell. You can do it to me, but you are not doing this to our son.* "Listen to me, Chris. You get the grades and I promise, I'll get you through school."

Emily held Chris close to her, closer than he had allowed in a very long time.

"Promise, Mom?" he asked tearfully.

She prayed silently: *God, give me the strength not to disappoint Chris.* "I promise, Chris, I promise."

Chris whispered before pulling away, "Mom, everyone's looking at us."

Emily smiled, her thirteen-year-old had returned. "Now, which of the eight panels do you think you'll need?"

Chris said excitedly, "Physics, mathematics, metallurgy...can I have them all Mom? Can I?"

"You can have the moon, darling."

Maggie's love of animals never faltered. When swallows began to build a mud nest under the eaves of their home, Emily and Maggie had front row seats for the spectacle, sitting on lawn chairs in the backyard. A picnic basket holding their lunch and snacks beckoned atop a checkered tablecloth draped upon the ground. They were content to watch the swallows, flying back and forth, carrying mud in their beaks. At first, only a mud stain appeared, and then, after many trips, the nest began to take form.

Emily said, "Remember the story of 'The Little Engine that Could'?"

Maggie and Emily sang, "I think I can, I think I can." They looked at each other, laughed, and continued, "I know I can, I know I can."

"I think the swallows must know that song, because they don't give up," said Emily. She gave Maggie a kiss on top of her head, and as her eyes filled with tears, whispered, "Just like you. Never give up on your dreams."

Emily smiled inwardly when she thought about Chris and Maggie growing up, the future she wanted to give them. Somehow, it made her own loneliness tolerable when she thought of being able to make Chris and Maggie's yearnings a reality.

It was August, three weeks before the fall school semester would begin, and Chris and Maggie were off for a week at camp. Emily got up at 5:00 a.m. to drive Chris to the drop-off spot for Boy Scout camp at his school, Mark Twain Junior High. Maggie's sleepover camp would be held at the Valley Farm School.

"Have a wonderful time, darling," Emily cooed, hugging her son. She could feel the mortified boy pulling away to join his friends on the waiting bus. "Bye, Mom. Bye, Squirt," he said, patting Maggie on the head.

Maggie said, "Mom, am I a squirt?"

Emily noticed Mommy was changing into Mom...at least half the time. "No, it's Chris's way of saying he loves you and he'll miss you. Now it's your turn to go to camp."

"Mommy, is it still camp if it's at my school?"

"Absolutely."

"'Cause Chris called me a baby."

"What did you tell him?"

"That I loved him."

Emily smiled. "Good girl! That'll stop his teasing every time."

By 8:30, the kids were safely on their way to what Emily hoped would be a wonderful experience away from home. She would spend most of today inside. Record high temperatures were predicted, and their air conditioner had broken. The serviceman joked: "Tomorrow at the earliest, Mrs. Grant. You know, air conditioners only break down when the temperature hits over a hundred degrees. They're union...like me." Emily was not amused.

It was hot and humid; earthquake weather, some said. Sometimes a neighbor, new to California, would ask her what an earthquake felt like. Emily thought it was the way she was feeling now, as if the world was unstable and ready to fall apart.

They had cooled the house down by leaving the windows open during the night. Now, Emily moved from room to room, trying to capture the cooler air in the house by shutting the windows, closing the drapes, and turning on the portable fans. The house, now clothed in an artificial darkness, became a tomb; the stale air a shroud.

Emily wondered, without any distractions, would she be able to keep thoughts of Char away? The times they had spent together, the sound of her laughter when they had shared a funny moment. Sometimes at night, after she had moved from Mitchell's bed to hers, she would remember when they had said goodbye and Char had held her hands, so briefly, but the memory of that moment and the sensations that filled her had never left. What would it be like to be touched by Char instead of Mitchell? Would it feel different? What was wrong with her that she couldn't respond to her husband?

She read the book that Char had given her, *Man's Search for Meaning.* If Victor Frankle could find meaning in a concentration camp, then surely she could find meaning in her life, even if the situation was not ideal.

School would start soon. She would pull herself together and use this free time to prepare lesson plans, buy supplies, maybe sew new kitchen curtains.

She was cooking differently now. Emily remained a voracious reader and took to heart the recent reports on healthier eating. Salads and roasted chicken replaced casseroles made with creamed condensed soup. Mitchell still enjoyed barbequing steaks, and the kids loved hamburgers and hot dogs. She tried to balance it all.

"Pass the butter, please." Emily handed Mitchell the margarine. She had quit buying real butter long ago in favor of lower fat margarine, but her husband was none the wiser. He proceeded to put a large blob on his baked potato until it ran over and dribbled onto the rest of his dinner.

Emily thought, *Mitchell looks more like his father every day. His hair is receding, his stomach is paunchy, and his eyes have become cruel.*

She thought about his mother, a kind but sad woman who had died only last month. "Mitchell, do you remember when we would study together and your mother would have freshly baked chocolate-chip cookies and ice-cold milk waiting for us?"

Mitchell barely glanced up. "That was a lifetime ago. You live in the past, Emily." He continued cutting his food, putting it in his mouth, chewing and swallowing, chewing and swallowing: a predictable, boring, methodical machine not unlike the ones that sorted the mail by zip code.

"I was feeling sad, remembering how kind she was, and now she's gone."

Mitchell shrugged his shoulders. "Did you get the kids off to camp okay?"

"Yes."

"You have a week off; no kids and no teaching." Mitchell laid down his silverware, his hazel eyes fixed on her; they looked to Emily like two once-bright pennies that had been in someone's pocket for too long and lost their luster, set in a face devoid of emotion. "Any plans?"

"I thought I'd sort through the kids' rooms, clean. Maybe sew some new kitchen curtains. Get school supplies and start my lesson plans."

He nodded and looked at her appraisingly. "Your hair's getting too long. You're starting to look like a damn hippie. Get it cut this week."

"I like it longer, Mitchell. I can keep it in a ponytail."

"Well, do something, for Christ's sake." Mitchell stood up, knocking his chair over. Emily saw his face turning red, his eyes changing into two dark, bulging marbles. "The school forwarded some of your mail here. You've been writing to her. Love letters, *Em?* Are you planning on spending the rest of your summer vacation in bed with her?" he said as he waved the letter above her head.

Emily stammered, "I-I h-haven't seen her since the party. Pen pals, Mitchell, we're only pen pals." Emily stood up, reaching for the letter. "It's my letter, Mitchell...mine...you had no right to open it."

"Sit down," he bellowed. "Doesn't sound like pen pals to me."

He removed the letter from the ripped-open envelope and read, his voice filled with hateful venom.

171

Hi, Em,

Sorry I haven't written sooner. Time has slipped out of my hands.

Here's a photo of the Girls. We took our annual vacation to Maui. I wish you were here. Beautiful waterfalls, hiking trails and the beaches! Lots of wonderful Kodak moments.

I got a letter from Lawrence on Mother's Day. Not exactly a loving letter. He asked me to stop sending him birthday and holiday gifts. He doesn't want anything to do with me. It hurts, but I know I have to let him go. I pray you never experience the pain of losing a child.

Hope your Mother's Day was sweet. Miss you and the kids.

"Miss you, wish you were here," he said mockingly.

Emily looked up, her eyes meeting Mitchell's. "It's my letter, Mitchell, my photo. You had no right to open it...no right."

"I have every right. You're my wife. Some wife—goddamn frigid lesbian. *You* shouldn't be near *my* kids. *My* kids, do you get it?" He grabbed her hair, pushing her to the floor. She remembered the chair falling over; she remembered his hands, pummeling; his feet, thumping. She stopped remembering.

When Emily was a little girl she saw a grandfather clock at FEDCO and became mesmerized by the sound of the ticking and the chimes that struck every fifteen minutes. She bought a miniature reproduction at a garage sale for twenty dollars and hung it on the kitchen wall. Mitchell said she had overpaid, but she loved to hear the chimes and the ticking that soothed her late at night when she couldn't sleep.

She woke to the sound of the chimes. She tried to count them but couldn't get past three. The house was quiet and the air, oh so hot and heavy. She knew she had to try to stand up. *The kids, where were the kids?* She remembered: camp. *They're safe, don't worry.* She struggled, kneeling on one knee, then the other. *Good, Emily. Hold onto the table.* She groaned as she pulled herself up. She needed help. She needed Char. She found her keys—could she drive? *You have to drive, Emily. You can do it. Fifteen miles, take the side streets. Take the side streets.*

Char's house was dark except for the porch light that shined like a welcoming beacon. What if she wasn't home? What if Char didn't want her here? What if she was *with* someone? She hadn't thought about that. *Emily, walk from the car to the courtyard gate. It's only ten feet.* She counted the steps. *Three steps more to the bell, Emily, one at a time, one at a time. Don't ring the bell—push the buzzer below.*

The hall light went on and Emily could see a shadowy figure moving across the courtyard. Char opened the gate and looked at her with unbelieving eyes. "Em? Oh, Jesus Christ, Em." Char's arms were around her, holding her, supporting her, helping her into the house.

Em's eyelids fluttered open; she was lying on a bed. *How did she get here?*

Char was holding her hand, stroking her brow. Max and Lesley were hovering over her. She could see Lesley's mouth moving, shaping words, but she couldn't understand what she was saying. Her words, suspended in space, sounded like angel wings fluttering to catch the breeze.

Lesley leaned over, her words becoming more distinct. "Em, can you hear me?"

Em nodded.

"Who am I?"

She croaked, "Dr. Lesley."

Lesley smiled at her. "Good girl." She flashed a penlight in Em's eyes. "Follow the light for me, Em. Excellent."

They undressed her, covering her with a soft blanket. She kept moaning. She didn't mean to; she wanted to be quiet so the children wouldn't wake up.

Lesley was examining her back, arms, and legs. "I'm sorry, Em. I'm almost done. You've got a cut over your eye. I'm going to numb the area and take a couple of stitches. Okay?"

Em whispered, "Okay."

Char said, "Em, where are the kids? Are they with Mitchell?"

Em tried to remember. *Focus, Em, you have to focus.* "No," she whispered before closing her eyes, "they're safe."

Lesley reached into her doctor's case for her stitch kit. "Char, keep holding her hand. She needs to know you're here."

Bamboo-slatted shades covered the bedroom windows. Once tightly woven, they had weathered over time, allowing the relentless sun to sneak through.

Em woke up with the sunlight shining directly in her eyes. She turned her head, at first confused. *Where was she?* She remembered this room from Char's party: black lacquered furniture and bamboo plants in large tubs. Then, the bed was piled high with coats and purses. Now, she was in the bed. Every part of her hurt, as if she had tumbled out of the highest peppertree on the lane.

Lesley opened the door, carrying her black bag. She sat on the side of the bed, stroking Em's head and holding her hand.

She spoke as gently as a warm summer breeze. "Do you remember how you got here?"

Em blinked, trying to gather her thoughts, her memories. "I drove."

Lesley nodded. "There's nothing broken, but you had a cut over your eye. I closed that, and now I want to check your bruises."

Lesley examined her, exposing small parts at a time. She helped Em to sit up and held back her own tears when she heard Em's groans. "Em, try to take a deep breath and hold it for me—good girl." Lesley sat back and held Em's hand. "Everything sounds good. Do you know where you are?"

Em looked around the room. "Char's."

Lesley nodded and smiled. "We'll get you some breakfast: toast, tea, and applesauce. And I want you to drink lots of water for me. Okay?"

"Okay...thank you, Dr. Lesley."

"For what?"

"For not leaving me alone when Maggie was born and for being here now." She sobbed. "I don't know why I'm crying."

Lesley put her arms around Em. "It's good to cry. Do you remember what happened?"

"He had my letter from Char. I told him it was mine." Em grabbed Lesley and cried out, "It was only a letter! *My* letter and *my* picture!"

Lesley held her, waiting for the sobs to play out.

"I remember him pulling my hair, hitting me, kicking me. Then, driving here, but I don't remember anything else. Except, I had a dream about three angels holding me."

"It sounds like a lovely dream. You need to know you have friends; you're not alone."

Em rested her head against Lesley's chest and nodded.

Lesley stroked her head. "Em, don't you think it's time you called me Les? All my friends do."

Char was in the kitchen, measuring coffee for the twenty-five cup percolator. The Girls were all coffee hounds and Ray—my God, that man could drink the whole pot by himself!

"How is she?" Char asked when Les walked in, her stethoscope bobbing around her neck.

"Confused, angry, in pain...grateful..."

"I'm glad she's angry. Maybe it will motivate her. I've called the Girls; they'll be here at four. Do you think she'll be up to it?"

"I think we need to give her some options. We can't let her go home." Les shook her head. "She's in a deadly situation...and so are you."

"Crap, Les. I'm fine."

Les ignored her. "Yeah, yeah, yeah. How much sleep did *you* get last night? I don't need two patients on my hands. Come on, humor me." Les guided Char to a chair and put her stethoscope to Char's chest and back. "You constantly amaze me. Your heart sounds stable. Are you going to tell her?"

Char sighed. "Tell her what? That I had rheumatic fever when I was five? That I might die? Tell me when—tomorrow, a year from now? Ten years from now?" A look of defiance crossed Char's face. "So far, I've beaten the odds. I should have been dead by fifteen. No one believed I could have a child. If I gave in to what everyone thought, I would have been dead years ago.

"Les, I think she has enough to handle right now. No one knows about this ticker but you and me. And, since you're my doc, you're stuck with the secret. I'm going to bet on another ten years: ten years to be in her life, to help her as a friend. Ten years can be a lifetime if you live every day to the fullest."

Les leaned against the kitchen counter and sighed. "Char, I've known you a long time." She smiled. "You brought me out."

"I haven't forgotten. What a month that was!"

"It was, wasn't it? Someone should have warned me. When that light got turned on..." Les shuddered. "Jesus, the only time we left my dorm room was to run to the bathroom and run back. I was the proverbial wunderkind, flunking out of med school at eighteen."

Char held Les's hand. "You were a wild woman. Remember how we kept ordering pizza?"

"And stacked the boxes in the corner. We called it the Tower of Pizza. Then, the dorm mother started banging on the door...didn't you almost die?"

Char chuckled. "I dove under the blankets. She didn't know it was a woman you had in bed. All she saw was my feet."

"Well, at least you didn't have to meet with the dean...and your parents. They kept asking me who you were, until I finally blurted out your name, 'Char.' You should have seen their faces. My parents looked at each other, hugged, and said, 'Thank God. *His* name is Charles.' I was finally normal. Then they begged the dean to give me another chance, and my mother took me out in the hall to lecture me on birth control, while Daddy wrote out a very large check toward a building fund."

Les became pensive. "They've never admitted the truth about me. Makes it harder, doesn't it? Having to hide who you are, who you love. To family and friends, I'm the old maid who chose a career over a family."

"Yeah. My mother died denying everything that was in the newspapers. I made the headlines: LESBIAN MOTHER FIGHTS FOR CHILD CUSTODY. I lost my son, Les. What a price to pay, and for what? Loving someone? Shit, life is hard enough without having to deny...to lie. You and I, all the Girls, we've made a family."

Les nodded. "Quite a family, I'd say. You know, Char, I still love you. That never completely goes away. Are you serious now, about wanting to buy time?"

Char nodded. "I know I've pushed the envelope, but I've haven't had anything...anyone to live for...not since Lawrence. And back then, the docs gave me little hope."

"There's a cardiologist at UCLA I want you to see," said Les. "New meds are coming out, and there's a trial study beginning for congestive heart failure. It's a mind/body program and it'll mean making a lot of changes. This'll have to go—" she waved a disapproving hand at Char's usual breakfast, a large cinnamon roll and a mug of coffee laden with sugar and heavy cream, "*and* fifteen pounds, Char. No more bullshit and no more ribs. Fifteen pounds. Promise?"

Char crossed her heart. "Promise."

"I've sent your records to UCLA. They'll accept you if you go. If you want time, it'll buy you time."

Char hugged Les. "Les, I know I haven't been the best patient—"

"I'm an obstetrician, not a cardiologist. Do you know how many times I've tried to get you to have a workup? You're the most stubborn woman I've ever loved...and a major pain in the ass." This last was said with mingled truth and affection.

"I want to change that," Char said sincerely. "I know I can help Em if she'll let me. All I'm asking for is time. I'll do whatever you say, whatever this new doctor says—"

"Time...that's the big commodity, isn't it?" Les shook her head, "I've never seen you so loopy. When you fall, you really fall, don't you—a straight woman with two children and an abusive husband. The perfect formula for disaster, *and* she doesn't know about your 'ticker,' *and* she doesn't know you're head over heels in love."

"You know I don't mess with straight women. I love her and I love her kids. That'll have to be enough."

Les shook her head. "It feels that way for now—but later..."

Les leaned over, kissing Char on the cheek. "Max and I are going home to change and catch some shut-eye. As your doc, I'm ordering you to take a nap. I've got a big investment in keeping you alive."

Max opened the passenger door of their candy apple red 1967 Mustang convertible, waiting patiently for Les to sit down and buckle up before she closed the door. She sank into the black leather bucket seat, listening to the purring of the 390 big block engine before driving off.

Max Junior, as her family called her, grew up hanging out with her dad, Max Senior, at his auto repair shop. Out of five daughters, Maxine

Juanita Tracey was the closest he would ever get to having a son. She learned everything about cars from her dad, and after graduating from high school, she applied to Westlake Community College for a certificate in the Automotive Service Technology program. She signed her application *Max Tracey Jr.* and received her acceptance letter within a month.

It was September 1960 when she entered the classroom filled with young men—some fresh out of high school, some veterans returning to school trying to better themselves.

The instructor, Mr. Phillips, glared at Maxine, a contemptuous expression crossing his face. "You're in the wrong room, little girl," he said snidely.

Laughter followed, some hooted, some snickered.

Max didn't pay attention. She was used to being laughed at. Her overall appearance, her gait that had a slight swagger, and shoulders that swayed as she moved. The men's clothes she favored prompted the frequent question: Is that a man or a woman? All invited ridicule.

She'd show them. She knew more about cars than all but the most seasoned grease monkey. She remained silent and handed Mr. Phillips her enrollment form.

Mr. Phillips said, "There's a mistake here, girly. Maybe sewing class, but automotive—not in my lifetime." His voice became patronizing. "Now, you head on back to the registrar's office like a good little girl and get this fixed."

The class roared as Max left. On her way to the office she stopped at a payphone to call her dad.

By the time she had walked over to the administrative offices' waiting room, the Cordoba-Tracey clan was beginning to assemble. Her parents, siblings, even her grandmother gathered around her.

Max put her head on her grandmother's shoulder. "Abuela," she said tearfully.

Dean Andrew Rush had just finished changing into his navy-blue Polo golf shirt and yellow linen slacks. He screwed up his face when his third phone line lit up. It only meant one thing: trouble. *Damn it!* He was all set to leave for an afternoon on the links and was eager to try out his custom-made two-toned kilties with fringed tongue, which the shoe salesman swore would improve his golf game.

He picked up the phone and listened. "I'll be right there."

He thought, *Another person screaming discrimination.* These cases were coming up more and more often. Didn't people understand where they belonged?

He took a deep breath. Getting angry would not solve the problem. Rational talk, appeal to their senses. That would work.

The number of people gathered in the front office took him by surprise. Ten? Fifteen? All chattering as if it were a day at the beach.

He said "Hello" to the group and smiled amiably. "I'm so sorry for the confusion, but I'm certain we can get this issue straightened out." He scanned the crowd and called out, "Maxine?"

Max raised her hand.

Dean Rush had learned over the years to be personable and to use a carrot instead of a stick. "Maxine, I am so sorry for the confusion. You see, we have regulations we have to go by and girls, umm...young ladies...umm...women aren't allowed into the automotive classes. There are other options, viable options. Why, you can choose almost any other major. What about nursing? That's a great profession for a young woman."

He went on seductively. "Of course, that is one of our most popular programs and the classes are filled. But I will make an exception for you, Maxine."

Max stood firm. "No, sir. It's not what I want. I was accepted into the Automotive Certificate Program."

"A simple clerical error, Maxine, and one that needs to be corrected."

Dean Rush's voice softened as he addressed the family. "Now, we all have the same goal. We want Maxine to have a good education and to be out of danger." He shook his head and tsk-tsked. "For a girl to be around automobiles...why, it simply isn't safe. There's heavy lifting and sometimes the men—well, boys—will be boys, and girls," he eyed Max's manly costume dubiously, "will, *ahem*, be girls."

Max Senior said, "Not in this family. Max Junior has been around cars since she was six. She could probably *teach* the damn course! She is not a nurse, she is a mechanic, and it's a damn fine profession for men *and* women."

"Now, now, Mr. Tracey, I understand your feelings, but there are rules and regulations."

Her grandmother, a diminutive woman with skin that bespoke her Hispanic and Native American lineage, stood a head shorter than Max, but towered over everyone in the room by dint of her fire and vigor. She held her hand up to hush everyone. In that moment of silence her eyes glowed with the passion of a woman who had suffered a lifetime of discrimination.

"Dean Rush, you have to understand the Cordoba-Tracey clan. There are a dozen of us here and more are on their way. In half an hour there will be twenty of us. And by the end of the day, we will be fifty strong. Reporters will follow; Hispanic and women students will picket."

Abuela raised her head in order to look directly into Dean Rush's eyes. "All we ask is that you give Max Junior a fair chance, let her stand or fall on her own merit. Don't turn her away because of some outdated rule meant to discriminate. Do what's right, Dean Rush. We aren't going away."

Max was the first woman to be accepted into the Automotive Technology Program and her laminated Associate of Applied Science Degree was proudly displayed on the wall of her office at Max's Garage.

Max kept the top of the Mustang up, drove along the side streets until they were further into the hills. She parked next to a secluded pasture where horses were grazing and eucalyptus trees shaded the street.

She undid her seat belt, leaned over, and in one smooth motion, unhooked Les's seat belt and held out her arms.

∞

Les's gift to herself for becoming Board Certified in Obstetrics and Gynecology was a 1969 black Karmann Ghia convertible. She was taking her morning run past the car agencies that lined Van Nuys Boulevard and happened to glance at the sleek car with its top down, exposing the tan interior. With its headlights beckoning, its chrome grill smiling, the Ghia seemed to be staring directly at her, softly speaking her name.

She ran another block, stopped in her tracks, turned around, and jogged back to the agency. She cupped her hands on the front window to ward off the morning glare and stared at the car sitting on the showroom floor. The sleek body appealed to her, and she could feel the ocean breeze on her face as she took the coast route on a Sunday morning to Santa Barbara. The back seat had been folded down and for a moment, she could see the space filled with her gym clothes, dry cleaning, and groceries. Ideal, she thought. She glanced at her watch: 8:00 a.m. The agency opened at nine.

She ran home, her heart pounding, infected with the dreaded disease known as New Car Acquisition Syndrome. She raced through her shower, threw on a set of scrubs, and drove her battered car—filled with a week's worth of take-out food boxes—back to the agency precisely as the small hand moved to nine and the big hand touched twelve.

The bank approved her loan and the salesman, thrilled at how little bargaining he had to do, had the car rolled out of the show-room and onto the car lot for prepping.

Les loved the way the little German sportster wrapped around her lanky figure, and the way the wind blew her long blond hair when she put the top down. Her Karmann Ghia, a busy practice, and an almost empty apartment: That was her life. She dated—when she had time—which was almost never. She had brief affairs with some incredible women she met at professional seminars. Great sex, to be sure, but no one seemed to get her heart. She told herself she was still young, only twenty-eight. Maybe, one day, love would find her.

It was late on a Friday afternoon and Les had just finished delivering twins. She was passionate about her work, never got over the thrill of seeing new life brought into the world, and prayed each and every time that she would not have to be the bearer of bad news. Her Friday appointments had been rescheduled and unless she had an emergency, she was off for the weekend. Dreams of breakfast in bed...*did she have any food in the house?* She made a mental note: Stop at the market. She could feel the silky sheets caressing her legs, the fluffy pillow that was like floating on a cloud—everything exactly the way she liked it. No alarm, just sleep, wonderful, wonderful sleep.

She eased her body into the Ghia and turned the ignition. Nothing. She tried again. Nothing. *It wasn't cranking.* On the fifth try she called a tow truck. *Fuck,* she thought. *There goes my weekend.*

She was tired, she was sweaty, she hadn't eaten, and here she was sitting in the front seat of a tow truck listening to blaring honky-tonk music arguing with the static of incoming calls.

The driver held out his hand. "I'm Brewster, ma'am. I'm gonna take you to Max's Garage. It's out of my way...but Max is the best." Les was loath to shake the grimy paw, but then she saw that Brewster had other ideas. He stared at Les with a look that said: "Tip expected." She fished in her wallet and took out her last ten dollars.

∞

Les watched the sun setting as intense colors of orange and red filled the surrounding sky. *What a waste*, she thought, *to be sitting in a tow truck and sharing this romantic sunset with the missing link.* She sighed quietly, longingly.

It was twilight before Brewster took the freeway exit to Sepulveda Boulevard and entered a street that led to an industrial neighborhood in Van Nuys. Les felt lost as the truck followed a labyrinth of alleyways into an area filled with automotive repair shops. There was an eerie sense of having been transported into another world where cars were the masters and service technicians, their slaves. Building after building painted in bright colors, meant to entice customers, announced their areas of expertise: Brakes and Mufflers; Transmissions; Body Work / Mechanical Service / Routine Maintenance; European Cars Only.

The tow truck stopped at an expansive white cinderblock building with a gleaming metal sign announcing Max's Garage in black Coneria Script. *Pretty fancy lettering*, Lesley thought, *for a garage.* Five empty bays faced the street. A man and a woman in white uniforms and black bow ties were busy cleaning, power washing the floors, removing all signs of oil and other fluids that might have dripped onto the floor during their day's work. Lesley thought they looked like operating rooms getting sterilized, ready for the next patient.

Lesley handed Brewster the ten dollars and thought, *I am now officially broke*, thanked him, and followed his gesture that told her where to wait while they positioned her car in the bay.

She expected Max to be a man, as most new customers did, when they saw the name on the sign, the script font notwithstanding. Lesley felt an immediate attraction to this somewhat strange-looking woman wearing a short-sleeved white shirt with *Max's* embroidered on the shoulder, navy-blue double knee work pants, and black steel toe boots. She could see that Max's arms were muscular, but they seemed incongruent with the small rolls that threatened to find their way over her black belt. Her black hair had been pulled back into a ponytail while her long bangs threatened to droop over her Ben Franklin glasses.

Max peered at the Karmann Ghia's engine, clucked her tongue, and shook her head. Then she rubbed her hand over the car's fender and spoke to it. "Don't worry, we're going to fix you up, good as new." She looked at Lesley and smiled. A fleeting wisp of a smile that lasted barely a second but which lit up Lesley's world as it had never been lit up before.

Max looked at Lesley the way Lesley would look at a patient's family when she had to deliver bad news. "Let's go to my office," Max said in a hushed tone.

Out of earshot of the patient, Lesley thought. She was surprised at the way the office was furnished. She expected to see leather chairs with deep cracks and a grease-stained metal desk: the barebones trappings of a grease monkey. Instead she saw an immaculate, tastefully furnished office not unlike her own. Framed and laminated academic certificates hung on taupe walls alongside sepia-toned lithographs of historic world's fairs. The comfortable, inviting atmosphere made her sigh as she sunk and relaxed into the soft leather club chair.

Lesley's eyes drifted to a low oak bookcase. Books of poetry by Shelley, Keats, and Dickinson, Maya Angelou's *I Know Why The Caged Bird Sings*, and a neat stack of *The Ladder,* the first monthly lesbian publication in the United States.

Max said, "I didn't want to talk in front of the patient."

Lesley nodded. She had entered the Twilight Zone.

"That's a great car you've got. Deserves the best of care."

Lesley felt the blood rush to her face. Had Max seen the interior of the car? *Crap!* Two weeks' worth of take-out lunches, empty coffee cups, and candy wrappers thrown on the floor mats. *Shit!*

"Oh, God, Max, I'm so sorry the car's a mess. I haven't had a chance to get it washed." Lesley hung her head, a mother guilty of neglecting her child.

"No, no, Lesley. Not to worry. We'll detail your baby for you. Every car leaves Max's as clean as the day it was born."

Max walked over to the espresso machine. She fixed a cup for Lesley; she didn't ask how she liked it, but instinctively made it perfectly. She placed two biscotti on a milk-white glass plate.

"Thank you," said Lesley, taking a small bite out of the chocolate-covered twice-baked cookie.

Max said, "You'll need a ride home and a loaner for a week."

"A week?" Lesley felt her knees turn to mush and her heart rate bounce up a notch.

"I'll have to order the parts. The repair won't be that difficult—it's just getting parts for a Karmann Ghia can take a couple of days, and I won't be able to order them until Monday. Look, I was just about to leave. If you'll drive home with me, you can use my car."

Lesley said weakly, "What will *you* use?"

Max chuckled. "Let's see, I have two more cars in my garage at home and a Kawasaki J1T—in red." Her face glowed with pride as she flashed the smile that melted Lesley's heart.

Max saw Lesley's expression that said, *What's a Kawasaki?* Max added, "That's a motorcycle."

"It's so sweet of you, Max, but I can't do that."

Max sat on her desk facing Lesley, her legs slightly apart. "Can't or won't?" She dangled the keys in front of Lesley. "No strings, no rental fee. Just drop me off."

Max drove her 1969 burnished bronze metallic Jeepster Commando. "My house is only about ten miles from here. Won't take us long—I didn't want to live too far from the shop. You know, in case of an emergency."

Lesley thought. *Just like any dedicated physician, on call 24/7.*

"I just acquired this Jeep. Great for camping. Four-wheel drive, V6 engine, and a three-speed stick. It's a real honey. I thought you'd enjoy driving it for a few days."

"It's very generous of you...I mean..." Lesley sighed. "I'm exhausted, and the thought of waiting for a rental car...I don't know how I can thank you. Plus, I'm officially broke. I gave the tow truck driver my last ten dollars."

Max shook her head just before stopping in front of a Spanish-style duplex. "That's Brewster the Butt-head, all right. He does it every time. Well, this is it." She leaned over and handed Lesley the keys. "I don't suppose you'd like to come in for dinner? My mother stopped over this morning with a care package. Do you like authentic Mexican food?"

"Authentic?"

"Mm-hmm. My mother is Mexican, and when I say authentic...well, she uses my grandmother's recipes from Guadalajara."

"It's awfully tempting, but I should go. I'm so grungy I'm bordering on toxic."

"You and me both. A day in surgery, a day inside engines. Guaranteed grunginess."

Max thought for a moment. "I'll tell you what. You come in, use the master bathroom; take a shower or a bath. I'll use the guest bath, and by the time you're done, we'll both be clean and dinner will be ready. It'll be safer for you to drive home if you've eaten."

A tray holding a glass of white wine and a plate filled with cheese, grapes, and crackers sat waiting on a tea table next to the tub. Lesley eased into the oversized claw-footed tub filled with scented oils and bubble bath. Letting out a sigh, she reached for a slice of cheese and cracker and took a sip of wine. She giggled when she heard the water running in the other bathroom. *This has got to be the mother of all lesbian fantasies,* she thought.

Here she was, naked in a stranger's tub; her scrubs whisked away to be laundered. She thought about Max and let out a quiet "whoo-pee" before ducking under the water to blow bubbles.

Max knocked on the door. "Dinner's ready. There's a terrycloth robe hanging on the hook. Your clothes should be dry soon."

A square dining table covered in hand-painted Mexican tiles, in black, gold, and white, was set with porcelain dinner plates in a white and blue pattern, bordered with deep red carnations.

Max had changed into a pink, long-sleeved Ralph Lauren shirt, chinos, and dark brown loafers. She held the chair for Lesley as the flames from the stucco and brick fireplace danced to the slow rhythm of the dance music playing in the background.

Lesley felt her throat tighten and tears begin to well up. *I'm being seduced. Damn, it's been such a long time, and damn, it feels good!*

Max said, "I should warn you; my mother overcooks. We'll start with *ceviche*. Halibut, cooked without heat."

Lesley nodded. "Cooked through marinating." She lifted her fork and slowly guided it to her mouth. She closed her eyes for a moment, taking in the full flavor of the food. "It's wonderful. Don't tell me you eat like this all the time."

"We usually have dinner on Fridays. The whole family: my four sisters, their husbands and kids, my parents, of course, and sometimes, aunts and uncles, too."

"What happened today?"

"I was planning on working late, get caught up on paperwork, things like that. That's why Mom brought over all the food."

They ate slowly, savoring the *mole poblano*, chicken smothered in a sauce made of dried chilies, dark chocolate, and roasted nuts.

Conversation came easily. They discovered they had a soft spot for the same poets, liked watching black and white Universal horror movies from the thirties and forties, usually starring Boris Karloff or

Bela Lugosi, while eating popcorn, and were equally passionate and dedicated to their careers. They ended their meal with flan, the traditional Mexican custard dessert topped with soft caramel, whipped cream, and fresh strawberries.

Lesley said, "This was incredibly delicious. I have to say, I'm feeling a little guilty about keeping you from your work."

Max filled Lesley's wine glass and shook her head. "You saved my life. I hate paperwork. I'd rather be tinkering with an engine. It'll all be there on Monday."

"Your family is okay with you?"

Max smiled. "Sexual preference" was inferred in the question. "They'd kill for me. What about yours, Lesley?"

"I'm the old maid aunt, married to her profession. They pretend...they know, but don't want to know." She put down her wine glass. "The dinner, the evening, everything has been extraordinary. How can I thank you, Max?"

"Dance with me, Lesley? One dance before you leave?"

"In only a bathrobe?"

Max didn't respond. Instead she went over to the stereo and put in a new cassette.

The Flamingos sang the achingly romantic ballad "I Only Have Eyes for You." She held out her hand to Lesley. "In only a bathrobe."

Max held Lesley, but not as close as she longed to. "I'm not so good with words, Lesley. Most of my education has been around cars; the rest is self-taught. I know I'm not the beauty of the week, and I have to warn you, this is the way I dress all the time. But, God, I'm attracted to you." Max murmured, "Spend the night with me, Les."

Les didn't leave Max's home until Monday morning. No one, but *no one* could understand how Max made her feel. The way she instinctively knew what to whisper in her ear, or how to touch her until she thought her body would explode. The way Max's family welcomed her and accepted them as if they were the same as any of their other children. For the first time in her life, Les knew what it was like to be valued for who she was, not for what others wished her to be.

Now, years later and sitting in the Mustang under the shade of the eucalyptus trees, Max gathered Les as close as the bucket seats allowed, and waited patiently for her sobs to begin.

Chapter 19

1977

The open bedroom door allowed a view of Em, a fragile figure lying on her back, her eyes half-opened.

Char held a breakfast tray in her hands. "Hey, Em, how you doing?"

Em spoke hoarsely. "I got into this position and now I'm afraid to move."

Char placed the tray on the nightstand. "Put your arms around me, Em, I'll help you sit up."

"I'm not sure I can lift my arms." She began to cry.

Char sat on the edge of the bed. "It's okay, Em."

"It's not okay to cry."

"Says who?"

In spite of the pain, Em chuckled. "Jesus, it hurts to laugh."

"I can help you sit up; I learned the technique in high school."

"In high school?"

"Yep, we had to take a home nursing course. You know, women always take care of the sick. I've never had a chance to try it out. Wanna be my guinea pig?"

"Char, don't make me laugh."

"Okay, no laughing. You put one arm around my shoulder. Now,

I slip my hands under your pillow and raise it and you at the same time. Em, if this doesn't work, we'll both be on the floor. Ready? One, two, three..."

With a grunt from both of them, Em was in a half-sitting position.

"Well, we aren't on the floor so it must have worked."

"I'm lopsided," said Em, tilting to one side.

Char tucked pillows around Em. "Better?"

"Yes."

"Les left you some pain meds. She said they're mild, two every four hours; take them with food. And breakfast is here. Doc's orders, light meals for a day or two. You'll feel better after you eat."

"Char, thank you for last night and for being my friend. I didn't know where else to go."

"You did the right thing, coming here."

"I can't stay long, though. Mitchell will expect me home to fix dinner."

Char sat down on the edge of the bed. *God, how I want to reach out, to touch her, comfort her.* "Listen to me, Em. You can't go home and neither can the kids."

"He won't do it again. Things got out of hand. I shouldn't have pushed him."

"This isn't the first time. It'll only get worse, not better."

Em looked down. "Once before, it was my fault."

"Never anyone's fault to get beat up. You really need to think carefully about this one. I've put a mirror on the nightstand and after you eat, I want you to really look at the bruises. Next time, he can kill you or go for the kids. No one is safe."

Char's earliest memories were of conflict, not of safety.

Her childhood home was a small apartment in East Los Angeles: one bedroom and a small alcove barely large enough for a youth-sized bed and a small chest of drawers. She'd lie in bed, listening to her parents arguing over moving, sucking her thumb faster and faster in cadence to the sound of cheap dishes being thrown by her mother in a fit of rage.

"I won't raise my child in this...in this neighborhood. We have to better ourselves. All our friends are moving. The schools, Saul—the schools are better in West Los Angeles. Don't you want the best for our Charlotte?"

"Sarah, darling," he pleaded. "We don't have the money, we don't have the money."

"Do something to get it. I don't care what you have to do, just do it!"

Char didn't want to move because Bubby and Zaide lived upstairs, and she only had to climb the steps to sit on Zaide's lap while Bubby handed her a "nosh" warm from the oven. "Es, es, mayn kind" *(Eat, eat, my child)* her Bubby would say. What a moment of sublime caring, to be served with such love while being rocked by her beloved Zaide.

Bubby and Zaide were Daddy's mommy and daddy. "Call them Grandma and Grandpa," her mother would say. But Char liked the sound of Bubby and Zaide, and she liked the way Zaide would hold her on his lap, his long, gray, curly beard tickling her face as he told her stories about coming to America from Russia. His beard was so long and his head so bald, that Char was sure his hair had somehow traveled from his head to his face.

Char always knew when it was Friday because the fragrance of roasted chicken and *knishes*—dumplings stuffed with rice or potatoes—would drift down from Bubby and Zaide's to the unhappy apartment below.

Char's mommy, Sarah, didn't like climbing the stairs every Friday night. "They're your parents, Saul, not mine! Do we have to go there every Friday night? Why can't we have *our* friends over?"

Daddy would shrug his shoulders and say, "It's tradition." He climbed the stairs, his shoulders slumping in defeat, a man caught between the old and the new worlds.

They moved from East Los Angeles to West Los Angeles when she was four. Mommy said to call her Mother because it sounded nicer.

Char liked the duplex with its high ceilings and thick, white stucco walls. She had her own bedroom now, but there were no smells from Bubby's cooking to remind her it was Friday, and no Zaide to hold her on his lap.

Instead of Sabbath dinner, Mother and Daddy had friends over every Friday night to play cards, smoke, and laugh.

Char only saw Bubby and Zaide for two special holidays, Passover and Yom Kippur. On Passover they would go to Bubby and Zaide's. The whole family—cousins, aunts, and uncles—would crowd into the tiny apartment in East Los Angeles for the Ceremony. Char didn't like sitting still for over an hour while they read from the Haggadah—the book that told the story of the Jewish people being slaves and escaping from Egypt. She liked it when the sea emptied and they could walk across in their bare feet—she thought it would be like going to the beach—but she didn't like it when they had to walk in the hot desert for forty years.

She sat at the children's table, kicking her cousin Benny for entertainment, until he cried. She would hold the Haggadah up to her eyes with an innocent, holy look and Benny's momma would hit him on the side of the head for being a bad boy.

On Yom Kippur, they would visit Bubby and Zaide in the synagogue. Mother would make her dress up and curl her hair like Shirley Temple's. Everyone would make a fuss over how big she was getting and said she should be in the movies. Afterward, Mother and Daddy would take her to C. C. Brown's for a sundae. No fasting for them, not even on the Holiest of Holy Days.

When Char was five, the war started and she became sick with the fever. Her body shook, and she had nightmares about purple and green monsters.

Quieter arguments, not meant for her to hear, drifted across the house to her room.

"Do it, Saul. You have a sick child."

"I can go to jail," her father whined.

Contempt wrapped around her mother's words. "Be a *mensch* for once, Saul, be a goddamn *mensch*. Go into business with my brother Abe; he said there's no risk. You know what the doctor said. It's her heart. What if she dies? We have to move, she needs a drier climate. Do it, Saul, just do it."

Things changed after that. Her mother got a fur coat and paid for everything with cash from a thick white envelope.

Char peeked in on Em. She was curled up into a ball, sleeping soundly, except for an occasional groan that brought tears to Char's eyes. She closed the bedroom door and began to get ready for the Girls. Char took out her mother's china, gazing at the hand-painted specimens of birds from around the world, each depicted in their native habitat. A wide band of gold encircled the edge of each plate. Her mother had bragged to her mahjong friends: "Twenty-four-karat gold."

***

Hand wash, she reminded herself, placing the china on the dining room credenza.

Her mother had bought the dishes at Bullocks Wilshire Department Store. Char loved going to Bullocks. A man in a general's uniform opened the car door and a lady wearing a jacket with gold buttons got to drive the elevator. "Second floor, toys and children's clothing," she announced. Her mother always let Char walk through the toy department. She saw a tiny doll that came with a carrying case filled with equally tiny outfits. She lingered for a moment, afraid to touch the fragile doll.

"Third floor, housewares and fine china," the elevator lady announced. Now they were in Mother's toy department. "Twelve to keep and six to break," her mother had joked with the saleswoman as she ordered the fine china that now resided in Char's cupboard. Char knew, even at that early age, that the dishes would break not from an accident but from angry outbursts.

When they returned to the car, the man in the general's uniform opened the door and handed Char a bag. "For you, missy, from your momma." Mother gave him a whole dollar and when Char looked in the bag she saw the fragile dolly packed away safely in her protective case.

When Char was nine, the war ended and Daddy had to go on a long business trip, for a whole year. Mother cried, but after he left, they went shopping and Mother bought a fox stole, complete with two heads and tails.

When Daddy came home, he looked thinner and smaller. He cried when he hugged Char and told her how much he had missed her. It wasn't until after her father died that she discovered his business trip was a twelve-month prison sentence for black marketeering.

They moved to Studio City, where it was drier and hotter—weather not tempered by damp ocean breezes from the west, but heated by the Santa Ana desert winds from the east.

Like the doll from Bullocks, Char's mother tried to keep her in a protective case, only to be taken out for special occasions, never to be allowed to run or ride a bicycle or play jump rope.

Char fought her on every battlefront. She had learned from an expert how to scream and how to throw dishes until her mother cried and gave in.

She wanted to attend New York University to get her bachelor's degree in psychology. What a fight she had with her mother! "Leave the state with your condition?" her mother had raged. "Over my dead body!" The dishes flew, the screams echoed, but off she went to New York. Char never told anyone about her heart condition. Her philosophy was simple: "Fuck it."

Char and Helen, with her long, curly hair and legs that went on forever, roomed together and became best friends. They went ice-skating, ate out, and saw every movie that played in the small college town of Winston. It was during the Halloween Midnight Horror Show that Helen reached over and held Char's hand. Char thought, *She must be frightened of the Wolf Man*, but Helen didn't let go of her hand, even when Lon Chaney, Jr. wasn't on a murderous rampage through the London countryside. Instead she turned Char's hand over, holding it gently in one hand while the fingers of her other hand moved softly across Char's palm. Char gasped as an unfamiliar electrical feeling jolted through her body. *God,* she thought, *just like in* Frankenstein.

They returned to the dorm in complete silence. They never said a word, not as they undressed each other, not as they got into Helen's twin bed. Char tried to muffle the animalistic sounds—shades of the Wolf Man!—that came from deep inside her. She wasn't too successful. They made love until morning, slept for two hours, and missed their classes the next day.

It was the most intense experience Char had ever had, but she also knew her destiny.

She transferred to UCLA the next year, met Paul Owens at a sorority party, and got married two weeks after she graduated with her BA in Psychology.

Char tried to understand why she decided to use the dishes today, of all days. She knew they were purchased with money earned illegally during WWII. Why did they do it? People were suffering all over the world and her parents profited. Was it her fault because she had been so ill? Did they really do it for her, or because her mother would finally stop nagging and could buy anything she wanted with cash from a thick white envelope?

She wondered if paper plates wouldn't be more appropriate. Paper plates and deli food seemed to go together.

She arranged the trays and bowls on the dining room table and stood back, pleased at the way the room looked. Platters of corned beef and pastrami, bowls brimming with potato salad, coleslaw, and a green salad overflowing with vegetables weighed the table down. Colorful floral paper plates complemented the setting; dishes not tainted by shame, but signaling friendship and hope.

She picked up one of the kosher pickles, took a small bite and remembered her promise to Les. *No more salt for you,* she told herself with a feeling of satisfaction as she threw the pickle into the compost bin and returned her mother's dishes to the cupboard.

The Girls drifted over in pairs, except for Ray and Iris. Char knew Iris sometimes played both sides of the street, and for a moment wondered if Iris and Ray had ever hooked up.

Frankie and Bobbie pulled up first; Char could tell from the sound of their Harley. "How is she?" Frankie and Bobbie said in unison after a quick hug.

"Napping."

Frankie took off her helmet and jacket. "I think this should be a short meeting. We kill the sonofabitch."

"That's too quick and easy," Bobbie said, brushing her hand through her crew cut. "I'm thinking of slow torture." She turned to Char. "Where should we put our stuff?"

Char sighed. This would not be an easy meeting. "In my office...in my office," she replied.

∞

The shades had been lowered and the bedroom was dark except for the waning afternoon light that trickled through the bamboo slats. Char watched Em breathing; a soft rhythm that told her she was in a peaceful place. She touched Em's shoulder and whispered, "Em, the Girls are here." Em grunted, then drifted back to sleep. Char thought, *Maybe this isn't a good idea, maybe it's too soon.*

"Em," she said, "it's time to wake up." This time her voice was firmer.

Em stirred, her eyes trying to focus. "Everything hurts."

"Em, you don't have to do this."

"I do," she croaked. "I looked in the mirror. What if he does it to Chris or Maggie?"

"Max needs to come in and take the photos."

"Help me sit up?"

Char sat on the bed. "Put your arms around me. Okay?"

Em put her arms around Char, moaning as she sat up.

She said, "Stay here. Please don't leave me."

"Em, I'll always be here for you."

Chapter 20

Tuesday, October 6, 2020
Studio City

"There were eight of us that afternoon, including Ray," Em told Treat. "We gathered in this room; it was a solemn group that day. Max asked me if she could pass the Polaroid pictures around. I agreed but I felt exposed, ashamed, as if it were my fault. I could see their expressions change as they saw the photos. Ray wouldn't look at them; Bobbie and Frankie wept."

Treat sat quietly, mesmerized by Em's story.

"They encircled me; each one took me in, wanted to protect me. Suggestions were flying around the room like crossed telephone lines. The first suggestion, which today would make sense, was to go to the police. Someone else, I can't remember now who said it— I think it was Ray—suggested going to the hospital to establish evidence of the beating. I refused: no police, no hospital.

"I was terrified that things would get turned around. Mitchell had accused me of being a dyke and said I shouldn't be near *his* children. I knew if that became a court issue, Pastor Lockner and my own parents would side with Mitchell. I had to think of Maggie and Chris before I thought of myself. What if I lost custody of them? I couldn't stand that, and I didn't want them thrown into the anti-gay undercurrent of the church.

"Well, it was getting pretty chaotic and I was fading, close to tears." Em dabbed her eyes with a tissue. "You see, my body wasn't the only thing aching. My heart was broken, and so was my soul."

Emily looked at Treat, an empty pad of paper dangling from her lap, a shocked expression frozen across her face.

"Are you all right, Treat?"

Treat looked down. "I've never known anyone to be abused like that. I'm so sorry." She looked down, whispering, "Emily, I forgot to take notes."

Em said softly, "Forgetting to take notes is nothing to be ashamed of. You got caught up in the feelings of the story; that's a good thing. Now, you're on your path to becoming a writer."

Chapter 21

1977

The Girls were wearing casual clothing, jeans or sweats with T-shirts; even Bobbie and Frankie had changed from their leather motorcycle pants into sweats, but Iris went everywhere dressed as if there was a photographer or potential client waiting around the corner.

Casual for Iris was a pair of gray flare leg pants, a soft, white, silk crepe blouse, and a tomato-red linen jacket. White flats still guaranteed that she would be the tallest one in the room.

Iris waited until the din had slowed down and sputtered to a stop. She stood up, squaring her shoulders to make the most of her five feet eleven inches.

"It's time to stop this bullshit and get down to business," she commanded, dramatically flipping her (this week's) black hair away from her face. "Look at who we are, and we're acting like a bunch of silly schoolgirls—including you, Ray."

Iris was the conductor of an elite orchestra, getting ready to lead them in a concerto. "Look at this woman—a woman who wanted nothing but to take care of her family and have a friend. Now, take a closer look: She's fragile, injured, bruised outside *and* inside."

Iris was using her courtroom persona, passionate at times, seductive at others: an attorney presenting her case in front of a bewitched jury. "Ray, would you please move Char's white board next to me?"

Char thought, *Shit, here she goes. Perry Mason closing in on the kill.*

Iris smiled seductively when Ray returned, board and markers in hand. "Thank you, darling." She turned to her jury. "Char, as a therapist, how do you see Mitchell?"

"He's been bullied and abused all his life, now he's the bully and abuser. I'd say he's a scared little boy who's identified with the role of the aggressor and finds power and safety in it."

"Good! We know he's scared." Iris wrote the word *scared*, and with a dramatic flourish, circled it several times in red.

She turned to Les. "Physician, what happens to abused women when they return home?"

"Usually there's a honeymoon phase and the victim can't believe it will happen again. But it does. It may start as anger, intimidation, then move to beatings." Les looked directly at Em. "It usually escalates and can lead to death."

Iris wrote the word *death*.

Em became caught up in Iris's drama. "He's scared to death of his father," she offered weakly.

"Excellent, Em." Iris beamed at her star witness. She circled the word *death* in red. "Anyone else?"

Ray stood up. "We'll scare him to death. That's where *I* come in."

Iris nodded. "This is a guy whose life is built on quicksand. Our goal is to scare the shit out of him, convince him to let go of Em. Now, how do we do that?"

Ray rubbed his closely shaved chin. "I served under Sergeant Grant. Tough SOB. Kept us alive, but scared the toughest of us. I spent the afternoon with Mitchell at Char's holiday party. Em's got it right: Mitchell is terrified of his father. I think I can put the fear of Sergeant Grant into him."

Iris said, "Em, it's up to you."

Em began shaking. "It's happening too fast. The kids are coming home from camp in a few days. What do I say? 'Hi, Maggie. Hi, Chris. Welcome home! Your father and I are getting a divorce, and you don't have a home.'" She wiped her tears away. "Maybe this is a mistake. Maybe he'll never do it again."

Les leaned closer to Max, whispering.

They exchanged looks. Max at first looked surprised, then nodded and walked over to Em. She knelt in front of Em and took her hands. "Believe me—he'll do it again. It happened to me."

"I thought you were always—"

"It isn't just men who abuse. I've never told anyone except Les." Max looked at Les, whose smile and small nod encouraged her to continue. "I stayed in an abusive relationship for a long time before I realized I had to leave if I wanted to survive. That probably surprises you and everyone else."

Max glanced around the room. "I know the way you guys see me—the way I dress, the fact that I'm a mechanic. But underneath I'm the same as everyone else. And I fell hard and paid the price. Em, this room is filled with people who care about you and who want to help you and the kids. As hard as it seems—and it will be hard—you're not alone."

Iris said, "Thank you, Max. Beautifully expressed." She clapped her hands, taking charge again. "Here's the plan, Em. If you're unhappy with any of it we'll change it. One, Ray pays Mitchell a visit. Shows him the photos, gets him to see the light. Ray, no threats, no violence, only persuasion."

Ray nodded. "I know what to do."

"Two, I'll draft up a divorce agreement. Any way you want it...to keep you and the kids safe. I'd suggest letting Mitchell have supervised visits, every other weekend. We'll start off slowly—a short visit, perhaps going out to lunch or a walk in the park."

"But, who will we get to supervise?" Em asked.

Ray looked at her. "I'm your man. Twice a month until you get something else in place."

Frankie said, "Bobbie and I volunteer our moving vans."

Em was flummoxed; everything was moving so fast. "How do I tell Chris and Maggie, and where do we live?"

Char said, "Em, one step at a time. We'll figure out how to tell the kids. I have two extra bedrooms. You have a place to stay for as long as you want. Live here."

Chapter 22

October 6, 2020
Studio City

E m said, "That's how I came to move into this house."
        Treat looked dazed. "I'm at a loss for words, Emily."
"Feelings tend to do that. Perhaps staying in your feelings will open new doors for you. It's getting late, way past my bedtime. If you hear noises early in the morning, don't be alarmed, that will be Madeline delivering our meals. Treat, is there anything you need before we go to bed?"

Treat shook her head.

"Let's try to sleep in. I think this might have been a difficult day for both of us."

"Thank you for everything, Emily...for rescuing me from that roach motel and letting me stay here."

"It's my pleasure, Treat. Make yourself at home."

Treat turned on the brass lamp on the nightstand and closed the door to Maggie's bedroom. Small posters of animals interspersed with larger posters of Michael Jackson and Madonna hung on the walls. *Maggie in transition*, she thought.

A single photo of four people standing in front of a fountain was placed on the white French provincial dresser. The frame, made of cardboard, was decorated with hand-drawn flowers and glitter. Maggie's project, she was sure. She turned it over and read the precise cursive on the back: *Hollywood Bowl: Emily, Char, Maggie and Chris, 1975.* Emily's writing, no doubt.

She lay on the bed and glanced at the mural painted on the ceiling—birds flying through fluffy white clouds. *What a nice last thing to see before falling asleep*, she thought as she turned the lamp off.

Lying in the darkened room, she began to wonder about Emily's theory of connection. It wasn't new to her; she had heard it called by many names—the red string of fate, the red thread of destiny, or the red thread of fate. Movies, television shows, and philosophers had all espoused the idea that certain people are connected and destined to meet.

Treat thought her life could be called the theory of disconnection. Her chest became tight; a lump rose in her throat.

When was the last time she cried? *Two last times*, she thought. *Once when she was seven and once when she was eight.*

Mommy tucked her in, read her very favorite book, *Goodnight Moon*, and kissed her goodnight. "You are my Treat," Mommy said, kissing her face until she giggled.

She could hear Mommy and Daddy talking. They were using their inside voices so she wouldn't hear, but she knew what was happening: Daddy was getting sick again. She liked the Daddy that was here now. He kissed her on top of her head and told her how much he loved her.

Why did that Daddy have to go away, and why had the other Daddies come to live with them? The Daddy that would be so sad that he would cry and smell bad. Or the Daddy that would want to go bowling while everyone else was sleeping.

She turned on her side and began to hum and rock. It was what she did when Mommy and Daddy used their inside voices and Daddy was getting sick again.

When she woke the next morning, she got dressed in her stone-washed blue jeans, red tartan flannel shirt, and high-top black sneakers. Mommy liked it when she dressed herself for school.

Daddy was sitting at the kitchen table, holding a letter.

He said, "Mommy's gone away, Treat."

"To the market?" she said, hoping Mommy would buy her favorite cereal, Cap'n Crunch.

"No, Mommy had to go away and she doesn't know when she'll be back." He spoke slowly now, depressed words spoken in slow motion. "Treat, she may never come back. It'll be the two of us, just the two of us."

"I want Mommy," she cried, sobs coming from somewhere so deep it hurt when she breathed. Only Mommy could brush her hair and make the single braid she liked so much. Only Mommy could pack her lunch and draw a heart on her brown bag next to her name. Only Mommy, only Mommy.

"Honey, I'm sorry. I'm really sorry."

Daddy tried to hold her on her lap, but she jumped off, ran into her bedroom, and slammed the door.

Had she been a bad girl? Didn't Mommy love her anymore? She cried that day, inconsolable sobs that lasted late into the night, until exhaustion took her and she fell asleep.

At first, Daddy took his medicine and the nice Daddy stayed. Treat went to school and Daddy went to work, did the shopping, and helped her take her bath. Sometimes, Daddy would have to go away, "On business," he said.

"I'll be gone for three days, Treat. Mrs. Reagan is going to take care of you."

Treat liked it when Mrs. Reagan stayed with her. Mrs. Reagan was big and soft like a squishy pillow. Sweet smells came out of the kitchen that reminded her of when Mommy lived with them. Mrs. Reagan knew how to brush Treat's hair until all the tangles were gone, and then make the single pigtail that dropped to her waist. She would tuck Treat into bed at night and read her three stories because she had been such a good girl.

When she was eight, Daddy returned from one of his trips and brought her a soft-bodied dolly wearing a red and white checked dress. "Every little girl should have a dolly like this," he said.

He held out his arms, beckoning, "Come sit in my lap." She did, and he kissed the top of her head. "You know I love you. You are my best girl. Treat, I've got a new job, and I'm going to have to travel a lot. Not like before, just one or two days at a time—a lot. I won't be able to take care of you."

Treat held Dolly tightly to her chest as she looked at Daddy with stricken eyes. "Mrs. Reagan, Daddy?"

"Mrs. Reagan can't do it, and you need someone who will look after all of your needs. You're growing so fast, someone has to take care of you all the time. Buy your clothes, make sure you're eating right—not just Cap'n Crunch cereal. Sometimes, Treat, boys and girls go away to school. Remember when your friend Joanne went to camp?"

Treat remembered that Joanne went to camp for a whole week, and then came home. Joanne talked about how much fun they had, playing games, swimming, and singing camp songs. She would like that.

Her light brown eyes grew wide and began to sparkle. "One week, Daddy? Like Joanne?"

"No, Treat. You'll live at the school and come home for vacations. It's a wonderful school in the mountains, and you'll learn so much, like how to swim and ride horses. And you'll be with other girls. And we can write to each other...would you like that?"

Treat didn't answer the question. She got off Daddy's lap, went into her room, and shut the door. She rocked and cried, her dolly held tightly over her shoulder, absorbing the tears that streamed down her cheeks.

Everyone that came into her life left. Mommy, Daddy, even Mrs. Reagan. Even Dolly would leave. She took Dolly with her red and white checked dress and put her on the top shelf of her closet. She decided she would never cry again or let anyone get close.

When she opened her eyes the next morning, they no longer shined. Instead, her large brown eyes gazed out at the world with a glassy stare.

Like a dolly's eyes.

Chapter 23

Wednesday, October 7, 2020
Studio City

Treat stirred, looked at the clock on the nightstand: 11:50 a.m. *Crap*, she thought, bolting up. She overslept and had broken the ten a.m. rule.

Em was in the kitchen, still in her robe and slippers. "Treat, you look absolutely panic-stricken. We both overslept—no big whoop. I said we should sleep in, remember? Sit," she motioned, "and have your coffee. Did you hear Madeline this morning?"

"I didn't hear a thing, and I haven't slept this late in a long time."

"It's the magic of the room. And you seem more relaxed."

"Do I?"

Em surveyed Treat. "Looser. It must be my bad influence." She smiled. "Are you scowling, Treat? Looser is a compliment. Bit of a grump this morning?"

Treat thought, *Have I dropped into the Hansel and Gretel fairy tale? Is Em the witch?*

"Have your coffee and put on your bathing suit. We'll have brunch on the patio. We can have an early swim, and..." she lowered her voice, "I have a surprise for you."

"Really?" Treat hated to admit she felt looser. Was it the brandy or was it because of her feelings getting stirred up? "I'd like that, Emily."

Em said, "That suit's perfect for you, Treat. In fact it looks as if I had picked it out for you instead of Charlene."

Treat looked down doubtfully at the multi-colored striped bikini. "It isn't something I would have bought, but I really like it."

"Make sure to take it home with you. It will be a memory of your visit."

"Thank you. I think I'll have a lot of memories of this visit."

They worked together, companionably, setting the patio table, and carrying the cold basil tomato soup and pasta salad prepared by Madeline outside.

Treat relaxed back into her chair. "This lunch is perfect for a warm day."

"Another bull's-eye for Madeline." Em jingled a plastic container filled with quarters. "These are for you to dive for. Charlene loved to play the game. The best part is, you get to keep the quarters."

Treat smiled. It sounded childish, not like something that would interest an adult, but she *felt* childish—giddy, even. "I'd like that, Emily, it sounds like fun. But are you sure I don't have to wait for an hour before diving for those quarters?"

"Absolutely. Don't worry, if you get a cramp I'll jump in and save you."

Treat eased back into the patio chair, a large stack of quarters neatly placed in front of her. She smiled shyly. "I really enjoyed the swim. It was a real treasure hunt. Thank you for letting me keep the quarters."

"Does make it more fun, doesn't it?"

"Yes. I think I can get used to this, having fun. I am a little worried though. The day is getting away from us, and our schedule has fallen apart."

Em threw up her hands in a who-gives-a-damn gesture. "Why don't we continue out here? It's such a beautiful day; it seems a shame to spend it inside. Treat, I'm going to make a suggestion: no notes. Let the words reach deep inside and then, tonight, write from your heart, not your tablet."

"I'll try it, Emily, but if it doesn't work, will you repeat the story?"

"I promise. And I still have some quarters left. You can do some more diving this afternoon."

Treat stretched her legs out to catch the sun. "Do I really get to keep them, Emily?"

"Of course! The quarters and the stories are yours to keep forever."

"I wasn't sure what my life would be like," Em said, "once I had made the decision to leave Mitchell, but Chris and Maggie would be safe, and in the midst of pain and despair, I began to have hope. I'm sure it's hard for you to understand...so much has changed for women since then. You see, there wasn't one of us who hadn't been abused in some way."

"How?" asked Treat.

"Let's start with Lesley and Iris. Professional women, each brilliant in their own right. It was not easy at that time to be a woman trying to break into male-dominated professions, and if you added the lesbian factor...it could be downright dangerous. Iris was in law school in the late fifties, early sixties. Les was fifteen when she was a premed student at a very prestigious university on the east coast and was accepted to UCLA's medical school at eighteen. Perhaps, Les suffered more than most of the female students because she was still a child and at that time was struggling with her attraction to women. We were trying to break into professions, and some men felt threatened. Not all, of course, but some. Work sabotaged, left out of study groups. You could write another series on that subject alone.

"I told you about Max. Try being a female mechanic in the sixties. Bobbie and Frankie met while they were in the military and had to hide their love." Em chuckled. "Not too carefully, I might add."

"You didn't mention Char. How was she abused?"

"She had an affair with a woman and lost custody of her son." Em paused. "Everyone involved suffered."

"You seem to know so much about each one of the Girls. Their history, their relationships."

"Not surprising. I'm the historian in the group. There's nothing I like better than to hear everyone's story. Char used to say I should have become a therapist, but I thought one in the family was enough. Tell me, Treat, what drew you to this assignment?"

"There was a class at Latham University on *The Girls*. It was part of the Women's Study Program, and I was completely enamored. Not only by the stories, but also by the fact that there could be a group of women who could be so diverse and yet maintain such a strong bond through time. Most of the Girls, according to the series, were so horribly rejected by their families. And the way the books followed them over the years; the group never fell apart."

Em chuckled. "Oh, believe me, we had our moments. As in any family there was gossip and alliances formed and broken. But we always forgave and we always regrouped. Treat, tell me more about your class."

"The class was very small, twelve in all. Our assignment during the semester was to try to replicate the Girls' relationships. We were housed together for one month and had to work as a family unit. The goal was to solve problems as they came up, and support each other. Instead, fights broke out, jealousies sprang up among the group...it was a disaster. The Girls seemed to have something that the women in class couldn't recreate: a bonding, a lasting friendship."

"It sounds like one of those dreadful reality shows."

"It does, doesn't it?" Treat spoke softly. "We tried to get you to speak at graduation. We thought you could address the issue of how, after so many years, you remained the Girls. It would have been a coup, to have you speak."

"I was contacted by Latham University, a few years ago, I think."

"That was my suggestion. It was the year I graduated. I'd still like to hear the answer."

"Off the top of my head and only about our group—our time and our family?"

"Please."

"People are not meant to be isolated. Most of our families had either rejected us or didn't acknowledge us. We needed a social group that we could rely on. There was only one among us whose family not only accepted her, but also embraced all of us."

"That would be Juanita?"

"Yes. That was Max's fictional name. Don't think for a moment that we didn't bicker. Oh, my, *how* we could bicker! We argued, but we took care of each other when someone was ill, and no matter what, we forgave. Isn't that the very definition of a family?"

"I wouldn't know," Treat said, wiping away an unexpected tear.

Em said tenderly, "What about your family, Treat?"

"Chapman's was my family."

"Perhaps another time you'll tell me your story."

"It's something I don't share, Emily—ever."

"I'll try to remember that, Treat. Now, I've lost my place again. Where were we?"

"You had just been rescued by the Girls."

"Oh, yes. Everything happened so quickly—in days, actually. The Girls were amazing. They stepped in as if they had known me forever. They never questioned, they never complained. I felt so cared for. Les insisted I rest during the day. I was in so much pain, physically and psychologically. I had lost my balance. My old way of life had disappeared, and I didn't know what to expect from my new life. It felt as if I had been set adrift without a compass."

Em paused. "Were you raised with any religion, Treat?"

"We learned about every religion at Chapman's but practiced none."

"Hmm...unusual."

"Chapman's was an unusual school."

"How?"

"It's in the Adirondack Mountains, two hours away from New York City. Originally a summer camp, it was converted into a girls' school."

"Did you have fun there?"

"Fun? I've never thought about it in that way. We were taught how to survive, in the wilderness and in New York City—which is a different kind of wilderness, of course." Treat chuckled. "We foraged for food during summer campouts. We could identify every specimen of fauna and flora. Then there were the visits to New York City, where we were taught how to order from the menu at the finest restaurants, and coached on the etiquette of dining. We had trips to museums, the opera, and learned how to shop for clothing.

"Winter was spent at Chapman's. We could cross-country ski, and there was an indoor riding arena. Everything was very structured, contained. But fun?" She shook her head. "I'm not sure I know what that is, Emily."

Em shifted in her chair. "I think we may have many things in common. I had to learn how to have fun as well. I was raised in a fundamentalist home. A lot of what I was taught I later determined was wrong, but certain things have stuck with me all these years. In particular, something from Matthew 17:20, if memory serves me correctly. It's about faith being able to move mountains."

Treat quoted from memory: "'If you have faith as small as a mustard seed, you can say to this mountain, 'Move from here to there,' and it will move.' I took a few classes in religious studies at Latham."

"You're well rounded...a good thing. You asked what kept the Girls together. Faith, I think. Faith in what they could do. It was a few days after I had been beaten, and I was beginning to feel better, healing physically, feeling more hopeful. That evening, Char drove me to Iris's office in Beverly Hills."

Em chuckled. "Iris looked worse than I did. I don't think she had slept in two days. Iris was always the most intense one among us. A bit of an edge about her, but that evening I saw a different side."

Chapter 24

1977

The law firm of Bentonfield and Associates was located in the penthouse suite of the prestigious Larkin Professional Building in the heart of Beverly Hills. Known for housing the most esteemed attorneys and physicians, it was perfectly positioned for the convenience of the most influential and sought-after clients. A guarded underground parking structure protected the rich and famous from the benign—fans hoping to get a glimpse of their favorite star—and the ridiculous—the relentless paparazzi hell-bent on snapping a candid photo of the latest celeb to fall from grace and sell it to the tabloids.

The bonus, for Iris, was that it was close to Rodeo Drive, her favorite place to shop. She dressed the role of a powerful divorce attorney to the stars, but chose not to discuss her side business of taking high profile pro bono cases—social causes—that also gave her the notoriety she craved. These cases spoke for themselves through television and newspaper interviews.

Her secretary knocked on her office door, announcing Mrs. Grant.

Iris nodded and said, "Give me ten."

She went into her private bathroom and reached for one of a dozen white washcloths neatly stacked in the storage cabinet. She took out the container of facial cleanser—formulated by Dr. Allison Magmas, plastic surgeon and dermatologist to the elite—put a dollop on her face, and massaged it with small circles, exactly as personally instructed by Dr. Magmas. Splashes of cool water removed the cleanser and some of the fatigue that had been built up during the day.

She put on a thin layer of foundation and lipstick, opened the closet door, changed her blouse, and was ready to see Em. She had to remind herself to stay cool; this was Em's divorce, not hers. She could only advise, but she had to work hard to wipe away the fantasy of getting even. She knew she could destroy Mitchell Samuel Grant, and for a moment her imagination ran free. Perhaps it was revenge that motivated so many of her causes.

Slatterville, CA

Slatterville, California, is located one hundred miles north of Sacramento and twenty miles east of Route 99. Once a flourishing copper and iron mining town, the population dwindled as the mines closed one by one.

There were no railroad tracks that went directly to Slatterville, but if there were, Iris would have been born on the wrong side. That she was born in the charity ward of Saint Francis Hospital, and then sent home with her sixteen-year-old mother to an ancient aluminum trailer set up on blocks, was proof enough of her troubled beginnings.

In 1940, the usual hospital stay for new mothers and infants was seven to ten days, and for the next eighteen years, it would prove to be the best nine days in Iris Fields's life. At twenty-two inches and barely six pounds, Iris was longer and thinner than most baby girls.

The hospital sisters tried to get Eugenia Fields to nurse Iris, but she steadfastly refused. "It'll ruin my figure. Take her away."

The Children's Relief Society provided Eugenia with formula and the hospital sisters of St. Francis Hospital prayed every day that Iris Fields would survive her first year.

Eugenia told Iris that she took after her father, name unknown, who played on the varsity basketball team. A complexion that was darker than most of the kids in town, towering over the girls and boys in grade school, and wearing dresses that were too baggy for her stick-like body. All these things made Iris an easy target for bullying.

Every day after school, Iris ran home, her long legs churning as she tried to escape the boys chasing her. Breathing hard, she prayed that the DO NOT DISTURB sign was not hanging on the trailer door. If the sign was off, it meant she could seek refuge inside, and maybe there would be something to eat to fill the emptiness in her stomach, and in her heart. She could see the trailer from a distance, and by its telltale rocking motion knew the sign was on the door.

Thankfully, the boys had given up the chase. She waited on the hot steps, gasping for air, and then, as her breathing slowed, rested her head in her hands, hoping the door would open soon and Mr. Slattery would leave. She could tell when that was about to happen, because the rocking of the trailer slowed and then stopped.

Mr. Slattery, descendant of the founders of Slatterville and owner of most of the town's property, stood on the top step, patted Iris on the head, put a dollar bill in her hand, and thanked her for being such a good girl.

Her mother waved goodbye, oblivious to her ten-year-old daughter, covered in dirt and with scraped knees and elbows.

After Mr. Slattery drove away, Iris whispered, "Momma, I got beat up again." Iris looked at her mother, her eyes dripping tears as she wiped her nose on the sleeve of her dress.

"Look at you, Iris. How you ever goin' to get a boyfriend?" said Eugenia Fields as she tightened the tie on her chiffon print robe—a Christmas gift from Mr. Slattery—and went back into the trailer.

Mr. Newly from across the dirt road sat in his web lawn chair. He held his cigarette in one hand and motioned to Iris with the other. Mr. Newly was an unkempt-looking man in his late fifties or so, who wore a ribbed, sweat-stained sleeveless undershirt and had a tattoo of a ship's anchor on his right arm. Mr. Newly had retired from the Navy and spent his days "taking it easy," which meant that he saw everything that went on in the Bit of Heaven Trailer Park. Iris scuttled across the dirt road that separated her from Mr. Newly.

"Iris, who's beating you up?" Mr. Newly said, taking a long drag on his non-filtered cigarette and exhaling luxuriously. With his ruddy face and short, wiry black hair that formed a widow's peak, he looked to Iris like a friendly devil, wreathed in the smoke of fire and brimstone. Iris liked him and counted him as a friend.

She looked down at a dirt patch and kicked up the dust with the toe of her sneakers. "Tommy...Tommy Connors beats me up."

"That red-headed kid with all the freckles?"

Iris kept her head down, continuing to kick the ground and watched the dust swirl around and land on her once-upon-a-time white sneakers. "Yeah," she muttered.

"Is he the head jerk?"

Iris nodded.

"That kid's a cream puff. All bluff. You have to take him down. The kids still might not like you or play with you, but they won't beat you up."

Mr. Newly drew deeply on the stump of the cigarette dangling from the side of his mouth and blew smoke rings into the air. "Have a plan and hit 'em with surprise. Here's what you do."

The next morning Iris walked to school with her two schoolbooks balanced on her hip and her lunch bag held tightly in her other hand. She thought about how hungry she was, and if she weren't so scared of being waylaid by bullies, would have eaten her lunch on the way to school. She hoped there was more than a bread and butter sandwich in the paper sack that felt so light she feared it might be empty.

Iris shuffled along on her usual route to school, the neighborhood gradually changing from run-down trailer parks to houses ordered out of the Sears catalog and assembled from kits that contained almost everything needed to build a multi-story suburban palace or a quaint bungalow—precut lumber, drywall, asphalt shingles—on scattered vacant lots.

The closer Iris got to school, the more nervous she became. Sweat began to form under her armpits, even though the temperature hadn't quite reached seventy degrees. The landscape changed as she got closer to town and school. Neighborhood produce stands, Jim's Meat Market, and clothing stores dotted the street, but none could compete with Mr. Slattery's General Store. Then there was Mr. Slattery's Legal Offices and Slattery Town's Civic Center, an ancient brick building that held the sheriff's and mayor's offices with Mr. Slattery's name permanently etched on the glass door.

Tommy Connors and his friends caught up with Iris a few blocks from school and began their daily ritual of taunting rhymes.

Iris's Momma, naked as a whore,
Swingin' on the outhouse door
While Mr. Slattery's yellin', "More, More, More!"

They roared with laughter and punched each other's arms.

Iris, Iris, skinny as can be.
Like a monkey hanging from a tree.
Iris, Iris, who your daddy be?
We don't know and neither does she!

Guffaws rang throughout the morning air.

As they drew closer to school the crowd of kids began to thicken and the taunting spread like a wildfire on a dry summer day. Iris stopped dead in her tracks and turned around to face Tommy Connors.

"Tommy Connors, I challenge you."

Tommy laughed. "You what? You *challenge* me?"

"That's right, you and me right here, right now."

That's what Mr. Newly told her to say, but Iris felt a sudden and overwhelming urge to pee.

Tommy Connors paled. Challenged by a girl, a stupid trailer-trash girl. The kids surrounded Tommy and Iris, now chanting for blood.

Mr. Newly's words echoed inside her brain: "Surprise, Iris, that's what it's all about."

She did exactly what Mr. Newly had told her to do. With a shrill yelp, she suddenly leaped up, using the element of surprise to knock Tommy flat on his back. While Tommy was caught off balance, she reached between his legs, grabbed, and squeezed as hard as she could.

Tommy screamed from the pain and the shame. Whipped by a girl, a trailer-trash girl, who didn't follow the rules of fair fighting. The kids broke the circle and scattered, leaving an opening for Tommy Connors to run home, crying for his momma.

Not one to pass up a meal, Iris picked up Tommy's sack lunch, felt the weight of it, and knew she would not be hungry today.

That was the last time anyone teased or tried to beat up Iris Fields. Mr. Newly was right, though. It didn't mean that anyone would want to be her friend, and nobody did.

Iris was fourteen and suddenly stopped growing. She was five feet eleven inches tall and weighed 110 pounds. Her mother piled her plate with mashed potatoes and gravy and called her skin and bones. Once her growth spurt stopped, Iris began to fill out and one day, she opened her eyes, looked in the cracked mirror hanging on her cubbyhole bedroom wall, and saw the reflection of a young woman staring back. The dresses that were once baggy began to cling to a curvaceous body.

The change in Iris didn't go unnoticed. Now, when Mr. Slattery left the rickety aluminum trailer, he put two dollars in Iris's hand, instead of one. His hand would linger in hers longer than necessary as he made his stock comment: "You're becoming a bea-u-ti-ful girl, Iris." He would smile and pretend to take the money back, finally releasing his grip and lumbering the two hundred yards to where his car was partially hidden under a weeping willow tree. He sank into the soft leather seats of his black 1955 Cadillac sedan, his head no doubt filled with impure thoughts of Iris Fields.

Every Friday, Eugenia Fields would take her week's receipts out of the Folgers' coffee can, drive into town in their rusted-out car to buy groceries, and spend the rest of the day and well into the night at Barnum's Bar and Grill.

One Friday afternoon Mr. Slattery pulled up to the trailer park, anticipating, hoping—certain he could convince sixteen-year-old Iris of the benefits he could offer.

Breathing hard, he left the safety of his car and climbed the sloped road toward the Fields' trailer.

Iris was lounging in the lone, woven collapsible chair, shaving her legs and sipping the last few drops of a cola. She fiddled with the dial on her bright-red Motorola portable radio, a gift from Mr. Slattery for her sixteenth birthday. She knew that there would only be two stations to choose from, Christian radio or country-western music. She listened to Tennessee Ernie Ford singing "Sixteen Tons." She wasn't sure what it meant, but she got a twitch inside her belly when Ford sang in his impossibly deep bass voice about his soul being owned by the company store.

She saw Mr. Slattery tottering toward her. "Howdy, Iris," he said, mopping the sweat from his forehead with a red western-style bandana. "Your momma home?"

Iris wondered what Mr. Slattery was up to. Everyone in town knew where her momma was on Fridays. Iris glanced up, shook her head, and returned to shaving her legs.

"You're a big girl now, Iris...shaving your legs and all." Iris saw his bug eyes roving to where her dress was tucked between her legs, straining to see what lay beneath.

He leaned against the rickety stair railing. "A young woman like you must want things, eh, Iris? Clothes, perfume...nice soaps, lotions and such. Frilly things."

Iris looked up. "Got somethin' in mind, Mr. Slattery?" she said impudently, making no effort to hide her disgust.

Mr. Slattery was taken aback. He had come prepared to seduce Iris, not to be confronted.

He forced a smile. "You're a smart one, Iris. Knowin' what you want early in life. That's a good thing."

Iris put the razor back in the pan of water, picked up the small towel, and began to dry her legs. It was impossible not to observe Mr. Slattery's desire rising; the telltale bulge of an erection pressed against the nappy fabric of his khaki pants as he knelt down next to Iris. She steeled herself for what might happen next.

"I'll bet I can guess what you would like, Iris," he said, his voice flattering, seductive.

"Guess away," she said, intrigued by a newly acquired sense of power.

"My guess is a nice motel room with a shower and tub. Bubble bath and shampoo for a maturing woman...lotion, too. Not that cheap stuff you get at the General Store. Something from a big department store, all the way from Sacramento. Something fittin' for a woman of class...like you. Did I guess right?"

Iris shrugged. "Kinda. But you left out a coupla things, Mr. Slattery."

"Anything you want, Iris. Anything at all."

"You won't tell my momma?"

He crossed his heart.

"Or no one else? Like your friends?" *If you have any, that is.*

"I promise."

"Twenty bucks."

Slattery cocked his head quizzically. "What?"

"Everything you said sounds fine: the bath, the motel, all the fixins. I'll be yours for every Friday. In return I want a good dinner and twenty bucks." She stared at him with green cat eyes, watching him fairly salivate. "That's one ten and two fives. Have we reached an agreement, Mr. Slattery?"

He didn't hesitate. "Why, yes, Iris, I do believe we have. Next Friday—after school. I'll leave my car door open. You scoot down on the floor in back." He couldn't help but gasp as he stood and tried to catch his breath.

"Okay," said Iris. She returned her attention to the bright red Motorola portable radio, hoping to find something other than static.

Mr. Slattery never broke his promises to Iris. Every Friday she crept into his car and hid while they drove to the motel. She would soak in the tub, then shower until she felt cleaner than she had ever felt. She liked that he brought her little presents every week: a new kind of shampoo that he thought she would like, a lotion to keep her skin soft.

She couldn't understand the fuss that everyone made about sex. It didn't feel like anything special to her. A huff, puff, and a couple of comical ape-grunts and it was all over, then he would relax his full weight onto her slender body. She didn't especially like that he was fat and covered with dark curly hair, but Iris was pleased with her arrangement and, after all, business was business.

Mr. Newly watched Iris leave Mr. Slattery's car and walk toward the trailer. He motioned her over. "I know what you're doing, Iris."

Iris became frightened and pleaded, "Please don't tell my momma."

Mr. Newly took a deep drag from his cigarette. Iris watched as three smoke rings drifted upward in the evening air.

"Do you like what you're doing?"

Iris had never thought of it as a like or not like proposition. "It's a means to an end." She had overheard a guest at the motel—dressed like a gangster and with a painted floozy on his arm—use the smart-sounding phrase and used it herself whenever she could.

"Ever thought of what you want in life?"

"Just to get the hell out of Slatterville, Mr. Newly."

"Iris, that's a wish. Now wishes are okay, but if you don't want to become like your momma, you need a plan. You're a bright girl. Make a plan."

A plan meant you had hope for a future. No one had ever told Iris Fields that she could have either—hope or a future.

Iris sat in the curtained-off corner of the trailer that served as her bedroom. A twin bed, a small table and chair, and a scratched dresser—missing one drawer—filled the small space. She took out her notebook and wrote her age: sixteen. Twenty-four months to graduation at eighty dollars a month. If she didn't spend any of it, she would have almost two thousand dollars, and that would be her ticket out of Slatterville.

Iris thought about her last name: Fields. *A common name*, she thought. She went to the library and checked out a book on genealogy. She liked the name Benton. It had an aristocratic sound and made her think of English lords and ladies. She continued her search through the phonebooks the library kept: page after page of Fields, not as many for Benton—but still too many for Iris's taste.

She wanted a name that would be unique and belong to only her. Benton...Fields...Bentonfield...Iris Bentonfield. That was it! She loved its noble ring and imagined a snooty butler announcing her arrival at a posh ball: "Ladies and gentlemen, Miss Iris Bentonfield."

Mr. Newly and Iris sat at the small kitchen table in his trailer. "Changed your name, did you?" Mr. Newly asked as he ladled squirrel stew into a chipped crockery bowl and served it to Iris. "Iris Bentonfield sounds real fine."

"Yes sir, Mr. Newly. I got me a new name, and by the time I'm eighteen I'll have enough dough to get to Sacramento."

He automatically reached for the saltshaker, shook, then shook again. "Okay, Iris, that sounds like a start. So now you're in Sacramento. What's next?"

"I'll get me a job, Mr. Newly."

Mr. Newly nodded thoughtfully while he chewed. "Damn fine stew, if I do say so myself. Do ya like it?"

Iris stared at the stew, brimming with unidentifiable chunks of mystery meat. Mr. Newly took great pride in shooting the plentiful squirrels himself with his Crosman pellet rifle, with which he was a dead shot. It was best not to conjecture what parts of the squirrel they came from. She took a bite and managed a brave, "Mmm."

"Here, then, have some more!" He leaned over to heap more stew in Iris's bowl. "Good thought, Iris, to get a job."

Iris smiled. She was proud of the plan and it seemed doable.

"Well, girl, what kind of job you gonna get?" Mr. Newly urged.

Iris stopped eating. *What kind of job?* She hadn't thought that far ahead.

She thought for a minute. "Cleanin' houses, takin' care of kids. Somethin' like that." Her voice trailed off. This planning business was getting more complicated.

"Well, that's good for a start, but you can do better. You got too much smarts to be somebody's maid." Mr. Newly put down his spoon, reared back, and let out a satisfied belch. "How's school, Iris?"

"Fine."

"Getting good grades?"

"All A's, Mr. Newly."

"I'm proud of you, girl. All A's. Seems to me you should be doing some thinking about college."

Iris looked down. "The Fields don't go to college."

"Well, someone's got to be the first one. Every plan has more than one part. You've done part one, now you have to do part two."

"Uh, Mr. Newly, how many parts to this plan?"

"As many as you need, Iris, as many as you need."

Iris was eighteen when she left Slatterville.

A short, unsweet note and twenty dollars summarized her relationship with her mother: "Goodbye, Momma. Your daughter, Iris."

Everything she needed fit nicely into the worn suitcase Mr. Newly had given her, accompanied by a characteristically laconic bon voyage: "My traveling days are over. Yours are just beginning."

Mr. Newly was waiting outside. "I have to make a stop at the cemetery. We have plenty of time; your bus doesn't leave for two hours. You have all your papers? Your checkbook? Everything you need?"

Iris smiled. "Yes, sir, Mr. Newly. I'm prepared to execute my plan."

The burial grounds were like the rest of Slatterville—muddy and slippery during the winter and dry and dusty during the summer. There was a window of time, between winter and summer, when yellow and orange poppies and purple lupine covered the hills and wild, dark green grass blanketed the cemetery. The rest of the year a brooding sadness hung over the neglected graves while stunted trees hosted noisy crows. As they trudged through the grounds, the grass flattened then sprung up again, removing all traces of their footprints.

"The grass is a lot like life, Iris," Mr. Newly observed. "You'll get beat down, lots of times. Always think about springing back to life."

Mr. Newly stopped by a plain granite headstone with two names chiseled into the hard stone.

JUNE NEWLY, BELOVED WIFE
AUGUST 7, 1900—JUNE 1, 1934

ALFRED NEWLY JR. BELOVED SON
JUNE 1, 1934—JUNE 3, 1934

"This is where my wife and son rest," he said, folding his hands reverently across his barrel chest.

Unexpected tears filled Iris's eyes. "I'm sorry, Mr. Newly. I didn't know."

Mr. Newly nodded. "Would you pick some wildflowers while I weed?" He knelt down and began to pull the dandelions that were rampant around the plot.

Iris had never been to the cemetery before. She wandered around, looking at the old granite markers, some so old that, in spite of the deep chiseling, the writing was beginning to fade from sight. Iris had a sudden moment of truth when she realized that, over time, everything in life would fade away and no longer exist. The granite markers, the wildflowers she was picking, and even Iris Bentonfield. She felt a weight on her chest that hadn't been there before. She didn't have a name for it, but she suddenly felt like crying.

Mr. Newly held out his hands for the flowers. "I like to spread them out, like a blanket, keeping their memories warm." Iris knelt down, sharing the flowers with Mr. Newly, her hands creating a pattern of spring colors across the graves.

"You're starting a new life," he said. Iris heard his voice crack a little and knew he was thinking of his wife and son. "Life has many beginnings, but only one ending." He put the last of the flowers on the ground. "Looks beautiful. My June loved flowers. Iris, I want you to promise me one thing. What you did with Mr. Slattery—don't do it again, not for money. Next time do it for love."

Mr. Newly held out his arms. Iris wasn't sure of what he meant about love, but she knew she felt something new when she rested her head against his chest.

Iris Bentonfield arrived in Sacramento, a naive girl barely eighteen, grasping a worn suitcase in one hand and her admittance papers to Sacramento State College in the other. She saw the campus looming ahead. She smiled as tears leaked from her eyes. The first sight of her new life; step one in her plan had come true.

She stopped at a busy donut shop, filled with students. She shivered; they didn't look anything like her. The boys had on pressed short-sleeved shirts and jeans or khaki pants. The girls wore skirts and soft-looking sweaters with saddle shoes or loafers. She saw them glance at her out of the corners of their eyes and quickly avert their stare.

Suddenly, she felt like trailer-trash. She took her donut and cup of coffee and sat at the bus stop away from the front of the donut shop and the well-dressed kids from the right side of the tracks. She munched on her Bavarian cream donut, thinking about how life wasn't so simple. She could change her name to Bentonfield, but inside and the way she looked made her Iris Fields.

The sidewalks became congested with students on their way to registration. Small shops, hoping to entice students, had their windows dressed with mannequins showing the latest fall fashions.

Iris stopped at the first store that didn't look flashy or expensive: Hardy's Clothing Emporium. The window was decorated with two mannequins: one wearing a beige, eight-gore skirt, a white short-sleeved blouse, and brown loafers; the other, rolled up blue jeans with a white polo shirt trimmed in navy-blue. Babydoll nightgowns, flannel pajamas, and bathrobes were artfully arrayed on fixtures elsewhere in the display.

Miss June Hardy, proprietress of Hardy's Clothing Emporium, heard the bell ring as the door opened. Business had been slow; she hoped to make a sale. She looked at the girl standing there, not knowing what to do. *A country bumpkin, probably, without any money.* Last Sunday's sermon suddenly popped into her head: *Judge not, that ye be not judged.*

She smiled at her customer and said, "How can I help you?"

Iris left holding an embossed shopping bag with a basic navy-blue skirt, a pair of jeans, and two blouses—white and a soft robin's egg blue— two T-shirts, and one ivory sweater set.

"Flats, Iris. Always wear flats. You don't want to appear taller than the men," the helpful proprietress had whispered to her. "Men always want to be taller and think they're in charge. I'm going to show you how to coordinate your outfits. Oh, and Iris, now that I know your sizes I'll keep my eyes open for a winter jacket."

In this fashion June Hardy had become her first friend in the bustling capital of California. With renewed hope in her heart she set aside the familiar feeling of worthlessness and continued on her journey to California State College at Sacramento.

Iris held her admission papers tightly in her hand, stated her major—Political Science—and enrolled in her freshman classes. She was directed to student housing: Building B, Room 210. She was surprised to find an office empty, save for the clerk.

"Admission papers, please." The woman held out her hand without looking up. "We don't have much left. Housing applications were due a month ago."

Iris felt her heart sink and the color leave her face. "Please," she squeaked. "I didn't know." The woman looked up to see a young girl, her pale face contorted, trying not to cry. "Let me get the supervisor." She looked at Iris's papers. "Iris, I want you to sit down on the chair. Have you eaten today?"

"I had a donut this morning."

"Well, it's now two in the afternoon." She reached under the counter and handed Iris a paper bag. "It's leftovers from my lunch. Half a sandwich, some fruit, and juice."

"Thank you." Iris suddenly felt frightened at being alone in a strange city with nowhere to sleep. Mr. Newly had said to make a plan, but she knew now that even the best of plans could not always be counted on.

She ate quickly; she hadn't realized how hungry she was.

"Iris, Iris Bentonfield?"

Iris stood. "Yes, ma'am."

The woman walked around from the counter and held out her hand. "I'm Betty Shapiro. I understand we have a bit of a problem. Come with me."

Iris followed her to a small office. Iris had never seen anyone like Betty Shapiro. She tried not to stare at the woman with a round face, red cheeks, and wearing men's clothing—black pants, a short-sleeved, white dress shirt, a black leather belt, and men's black Oxford shoes. Her short black hair was held down with pomade and slicked away from her face.

"Didn't you get your housing packet?"

"No, ma'am."

"The packets were sent out two months ago. Housing requests were due a month ago." Betty sat back in her chair. "There's nothing left, Iris. I'm so sorry. Perhaps you need to go home and enroll for next term."

Iris started to stand up. How could her plan have fallen apart so quickly? She sat back down. "Mrs. Shapiro, I don't have a home."

Betty looked at the girl with scraggly brown hair, wearing a faded print dress that hung unevenly below her knees, holding on tightly to a ratty suitcase and a shopping bag. "Wait outside, Iris. I have an idea."

Iris regretted having eaten the leftover lunch. The food lay heavy on her stomach and wouldn't move. She couldn't remember ever being so scared, not even when Tommy Connors was beating her up every day. If she stayed at a hotel, her almost two thousand dollars wouldn't last six months. And she needed to pay tuition and buy books...and eat.

Betty came out and waved Iris back into her office. "Iris, would you be willing to exchange housework for room and board?"

"Yes, ma'am. I'm not afraid of hard work."

"Glad to hear that. I have a friend who has a boarding house for female students. Her rooms are full, but there's the attic. We'll have to clean it out and fix it up a bit. Interested?"

"Yes, ma'am."

"As for tonight...look, Iris, if you want, I have a couch. It's yours for tonight. I've got some extra furniture, not much, but enough to get you started. Tomorrow we'll tackle the attic. You'll be settled by the time school starts on Monday. Deal?"

Iris broke into a wide grin. "Deal."

The next morning, Betty and Iris filled Betty's truck with spare furniture. It wasn't much, but it was more than Iris had ever owned and the small dresser, now filled with extra towels and sheets from Betty's linen closet, had all its drawers.

It was a short ride to Alice Wonder's Boarding House for Young

Women. It didn't take long before Iris realized that Betty Shapiro and Alice Wonder were more than friends. Iris never knew that two women could be in love, but she saw the way Betty and Alice's eyes shined and their lips curled into small smiles when they saw each other.

Alice warned her that the attic was freezing cold during the winter and steaming hot during the summer. Iris didn't care; it was no worse than the aluminum trailer and actually better, because there was no Mr. Slattery and no drunken Momma.

Iris began to go to the movies once a week with one of the girls that no one seemed to like, Melanie. Melanie wanted to be called Melly, just like Melanie "Melly" Wilkes, Scarlett O'Hara's sweet-natured friend and sister-in-law in *Gone with the Wind*. Melly thought she would go to Hollywood after graduation and become an actress. Iris knew that no plan could make that happen.

Melly, with her small, ferrety eyes, and chubby, dimpled hands like a baby, insisted on helping Iris with her housework.

"You don't have to do that, Melly," Iris protested to no avail. "It's my job."

"But I like to be with you, Iris. Otherwise, I'm too lonely."

"Okay, but you have to do it right. No sloppy work."

"Thanks, Iris. I'll be the best assistant you ever had."

Miss Alice called Iris aside one day. "Iris, I'm pleased that you've taken Melly under your wing, but I trust she's not causing you any problems."

Iris looked apologetically at Miss Alice. "I hope you're not mad. Melly insisted on helping. To tell you the truth, Miss Alice, she *is* more of a hindrance than a help."

Alice Wonder smiled at the change in Iris. Her vocabulary was growing by leaps and bounds, and her hometown accent had disappeared. "Let me know if she becomes a nuisance," she said with a twinkle in her eyes.

∞

Iris and Melly went to see *Love Is a Many-Splendored Thing*, with Jennifer Jones and William Holden. Melly was starry-eyed and moony over the movie. Iris wondered if she was capable of that elusive feeling called love. What would it feel like to be in love? What would it feel like to lose that love? Would it be worth it?

It was late by the time they walked home to Miss Alice's. It was a new moon and the sky was dark except for the millions of stars that seemed to have gathered directly over Sacramento.

"It's a beautiful night, Iris," Melly said, gazing up at the sky. "See all the stars? Every time a star twinkles, someone falls in love."

Melly sighed. "Wouldn't you like to be kissed the way William Holden kissed Jennifer Jones?" She puckered up her lips.

"You look like a goldfish, Melly. Haven't you ever been kissed?"

Melly suddenly seemed more mature, not like the silly Melly who followed her around like a puppy dog. "I've never been kissed, Iris, but I am in love."

"God, Melly, I hope it's not with Bobby Fenton, that jerk from our history class."

Melly shook her head and looked down at the sidewalk. "You know how Miss Alice and Miss Betty are?"

Iris stopped walking and stared at Melly. "*You*, Melly?"

"Will you hate me now?"

Iris thought about what she had done with Mr. Slattery. If Melly knew, would she hate *her*? "No, Melly, I won't hate you."

They continued to walk, lost in their own thoughts.

Melly reached over and touched Iris's hand. "It's you, Iris. It's you I love."

"Me, Melly? But I'm not like Miss Alice and Miss Betty."

Melly sighed. "I know, Iris. I know."

They ambled along the pathway to Alice Wonder's Boarding House for Young Women.

Iris wondered, *What would it be like to kiss Melly? She's homely as*

sin, and her little ferret eyes give me the creeps, but her lips look soft.
"Melly," she said impulsively, "if I kissed you, would you be happy?"

Melly nodded, her soft lips breaking into a smile.

"I ain't never done this before," said Iris, reverting to her coarse trailer-speak.

Iris pulled Melly into the shadow of a tree. They moved closer until their lips touched. Melly sighed, "Thank you, Iris. Now I know, for sure."

Iris looked at Melly. Her eyes suddenly seemed larger, her lips softer than before. She kissed Melly again, this time pulling her closer. "Melly," she whispered, "the attic is real pleasant this time of year. Sleep with me?"

"You mean like a pajama party?"

"Something like that, Melly."

Melly graduated two years before Iris and left for Hollywood to become an actress. They wrote regularly until Melly's letters began to change. At first full of brag and bluster about how she was going to take Tinseltown by storm, now her letters became filled with stories about church dances and dating. Melly's final letter said she wanted to be normal and was getting married. She hoped Iris would follow her dreams and be the way Melly was now: happy.

Iris had a plan, but it only went as far as getting a bachelor's degree in political science. Then what? Melly's letter made her think about having a dream to go along with her plan. A dream meant you could want to be anything in the world. That night before she went to bed, she opened the attic window and stepped out onto the Juliet balcony, a small platform only accessible through the attic window. In the hottest summer nights when the heat from the attic bore down and became intolerable, Iris would take the quilt off the bed and fall fast asleep.

This night, she looked at the stars and wondered if it was true that each time the stars twinkled someone fell in love. Even on a balcony whose namesake was history's most famous lovesick heroine, Iris had a hard time identifying with romantic love. Iris had never been in love, certainly not with Mr. Slattery and not even with Melly. Maybe love would never be part of her life, either as part of her plan or as a dream. She fell asleep on the Juliet balcony and woke with the sun heralding the beginning of a new day.

Professor Todd Garvin faced the front of the auditorium and the sixty-five—more or less—students, most of them awake—more or less. Political Science 242: *Lawyers, The Law, and Litigation*—a required course for Political Science majors.

Professor Garvin's pipe lay on the podium, his fingers drumming in a rhythm that matched the lilt of his pleasant baritone. His corduroy jacket was appropriately worn at the elbows, and from time to time as he lectured, he would run his hand through his thick blond mane. Iris guessed he was on the sunny side of forty and looked beautifully preserved.

"That concludes today's lecture on lawyers and the legal profession," Garvin said, a statement that finally roused some of the sleeping heads. "Now, many of you have no interest in joining that league of angels—or demons, if you prefer—or perhaps are teetering, waiting to be pushed over the edge. Your parents will probably be happy if you go in that direction—it gives them bragging rights. Plus, they'll be able to use your services pro bono for the rest of their lives...and probably into the great beyond."

Professor Garvin paused, waiting for the laughter he was certain would follow. He wasn't disappointed.

"How many of you chose Political Science only because you didn't know what else to do?"

The students looked around the room; only one raised her hand.

"Miss Bentonfield, thank you for being the only honest person in the room."

The class laughed.

"We tend to see lawyers in black and white, either as noble figures or accursed devils. In *Henry VI*, Shakespeare had one of his characters say: 'The first thing we do, let's kill all the lawyers.'" Wild laughter. "Certainly, lawyers have been the target of jokes throughout the ages; a necessary evil or warriors for just causes." He ran his long, artistic fingers through his hair, a gesture that stirred the passion of some of his more besotted female pupils. Iris felt a little tingle herself.

"Your assignment is to write a paper from two points of view. The first: Why you would choose to become an attorney. The second: Why you would *not* choose to become an attorney."

The obligatory moans and groans followed.

"Oh, come on, young people. Grow up! In another two to six years every one of you will be pounding the pavement looking for a job."

More groans.

"Papers are due next week. And in case you've got any ridiculous notions about half-assing this assignment, it's 25 percent of your grade."

Iris sat on the Juliet balcony, watching the sun set. She liked to rest there, allowing her thoughts to meander through the landscape of her mind. *Become a lawyer,* she thought. Iris Fields? She couldn't see that far ahead or that far up. *Don't become a lawyer.* That was easy. One sentence came to mind: Who would want me?

Professor Garvin had said in two to six years everyone in class would be looking for work. What work? Where would her BA take her? A clerk in an insurance company? Maybe a teacher. God, she would fail miserably at that. She wasn't even sure if she liked kids.

She had followed her plan, but never thought about what would happen when the plan ran out.

Professor Garvin liked it when she was honest in his class. She would skip the "why she would choose to be an attorney" angle— what was the use in indulging that pipe dream?—and would write from her heart about why she felt she could *never* become an attorney. *The hell with the grade*, she told herself as she stood on the balcony and slipped back into her attic bedroom.

Professor Garvin returned the students' papers at the end of class. Iris looked at her paper: no grade. Instead, she saw a note in Garvin's spidery handwriting: *Miss Bentonfield, please come to my office at 5 p.m.* It was noon and she had to work in the library until 5:30. She hoped she could get someone to cover the final hour.

Iris arrived at the faculty building and knocked on Professor Garvin's office door.

"Miss Bentonfield," Professor Garvin said in a deep, melodious voice that sent sudden shivers up and down her spine. "It was a delight to read your paper." He smiled at Iris. She had never realized how his smile sparkled and lit up his penetrating blue eyes.

"Please, Miss Bentonfield, sit down." She looked around the room. The two chairs were filled with books and papers. "On the couch, Miss Bentonfield."

Professor Garvin sat next to her. "While you didn't follow the assignment—and why am I not surprised?—you were honest, and honesty in any profession is to be admired. You wrote your paper with passion and yet got down to the essence, your feelings of not being worthy. Quite frankly, I think you would make an excellent attorney.

"I couldn't grade your paper because you didn't follow the assignment. However, I do want to give you a second chance. I want you to answer this question: If you could fix anything in the world, what would it be?"

"Professor Garvin, how long does that paper have to be? I work at the library. I'm carrying fifteen units, and I have to work for my room and board."

"Don't worry about the length. It's more about the process."

Iris watched as if in a trance as he sidled closer to her. She caught a whiff of his musky cologne. His eyes were smiling.

"Miss Bentonfield, your hair is falling over your eyes." He reached up and brushed away the strands of wayward hair, tracing her face with his fingertips. His touches, lighter than butterfly wings, made her shiver. He leaned over and kissed her, not the way Mr. Slattery did or even the way she and Melly had kissed. His lips drifted lightly over hers; his hands followed the curve of her body, finding their way under her skirt.

They made love on the office couch, with her skirt pulled up and her shoes, panties, and hose thrown somewhere on the floor. A new dimension was added to Iris Bentonfield's life. She wasn't sure where it belonged. Was it a new part of her plan or the beginning of her dream?

She remembered what Mr. Newly had told her that day at the cemetery. She didn't think she had found love, but she had discovered that she enjoyed having sex with men and women. She wasn't quite sure what that meant, but she thought she was doubly blessed.

Professor Garvin continued to "tutor" Iris every Thursday after class. They were lying in bed after a particularly enlightening session.

He raised himself on one elbow to face her. "Miss Bentonfield, you think like an attorney. Apply to law school."

Iris thought it wildly funny that he should continue to address her so formally, but it was part of their role-playing. "Objection, Professor Garvin," she retorted. "I'm just poor white trailer-trash. I don't know nothin' 'bout torts. I'm a tart."

There was no mirth on his face when he replied: "Objection overruled. You will be a fantastic lawyer."

"No shit?"

"No shit."

Miss Alice and Miss Betty helped her to complete her applications for law school. She applied to four universities and was accepted to two. She would be one of the few women to attend Harvard Law School, Graduating Class of 1966.

"Have a plan and hit 'em with surprise." Mr. Newly's words were engraved in her brain and on a wood plaque that sat on her desk, unnoticed by most of her clients.

As a young attorney, her first office was located far from Beverly Hills in a storefront location run by Legal Aid. One of her first pro bono cases was Char Owens. Iris knew they didn't have a chance to win the custody battle, but the case put Iris and the plight of lesbian mothers in pinpoint focus in local and national media. She never forgot the people who helped her: Mr. Newly, June Hardy, Melly, Betty and Alice, and Professor Garvin. She hadn't found love, but she had found her dream. She would fight for the rights of the underdog.

After all, hadn't she whopped the crap out of Tommy Connors?

Iris hugged Em, stood back from her to eye her appraisingly, then kissed her on the cheek. Em's bruises were healing nicely. "Much better, much better! Come sit," Iris said, waving her to one of the white leather couches.

Em said, "Your office is beautiful."

"Thank you. Do you think there's too much white?"

Em looked at the white carpeting, white walls, white leather chairs, and the white couch she was sitting on. "It's all white, Iris.

Except for your desk, and that has a glass top so you can see the white carpet below. But it offers a wonderful contrast against your red suits, don't you think?"

"Exactly. Em, you're one of the few people who understand that concept. I want my clients to think purity and power when they come in. My office is the purity and my red suits are the power. Say, did you have a chance to read the draft?"

Em nodded. "I was glad that you put in increased visits, provided Mitchell attends anger management classes."

"I like to start there. It gives us an idea to see how motivated Mitchell really is to see his children."

"Iris, I don't want any of his pension, and I don't want any part of the house, or alimony."

Iris had heard this before: women so relieved to get out of their marriages that they gave everything away. "You understand you are legally entitled."

"I've thought it out. I'll have my retirement from the school district. I want him to pay child support, and help the kids through college, at least for their bachelor's degrees. *And* I want it to be the school of their choice."

Iris nodded. "It's your call, Em. But, I want some guarantee— perhaps an insurance policy with the children as beneficiaries."

"Mitchell has a good policy with the post office and good medical insurance. I want the kids on both of those."

"It won't take long to make the amendments." Iris wrote a few notes and then buzzed for her secretary to make the changes. "Where's Char?" she asked.

"She went to the market. She wanted to stock up for the kids." Em's hands trembled and she began to cry. "I'm sorry. This seems to be happening all the time."

Iris took her hand. "It's normal, Em. This is a difficult situation; it's as if you've been put adrift on the open sea. Look, I have something for you, for the kids. Well, if you want him."

"Him?"

243

"He's sleeping right now. I think he's exhausted after his visit to the vet." Iris smiled, went behind her desk, and returned carrying a small blue and white pet carrier.

Em opened the top and stared at the black and white kitten, curled up in a small furry ball. "Iris, he's so little and precious!"

"Eight weeks old. He's a tuxedo cat, very special and exceptionally smart. I thought he would be a perfect match for your family."

"Can I pick him up?" Em said as she reached for the kitten. She held him next to her face as he opened his green eyes, stretched, and stared at Em with a serious expression.

Iris chuckled. "He's taking you in, Em. Deciding if he'll keep you."

"You said he's special. I mean, I can tell he's really smart."

"The first cat in the New World was a tuxedo cat named Asgard. Now, a little known fact—and I'm sure it is a fact, not an apocryphal tale—was that he actually led the Viking expeditions to North America."

Em couldn't care less if the story was true or not. "Iris, we've never had a pet. I love him, I love him!" she exclaimed. "Oh, Iris, I'm so ashamed. I don't want to share him."

"Exactly my sentiments." Iris went into the corner and returned holding another pet carrier. "Box number two, for Maggie. I understand Max is looking after Chris."

Em opened the carrier and admired the tiger-striped kitten as it slept. "Leonardo da Vinci said, 'The smallest feline is a masterpiece.' And he sure is!"

"Correction, *she*. I thought she'd be *perfect* for Maggie—a real tiger, so to speak, to go with all her stuffed animals."

"Do you think Char will mind two kittens?"

"I checked with Char yesterday. She thought it was a fabulous idea. She isn't just shopping for food—she's also getting kitten supplies. You know, Char's really good at keeping secrets. There is one condition, though."

Em chuckled. "Uh-oh. Just like an attorney, always a condition."

"It's good to hear you laugh again. This is a small one: I want you to call your kitten Mr. Newly."

Em lovingly stroked the purring kitty. "With pleasure."

Chapter 25

"**M**r. Newly was exactly what I...*we* all needed. The kittens allowed me to see a sweeter side to Iris: one that she hid from everyone, including the Girls."

Em chuckled and went on as Treat listened raptly, obeying Em's edict of not taking notes. "Les and Max spent the weekend painting the bedrooms. Max took charge of Chris's room. They painted it taupe, and Max added some dark wood shelves. And, she gave Chris some of her Hot Wheel cars, the ones she knew he would love. Maggie's room—the room you're staying in—was initially the room Maggie and I shared, in case you're wondering about my relationship with Char."

Treat cocked an eyebrow. "I have to admit, I've been wondering how you and Char became lovers."

"All in good time, all in good time."

"I'm sorry, Emily. I didn't mean to push."

"An inquisitive mind is nothing to apologize for. I promise you'll get everything you want from this interview and who knows, perhaps even more."

Em reached for the pitcher. "More ice tea, Treat?"

"Yes, please."

Em filled their glasses and settled back into her chair. "Did you notice the ceiling in Maggie's room?"

"Yes, it is quite a work of art."

"Les did that. I only knew Les as my doctor, not really as a person. For the first time I got a glimpse of her in different surroundings. She was Michelangelo, painting the Sistine Chapel."

She sipped her tea and continued. "There was still so much to do. The kids were coming home in a few days. I had to go back to the house and make sure everything was packed. I decided not to take much—our personal belongings, books, photos, and my grandfather clock."

Em wiped a tear away. "That was hard, so hard. Going through things, worrying about Chris and Maggie, watching their rooms being broken down and packed away in boxes. I was still blaming myself for breaking up our family, and I still had to find a way to tell the kids."

"One question, Emily. How *did* you tell them?"

Em sighed. "Well, as Char always said, 'When all else fails, tell the truth.'"

Chapter 26

1977

The bedrooms were painted; the moving boxes were neatly stacked next to the walls.

The Girls sat around the octagonal kitchen table, their plates heaped with roasted chicken salad and freshly baked yams.

Bobbie said, "I worked up an appetite."

"From what?" Frankie sneered amiably. "All you did was point to the guys and say, 'Pack this, move that.'"

Bobbie stood her ground. "That's work, too. That's *brainwork*—something you know nothing about. Say, Char, these yams are really good. What's in them?"

Les and Char exchanged a knowing glance.

Char said, "It's about what's not in them. No butter, no sugar."

"You're kidding," Frankie mumbled around a mouthful of the yams, "'cause they taste really sweet."

"Les gave me her recipe. Wrap in foil, slow bake. Mash. *Au natural.*"

Bobbie quipped, "God, that reminds me of the time we went to Elysium Nudist Colony—that sure was *au natural.*"

Frankie kicked Bobbie under the table.

"Ouch! Did I say something wrong?"

"I *know* what that means, and I *know* about Elysium, and I'm *fine* with nud...the *au natural* body," Em huffed. "I'm not made out of glass, you know."

Mr. Newly meowed at Em's feet. Em bent down and gave him a tiny piece of chicken.

Iris scowled. "Em, you have now created a beggar forevermore."

"Poor darling, I think he felt left out."

Max said, "When do you pick up the kids, Em?"

"Chris at four, Maggie at five-thirty."

Char insisted that everyone take care packages home for dinner.

"Em, you really handled that *au natural* business well," she said.

"Thanks, but actually I'm not that fragile. But I am nervous. What if I can't get through to the kids?"

"There's no simple way to handle this. It's one of those things you just have to get through."

"I just pray I have the strength to find a way that won't make Chris hate his father...or me."

Em pulled into the parent pick-up zone in front of Chris's school—Mark Twain Junior High School. Em had always looked forward to seeing Chris returning from camp, bounding down the steps of the bus. His hair would be bleached almost white by the sun, he would have grown at least a foot—or so it seemed—and his face would light up when he saw her. *Would it be the same this time?* she wondered.

The families were out in full force, gathering to greet their returning heroes. Em moved around the crowd, saying "hi" to some of the parents, answering the same question over and over again: "Are you all right?" She couldn't hide all the bruises under makeup, and a bandage still covered the stitches. She had prepared a plausible lie:

"A minor car accident. I'm fine, thank you for asking. It looks worse than it is." She wondered if she had really fooled anyone.

"There they are, there they are!" someone shouted. Parents, cameras in hand, began to snap photo after photo. Every bright yellow bus, every move, was a moment to be captured for future photo albums.

Chris was on bus Number Three. Em hung back from the crowd, longing to see Chris, dreading his reaction. She saw him step off the bus, taller, tanned, looking around for her. She waved. "Chris, Chris, over here!"

He smiled and waved back, stopping to exchange friendly arm punches with friends before collecting his backpack and duffle bag.

They walked toward each other. Em put her arms around Chris, drawing him close. He hugged her for a minute, then backed away. "Gee, Mom, not in front of the guys." Em couldn't help but chuckle; she saw the same dance being performed by all the families with teenage boys.

Chris's smile left; his expression became sullen, his voice surly. "Mom, what the hell happened?" he said, staring at her. The boy looked around almost frantically, his voice becoming louder. "Where's Dad? It's his day off. He said he'd be here."

Em couldn't answer.

Chris's face twisted into a scowl; hot tears stung his eyes. "You don't have to tell me what happened, I know."

The other parents and Chris's friends turned to stare at them.

"Chris, it's not a good idea for us to talk here in front of everyone," Em warned.

"No questions now. Let's go."

Chris threw his gear into the open trunk, the automobile lurching as he slammed the lid. Gloom filled the car as he sat in the passenger seat, his head turned away.

Em said a silent prayer to find the right words, slid into the driver's seat, and spoke softly. "Chris, something happened while you were gone."

Chris scanned her face. "He's hit you again, hasn't he? I remember the first time it happened. You thought I was sleeping. I wasn't, and I've hated him ever since."

Em started the car. "I'm getting us out of this parking lot. I don't need half of your troop and all the parents staring at us. There's a park around the corner."

She pulled into the parking lot, tried to find a spot with some shade, finally settling for the only space that was available. She pulled the visor against the side window, hoping to protect them from the sun, from the prying eyes of passersby.

Chris leaned his head against the car window, his lower lip trembling.

"Chris, I'm going to tell you the truth because I think, in the long run, it'll be easier for you to cope with me and your dad."

"He's a fucking coward, and I never want to see the bastard again."

Em was surprised by her son's language but let it go. She sensed he had matured in camp, perhaps even had a sexual awakening, which wasn't uncommon, or so she'd heard. He was becoming a man and deserved to be treated like one.

"So now what?" he demanded. "I hope you're getting a divorce."

Em reached out to Chris. "Darling, it's not that simple."

"It is for me. Has Dad moved out?"

"No, Chris, we have."

Chris began to cry, the façade of bravado and adulthood disappearing: no longer the child-man; he was just a child again—hers.

"Where, Mom?" he sobbed. "Are we moving in with Grandma and Grandpa?"

"No, Chris, we're moving in with Char."

"Then Dad was right. I heard him that night. She's a *dyke*." Em hated the nasty way he pronounced the word. "That means you're one too. I won't live with you, and I won't live with Dad. I'll live with Grandpa Grant. Now that Grandma's dead, he's alone. He'll need me."

"Chris, I need you and your sister needs you."

"I'll have to change schools, won't I?"

Em nodded.

"That's perfect. I can just picture it: 'Hi, everybody, my name is Chris. My dad beat the shit out of my mom, and now I'm living in Dyke Land."

His sarcasm stung. "Chris, you listen to me. You can be as angry as you want to be—with me, your dad. But, you are never to use that word: *dyke*. I know this is a lot for you to take in. Char and I are friends, and she has two spare bedrooms. You'll have one, and Maggie and I will share.

"You met Char's friends at her holiday party, remember? Max and Les have spent two days painting your room and building shelves. Frankie and Bobbie packed up your room and all your things. Everything is waiting for you at Char's. These are people who care about you, about us; they don't deserve to be called names."

"I'm sorry, Mom," Chris said, sniveling. "Mom, if I'm living with Char...can I catch it?"

"Catch what?"

"Will I become like Char and her friends? Some of the guys at camp were saying it's a disease, and if you're around homosexuals you can catch it."

Em ached for her son, trying to make sense of what his young mind naturally saw as alien, nonsensical. "Chris, it's not a disease. Char and her friends are attracted to women. They were born that way—it's natural *and* normal. And, they fall in love the same way as heterosexuals—with their hearts and souls. Okay?"

He sighed. "Okay, Mom. Have you told Maggie?"

"We're going to pick her up in about an hour. I want us to go somewhere where we can talk. You can ask me any questions, and I promise to answer you honestly. Are you hungry?"

"Starving. Can we go to In-N-Out?"

"You bet. I'd like a burger myself."

Chapter 27

Wednesday, October 7, 2020

Em and Treat were beginning to settle into a routine, not unlike the evenings Em had shared with Char: sitting in the living room after dinner, drinking brandy-laced coffee.

"Em, I really want to thank you for sharing your home with me and feeding me, as well," Treat confided. "Are you sure Madeline is cooking low fat, no sugar? My clothes seem to be getting snug."

"Why, of course, dear."

"And these coffees—I hope I can break the habit when I go home."

"Not all new habits are bad. Perhaps we tend to see the world in black and white, when in fact, it is almost always gray."

"Is it okay if I ask you a question? That is, if it's not against the rules..."

"Now, Treat, are you teasing me?"

"No, I'm just a little confused about your rules."

"They do seem to fluctuate, don't they?"

"God, do they," said Treat, more tersely than she intended. Em only looked amused. "Returning to my question, *Book One* was about how the Girls rescued you and your children. They seemed to be initially disorganized, not really a vigilante group but merely friends helping a friend. How did you actually become a formal group?" She looked up and added dryly, "Probably with copious bylaws and rules, I suspect."

"Touché," Em said softly. "Perhaps someday you will come to understand and appreciate the subtlety of rules. But as to your question: It was a couple of months after we moved into Char's, a Saturday night, I believe. Things were finally calming down a bit, but it was a difficult adjustment for all of us.

"I was entering Char's space: her house, her kitchen. We ate differently, at least in the beginning. When we loaded the dishwasher, she put the silverware handles up, and I put the handles down. The toilet paper roll: over for her, under for me. She folded bath towels in half; I preferred thirds, then in half. Little things like that can drive the strongest of us to commit mayhem.

"Chris and Maggie—each acted out in their own way. Maggie regressed, began to wet her bed at night, and wouldn't stop nagging for a pony. Chris didn't want to see Mitchell at all...I think you get the picture."

"It's amazing you all lived through it."

"Barely, but we did, and I guess it is pretty amazing. Well, things were beginning to settle down, and Char wanted to have one of her impromptu dinners to celebrate the New Year. All the Girls were over, including Ray. Chris was at a Boy Scout outing; it was his one place of stability in those early months. Maggie was sleeping in our room. My, how she loved that ceiling.

"It was November, and the nights were quite chilly, at least for Southern California. We had finished dinner and were sitting around the fireplace, having a glass of wine or beer. My bruises had faded by now, but my heart was still aching. It felt as if it had been broken over and over again. I didn't think anything could ever repair it."

Chapter 28

"The dinner was double dee-*licious*," declared Bobbie. "Em, I think you're a good influence on Char. Hey, Char, you losing weight?"

Char threw another log on the fire. "Oh, a few pounds here and there," she said casually.

Frankie rested against the large pillows in front of the riverstone fireplace, patting her lap for Bobbie to lie on. She was on her second beer and doing what Frankie loved to do: Monday morning quarterbacking. "Christ, that was quite an escapade we had. I haven't enjoyed myself that much since Bobbie and I were in the Army."

Frankie reached up to stroke Bobbie's face. "Remember those days, dearest?"

"How could I forget? Especially getting a dishonorable discharge."

"We were lucky we didn't get the firing squad."

Iris said, "The two of you have never told us how or why you got your dishonorable discharges. Wanna spill?"

Bobbie laughed. "Should I, dearest?"

"Oh, what the hell," Frankie shrugged. "It's only us girls."

"Excuse me, girls," Ray interrupted. "I may be *part* of the Girls but I'm not *one* of the Girls. I am going outside to enjoy my annual cigar."

Bobbie said, "Before I tell the story, are you okay with this, Em? You know Frankie and I can get a little raunchy."

Em feigned a wounded look. "I thought I was one of the Girls now! And, for everyone's information, I took sex education courses in school and read all the textbooks. I know what parts boys have...and girls."

Iris said dryly, "That does qualify you, Em. You are indeed one of the Girls."

Bobbie chuckled. "Okay, girls, here's the story. You know the Army's health rule of the bunks alternating head to toe, head to toe?"

"Yes," said Les. "It keeps communicable illnesses under control."

Frankie and Bobbie looked at each other, somehow managing to maintain deadpan expressions.

"Exactly," said Bobbie. "So there we were, head to toe, toe to head."

Les choked and put down her glass of wine, "Uh, toe to head? Oh, Christ, they didn't catch you in the same bunk, head to toe and toe to head?"

Bobbie and Frankie nodded. "Yep," they said in unison. "A midnight surprise inspection that ended our Army careers."

The titters turned to giggles, turned to laughter, turned to hysteria.

Char said between peals of laughter, "Oh, God, that's the best story yet! Now I know why I keep you all around. I'll be laughing for days." She rose, saying, "I'm going to get Ray and tell him it's all clear."

The Girls were still laughing when Ray and Char returned.

Ray said, "I can only imagine what set you hens off, and no, I don't want to know."

Char kissed him on the cheek. "You're a good sport, Ray, and you *are* one of the Girls whether you like it or not."

Frankie said, "Look, I know I'm getting a little buzzed, but damn it, we should become a vigilante group. You know, swoop in and rescue damsels in distress." Frankie's eyes were gleaming; she was on a roll. "We could even have code names."

Everyone laughed at the quaint "damsels in distress" expression; it was so Frankie. Then the room became unusually quiet.

"For once, I'm being serious," Frankie insisted. "We have all the equipment we need and the perfect team in place. A doctor, a therapist, Max—who can do anything with computers and getaway cars—moving vans, an attorney...and Ray, the Hit Man. Em, you're always keeping lists; you can be the Planner."

"I could do that," said Em seriously. "I've read tons of mystery and spy novels."

Ray took a sip from his bottle of Dos Equis. He never could understand drinking wine. "Dangerous ground, ladies, dangerous ground. It worked with Mitchell because he was terrified, and I knew his father. He had a lot to lose. But what about the guy who's crazy, violent? I saw it in Germany, and I saw it in Korea—the guys who are more than assholes. The guys who don't give a shit about anything or anybody." He shook his head thoughtfully. "You lucked out on this one. Your best bet is to try to tighten the laws, start a women's shelter. If you go ahead with this scheme, count me out."

Chapter 29

"And that's where it ended," said Em with a note of finality. "Ray went home, but some of the Girls were a little too buzzed to drive, so we had a sleepover—bodies on couches, in sleeping bags, but definitely only head to toe. When we woke up, we laughed about the night before, had breakfast, and everyone went home."

"This must have seemed foreign to you, Emily—coming from such a strict background," Treat observed. "Were you embarrassed? Did you feel out of place?"

"In the beginning. You know, I was taught to hate, to fear. I sat through many a sermon on the sins of homosexuality. But then, when Maggie went to the Valley Farm School and I saw same gender couples with their children, I began to question the teachings of Pastor Lockner. He preached love but taught hate. That's when I began to think for myself."

Treat mused. *Think for yourself. What would it be like to throw everything to the wind, all the rules at Chapman's...* She giggled silently. *All the rules imposed by Emily Elizabeth Scott.*

"The next year was unremarkable," Em was saying. "I was teaching fourth grade. Maggie and Chris were settling in—adjusting. We were all busy and pretty much—just doing life.

"I had been having lunch with one of the other teachers, Isabella, for quite some time. We had become friends—well, more friendly than close friends, but we shared our love of teaching and museums. Occasionally we'd see a foreign or classic film at the Art Theater near Izzy's house.

"Izzy's husband Charles was an assistant soccer coach with the local league and knew all the kids and their families. They didn't have any children, but Charles would always ask about Chris and Maggie. Charles was the stereotype of a suburban husband: slaved away at a 'honey do' list on Saturdays, gardened on Sundays, had neighbors over for barbeques, and kissed his Izzy goodbye in the morning and hello in the evening. He was always pleasant to me, seemed about as non-threatening as anyone could be."

Chapter 30

1978

Em enjoyed the fifteen-minute drive from Studio City to Izzy and Charles's home in Encino. The Sunday traffic was lighter than usual, and she looked forward to a change in scenery once she turned off the freeway and continued south into the hills.

Estate-sized, ranch-style homes, in a countrified setting, spread across acre parcels. Signs announcing CHILDREN AT PLAY or HORSE CROSSING hung from the two-arm, three-light lamp-posts. Em automatically slowed down; she had seen children darting out or playing in the street on more than one occasion.

Charles and Izzy were waiting outside as Em pulled up. Charles was doing his usual Sunday gardening, but stopped to wave hello and say goodbye to Izzy. Em thought, *What an attractive couple*.

Izzy kept her hair cut medium-length in a fashionable pageboy style, her luminous eyes were the color of paper-shell pecans, and a warm, olive tone complexion lent her an aura of sensuality. Charles gazed at Izzy, his tight T-shirt clinging to his well-muscled body. He leaned toward Izzy, kissing her gently on the lips, and brushing stray hairs away from her eyes.

Charles blew Em a kiss, smiled, and waved as they drove off.

Em said, "You're lucky, Izzy. Charles is a sweetheart, the perfect husband. I'll bet he'll have dinner waiting when you get home."

"More like frozen pizza, but at least I won't have to cook." She smiled. "I'm excited about seeing anything with Woody Allen and Diane Keaton, but *Manhattan*! I can't believe we missed it when it first came out."

"That's what we both love about the Art Theater—it's always giving us a second chance."

"I wish I had the nerve to dress like her." Izzy looked at Em. "You know, Em, you could dress like Diane Keaton—it's a perfect look for you."

"Izzy, I think it's time for you to get your eyes examined," Em said playfully. "Look at Diane Keaton: tallish, willowy, with straight, light brown hair. Then look at me. Umm...short, definitely *not* willowy, and tight curls that have a mind of their own."

"Oh, I don't know, I think you're just right for the Annie Hall look," insisted Izzy. "I can see you in a vest, man's blazer, a Ralph Lauren tie, and puffy pants and boots. Oh, and a cool fedora. We should go shopping together and try it out."

Em shook her head and laughed. "Izzy, I adore you, but sometimes I think you're just a little bit off."

Izzy became serious. "Em, your friendship means so much to me. We seem to have so much in common. We like the same films, museum exhibits, and it's nice that we get to have lunch together during the week."

"I love you too, Izzy," Em said lightly as they pulled up to the Art Theater. "It's going to be a warm day. Don't you want to take your sweater off?"

"Oh, I've been a little chilled lately—probably my hormones starting to rage. I'll take it off later."

They shared a bag of popcorn and a box of malted milk balls. Dusk was falling by the time they left the theater.

Izzy said, "Do you want to stop for coffee? We can do our patented Em and Izzy postmortem on the movie."

"I'd love to, but I've got to get home. Char's been watching Chris and Maggie, and I don't want to take advantage of her—she might be having a meltdown at this very minute. You know, when those two kids get going—"

"So I've heard. How's that working for all of you?"

"Fine, actually. Char's really good with the kids and they—*we*—are all settling in."

"Em, I want to thank you for sharing your story with me."

"I trusted you, Izzy. I knew you wouldn't tell anyone, and we've been friends for a long time."

Em stopped the car in front of Izzy's house. Izzy continued to sit, not moving to open the door. Em said, "What's wrong, Izzy?"

"I trust you too, Em." Izzy pushed up the sleeves of her sweater. Large bruises—some fresh looking, some fading—covered her arms. She looked directly at Em, her eyes now swimming with tears. "It's happening to me, too."

Em reached out to put her hand on Izzy's arm, but before she could touch her or say anything, Izzy got out of the car, shut the door, and ran into the house.

Marvin Elementary had an active Parent-Teacher Association; proof was in the recently redecorated teacher's lounge. Bright blue storage cabinets with counters had replaced the folding table. New appliances, including a microwave oven and a thirty-cup coffee pot, helped to create a pleasant break room for the frazzled teachers who were now dealing with larger classes and budget cuts.

Em and Izzy sat at one of the smaller tables, grateful for the time to have an adult conversation and restore their energy. They knew their students would gobble up their lunches and run out on the playground for a game of dodge ball or jump rope. PTA volunteers were on yard duty; they would handle any bumps or hard feelings.

"The kids are unusually antsy," Em observed.

"They're all wired up about spring break, and I'm antsy, too," Izzy replied. "I'm so excited, Em. We're going to New York over spring break. Charles told me to buy a new wardrobe. Can you imagine, a new wardrobe?" She looked down. "What happened before, no one else knows about, and I know it won't happen again. Charles was having a hard time at work and things just got out of hand. He's been so sorry and so sweet."

"Izzy if you ever need me..."

Izzy put her hand over Em's. "Don't worry, Em. It won't happen again."

It was the first day of spring vacation, and Chris and Maggie were bouncing out of their skin with excitement.

Chris asked between mouthfuls of cereal, "Where are we going, Mom?"

"Chris, if you keep shoveling your food in your mouth we'll be going to manners school."

"But Mom, I'm starving all the time."

"Here, Chris," said Char, "bacon and eggs and raisin toast."

"Thanks, Char," said the teen, heaping his plate. "I really can't help it. I can feel my bones getting longer."

"You're only imagining it, Chris," said Maggie in a superior tone. "It's a physical impossibility to feel your bones lengthen."

Em said, "Maggie, put your book down. No reading during meal time."

"But Mom...it's on physiology. *That's* how I know Chris can't feel his bones growing."

Em took the book out of Maggie's hand. She thought, *What a difference in the kids since we've moved here.*

"Okay, here's the drill," she said. "Clear your dishes, clean your rooms, shower, and dress. Then, we'll sit down and discuss where we'll be going this week."

Em looked at the kitchen: a sink filled with dirty pots and pans, cereal dishes piled precariously on top, and crumbs all over the table and the floor. She sighed wearily as she sat down to her usual breakfast of sprouted grain toast, Greek yogurt with blueberries, and coffee.

"Quite a change in the kids, huh?" said Char, peering amusedly at Em over the lip of her coffee mug.

"I'm not sure I like all of it, but God, they're so normal now."

Char folded her fingers across her palm, blew on them, and wiped them across her nightgown comically. "Mission accomplished! Two wayward kids, tamed by the House of Char," she said with mock pride. "Oh, by the way, I finished the list of places to go and things to see."

Em looked at the list and laughed. "Char, we'll be dead by day three. You've got five major things to do with no downtime."

She read from the list:

Day 1:   Disneyland.
Day 2:   Knott's Berry Farm.
Day 3:   Drive to Lake Castaic with Max and Les and learn to waterski.
Day 4:   Horseback riding.
Day 5:   Drive to San Diego for Sea World.

"Char, you have no idea of what you'd be letting us in for."

"Too much, huh? We can knock one off...but which one?"

"The kids will be happy doing any one of these. Why don't you pick two outings *you'd* like, and leave the rest for some other time?"

"Well, I've haven't been to Disneyland for years."

"Okay, that's one. What else?"

Char tapped a finger against her lips. "Max and Les are looking forward to a day at the lake. Les is planning on teaching Chris to waterski, and there are lots of nature trails for Maggie."

Em said, "That sounds good for the second outing. What about the other girls? Will they be joining us at the lake?"

Char shook her head. "Bobbie and Frankie are going on a ride with Dykes on Bikes, and Iris," Char lowered her voice, "I think she's got a romantic weekend planned at Big Sur."

Em raised her eyebrow and whispered. "Boy or girl?"

Char winked. "She isn't talking." She looked down, suddenly pensive. "You know, Em, I would have been a terrible mother. Maybe it's just as well that Lawrence lives with his father."

"Don't talk that way, Char. This is something you would have learned along the way. Besides, it makes me feel good when I can teach you something. How about if, on the off days, we just hang. The kids should have to do some chores if they want to waterski. It'll be a nice time with just the four of us, okay?"

"Yeah, I like that idea, just the four of us."

Spring break went by too quickly. Both Passover and Easter Bunny paid a visit to One Peppertree Lane. Maggie got two real bunnies of her very own, and almost fainted. She named them Thumper and Flower after characters in Walt Disney's *Bambi*.

Chris got a radio-controlled airplane from the Easter Bunny's assistant, Max. The two of them had disappeared into the garage to assemble it and get it ready for a test flight near Lake Castaic.

Disneyland wore everyone out and the day of waterskiing, even though a few days later, finished everyone off.

It had been a hectic Monday, and Em felt relieved to get back to her workday routine.

Em thought, *What a morning.* She couldn't get Chris out of bed. He moaned and groaned, "My muscles hurt. Ten more minutes, Mom, please."

Maggie and Chris got into a fight over who would use the bathroom first. Lunches had to be packed, both kids dropped off at school.

Char shuffled into the kitchen. "Boy, Em, am I glad I talked you into doing fewer excursions."

Em looking at her exhausted crew and laughed. "You all look like you're going to drop." She went over to the blender. "I'm making you all smoothies with flaxseed. And Chris, stop making faces."

Char whispered to Chris, "How did she know that?"

"Mom's got eyes in the back of her head, Char. Don't do anything naughty," he teased.

Char laughed. "I won't."

Em said, "Chris, you go in and shower first. No dawdling. Maggie, make your bed while Chris is showering. No playing with the bunnies until after school. Five minutes for both of you. You've got your marching orders. Git!"

The kids got.

"Em, how do you do it?" Char asked as she sat at the kitchen table, her legs outstretched, her head drooping.

"I got my Ph.D. in scheduling. Here's some java for ya." She put the mug down. "Black and extra strong. Can you drop Chris off at school?"

"Yeah, can I drive in my jammies?"

Em was probably every bit as tired as her crew, if not more. Over the years she had learned to put one foot in front of the other and just do it.

The students were either over-stimulated or exhausted from their spring break. It was close to the lunch hour and nothing was getting done. Em had learned a forced lesson was of no value and decided to have the kids put their heads down on their desks while she read a chapter from *The Little Prince*.

Em opened her bright yellow Tupperware lunch box and placed the containers on the lunchroom table: green salad with breast of chicken, soda crackers, a peeled and sliced orange, and a small banana for her afternoon snack. She saw Izzy and smiled broadly as she waved, eager to share their holiday adventures.

The smile faded in a hurry.

Izzy, her arm in a cast from her elbow to her hand, worked her way across the crowded room. Along the way she murmured excuses to the curious: "A small accident while seeing the sights of New York. Slipped down some steps." A pasted-on smile hid her pain.

"Hi, Em," she said, sitting down. "Dumb accident, huh?"

"Oh, Izz—"

"*Please*, Em. Not here. Everyone is looking. Smile—laugh a little—please. Help me."

Em forced a laugh. "Izzy, you are such a klutz. Only you..."

Everyone in the room relaxed and went back to their lunchtime conversations.

"So, Izz, how was New York?" She knew her voice was louder than necessary, and she was sure her eyes must have betrayed her worry.

Izzy smiled, but spoke barely above a whisper. "Em, is there anywhere we can meet? I need help. Em, I really need help."

Chapter 31

Wednesday, October 7, 2020
Studio City

"I have to admit I was scared," said Em. "I remembered what Ray had said about the crazies that don't stop. Still, I met Izzy the next day because I was more frightened for her than for me."

"In *Book Two,* you wrote that Izzy's husband was well connected to drug dealers," Treat replied. "Was that true?"

"Charles was well connected, but not to drug dealers. So much of *The Girls* was fictionalized to protect identities. I don't think it matters now, telling you, as long as it's off the record."

"Yes, of course. I'll send you the draft for proofing."

Em nodded. "Good. I have to protect the innocent, and in a way we were all innocents. It wasn't drugs Charles was connected to: It was to the government. Members of his family were heavy political contributors and had influence with the police force and city council. On a national level—let's just say that the connection went all the way up the ladder. What chance did Izzy have to escape?

"I called a meeting that night, and that's when we decided to officially create the Girls.

"You know the part in the second book, where I describe the cycle of abuse?"

"Yes, the four phases or stages of abuse. You want to hear them from memory?"

"Please."

Treat half closed her eyes. *Was she beginning to pick up Em's way of processing?* "One, tension builds between the couple and escalates. Two, the abuse begins, often times verbally, but can escalate to physical abuse. Three, the abuser apologizes afterward, is contrite, promises it will never happen again. Four, that's the honeymoon phase—the calm before the next storm builds up. The abused wants to believe, and the abuser does everything to make his victim think it will never happen again. Perhaps, somewhere in the abuser's mind, they really do believe they can control their impulses."

"Very good. Did you memorize the books?"

"Almost. I did my Master's thesis on them."

Em looked surprised. "I'm flattered. I'd like to read it sometime."

"I'd love that."

Em nodded. "We thought Izzy would be safe as long as she had the cast on. This would be the honeymoon phase, and in fact, Izzy and I spoke every day. She would stop at a payphone on her way home and check in with me—payphones, another artifact lost to time.

"The honeymoon phase was in full swing; Charles was sending her flowers, telling her how sorry he was, and how it would never happen again. The doctor said it would be six weeks before the cast would come off, and we knew we had to have everything in place sooner if possible.

"We were in new territory. We needed time for research, to make a plan. Max was able to get hold of the police records that showed a string of calls from neighbors complaining about the violence. Everything indicated that the authorities weren't going to do a thing. We knew Izzy didn't stand a chance."

Treat was writing furiously, trying to capture as many words as she could.

Em stopped abruptly. "Treat if you're trying to operate like a soulless tape recorder you'll miss the essence, the feel of the stories.

That's why I didn't want you recording these interviews in the first place."

Treat looked up, surprised. "It was one thing not to take notes this afternoon, but are you suggesting I not take any notes *at all*?"

"Tell me what you're feeling about the story, so far."

"Feeling?"

"Without feeling, you'll just be writing a list of facts, and I'll tell you right now, your readers will be bored."

Treat put down the tablet and pen. "Is not taking notes a new rule?" she said sarcastically.

"Rules need to be bent, and/or changed, according to the situation." Em softened her tone. *Perhaps, Treat was more fragile than she seemed.* "Any feelings coming up for you?"

Treat stopped. *Feelings? I try not to have them. Shit, now she wants to get into my feelings.*

"Angry—I think I'm feeling angry."

Em nodded. "About what?"

Because, you bitch, you keep changing the rules, Treat thought. *One half of the truth is all you're getting from me, Ms. Em.*

"Because the system failed to protect her," Treat said.

"Good. Now that's what you want to get across to your readers. You want to raise consciousness. Yes?"

Treat nodded but felt her face begin to flush. That really had not been her goal.

Em continued, as if unaware of Treat's embarrassment. "Iris was gaining power as an attorney and as a public figure. She knew about the underground railroads, and she knew how to find them."

Treat slipped back into the role of hardened professional. "Underground Railroad...that was the secret network during the Civil War that helped slaves escape from the South to the North. I'd like to know more about the ones that existed for the abused."

"There were a few, and the men and women who ran them took big chances. The victims, usually women and children, would be moved from house to house, only staying a day...sometimes only hours. Eventually they'd be issued new identities and start a new life. It meant leaving everything and everyone behind.

"Iris gave us an initial contact number and we decided, as the Girls, to move forward and help Izzy to disappear. Her husband was showing a familiar pattern: beginning to drink and coming home surly, complaining about everything. The honeymoon was definitely over. Izzy was due to have her cast removed in two days and timing now became an issue. We put our plan into action.

"Izzy went to a shopping center, parked her car, and went shopping for a while. Then she walked out a different exit and got into a car driven by Bobbie. Bobbie drove Izzy to Les's office. It was Les's half day and the office was closed. She removed the cast and Bobbie dropped her off to a prearranged location, where Char was waiting."

"Why did Les remove the cast?"

"When Izzy was reported missing, they would be looking for a woman with a cast," Em explained. "And if she had gone to her own doctor, there would have been a trail for her husband and the authorities to follow.

"We followed the underground railroad's instructions for getting Izzy to the safe house. We changed cars several times, stopping at shopping centers, entering and exiting only to transfer Izzy to another car, another driver. Always making sure we weren't being followed. The last driver, that was Frankie, made a phone call and got the drop-off address. After Frankie got Izzy to the safe house, our job was done. We could only pray she would find a new life and be out of danger."

"Emily, thank you for the tip about my feelings," said Treat, a little sheepishly. "Right now, I'm feeling sad for Izzy and for you because you both lost your friendship. You all risked so much."

"More than anyone can ever know." Em became quiet, more thoughtful. "You know, I think about Izzy every now and again, but once she had a new identity...I could only hope she was okay. Sometimes, I fantasize about what her life was like. I like to think that Izzy was able to start over. I hope she made it.

"After *The Girls,* was published, we decided to donate the profits to our cause. The money went toward women's shelters, and we supported the Equal Rights Amendment. Then there was the AIDS epidemic. We lost so many, so many. Our community was blamed for that, but we pulled together because that's what family does.

"An uphill battle, Treat, but one I wouldn't change for the world. I just wish that Char was here now to know we have the right to marry."

Treat said, "Emily, I'm very curious about something. You and Char: best friends...then lovers. How, umm, how did that change?"

"Politely put, Treat. It may sound like an odd situation to you, and I guess to a lot of people. Two women: one lesbian; one with two children and recently rescued from a bad marriage." Em shrugged her shoulders. "I began to fall in love with Char. I think I had loved her all along and wasn't able to recognize it. I discovered she loved me deeply in every sense of the word."

Em stifled a yawn. "It's way past my bedtime. I'll see you in the morning for breakfast. Good night, Treat. Sleep well."

Chapter 32

The Girls gathered in the living room with bowls of popcorn on the tables and colas in their hands.

"Cool set," said Max, admiring the new twenty-five inch television—and the gadget on top. "This is state of the art equipment, Char. Jesus, a Magnavox 4-Head VHS VCR with a remote control." She stared in annoyance at the 12:00 flashing on the display. "I bet you don't even how to use it."

Char planted a kiss on Max's cheek. "No, but you'll figure it out. That's why we keep you around."

Max said, "Lessons are extra. Hey, Iris, you got the tape?"

"Of course, darling." Iris handed Max the tape of *Magnificent Obsession*, starring Rock Hudson and Jane Wyman. "There is, however, one condition."

Everyone moaned and groaned out loud.

"No talking during the movie," she said, directing her gaze toward Bobbie and Frankie.

Bobbie and Frankie rolled their eyes.

"Who brought dessert?" said Bobbie.

Les said, "Max and I. Fresh strawberries, whipped cream, and homemade angel food cake."

"My mom said it's for her seven angels," Max added.

Les laughed. "We finally got that 'good-enough mother' Char is always talking about."

They settled in, following Iris's condition until the last scene. Then Bobbie and Frankie broke out into sobs.

Char said, "Okay, girls, let's rewrite the cast. Nominations are open for the two best women to play the lead roles of Rock Hudson and Jane Wyman. Whoever wins gets the prize."

"Why change Rock Hudson?" said Iris. "He's about as femme as you can get."

Iris was immediately showered with good-natured boos and a hail of popcorn.

Em said, "What are the rules for nominating?"

"No rules, Em," Char replied. "They can be living or dead, as long as they fit the part."

Max said, "I can't see Jane Wyman kissing another woman. I'm going to nominate Joan Crawford."

"Ha!" scoffed Char. "She could never play that role. We need someone who can be strong one minute and suffer the next."

Les said, "I'm going to nominate Susan Hayward for Jane Wyman's role. No one can suffer like Susan Hayward, and she can be damn strong—both at the same time."

Iris agreed. "She would definitely be able to kiss another woman. Shall we vote?"

Everyone raised their hands.

"Now," said Char, "the Rock Hudson replacement?"

The nominations came in a staccato rhythm: Sigourney Weaver, Bette Davis, and Susan Sarandon.

"There is only one woman to play that role: Greta Garbo." It was Em speaking. "Can you see that scene where Jane Wyman is in an evening dress and Rock Hudson is kneeling with his face resting on her chest? Now picture Susan Hayward in a low-cut, black, knockout evening dress, and Garbo in a white tux, kneeling, her head resting lightly against Hayward's breasts."

The room became silent—too silent. All eyes froze on Em.

"Jesus, Em," said Bobbie. "I didn't know you had it in you."

Em looked from shocked face to shocked face. "Did I say something wrong?"

Char said, "Not at all, I think you just nailed it."

"Before this goes any further," Frankie put in, "let's put it to a vote. Who wins tonight?"

"Em!" sang the chorus.

Char handed Em a small box wrapped in rainbow paper. "And the prize is..."

Em unwrapped the package. "What could possibly be in here?" She laughed when she saw the mug: two stick figures wearing dresses, kissing.

"This is really cute. Thank you, girls."

Char closed the door to her bedroom. *What a group,* she thought. But, she wasn't quite sure of where to put Em's comments. She was right on, but coming from prim and reserved *Em?*

She shook her head as she followed her nightly routine: lifted her ten-pound weights for fifteen minutes—as prescribed by her doctors— stretched, brushed her teeth, and took a shower. The extra pounds were gone, her body was firmer, but the pain from wanting Em intensified with each passing day.

She cried in the shower, as she did almost every night. Tears beyond count, welling up, trickling down her cheeks. Then came the sobs, so violent they hurt—and all to the sad, sad tune of her forbidden desire.

She wondered if she shouldn't have listened to Les. Les knew her better than any of the other girls; her words echoed in her mind: "Char, you are the best-meaning person I know, but you are looped about this girl. Now she's going to be here, every day, every night. Can you handle it?"

She had been so certain she could *just* be friends with Em and help her with the kids. She thought, *It isn't fair...why can't I have what others take for granted?* Then, as if answering her own question: *Life isn't fair—we have to play the hand that was dealt.*

In so many ways they acted as a couple. They marketed together, were involved in the day-to-day dealings with the kids: getting them to school, helping with homework. At night, after Chris and Maggie went to bed, she and Em would sit in the living room drinking their decaf coffee laced with brandy and topped with whipped cream. They would recap the day in front of a fire, or watch television. They got involved in the delicious melodrama of *Dallas,* analyzed the characters and tried to guess how the hour would end. Em would get a mustache of whipped cream and Char would lean over and wipe it off with a napkin. They would smile and go back to watching their show.

Now she imagined leaning over and wiping Em's lips with her finger, moving closer and kissing her. Soft kisses that would slowly change to urgent kisses that said how much she wanted her. Char made the water colder and wondered if cold showers worked for women the way they were supposed to work for men.

Char chose her black silk pajamas and the Japanese kimono with white herons on a red background. She looked inside her closet where she kept her robes. They reflected her travels: a robe for each place she had explored. Disavowed parts of her suspended from wooden hangers. She held up the silk robe from Paris, the city of love. She touched the material, feeling the pangs of desire conflicting with her vow to remain Em's friend...and only a friend.

She sighed, burying her face in the fabric. She thought of Em wearing the robe, walking over to her and loosening the tie slowly, slipping it away from her shoulders and letting it drop to the ground. She imagined holding her, their bodies touching, lingering until they moved to the bed and made love.

Char opened the bathroom window, knowing the night breeze would stir the reeded window shades in a rhythmic way that would lull her to sleep. The shades began to flutter, as if they were reaching, dancing, beckoning for a partner. *Come dance with me,* they murmured. *Dance the dance of love; dance the dance of passion.*

With a sigh, Char eased into bed. Had she been wrong to bring Em into her home? Was it right to pretend they were just friends when she wanted her in every way?

Char randomly opened her book on family systems theory. She often read that way, not from beginning to end. She liked the surprises that came from randomness. She opened a page comparing a family to the mobile over a child's crib. Five figures perfectly balanced: remove one and everything becomes out of kilter—confused, disoriented, until a new balance is found. She thought, *That certainly describes me to a T. Does it describe Em?*

She tried to concentrate, but found that her eyes wouldn't stay open. She turned off the lamp, hoping for sleep without dreams. Images of Em danced behind her closed eyelids: Em's face when Char would make love to her; falling asleep wrapped in each other's arms; drifting apart during the night, only to reconnect before they awakened.

Lost in her fantasy, Char didn't hear the knock or the slight movement of the door as it opened.

Em peeked in. "Char...Char...are you awake?"

Char woke from her reverie with a start. "Em? Is everything okay?"

The moonlight shone through the bamboo shades, casting a dim glow in the room. Em was wearing a cream satin nightgown with a low-cut neck and spaghetti straps. Not what Em usually wore, but Char liked it...too much.

Char motioned for Em to sit down next to her. "New nightgown?"

Em kept her head down as she whispered, "Yes."

She could tell Em had been crying. She wanted to wrap her arms around her, hold her close to soothe her, but she knew if she touched her she wouldn't be able to stop. "Em, what's wrong? Are you missing the kids?"

Em's voice was soft, timid, unsure. "No. I know they're having a good time with my parents. Char, did I make a fool of myself tonight?"

"You mean with the movie?"

Em nodded.

"You were wonderful. You know, everyone really loves you."

"It bothered me, because I really didn't know where it came from."

Em reached out, touching the trim on Char's kimono. "You have so many robes. One for each girl in a port?"

The wry remark jolted Char. "Is that what you think?"

"I don't know what to think."

Char spoke gently. "What are you thinking?"

Em whispered, her head down, tears filling her eyes. "Char, do you like me?" Her lips quivered.

"Like you? Em, you're my best friend."

"I don't mean best friend way. I mean the other way."

"The other way?"

"The way you've liked Les."

Char was stunned into silence.

Em, stood up, mumbling, "I'm sorry, it was wrong of me to come here, to ask you that question. I should go."

Char grabbed her hand. "Don't leave. I got caught off balance. Em, where is this coming from?"

Tears were streaming down Em's cheeks. "For a long time now, I've been thinking, wondering..."

"Em, look at me. I don't like you the way I've liked Les, and well, some other women. I like you in a different way."

Em hung her head. "I know I'm not very pretty."

Char put her finger under Em's chin and lifted her face. "The way I like you... Damn it, Em, I'm in love with you, and you're more than pretty. You're beautiful."

Em looked up, her eyes smoldering hungrily, coming to life. "You've never said anything...you've never really touched me. Only once, when you told me we couldn't see each other anymore, you held my hands. I've never forgotten how that felt."

Char stroked Em's face, moving her hand to one of the gown's straps, lowering it slowly until Em's shoulder lay bare. "I'm touching you now," she said hoarsely as she brushed her lips against Em's shoulder. "I know I should stop."

Em moved her hand to the remaining strap. Char watched as the gown slipped to Em's waist.

Char felt heat surging through her body, the tempo of her heart increasing as her hand drifted to Em's breast. She felt Em trembling as her fingertips explored the pale, velvety dune.

"Are you okay, darling?" she said softly.

Em nodded, whispering, "Make love to me, Char. Make love to me."

The sun peeked its way through the shades, warming the room. Em lay on her belly, arms and legs askew. Comforting sounds and smells drifted from the kitchen to the bedroom: a cupboard being opened and closed, coffee brewing.

Blankets had been lost to the floor during the night, leaving a single sheet to cover Em, a gossamer veil, barely in contact with a newly aroused body. The memories of touching and being touched swirled together, separating and connecting until they merged. She remembered Char making love to her and soft moans escaping as her body awakened to new sensations, her legs relaxing not because she wanted it to be over, but because she wanted more of Char, all of Char. Char murmuring how much she loved her and holding her until her eyes slowly closed and she fell asleep. When she woke, it felt as if she had slept the night away, but it had only been a few minutes.

She whispered to Char, "I think the earth moved."

"The earth moved?"

"Hmm, you know. Hemingway, *For Whom the Bell Tolls.*"

Char nodded and chuckled. "Darling, there's another word for that."

"I know, but I can't say it," Em whispered. She shifted, her hand tentatively circling Char's breast. "Will you do something for me?"

"Right now, I'd reach up and pluck a star from the sky."

Em began to cry. "Would you teach me how to dance?"

Char held her. "You never learned?"

Em shook her head. "I missed so much."

"We'll make up for everything you've missed."

Char reached up, kissing Em's tears away, breathing in her essence. "God, I'm in love with you."

"I think I've always loved you, too. Char, I'm so afraid I won't know what to do...to make you...happy."

"You've already made me happy. My wonderful rule-bound girl," said Char, gathering Em until the distance between them diminished, then evaporated. "Here, there is no lesson plan and no rules to follow."

∞

Em heard Char's footsteps coming down the hallway. A sudden rush of embarrassment washed over her. "Oh, Jesus," she said out loud as she threw the sheet over her head.

Char came in the room, balancing a red-lacquered bed tray. "Em?" She laughed. "Are you hiding?"

"I'm embarrassed," was Em's muffled answer.

Char sat on the side of the bed. "It's strange what daylight can do."

"Do I smell coffee?"

"Coffee and Joe-Jo's croissants."

"I'm starving."

"I'll bet you are."

A hand shot out from under the sheet.

"Nope. Show yourself, Em."

"Don't laugh at me." She sat up, rumpled hair hanging over her face.

Char brushed Em's hair away from her forehead. "Christ, you're beautiful."

"Really?" she said as she reached for a croissant. "God, I can't remember ever being this hungry. Umm, last night?"

"What about last night?"

Em wiped the crumbs away and licked her fingers. "Was I, was I...okay?"

"Darling, you were magnificent."

"I was afraid, you know, if you compared me..."

"No one, and I mean *no one*, has ever made the earth move the way you did."

Em smiled, a small smile that lit up her eyes and made her skin glow. "God, this croissant is good. Did you go to Joe-Jo's?"

"Uh, Max brought them."

Em sank back under the sheets. "Oh, no, everyone will know! Did you tell her?"

"I wouldn't, and didn't have the chance. She took one look at me, dropped the bag on the kitchen table, and invited us to lunch at two. She was out of here like a turkey on Thanksgiving Eve."

Em popped up again, squinted at the clock that said 11:10, and reached for the second croissant. "Are you going to eat your croissant?"

"It's all yours. Lunch at two?"

She couldn't speak, her mouth was too stuffed. She swallowed. "That gives us less than three hours. Do you think Max will tell everyone?"

"Honey, all they'll have to do is take one look at you."

"Does it show?"

"Everywhere. Your eyes are shining, and you have that look."

"Look?"

"Yes, darling, that freshly-fucked look."

Em looked at the clock again, pulled the sheet away, and reached for Char. "That look. Hmm...will it fade by two o'clock?"

Joe-Jo's was a small breakfast and lunch cafe built in the 1950s. Joseph and Jo-Ellen Harper served the best breakfast in the Valley, and in spite of its rundown appearance people lined up every Sunday, waiting patiently for a seat.

Marble Formica tables and red vinyl kitchen chairs wore their years of service with grace. Gray asbestos tiles showed permanent scuffmarks as over-fed customers made way for the next wave of eager diners to settle in for Joe-Jo's unique experience. Newspapers and magazines, stacked in wooden crates, kept the patrons abreast of semi-current turmoil in the world—not that it mattered a damn to them. The unbeatable food and personable service made them forget all their troubles for a while.

Joseph and Jo-Ellen Harper had been married for thirty years; the cafe had put their children through the universities of their choice. Jo would stop by each table, photos of her kids in hand: Michael, the attorney, and Janice, the doctor.

Joe's gnarled hands cracked and hand-beat more than thirty dozen eggs a day. His cooking was a symphony, and Joe was the conductor. Each grill cook came in on Joe's cue, flipping pancakes, keeping the waffle irons hot, while trying to keep up with customers' orders for Joe-Jo's famous grilled-cheese sandwiches. Diners came in to watch the open kitchen as much as to eat the old-fashioned, forget-your-waistline food.

The Girls had put their usual two tables together in the back of Joe-Jo's and were busy trying not to look at Char and Em as they made their way toward them.

"I don't think I can face them," whispered Em.

Char held Em's hand. "Stay close to me. It's your initiation."

Max kept her head down, pretending to be engrossed in the October 1978 *Petersen's Vans & Pickups* magazine. Dropping off the croissants to Char earlier in the morning had been an impulse, and one that she regretted. She had walked into what was an obvious intimate moment and knew it the minute she saw the glow in Char's eyes. Max looked up briefly, turned a bright red, said "Hello," and put her head back down.

Char picked up her menu. "What looks good to you, Em?"

"Everything! I'm starving."

Em's face began to flush as muffled tittering spread around the table.

"Hungry, Em?" said Iris, a sly-as-a-fox expression crossing her face.

"Starving," she said before she realized where the conversation was going.

The waitress came over. "Take your orders, ladies?"

Em was sure she was staring at her. *Did everyone in Joe-Jo's know?*

Joe flipped his eggs, turned and nodded. Coincidence? *No, everyone knows! It's probably going to be on the five o'clock news.* She could see her image being flashed on the TV for the world to see— Chris and Maggie, her parents...oh God, my P.A.R.E.N.T.S. *Today's top story: Char and Em made love until the rooster crowed.*

Char ordered. "I'll have the oatmeal, grapefruit, and coffee."

The waitress went around the table. "And for you, Em?" she said, smiling. *She never smiles. She knows.*

"I'll have the Paul Bunyan Breakfast, extra bacon and coffee," she said, turning her coffee cup over. "I can't wait for my order— could you bring me a chocolate éclair?"

Max looked up, her embarrassment replaced by a deadpan expression. *I can't pass up this opportunity*, she thought. "Pretty hungry, Em?"

"Yes." Em's expression matched Max's. "Char says it's from being freshly fucked. Pass the cream, please."

Everyone laughed as they settled into their latest topic: the *All-Star Salute to Women's Sports*, a musical-comedy program on television that evening with an auction to raise money for the Women's Sports Foundation.

Bobbie said, "So, Helen Reddy? Yes or no."

"She doesn't play on our team," Frankie noted, "but she is *definitely* on our side."

Char said, "Dinner tonight at seven. We'll continue the debate as we're watching the show. Now, about Billie Jean King..."

Chapter 33

Thursday, October 8, 2020
Studio City

Em, startled out of her sleep, stared at the alarm clock on the nightstand: 4:30 a.m. *Damn, it was that dream that woke her.* The same dream she'd had for the past three nights.

She was in the Keane Eyes Gallery in San Francisco. The "Big Eye" paintings of children were displayed on the walls. Paintings of waifs, children with eyes larger than life, sad eyes filled with pain. Suddenly, one painting came to life and the child, a little girl no more than nine, walked out of the painting to stand by Em and hold her hand. Em turned, knelt on the floor next to the child, and drew her close.

That's where the dream would end. Tonight's dream went further. After she held the child close, she released her and looked closely at her face. It was Treat.

She was done sleeping for the night, and the minutes would begin to feel like hours. She was feeling uneasy. At what? A young journalist wanting a story, asking questions that should be asked? At leaking more than she should have? What the hell was it? She was the Planner, the one who didn't miss details. Something was off, and she couldn't put her finger on it. Max's e-mail had said the girl checked out. Okay, fine. But *Treat*: What parent gives a child a name like that? She got out of bed, sat at the small desk, started her computer, and sent a short e-mail to Max: *Treat Mason, dig deeper.*

"We're doing way too much sitting," Em said over their breakfast of fresh blueberries, scrambled eggs, and toast. "This morning's session will take place as we're walking."

Treat thought, *Thank God! I thought my body was going to become permanently locked in a sitting position.* "Sounds wonderful," she replied.

They settled into Em's 2013 Hyundai Sonata. "I bought this car because the driver's seat was height-adjustable. Now I'm as tall as you, Treat," she laughed. "In my next life I'll be at least five foot eight, with black hair that never turns gray, and deep blue eyes.

"We're going to Fryman Canyon; it's about four miles south of here. It's where Char and I walked several days a week. We would get up at five to beat the crowd and the heat."

Em turned onto Laurel Canyon Boulevard, keeping up a stream of chatter, acting as tour guide. They passed an area crowded with apartments and condos. "The Valley is really a hodgepodge of architecture in a lot of ways. Once we cross Ventura Boulevard the apartments will vanish and you'll see small, mid-century houses."

"Mid-century?" Treat queried.

"Oh dear, the former century, not this one. I keep forgetting we're well into the new millennium. The farther south we go, the more luxurious the houses will become, and if we kept going we would end up near Beverly Hills." She turned to Treat. "You know— Rodeo Drive?"

What kind of bumpkin does she think I am? "Yes, I have heard of it." She didn't care if her sarcasm went unnoticed or not.

A short jaunt down Laurel Canyon Boulevard led them to Fryman Canyon's parking lot. Em eased out of the car, fed the parking meter, and placed the printed day pass on her dashboard.

"It's all in the stretching," she said, limbering up with her tried and true stretching regimen. "We learned that when we trained for the Avon Three-Day Walk for breast cancer—sixty miles in three days. We didn't all do the actual walk. Bobbie and Frankie were on the support team, giving out water, snacks, and *attagirls*. They wore clown costumes to keep everybody entertained and in good spirits.

"It was after Char had died. We needed to do something, to regroup. What an event! Les, Iris, Max, and I did the actual walk, from Santa Barbara to Malibu. Almost two thousand people, mostly women, walking for a cure and sleeping in tents. Iris brought a blow-up mattress *and* silk sheets. We discovered Max snores like a buzz saw." Em laughed out loud.

Huffing, Em did a final backbend stretch, and reached over and almost touched her toes—which, at her age, looked a million miles away from her fingertips.

Treat smiled to herself. *Pretty limber for an old broad, but I'll show her for that Rodeo Drive crack.* Her competitive nature took over and she began to do yoga poses, easily bending her lithe body into a perfect inverted V, her head nearly touching the ground.

Em mopped her brow with a towel. "I'm impressed. I guess you don't need lessons from me."

"I think I can learn a lot from you, Emily." She paused meaningfully. "And maybe you can learn something from me, too."

Em's eyebrows rose a tad, but she held her tongue. "We'll take the three-mile hike. The beginning is kind of stark, but once we get past the dirt hill, you'll see all kinds of vegetation. Lots of California oak trees. We don't have to worry about mountain lions, although Char and I saw one, back in the late 1980s. This area used to be so open, but now it's over built and over civilized.

"Char loved to stop at the top and gaze out over the endless vistas. She liked to say Studio City was *her* city. She felt she owned it, and in a way she did. She lived here when there was nothing but chicken ranches and a scattering of homes. You know, her house is eighty years old. It belonged to her parents, then it was passed down to her."

"Char left it to you, then?"

"In a way, she did."

"In a way?"

"Yes, dear, it's a bit complicated. You see, Char was cut from a different cloth."

"How do you mean?"

"Small ways, mostly. The way she dressed, I guess. But, it was really the way she lived life. Maybe because she had known since she was a child about how ill she was. Somewhere, inside, there had to be a reminder of how temporary life is. We all know it, but choose to ignore or deny it. I don't think she had that luxury.

"Then there were her secrets. Surprises for the most part. And some deeper secrets that she kept to herself."

"Emily, is there anything more you can tell me about Char's secrets? Off the record, of course."

"Perhaps later...or not. We'll see."

They walked the trail, Treat setting the pace, Em huffing a little but keeping up. The dirt hill flattened out, then rose again to a higher level. To their right was a clearing with a wooden bench and a clear vista of the Valley below.

"Stop here," said Em, pointing to the bench. "This is where we would rest. Let's sit for a while." She sighed as she sat down. "Ah, this feels good. To sweat and then to rest."

Treat hesitated. "Emily, I want to ask you something."

"Go for it," Em said.

Treat looked down, a serious look crossed her face. "Why did you stop writing *The Girls* series? It was so popular."

"I was really done after Number Six. I wanted to try something different."

"I can understand that. But what about the fans? The women, young and old, that lived for the next installment—"

Em silenced her with an annoyed glance. "Hush and listen. This is one of those off the record moments. If I tell you this story, you have to take the most solemn oath of all. You do know how to do a pinky promise?"

"Um, I think they left that out of the curriculum at Chapman's."

"It's easy." Em held out her hand with her pinky finger extended. "Okay, Treat, hook fingers."

Treat looked puzzled but hooked her pinky with Em's.

"Do you promise to keep what I am about to tell you a secret?"

"Uhh, yes I do."

"You have just taken the most solemn of oaths. Now you get your story."

Em looked down shyly and giggled. "I wrote children's books under the name of Frankie En Stine."

Treat was slack-jawed. "*You're* Frankie En Stine?"

Em giggled like a schoolgirl. "Now you've got my biggest secret. You get the pun, of course: Frankie En Stine...Frankenstein? They're children's horror stories."

"You don't have to tell me! I read them all when I was a kid," Treat gushed. "Oh, Emily, I loved them."

"I wrote them for my grandson, Jonathan. He's just about your age. Kids like scary stories. I think it helps them to fight their fears, to see how they can conquer their little demons."

"Can I publish this?"

"We'll see. I'm not sure how far I really want to come out of the closet."

Em became serious. "I only wrote *Number Seven* for Char. I wanted to give her something—a going away present, you might say. I never really thought of myself as a writer. I always identified my-self as a teacher. Of course, I read constantly, everything I could get my hands on, but it's a leap from reading to writing. Then the idea for *The Girls* came to me late one night. And I started writing and rewriting. It's quite a process."

Em drank thirstily from her bottle of water. "There's nothing like water when you're thirsty. Well, much to my surprise, the books became an overnight success and not just with lesbians. People became more aware; laws were beginning to be put into place. To use words to change the world—not guns, not violence—is a powerful feeling."

Treat seemed surprised. "But *Number Seven* was violent. It's the only book about a woman abusing another woman and a murder committed by *The Girls*. Weren't you advocating violence?"

"Good question, and there are plenty of critics who would agree with you. But I'm not going there right now. Suffice it to say it was written for Char, in her honor."

"So, it was fiction then?"

Em ignored the question. "Let's finish our walk. How many calories do you think we've burned up?"

"Not many."

"Enough for an ice cream cone?"

Treat said with a twinkle, "Exactly enough. But I'm getting a yogurt."

Chapter 34

Thursday, October 8, 2020
Studio City

Em said, "The living room has become our room, hasn't it Treat? We have everything we need here. The chairs are cozy, the fire keeps the chill out, and we have our brandy-coffees."

"It's a perfect setting for a story, Emily," Treat agreed.

Em handed Treat her coffee and eased into her chair. "You've been patient with me. I've been avoiding talking about *Number Seven*."

"I hadn't noticed," Treat said with a newfound sense of humor. Sipping her coffee she thought, *Damn, this is good. Heavy cream, sugar, and coffee brandy. I'll have to put those items on my grocery list. Right next to those disgusting boneless, skinless chicken breasts.*

"It's difficult for me to talk about when Char died," Em was saying. "It was such a loss for me, for all the Girls, for Maggie and Chris. And, I'm rather ashamed of what transpired during this period of time. Before I begin, what I am about to divulge must go into the top-secret file. Do you understand?"

"Pinky promise, Emily?"

"On this one, I'll take your promise as a journalist."

"No notes, and I promise that nothing will be revealed in any of the articles. I appreciate your trust...I will not let you down."

Nodding, Em relaxed back into her chair, her voice now taking on a lulling, hypnotic quality. "In *Number Seven*, the character Sarah, aka Char, was the hero: the person who took out the one abuser who was portrayed as pure evil. For you to understand Char and *Number Seven*, we'll have to go back to the last time the Girls all took a vacation to Maui."

Chapter 35

1997

"First class seats again," Em sighed, surveying the jet's plush quarters. "Girl, you're going to spoil me."

Char, smiling, lifted the arm dividing the two seats, and drew Em closer. "You deserve it," she whispered. She brushed her lips against Em's, a gesture that had been made thousands of times over the years and yet felt as fresh as the first time they had kissed.

Em murmured, "I'll never get tired of your kisses."

Char shifted in her seat, finding her comfort spot, and began thumbing through the stack of toy catalogs she had carried on board.

Em raised a disdainful eyebrow. "Char, I'm afraid to ask you what you're doing."

"Early Christmas and Hanukkah shopping."

"Chris and Hillary will kill you!"

"Why? They're educational—"

"Jonathan will have a meltdown! For God's sake, our grandson is only going to be six. Remember last Christmas?"

"I wasn't the only guilty party. The other girls went nuts, too. Okay, you know I always listen to you: the Voice of Reason."

"Hmm...my newest nickname."

"I'll keep Christmas to twelve, for the twelve days of Christmas." Char crossed her heart. "Promise."

"And what about Hanukkah?"

Char shrugged. "That's eight more."

"And what about what the other grandmas will give?" Em shook her head. "One gift from each of us—no more, no less."

"Party-pooper." Char put the catalogs down and reached for Em. "We've got the big room again. You know, the one with the large shower with a window and a view of the ocean?"

"What view? I won't see anything but you, darling."

Les walked up the aisle, stretching her arms over her head and yawning. "How are my two lovebirds doing?"

"Arguing, of course."

"I heard every word, and I agree with Em."

Em said, "Thanks Les. What are the others up to?"

"Senator Iris is snoozing. Dreaming of her next California senatorial campaign, I'm sure. She sure aced that election. Bobbie and Frankie are doing their usual perusing of Harley magazines and catalogs. They wanted me to ask you if their one gift for Jonathan could be a battery-operated Harley."

Em laughed and shook her head. "They can run that one by Chris and Hillary. As for perusing: Getting mighty high-flown there, aren't you, Les? Just kidding. It's a good word—reminds me of our old days."

"You really were the champ, Em. *Inchoate.* I could never beat that one."

Em smiled. "It's my favorite word."

"You two and your words," Char yawned. "What's Max doing?"

"Max is on a mission."

"*Now* what?"

"She wants revenge. Remember the woman who abused her? She's her latest obsession. 'Find the bitch, find the bitch!'"

"I thought that issue was resolved," said Em.

Les laughed. "Not by a long shot. She's even talking in her sleep. Let's hope this settles it for her. I need a good night's rest."

The vacation house was located on the west side of Maui, with a view of the lush green mountains on one side and the Pacific Ocean in all its teal majesty on the other. It was the same house they had rented for the past fifteen years.

The Girls all agreed that they needed someone with plain, old-fashioned common sense, and Em had been elected to schedule the chores and dinners.

"Just like my dorm years," Les laughed.

"Not quite—I don't go inside a kitchen unless it's to mix a martini," Iris quipped. "The night I'm assigned to cook, we're eating out!"

"That's okay, Iris," said Em, handing out charts. "I've made you the Queen of Drinks. No dinner night for you."

Everyone was satisfied with the schedule. They hired a maid service for cleaning up and settled into a routine that had been established over the years.

It was their third night, and Bobbie and Frankie's turn to cook. They made it a rock and roll dinner and made their favorite foods from the 1950s. Elvis's hits played in the background. Bobbie donned an Elvis wig—replete with outrageous muttonchops—and Frankie strummed on her guitar, warbling an off-key version of "Love Me Tender."

"Time for time travel," said Bobbie as she brought out the no-holds-barred, fifties delights. Hamburgers, fries, and chocolate shakes were set on the buffet.

"Come and git it!" said Frankie.

Les and Iris exchanged pained looks. They had forced everyone into healthier diets, and now everything was going to hell in a hand basket.

"Oh, what the hell," said Les, pushing her way to the front of the line. "What's for dessert?"

"Chocolate brownies...homemade," said Bobbie.

"Oh, sure," quipped Iris.

"Well, *someone* made them."

They sat around the dining room table, moaning and groaning about how full they were.

In a rare moment of kindness, Iris said, "Wow, that was the best meal I've had in a long time. My hat's off to you two," she added, slurping the last of her shake.

Bobbie and Frankie exchanged looks that said, "The sugar and fat did Iris in."

Char said, "I don't know about the rest of you, but I want to dance with my girl." She held her hand out to Em as Johnny Mathis's "Chances Are" began to play.

Char's hands circled around Em's waist, their bodies touching in a familiar way. "You'll always be the only one for me," she murmured.

Em whispered, "Thank you for teaching me how to dance...and other things, too."

"Darling, you were a natural."

"Chances Are" ended and "The Twist" by Chubby Checker began to play.

Char said, "I'm going to sit this one out."

"Are you okay?"

"Just a little tired. Why don't you dance with Iris? The rest of the Girls are really going at it."

Em gave Char a light kiss, turned and held out her hand to Iris. "C'mon, let's twist, Iris!"

"I'd like that, Em."

The Girls lounged around the living room, some on cushions near the flagstone fireplace, some sprawled out on couches, their stomachs filled with slurp-down food and Iris's martinis.

"Geez," said Bobbie. "These bodies aren't as young as they used to be. That dancing pooped us all out."

"Speak for yourself," retorted Frankie. "I'm as young as the day I was born."

"Yeah, and still needing diapers."

Max abruptly broke the bickering with: "I've got an announcement."

Everyone became quiet.

"I found the bitch."

They all knew what Max meant. She left the room and returned with a stack of papers neatly stapled together in packets. "Here's the lowdown. Everything she's been up to since she was twelve. Her string of crimes began with shoplifting, bullying, and then grew into adult atrocities. She's like a cancer in the lesbian community and still going strong."

They looked at the list of crimes: the families she had broken up, the women she had abused and stolen from, the hearts she had broken.

Max said, "I'm calling for an official meeting of the Girls. Tomorrow night at midnight."

Chapter 36

Thursday, October 8, 2020
Studio City

Treat held her breath. "Midnight? Why midnight?"

"That was one of the Girls' rules." Em laughed. "You were right: We certainly had our share of 'em.

"Midnight meetings meant we were about to do one of our rescues. Except that particular meeting had to be postponed. You see, the next morning, I overheard Char and Les arguing. And I found out one of Char's darkest secrets."

Em got the bottle of brandy from the bar. "I think this story calls for a little more liquid courage."

Chapter 37

1997

Em woke the way she had for the past nineteen years with Char spooning against her back. They fell asleep that way, naturally moved during the night, but always returned to that position before morning. She thought she would never tire of the feel of Char's arm around her waist, sometimes moving to caress her breasts, her leg resting gently on top of Em's.

Em turned over and whispered, "I'm going to get some coffee. Do you want a cup?"

Char groaned lightly. "Honey, I'm not feeling too well. I think I'll rest today, spend the day in bed."

"You haven't been feeling well for a week." Em put her hand on Char's forehead. "You don't feel warm. I'm going to make you a cup of tea and ask Les to come in."

Char grabbed Em's hand. "The tea sounds perfect, honey, but don't bring Les into it. I'm fine, just a little tired. I'll nap, and by tomorrow I'll be back to normal."

Em wandered into the kitchen and poured coffee in her mug. Max was hunched over her computer. *Probably gathering more evidence*, Em thought. She smiled to herself and started to make a cup of tea for Char.

Les was at the kitchen table, reading the morning newspaper. Another Girls' rule was to always be quiet in the morning. Give everyone a chance to wake up. Em sat down next to Les.

"Les?"

"Hi, Em." Les looked up and then went back to reading her newspaper, a not so subtle cue for silence.

"*Les*?"

"What *is* it, Em?" Les said, annoyed at the interruption and the flouting of the rule.

"Char's not feeling well. I thought you could check on her a little later."

Les stood up with a sudden sense of urgency, the kitchen chair rocking before it settled back on its four-legged stance. "Stay here, Em," she said as she rushed to the back of the house.

Em followed, keeping out of sight, standing quietly next to the open door of their bedroom.

Les had her bag next to her and held the stethoscope to Char's back and chest. "I'm calling 911. You need tests, and your meds need to be adjusted."

"I'm fine, Les."

"Bullshit! I'm calling Dr. Satou. He's our contact here. Then I'm calling 911."

"Can't you adjust the meds?"

"No, and either you tell Em right now or I'm telling her *and* all the others. Enough is enough, Char."

Em stepped into the room. "Tell me what?"

Em opened the drapes to the bedroom. She wiped her eyes before returning to sit on the bed next to Char. She held Char's hand and then lay down to snuggle next to her. "Look at the sunset, darling," she said, raising Char's hand to her lips. "I think it's the most beautiful one I've ever seen."

They shared the palette of colors blazing across the sky—red, orange, pink, and blue—as the sun made its way toward the horizon. Their fingers tightened, tears rolling down their cheeks.

Char said softly, "In a moment we'll see the green flash."

They sat silently as the sun disappeared from view, as if it had dropped into the sea, for a fleeting moment an intense emerald light flashed in its wake.

"I think we just witnessed the meaning of death." Char's voice had taken on a dreamy quality. "We sink beneath a horizon, there is a flash of energy, and then we disappear to be transported somewhere, to be with others we have loved and who have loved us. Life and death is all around us, if we take off our blinders and look." She turned and saw her lover's anguished face. "Em, please don't be angry with me."

Em wiped her tears away. "I'm trying not to be angry, but how could you not tell me? All these years, you carried it alone. It wasn't fair to you, and it wasn't fair to me."

"I'm sorry, Em. I wanted to put this off for as long as I could. I know you so well. You would have been worried for all these years. You would have monitored every move I made." She smiled before nuzzling against Em's cheek. "You would have never learned how to ski."

Em laughed in spite of the pain. "I never did. Remember when I lost control getting off the ski lift and knocked down the people in the ski school?"

"You were a bowling ball and they were the pins. *That* was a sight and a day to remember."

Em wept. "I can't lose you, Char."

"Dr. Satou adjusted the meds and the tests show we have...some time." Char was being brave for both of them. "I prayed for ten years, and I've been given nineteen. It doesn't get much better than that. Let's not waste a moment in regrets. When I'm gone you'll have memories. We have so many wonderful ones; I'm going to take them all with me. Right now hold me, so I'll never forget how you feel. I'll take that with me, too."

Em snuggled in, as close as she could get, resting her head on Char's chest. "I don't want you to leave me."

Char sighed as she kissed Em's face. "That's the hardest part of a relationship. One always has to leave first. Sweetheart, all in all, it's been a good life. I do have one regret."

"Only one?"

"Well, more like two. One, we couldn't marry. That has broken my heart every day we've been together. Do you ever think it will happen?" She spoke huskily. "In our...in your lifetime?"

"Darling, we'll keep fighting. They can deny us the license but we have each other, our kids." Em stroked Char's face. "Remember the day Maggie decorated your desk?"

Char laughed. "I'll never forget that one. We had walked out to the garden; I think we were picking fresh tomatoes. When we came back to my office, Maggie was standing there with the widest grin."

"A bit of a toothless grin if I recall."

"A slight gap. She was so proud. 'Look at your desk, Dr. Char,' she said. 'I drew you flowers.'"

"Hmm...with permanent markers. I thought I would die."

"I was delighted. A memory to savor. Em, all of our memories, so wonderful."

"Tell me your other regret," Em said, stroking Char's face.

"Lawrence. It hurts so much." Char began to cry. "I tried to make him understand."

Em held Char close, comforting her with soft, melodious sounds.

"Darling, you need to know that Iris has Lawrence's address and phone number. For...afterward. I gave it to her when I had my will drawn up."

Em put her finger to Char's lips. "That's all I can bear to hear. Right now, I want to hold you close and tell you how much I love you."

Chapter 38

Thursday, October 8, 2020
Studio City

"We agreed to live as normally as we could; it was what we all wanted. We changed our meeting time to noon instead of midnight. Max said it was midnight somewhere in the world." Em looked at her watch. "It's getting late. I think it's time to stop."

"Em, can't we bend the rule?" Treat pleaded.

Em hesitated. "Only because you called me Em."

Chapter 39

1997

Char insisted on getting dressed for the meeting. "I'm not dead yet, and I will *not* wear pajamas and a robe to a meeting."

"All right," Les agreed, "but I insist on one condition: The oxygen tank goes with you."

Char knew she would lose that one and mumbled, "Okay."

Em and Les helped her into a pair of lightweight black sweats, T-shirt, and a white long-sleeved blouse. "I don't want the bruises from the IVs showing. And, I want to wear my spectators," she was already slipping on the black and white shoes. "I'll need help tying the laces—crap, I love these shoes— and don't forget my fedora! If I'm going down, I'm going down in style."

Max's research showed a woman who had crisscrossed the country many times, leaving her mark wherever she went. A string of aliases accompanied Linda Blackstone on her path of destruction: seducing, stealing, physically and mentally abusing her victims along the way. She served a few days in jail in various places, but seemed to have the ability to avoid any lengthy sentences. The records showed that some of the victims recanted their testimony on the witness stand.

Les held Max's hand. "I think we create a snare: seduce her, set her up, and after she forges Iris's checks or steals her jewelry, we call the cops."

"What!" said Iris, snorting. "*My* checking accounts, *my* jewelry. Why not *yours*, my little princess?"

"Because, Iris, you are the only one with diamonds and sapphires."

"*And* a reputation to spoil. Get another sucker." Iris downed her martini in one smooth gulp.

"You guys are forgetting the power of a sociopath," Char interjected. All heads turned to listen. "Seducing women and juries—she's wiggled out of every court case so far. Her time in jail has been for minor offenses: shoplifting, DUIs. I'd say your chances are slim to none."

She suddenly became quiet. From time to time she would use the oxygen cannula for a few minutes, closing her eyes—dozing off, everyone thought. Then, Char's eyes opened, glowing with fierceness.

"There's something I want to do before I die, and I don't want anyone else involved in it!" she said defiantly. "I'm going to get rid of her evilness once and for all. It will be my final act before I leave this world. I'm going to murder her."

Everyone froze; a deathlike silence hung over the room.

Em broke the stillness. "You've already involved all of us, by telling us what you want to do. We've never hurt the abuser, physically. We've scared them, moved their targets, but *murder*? It goes without saying, that's a bit extreme. I thought we would gather the evidence and turn it over to the police. Have her put away."

"Lots of luck with that one!" Char snorted. "Look, I know you think I'm sick and probably suffering from a lack of oxygen to my brain. But I want you to look at me. My thoughts are clear—they've never *been* this clear. I'm the one with nothing to lose. What can they do to me? I could be dead any day now; I've got maybe six months if I'm lucky, or so the docs have told me. I'll write a confession. That will leave everyone else off the hook."

The Girls looked at Em.

Iris said, "Em, you're the Planner and the Voice of Reason. What do you think?"

"We're leaving in three days. Let this percolate. By the time we get home, I'll have some options in place."

The flight home was unusually uneventful and quiet. The Girls were stricken into silence: a group wanting to deny the inevitable. Seven minds bound tightly together for so many years had now fused into one.

All gatherings at One Peppertree Lane began with food. It was Char's way of life, and Em would carry on the tradition. She thought, *What to serve, what to serve?*

She remembered their picnic at Griffith Park when Maggie popped a grape in her mouth and asked for two mommies. *How would she tell Maggie and Chris that they were losing one of their mommies?*

She decided on fruit and salads, with baskets of bread and muffins. *Dessert?* She couldn't get past puddings, a comfort food that could go to where the pain was hiding and cover it with sweetness.

The Girls gathered, despair written across their faces. Foods that ordinarily would have been enjoyed and raved over were toyed with. Forks moved listlessly across plates, lifted to mouths that could barely open. A small taste to remind them they were all there, all of them alive.

Iris looked so solemn. All of her witty one-liners had disappeared, and the other side of Iris—the tender, sentimental, vulnerable side that belied her wrong-side-of-the-tracks upbringing—was peeking through. "It's your meeting, Em," she said, her voice quivering.

Em cleared her throat. She was not used to leading the meetings. "First, I want a secret vote. If anyone doesn't want to…" she cleared her throat again, "do the deed, we cancel the plan. It's all or nothing."

Em passed out pens and paper. The Girls wrote *yes* or *no* and placed the votes in Char's black fedora hat. "Okay, we're on," she said after tallying the votes. "The first step is to find Linda's weak link. We need to outfox the fox. No outside help—it has to be kept between us. Max, you've gathered a lot of information, but we need more. I want to go back all the way to when she was born. Let's capture those early years."

Max said, "She told me she was born in Iowa. It might be true, because she was drunker than a skunk when it slipped out."

"Good info, Max," said Em. "Can you create false IDs?"

Max grinned. "What do you need?"

"Depending on what you discover, we might need to purchase certain things, rent a car, and so on. It's hard to say at this point."

"I can get us birth certificates, Social Security numbers, driver's licenses, credit cards. That should do it, and I *can* do it."

"Okay, Max. You will be the researcher. I want every detail on Linda from the day she was born. We have to find her weak link. Start with false IDs for yourself. You know more about it than I do, but find a way to destroy any information you've already downloaded and make sure any new info you glean isn't traceable."

Max nodded. "Consider it done."

"Iris, after Max gets the info, I want the two of us to go through it. We'll be looking for patterns, weaknesses."

Iris said, "I'm with you, Em."

"You've added color to your office," said Em.

Iris laughed. "I know when you're teasing me. Just a few red pillows on the couches—more power and a little less purity. Being in public office is quite an education."

"Iris, you're really taking a risk with this. Are you sure you want in?"

"Darling, I wouldn't miss it for the world."

Em put a file on Iris's desk.

Iris asked, "What did our intrepid Max, the Detective, find?"

"More than we could ever hope for. Max was right: Linda's roots are in Iowa—Des Moines to be exact. And she seems to have found a wealthy widow in Santa Barbara; she's in the area."

Iris scanned the file. "Someone has to go to Des Moines and see if they can talk to the people who knew her, back in the day. Childhood fears can be covered up, but remnants are always left."

Iris thought about her own youth when hunger was a frequent visitor to the aluminum trailer she called home. Her condo was stocked with two refrigerators and a separate freezer, enough food to last for months.

"Les wants that job," said Em. "In fact, she's already booking a flight for Chicago. She'll drive to Des Moines from there."

Iris sat the file down. "Christ, we're really in it, aren't we? And Char? Is she still insisting she'll do the deed?"

Em moved away from Iris's desk and sat in the nearby white chair. "I'm really worried. This revenge thing is keeping her alive, but God, she's getting weaker every day."

Chapter 40

October 8, 2020
Studio City

Em heard the grandfather clock strike twelve. She felt a sudden wave of fatigue. Was it the time or the telling of the story? She stifled a yawn.

"Treat, are you getting tired? It's late, way past our bedtime."

"Please, Em, don't stop. I won't be able to sleep if you do."

"It is difficult to stop in the middle of a story," said Em, smiling. "Max had completed a thorough dossier on Linda—every detail, including all her old hangouts in Des Moines. Les flew to Chicago for a weekend seminar. She rented a car and drove the 350 miles to Des Moines, hanging out in Linda's old neighborhood."

Em's voice lowered to a whisper as if fearful of what she was about to divulge. "Well, she was sitting at the neighborhood bar and the guys were flocking around her. Les once told me she liked the attention, but that's a deep secret. Max would absolutely flip out.

"They're all bullshitting about their high school days, when they started talking about going to Dale Maffit Reservoir at night with Linda Temple and getting really drunk. They all laughed and as they were talking, Les remembered Linda Blackstone's birth name. Linda Temple and Linda Blackstone were one and the same.

"Now, the reservoir was built over an old gravesite and the coffins were never moved. So the coffins *and* the bodies are still out in the middle of the lake. Well, they decided to go swimming in the lake and Linda couldn't swim worth a damn and starts floundering and almost drowns. They all laughed but ended the story with, 'and that was the last time Linda ever went in swimming.' Les's ears perked up. Bingo! She discovered what Linda feared the most: drowning. She couldn't swim."

Treat's eyes were wide open, staring. *This is more than I could have ever wished for: the confessions of a murder!*

"Linda was finished with the widow in Santa Barbara," Em went on. "After emptying most of her bank accounts she had traveled to Los Angeles and was hanging out at the Blue Star Bar and Grill, a hot lesbian spot. We could only surmise she was on the lookout for her next victim.

"We came up with a plan. Iris had a boat—almost a yacht, I guess. Our plan was simple: We would lure Linda onto the boat, and once we got a few miles out, we would push her over. All that remained was to get Linda onto the boat. I was assigned to be the bait."

Em paused, rested her head on the back of the chair, and sighed.

"Do you want another brandy, Treat?"

She whispered, "Hand me the bottle, Em, and please go on with your story."

Em closed her eyes. "I remember that night as if it happened yesterday. An intimate bar, women dancing to the music playing in the background—the old torch songs, the blues singers: Ella Fitzgerald, Billie Holiday. Way, way before your time, Treat."

"I've heard of them."

"But never *heard* them?"

"No."

"A shame. It was a time when music reached your heart and soul. I sat at the bar with a glass of white wine, waiting. The music was so beautiful, and I was thinking about Char, wishing she was there with me.

"Then this lovely, elegant woman, with such a sweet smile, sat next to me. It was Linda. We talked for a while. I hinted at being a recent widow, and I saw a flicker in her eyes: such a deep blue color, as close to purple as I've ever seen—like Elizabeth Taylor's, but not quite as pretty. I thought, could we be wrong?

"I told her about the party on Saturday and invited her to be my guest. When she heard it was on a yacht, she paled. I could see the fear of drowning written all over her. I said I hoped to see her there. I held her hand for a moment and left.

"Our plan was simple: Take Iris's boat out, get Linda drunk, have Char push her over, and say it was an accident."

Treat was on the edge of her seat. "And? *And?*"

"We held one final meeting before Saturday."

Chapter 41

1997
Studio City

Char and Em sat on the sofa in the living room, curled in each other's arms.

"The Girls will be over soon," said Em after a long, exquisite silence that no words could improve upon.

"This will be my last meeting."

Em wiped her eyes. "No!"

"Don't pretend. I'm running out of steam."

"Please, Char. Maybe another doctor?"

"Darling, there comes a time in everyone's life when they have to say goodbye. This is our time. At least I'm going out with a bang."

"Are you sure you want to go through with this?"

Char kissed Em, a soft gentle kiss that betokened friendship as much as romantic love.

"As sure as I've ever been of anything."

Iris called the meeting to order. "This will be the final Girls' meeting before Adventure Number Seven takes place."

Frankie said, "Did you ever think of everything that starts with a seven?" She didn't wait for an answer before rattling off: "Seven Deadly Sins, Seven Wonders of the World—"

"The Seven Dwarfs," Bobbie interrupted. Her eyes grew big. "That's it, girls! We need those code names. There are seven of us. This will be our seventh adventure. What do you say?"

Frankie frowned. "I already suggested code names. Remember?" Six heads bobbed. "Okay, everybody agrees it was my idea. I say we should do it."

Iris said dryly, "First you have to name all Seven Dwarfs. If you can, we'll do it."

Frankie flicked an unconcerned hand. "That's easy: "Dopey, Sneezy, Doc, Grumpy...that's four." She stopped, stumped.

Iris said, "Frankie, when you can name all seven, *then* we will take a vote, as is the custom of the Girls."

While Frankie struggled to remember the other names, Em thought, *Iris's sarcastic nature has returned. It's feeling more like old times!*

"I want to go over our assignments one last time," she said. "Iris, you are going to beef up our alibi."

Iris essayed a sailor's salute. "Aye, aye, captain. I'll stroll from my condo to the marina. I'll make sure everyone notices me—*Senator* Iris Bentonfield on her way to a party on her boat."

Bobbie and Frankie giggled.

Em said, frowning, "Bobbie and Frankie? Know your parts?"

"Sure thing," said Frankie. "The catering is in place, and the decorators will be there at noon."

"Max, you're sure your fine with..." Em struggled for the right word, "*driving* the boat?"

Max had to hold in her laughter. She loved Em, and while she thought about correcting her, she only did so in her head: *Em, it's driving a car, piloting a boat.* "I'm good to go, Em. I drove the boat the other day, and if it's got an engine, I'm the driver. I doubt Linda would recognize me, but just in case, I'll lock the door to the cabin."

"Iris, what about us not wearing life vests?" Em asked. "You know if Linda wears one she won't drown."

"I'm going to refuse to wear one," Iris replied. "I'll bat my eyelashes and say, 'Why ruin a perfectly good outfit?' We'll have our drinks, and perhaps a dance or two, and then I'll position Linda the Rat at the railing."

"Max, the railing?" Em prompted her.

"That section's been loosened. I tested it when I took the boat out for a trial spin."

"Char?"

"Two hands and one shove."

Em nodded. "I think we have everything in order. We'll gather at the marina tomorrow at 4:00 p.m."

As everyone was leaving, Les took Em aside and spoke softly. "Char's too ill to do the deed." There were tears in her eyes. "I'll do it."

The seaside community of Marina Del Rey was one and a half square miles of one of the most sought after areas in Los Angeles, and State Senator Iris Bentonfield was one of its star residents.

Beach-style homes and high-rise condos afforded views of the marina and the Pacific Ocean. Iris walked the three short blocks from her penthouse condominium toward the marina and her fifty-foot convertible boat, the *Betty Alice*.

Quite a change, she thought, *from Slatterville.*

She usually began her day by walking early in the morning, before the crowds began to gather at the Burton Chace Park. It was late afternoon, and she wanted to check on the caterers and decorators—*and* Frankie and Bobbie. Em might trust them, but Iris didn't.

And, she wanted to provide a tighter alibi. Anyone who lived near the marina, or had their boats anchored there, knew Senator Bentonfield. It was hard to miss Iris, first because of her height, and second because she was something of a media butterfly—she was the first to admit she loved the spotlight—and was easily recognizable from her many appearances on network and cable "talking heads" shows.

Iris strolled toward the marina, stopping briefly to wave to the crowd at Burton Chace Park. She glanced up at the sky. It was a clear day. Gentle breezes made it perfect for the people flying kites from the beach, decorating the sky with confetti of many colors.

It was also an ideal day for a boat party.

On the way to her boat slip, Iris stopped to chat with neighbors and constituents. She was confident that, if any were questioned after the fact, they would remark that she was friendly, seemed genuinely interested in how they were doing.

Clearly not like someone on the way to commit murder.

Chapter 42

Thursday, October 8, 2020
Studio City

Em said, "I hope you don't think I'm making this up, Treat. It probably sounds a little over the top."

"Not at all. From what you've told me about the Girls, it sounds like another day in paradise."

"What a sweet way to put it."

Treat settled back on the chair, her face alight with anticipation. "I can't wait to hear what happened next."

"We got to the boat early," said Em, "went over the plan once more, and put on dance music to set the scene. Max went into the cabin and locked the door. We were all set—all we needed now was Linda.

"Last minute changes are never good with any plan. But I knew Les was right. Char was pretty weak at this point, but I have to say, she was dressed for the part." Em couldn't help but chuckle at the memory of Char's outfit. "She was wearing a sailor suit, right out of Gilbert and Sullivan's *H.M.S. Pinafore.*

"It was four in the afternoon and everything was in place. Char was resting on a lounge chair. I sat next to her, and we held hands and sipped our champagne. Les had slipped a sedative into her drink, and in a few minutes I saw she was nodding off."

Em looked glassy-eyed as she related the story. She shook her head as if she were returning from some far-off time and place.

"I'm sorry, Treat. That happens now and then when I'm thinking about all the memories."

Treat felt a rush of compassion for Em, so easily moved from the present to the past. *But, wasn't this happening to her, as well?*

"The music was playing, romantic songs from our time, some from our parents' time—the old love songs from World War II. I don't suppose they would have any meaning to you, but when they played 'I'll Be Seeing You,' I could only think how short our time together would be.

"Bobbie and Frankie began slow dancing and you could see the love in their eyes. All their bickering was nothing but a disguise for their love.

"Linda showed up right at five, with her fear of being on the boat and the water written all over her face.

"Max started the engines, and we cruised out of the marina toward the ocean. We were eating, drinking, and slow dancing. Actually, it was one of the best parties we had ever planned. I think we all forgot why we were there."

Treat leaned forward in her chair, caught up in the intensity of Em's story.

"As soon as Linda recognized Iris, she flocked to her like a moth to a flame. Linda wasn't shy about her interest in Iris—or about how much she could drink—and we got to watch Linda's seduction firsthand. Damn, she was good! Well, Iris was flirting right back and if I didn't know better, I would swear it was love in bloom.

"It was dusk, and the other boats had returned to the marina. Max had shut the engines off and we were getting ready to do the deed. Les came over to me and said, 'What the hell are we doing?' It was as if Les had thrown cold water in my face. I glanced at Iris and she had the oddest expression on her face: as if she had woken from a dreadful nightmare. Max came rushing out of the cabin with her hand held up like this." Em held her hand up like a crossing guard.

"Bobbie and Frankie stopped dancing; I'll never forget the look on everyone's faces.

"Linda began to shake. Les said, 'Jesus, she's having a convulsion.' Les rushed over and shouted at Max to call the Coast Guard. We looked at each other in horror as reality smacked all of us in the face.

"Les did everything to save her. Later, the autopsy showed that she had died from a drug overdose. Char slept through the whole thing."

"So, the murder was fiction?" Treat asked.

"Yes. You see, we were planners, not killers. In that moment, we came to our senses."

"And Char?"

"As we were returning to the marina she woke up and said, 'Did I do the deed?'

We were all stunned. Les stepped forward and held Char's hand. 'You bet, kid,' she said. 'And you were fabulous!'"

"Em, I don't understand. You were so determined and so thorough in your planning."

"Treat, I'm sure you have had some psychology courses."

"Yes, really basic ones. Nothing to explain this."

"Over the years, I've thought so much about what we almost did. Most of us were in some kind of socially concerned profession, and we all volunteered at women's shelters.

"Char was the center of the group—you could say the glue that held us together—and One Peppertree Lane was our home base. We were family, and she was the first...the first to die." Em dabbed the tears. "God, just when I think I'm done grieving, another wave washes over me.

"There is something in psychology—well, you know I'm not a psychologist, but I've read. Oh my, how I've read! It's called a *folie à deux*."

"I know about that one." Treat raised her hand enthusiastically, a student in Em's class on life.

Em relaxed back into her chair, her eyes twinkling, a small smile crossing her face.

"It's when two people share a delusion. I remember it from class." *I've got this one aced,* she thought excitedly. *An A plus in Ms. Em's class.* "It usually happens when two or more are strongly connected or live in a tight social group."

"Very good, Treat." Em applauded lightly. "We couldn't face her death. But, of course, now we had to—and we did, in the true fashion of the Girls."

"The next morning I started writing the book and fictionalized it so Char could see in print how she did the deed. I wrote for hours, usually at night while Char was sleeping, and then read the draft to her the next morning.

"Three months later Char died." Em buried her head in her hands and sobbed. "She slipped out of my hands. I couldn't stop her."

Treat reached over and put her hand on Em's arm. "I'm so sorry."

"Those last few months were incredible. The Girls talked about everything we had done, our lives, and our friendship. We thought if we did, we wouldn't feel the loss. Let me tell you, Treat, there is no way to avoid the pain."

Treat felt her heart move and thought about how she had avoided her pain for all these years. *At what price,* she wondered.

Em wiped her eyes and sat up straight. "We're almost to the last chapter of your visit. Perhaps we can wrap it up tomorrow. Why don't you look at your computer and see if you have any unanswered questions."

Treat smiled faintly. "My computer? Thought that was verboten."

"Another silly rule bites the dust," said Em, standing.

Treat held out her hand. "Thank you, Em. For everything."

Em bent over and impulsively kissed Treat on the top of her head. "Goodnight, Treat. Sleep well."

Treat lay on her back, staring at the mural of a blue sky, white fluffy clouds, and a flock of birds. She began to count them—seven stylized birds with great wingspans, represented as luminous white, winged shapes—like angels—plus two much smaller and more distinct sparrows. *The angel-birds were the Girls,* she thought, *seven caregivers hovering over two sparrows, escorting them through the clouds, through life.*

Now, lying in bed with her hands under her neck, she continued to stare at the ceiling. Treat had to admit she felt envious of the two little birds, surrounded by a loving family.

She had found out the story behind *The Girls,* and what a feature article it would be. Her name would be on the byline of the magazine—and, someday soon, she prayed, on the door of the corner office. She saw herself looking out of the office window, taking in the panoramic view of Manhattan. Her first task would be to fire Evan Perket.

She hoped he would grovel.

Chapter 43

Em woke to the fragrance of coffee wafting through the house. *What a delightful way to wake up.*

The first time she and Char had made love she had awakened to that same robust smell. She was so embarrassed that morning. Then, suddenly, Char was sitting next to her with coffee and Jo-Joe's croissants, and she knew it hadn't been a dream, and that she need not be embarrassed. Everything felt new that day. It was the first cup of coffee she had ever drunk, and the first croissant she had ever eaten. At first, her physical hunger was insatiable, but became overshadowed by a new hunger that couldn't be satisfied by food.

Em yawned and stretched, the movement of her legs interrupting Boots's morning grooming. He meowed with annoyance before jumping gracefully off the bed. Boots knew her routine as well as she did. A loud yawn to shake away the night's cobwebs, a quick trip to the bathroom, and then his bowl would be filled with his favorite food.

Em got out of bed, massaging the small of her back, before bending over to stroke his head. "Boots, you are quite the narcissist." He arched his back and purred at the compliment.

She splashed water on her face and put on her pink chenille robe that had been ordered from an online store. It reminded her of the robes her mother always wore and of their sweet moments—perhaps only enough to count on one hand, but sweet nevertheless. The Snow White sheets her mother had bought her for her fifth birthday, the dresses her mother had sewed for her, the time they went out to lunch and to a movie, and the necklace with the gold cross. Her hand reached up to touch the small cross, a soothing gesture that she frequently made. A grand total of four. Not a lot, but she would take them.

She tried to remember those times, not the ones of complete rejection that had broken her heart over and over again.

She still wondered why there was so much hatred and bitterness. Her parents, dead for many years, had chosen to keep their painful memories locked tightly inside, with only their bitterness seeping out from underneath the closet door.

Being gay is not the only closet, she thought. *So many closets in life, as she had discovered over the years.*

Em followed the fragrance that drifted from the kitchen to her bedroom, with Boots at her side. Em laughed to herself. *Boots and me: like Pavlov's dogs.*

Treat was in the kitchen, standing next to the stove. "Good morning, Em, and a special good morning to you, Boots."

"You're dressed," Em said, surprised. "No PJs with feet."

Treat smiled. "I got up early. They're in my suitcase. I hope you like French toast. It's one of the few things I know how to make."

"It's one of my favorites."

Treat handed Em her coffee.

Em said, "Am I going to get served this morning?"

"Absolutely. Boots, too."

Boots pussyfooted toward his bowl, stopping briefly to rub against Treat's leg. Treat rubbed his head and then ran her hand down the center of his back. "I like to see the way he arches. He does it every time. I hope you don't mind that I've filled his bowl. I think I put in the right amount."

Em opened the refrigerator, reaching for the fruit-only jam. "Mind? Not at all. Truth to tell, I think Boots has a crush on you, Treat." She paused, adding conversationally, "You said you were raised around animals."

"Lots of animals, but they all had jobs to do."

"Jobs?"

"Yes, the cats were there to catch the mice, the horses were there for riding. We even had a plow horse that pulled the furrow for spring planting. And the dogs were to protect us from intruders."

"Intruders?"

Treat hesitated. "Chapman's was completely self-contained and isolated. We raised most of our food and we all worked in the garden, milked the cows, and collected the eggs. Everything was routine." Treat felt her chest tighten and her lips quiver. "It wasn't cruel if that's what you're thinking. Just routine. Sometimes people would ignore Chapman's 'private road' signs and want to walk through the school grounds. The animals were there to perform a job, not to be pets."

"They were expected to work, then, but got no tenderness, no affection in return?"

"I never thought of it that way. They were well treated, but they might become confused if we made pets out of them—not be as efficient."

"That's too bad. We all need tenderness and affection. It's how we thrive."

Treat spoke thoughtfully, "I guess we don't always get what we need." *God,* she thought. *I was raised the same way as the animals. Well treated, but not shown the affection I needed. I never put that together before. Would I have been different if I had been raised in a real family—the way Maggie and Chris were?*

"Em, I've made reservations for the five p.m. flight. I hope that's all right. I've got an office full of work." She hesitated. "And a personal matter I have to handle."

"Love problems?"

"No, very much the opposite. It's actually a work issue that became personal."

"Well, then, let's get down to work. Do you have any questions left?" Em sipped her coffee and took a bite of French toast. "This is amazingly delicious."

"Thanks. I decided I had to learn how to cook at least one thing other than boneless, skinless chicken breasts."

"Well, I think you have a hidden talent."

Treat's usual serious expression quickly replaced her fleeting grin. "I do have a few minor questions and a couple of major ones. I'm curious about Ray. He was in *Book One,* and I've been wondering what happened to him."

"When Iris got into politics, she turned over her interests in the law firm to her associates. Ray was always a solitary man and didn't want to go along with her to Sacramento. He met a woman—Annabelle, I believe was her name. They got married and moved to Florida. Well, he's gone now, as are so many...so many others."

"And Mitchell?"

Em chuckled. "Mitchell is another story. He found his way back to the church. He's Pastor Grant now. It's what he needed: the structure, and the absolutes. He finally found his place. His father forgave him; my parents could never forgive me."

"Did they know about you and Char?"

"Not directly, but they knew. They met Char once when we went to pick the kids up from their house. They looked at her, they looked at me, and they didn't say a word. When we got home there was a message waiting on the machine. So cruel, so cruel."

"What was it, Em?"

"'Don't ever bring that woman to our home again.'"

Treat had to brush her tears away. "I'm so sorry. It sounds so heartless."

"It's been years, and it still hurts. I'm not sure that kind of pain ever goes away. What child does not want her parents to love and accept her? They tolerated me only because they wanted a relationship with Chris and Maggie. After they died, everything they owned was donated to the church. A few photos are all I have. A few memories, as well. Early on I learned to try to keep the good ones and let the bad ones go, as much as you can. Life continues whether you choose to hold onto anger and disappointment or not. It boils down to forgiveness, and perhaps that is the biggest lesson of all."

Treat nodded. "That's something to remember." She mused if she could ever move past her anger and into forgiveness. "You've mentioned Char's son. Did you ever meet him?"

"Yes, at Iris's office for the reading of the will. He refused to come to the funeral."

"Em, you always refer to this house as Char's. Isn't it yours?"

"No, not really. I'm simply taking care of it for her."

Treat burned with curiosity but decided not to press. *How could that be? Taking care of a house for someone who had been dead for more than twenty years?* She would see if there would be another opening, another chance to solve that mystery.

Em sighed. "I know that must sound crazy to you. You should leave here around two to make your flight. That gives us five hours if we forego our lunch break. We can eat peanut butter and jelly sandwiches while we work. Maggie used to call them 'my best.'" Em chuckled. "Those are the kind of memories I choose to hold onto."

"Thank you for breakfast, Treat. It was delicious. I'll take a quick shower and then let's plow through this. Shall we say thirty minutes, in the den? We can end our adventure where it began. I think we both have to get back to our lives."

Chapter 44

1998
Studio City

Les came out of Char and Em's bedroom. She held her arms around Em. "It won't be long now. She's in a quiet, peaceful place. Why don't you sit next to her and hold her hand?"

Em shook her head. "Les, I want to lie next to her and put my head on her chest. She would want that, I know."

"Of course. Do you want me to stay with you?"

"No, honey. This is a one-person job now."

Les hugged Em, pulling her close, letting her rest her weight against her. "We'll be in the living room."

Em stretched out on the bed, her head resting on Char's chest, listening to her breathing in and out, in and out. Hard breaths, soft breaths, skipped breaths.

She was amazed that tears still came: hot, stinging tears that flooded her eyes and rolled down her cheeks.

She put her mouth close to Char's ear and whispered, "Darling, I think you can hear me. I want you to know I will remember and cherish every moment we shared. You have been the most wonderful friend and lover I could have ever prayed for; you gave my life meaning. You made Chris and Maggie yours, as if you had given

326

birth to them. I couldn't have done it without you. Thank you for loving them, for loving me."

Em wiped her tears away. "Darling, we won't be separated forever. Save a place for me on the other side."

She felt the warmth of Char's body and the irregular rhythm of her breathing. Em's eyes grew heavy; she was so very tired. Had she slept at all this week? She only dozed for a minute, but was jolted into awareness by the complete silence. She didn't mean to, but the wailing came on its own: a sound that traveled through the house and entered the hearts of the Girls.

Les sat next to Em, holding her hand.

"I have to call the funeral home and make an appointment," said Em in a monotone. "Char wouldn't let us discuss anything before she died. She said it was a bad omen. Who do I call?"

Iris said, "Block Memorial Park and Mortuary, of course."

"Isn't that only for Jews?"

"Darling, Char *was* Jewish."

"Yes, but I'm not."

Block Memorial Park and Mortuary was the most sought after final resting place for affluent Jews in the Los Angeles area. At the height of the Depression, Rubin Block purchased two hundred contiguous acres of farmland, some flat, some rolling, some with views of the Pacific Ocean. Everyone in the family thought Rubin was crazy and no one in the family wanted to discuss his chosen profession, which they considered unsavory and morbid. "It's a calling," he defended himself, with a sincerity none could question.

Rubin's grandson, Matthew Block, stood at the window of his office, gazing out upon the large expanses of bright green lawns, dotted with flat grave markers made of marble or granite.

Visitors in the perpetual care cemetery could sit on nearby marble benches or on the lawn to pray or think about their loved ones—or anything else—and not be distracted by garish headstones or graveside decorations. Flowers were allowed, but only live ones, which were removed at the first sign of decay. No artificial flowers were permitted, no matter how closely they mimicked nature. *Dignity and Serenity Forever* was the motto of Block Memorial Park and Mortuary.

When kids at school discovered Matt's father was a mortician, they stopped calling him by his name and began to call him Morty, the Titian. His father sat him down, wiped his tears away and told him, "Our family provides a service that everyone needs. *Everyone.* Remember, Matthew, no one leaves this world alive."

Now, Matthew was next in line to be president of Block Memorial Park and Mortuary. Fulfilling an important social function, he ignored any slights or jokes about morticians. He never forgot what his father had told him thirty years ago. No one would leave this world alive, not even Matthew Block.

He watched the landscapers planting evergreen trees and laying down sod around their most recent development, Forever Peace. The marble benches would be in place in a few days. Matthew was partial to that particular site, it had the most incredible views of the ocean. The view would not be enjoyed by the interred, but it would bring peace to the most bereaved or guilty of families.

Yesterday a call had come from an Emily Scott, who explained that she was Dr. Charlotte Owens's "partner in life" and would be handling the funeral arrangements. He offered his condolences, made an appointment for the next day, and dispatched a vehicle to the home.

Matthew liked to think of himself as being socially enlightened and worldly. Dr. Owens would not be the first lesbian he had buried, although at times, he did struggle with the concept. He popped a fresh-breath mint in his mouth and continued to gaze out the window at Forever Peace.

∞

Leann announced Emily Scott and—she hesitated—relatives.

He would treat Emily Scott as any grieving widow: greet her first, offer his sympathy for her loss, and then introduce himself to the extended family.

He thought Dr. Walker, who was holding on tightly to one of Ms. Scott's hands, was attractive. Must have been hot in her early days. What a waste. Maxine Tracey held Ms. Scott's other hand. Definitely *not* hot. Then there was the lawyer, Iris Bentonfield, who was quick to shove her card in his hand. He recognized her from the newspapers and television: high profile attorney, now in the political arena. Then there were the two, er, *indescribables*—Francis and Roberta—wearing motorcycle jackets, sobbing and hanging on to each other as if they were conjoined twins.

Matthew Block escorted them into his office, offered them coffee or tea, and began the customary paperwork and formalities. A burial was decided upon; Ms. Scott visibly shuddered at the thought of cremation.

He ushered them into the casket room and explained the selection, ranging from a simple pine box, to a twenty-gauge all-steel casket. The quiet one, Maxine, looked dopey but wanted to know everything about the construction: materials, wood compared to metal, and interior linings.

Ms. Scott said, "Something dignified."

"I would recommend this casket." Matthew placed his hand on a solid oak coffin with a white velvet interior. "It offers both utility and understated elegance."

Em drifted toward the deluxe casket, rubbed her hand over the mahogany wood, and looked closely at the soft-pink interior. "Char would have liked this one," she said. "I'll take two."

"Two?"

"One for Char and one for me."

"Oh," Matthew replied, anxious not to let his delight show

through his professional mask, "you wish to preplan?" *Two*, he thought. *This will be a good day.*

They returned to the office. "Preplanning will take a bit of time. Please, allow me to have some refreshments brought in." He picked up the phone and in a soft tone said, "Refreshments, Leann." Leann would know what that meant, after all, Block Memorial Park and Mortuary was a business, and at the end of the day, they needed to show a profit.

Matthew shifted into a new level of sympathy. "At a time like this," he said, "the bereaved must remember to take care of themselves." He paused, adding hesitantly, "Uh, Ms. Scott, you do realize that this is a Jewish cemetery?" He glanced at the necklace with a gold cross, given to Emily as a gift from her parents upon the purity ceremony.

The attorney glared. "And?"

Matthew kept his eyes focused on Ms. Scott, ignoring Ms. Bentonfield's comment. "Perhaps I've made an incorrect assumption."

"No, Mr. Block. You're correct; I am not Jewish."

Matthew rocked slightly in his high back leather chair. "We have no problem allowing the burial of, er, Gentiles, but I do have to inform you that we only permit rabbis to officiate in our chapels. Services performed by non-Jewish clergy will have to be held graveside."

Leann knocked and rolled in a vintage maple drop-leaf teacart, brimming with delicate finger sandwiches, petit fours, tea, and coffee.

"Thank you, Leann. Ladies, please, have something to eat."

"Em, are you okay with these conditions?" asked Les, ignoring the call to food.

"I want to be with Char, and I couldn't give a *shit* about who says what after I'm dead."

Matthew felt his eyebrows itching to arch but maintained his plastic expression.

330

Iris said, "Em, how would you feel if I bought a plot next to you and Char? It seems we should all be together, in death as we were in life. What do you say, girls?"

Les laughed. "That is the perfect revenge on my family. I can see the obit now: 'Lesley Warren, physician and avowed lesbian daughter of the socially prominent Laguna Warrens, was buried today in a Jewish cemetery.' What do you say, Max?"

"I'm game. We can count on my family to bring flowers on Christmas and Easter."

Bobbie and Frankie looked at each other. Bobbie reached for a plate of petit fours. "Do you have a double-decker?" she said. "I want to be on top."

"You always did," said Frankie, elbowing her.

Matthew Block thought he had seen it all: bickering families, cheapskate families, families that didn't give a damn and just wanted to plant their "loved one" and get it over with. But he had never seen such unabashed candor as this. It was refreshing. And rather amusing.

His father had taught him another valuable lesson: "Strike while the iron is hot." No one in the history of Block's had brought in seven birds at one swat. This would guarantee his presidency. He just hoped they couldn't see the excitement in his eyes.

"Ms. Scott, we are in the process of completing one of our most picturesque locations, Forever Peace," he said in his most pleasant, I'm-here-for-you, no pressure voice. "In fact, the final touches will be completed before Dr. Owens's burial. I do have some family plots available that I believe will satisfy all of your needs. The site can be gated, if you wish, to give family and friends additional privacy."

Em could tell Iris was bridled up. "This will make seven in one day, Mr. Block. A company record, no doubt. There must be all sorts of rewards that go with salesmanship that skilled. The sale is yours on one condition."

"That is, Ms. Bentonfield?"

"We need to have private access to Dr. Owens the night before her funeral."

"Do you mean a private viewing?"

"That's not exactly what we had in mind."

The Girls were dressed in matching black sweat pants and turtlenecks.

"Don't we have to put dirt on our faces or something?" said Bobbie, stifling a giggle. "We look like a bunch of dime-store burglars!"

"Christ, Bobbie, you do that and you'll be sneezing all over the place," said Frankie.

"Oh, Frankie, stop being such a grump."

"Max," said Iris, ignoring the bickering lovers, "did you make the arrangements?"

"We're set. We have from midnight to two a.m. Mr. Block will be meeting us in front of the mortuary. Em, are you sure you want to do this?"

"Max, you know Char would have loved it. It'll be the final meeting with all of us in attendance."

"Okay, let's go."

They piled into Max's eight-passenger van, large enough to hold all of them plus accessories.

A moonless night with dark clouds hovering overhead sent shivers up and down the spines of the Girls. An eight-foot gray stone fence surrounded Block Memorial Park and Mortuary from the rest of the world. There was only one entrance, through the wrought iron gate that faced the street.

Max pulled up and blinked the headlights twice, a signal that the Girls had arrived. The guard, positioned to view any vehicles wishing to enter the cemetery after hours, responded to Max's signal by unlocking the gates and waving them in. He pointed to a parking spot in front of the mortuary. "Park there, ma'am. Mr. Block is expecting you."

Matthew Block, still dressed in his custom-tailored suit and looking as fresh as he had the other day—*as if he had been embalmed,* Max joked quietly to the others and had to beg them to stop laughing—waited by the mortuary side door and guided them to the elevator. He pressed the button to the basement.

"Two hours, ladies," he said. "I'll be back at two a.m."

Char lay on a table, a white sheet covering her body.

Em said, "She looks so peaceful. Char would have loved this." She leaned over to touch her.

Les put her hand on Em's arm. "Em, she'll be cold."

Em touched Char's brow. "Oh, God, she's *so* cold." Sobs wracked her body.

"It's good, Em," said Iris tenderly. "Char would have wanted all of us to cry. She would say it was cathartic."

Max said, "We should start the ceremony." She cleared her throat. "I would like to call to order the Midnight Meeting of the Girls. We, as Char's family and sisters, have gathered to prepare her for her journey to the other side.

"First we will participate in a ritual bath so that Char can leave this world as pure as when she arrived. Then we'll dress her in garments befitting one of the Girls.

"Finally, each of us will say something personal about Char to send her on her journey with love. May her spirit move with grace to the next universe."

Em said, "Make sure the water is warm, but not too hot. Char hated hot water unless she was in the hot tub."

Max said, "Okay, warm water, not too hot."

"Em, why don't you wash her face?" said Iris, handing her a soft infant's washcloth.

There was something soothing in the ritual, bathing a friend while saying goodbye for the last time.

Les said, "Bobbie and Frankie, do you have the outfit?"

Frankie held it up. "Everything is here, checked twice."

Bobbie nodded and giggled. "God, this is the best funeral I've ever gone to!"

They finished dressing Char, and satisfied with the results, held hands as they surrounded the table.

Les said, "Char, you were the glue that held us together. Thank you for making One Peppertree Lane our home. I'll miss you."

Max spoke next. "When Les brought me over to meet you, you welcomed me and made me one of the Girls. I've never forgotten that."

Frankie said, "Bobbie will speak for both of us."

Bobbie said, "Roses are red, violets are blue. Char, there will never be another you."

"Well, *that* was certainly original," Frankie groused.

"Oh, shut up!"

"Decorum, ladies, decorum," Iris scolded. She looked at Char. "Darling, you taught me how to keep a secret. And I will keep yours."

Frankie and Bobbie chanted: "What secret, what secret?"

"*Hush!*" the rest of the Girls chorused.

Max squeezed Em's shoulder. "Okay, Em, it's your turn."

"Char, I think we said it all." She touched a finger to her lips, and then to Char's forehead. "I love you."

Chapter 45

Em and Treat had returned to the den, sitting once again in the same places.

"The next day we held the funeral. Char had wanted a closed casket, but we knew what she was wearing."

Em looked at Treat with her inscrutable smile. "Can you guess?"

Treat burst out laughing. "You didn't..."

"Decked her out to the nines, just like her portrait. I'll bet she was having a good laugh, wherever she was."

Treat couldn't stop laughing. *God, these last few days, what a ride.* She had to force herself to return to serious journalist mode. "Em, you said that Char's son didn't attend the service."

"That's right. I met him a week later at Iris's office for the reading of the will."

"What was he like?"

"He reminded me a lot of Char. The way his eyes crinkled and his voice—a man's voice but with Char's inflections. It was his eyes...I'll never forget them. They were hazel, like hers, but her eyes shined so brightly, as if holding onto a joke or a secret. His were cold and filled with rage. They made me shudder."

Chapter 46

1998

With the exception of one client, Charlotte Owens, Iris had given up her practice when she ran for the State Senate. Although the estate was substantial, Iris handled this case pro bono. It wasn't because of their friendship; it was the right thing to do.

Her relationship with Char started that way, in the 1960s: a young attorney seeking justice for a mother who would lose her child because society had branded her a pariah. She had warned Char at the beginning. "Char, homosexuality is considered a mental disorder. You have to know, we don't have a chance."

"Well, then, I don't have much more to lose, do I? Let's go for it, Iris. If I'm losing my son, let's make a fucking statement to the world."

Iris felt her chest tighten as she fought back the tears. She had to stay strong now; she had to face Char's son, Lawrence Owens. She was certain it would not be a pleasant meeting.

"Mr. Owens, thank you for coming." Iris held out her hand. "I'm sorry for your loss."

He nodded and sat in the chair next to Em.

"This is Ms. Scott, your mother's partner in life."

"I'm aware of who *she* is," he said tersely. "Look, I'm not going to pretend to be happy to be in the same room with either of you. I'm only here because I'm in the will, and I came for what is rightfully mine."

Iris maintained her professional demeanor. "Let me begin by informing both of you that Charlotte Owens's will is a bit unusual, but remains a legally binding document. Because of some of the conditions, I had it reviewed by two of the finest estate attorneys in California. I have been assured that it will hold up in court, should it be contested."

Lawrence sat with his jaw and hands clenched, his knuckles bulging, his face turning red.

Iris continued, "Char left her interests in *The Girls* novels, to be divided equally between the remaining Girls. She states in her will: "'It should be kept in the family.'"

A small smiled crossed Em's face. *We really are a family,* she thought.

"Okay, okay," said Lawrence impatiently. "Get to the important stuff."

Iris looked at him, then to Em. "Emily, the house located at One Peppertree Lane has been left to you."

The blood drained from Lawrence's face as he sat in stunned silence, visibly shaking.

Em was no less shocked. She was so sure that Char would have left the house to Lawrence, as a way for them to connect, perhaps even to heal, after her death.

Iris continued, "Mr. Owens, you have been granted a monthly stipend—quite a generous one, I might add."

Iris handed each of them an envelope. "Char wrote personal letters to you. They will explain how she came to her decision and the conditions for your inheritance. The contents of the letters are to remain private. If you should share the information with anyone, outside of legal counsel, your inheritance will no longer be valid. I'd like you to read them now, and if you have any questions, I'll speak with each of you privately."

Lawrence read his letter, crumpled it in his fist, and threw it across the room. He turned to Emily, his face bright red, hateful words gushing out. "You...you...this is all your doing. You influenced her. The house should be mine...not yours."

Chapter 47

Friday, October 9, 2020
Studio City

Em said, "I never knew what was in his letter. My letter explained his arrangement, but the personal details were absent. That was the only time I saw Char's son."

"I'm curious, Em. What was in your letter?" Treat said calmly.

"Huh?" Em said, returning from a sudden reverie.

"Em, you're leaving me with a cliffhanger."

"Not fair, huh? Okay, as Paul Harvey used to say, here's the rest of the story."

"Who?"

"Never mind. It's a generation gap thing. I was shaking and could barely open Char's letter. It was another one of her secrets—her *final secret*." She paused a long moment for effect.

Treat pushed, her voice rising, "I'm going to miss my plane! What *was* in your letter, Em?"

"In a minute, dear, in a minute. Treat Mason, such an unusual name," she mused.

Treat looked down. "My mother told me I was her treat."

"I guess that could be taken in different ways. When you first called, Max investigated your background and everything checked out: your place of work, schools you attended, work...social history."

Treat scowled. "Social history? You're kidding! You had the nerve to check out who I've dated?"

"Not exactly who. You see, the Girls look for patterns. Patterns can be telling, and we learned to be thorough over the years. After I met you, there was something that didn't quite fit. The way you described your interest in *The Girls*—I kept wondering why? Such intensity. I asked Max to dig deeper. Max couldn't find a birth record for a Treat Mason. It seems your life began when you were eight and started school at Chapman's."

Treat said angrily, "Well, I guess you just aren't as smart as you think you are, *Ms. Scott*. My name is Treat Mason. End of story. I'm getting the hell out of here."

A gesture from Em halted her before she could rise. "Now Treat, you know and I know that you didn't float down from the sky when you were eight. I have to admit, you kept me up at night, thinking. Have I told you how I hate unsolved mysteries? There were clues, but I didn't put everything together until just now."

"Clues?"

"Yes, the way you kept staring at Char's portrait. Time after time I saw your gaze drifting back, captivated. Your interest in the Girls and now, pushing to know the details of the letter. It just seemed, well, let us say your interest seemed to extend beyond mere journalistic curiosity."

Treat slumped her head in her hands. Her voice faltered. "I've got a plane to catch. I have to leave."

"Not so fast. I've spent the last five days telling you all about the Girls. You've got enough information for a dozen articles. Now, it's your turn to tell me a story. Who are you?"

"I'm Treat Mason, *that's* who I am."

"Have you ever had an uneasy feeling when you've first met someone? As if you knew them from another time, another place? I felt that way when I held your phone message in my hand. A connection I couldn't explain, just feel."

340

Em's eyes drilled into Treat's. No longer an amusingly eccentric seventy-four-year-old woman, she was a no-nonsense parent needing to get the truth out of a recalcitrant child. "It's time now, Treat. Spill it."

Treat's face turned a bright red. "Spill it? Who the hell do you think you are?"

"I know who I am, and I need you to tell me who *you* are."

"I've told you who I am. Treat Mason...I'm Treat Mason. Do you want identification? My passport, driver's license?"

"As if names and documents can't be falsified." Em walked across the room. "Give me your hands, Treat."

"Don't you dare touch me!" Treat started to stand up. "I'm out of here. Fuck the Girls, and fuck the goddamn story. Oh, and by the way, *Em*, fuck you, too!"

Em demanded, "Sit down, *now*." Her wrinkled hands reached out for Treat's, holding them in a vice-like grip. Compelled, Treat sank onto the sofa, trembling.

"Leave me alone, please, just leave me alone. I'll go away. I won't bother you. *Please*."

"No, I'm not leaving you alone. You've been left alone too long."

"Please, Em. Let me go. I have to go home." The rage that had filled her eyes was replaced with tears. "I have to go home," she sobbed.

Em remembered that night, when she was seventeen, in a strange motel with Mitchell. She had cried, "I want to go home, I want to go home." What if she had? She thought of how that one night had changed the course of her life. Chris, Maggie—they would not exist. Char, all the Girls—she would not have met them. And she would not have been here to help Treat find her way home.

"I'm not letting go of your hands or of you."

Treat shuddered, her voice childlike, pleading. "I want to go home, I want to go home."

"Soon."

"Please, Em, don't hold my hands."

"Tell me your name."

She shook her head.

"We can sit this way all day. Now, tell me your name."

"My name is—my name is—I can't say it."

"Yes you can. My name is..."

"My name is...S...Sa...Sarah."

Em said softly, "Sarah, you have a last name, too."

Sarah shook her head, gasping. "Can't say it, can't say it."

"Yes you can. I'm right here, I've got you...nothing bad will happen."

Em released her hands, reaching up to touch Sarah's face. "Look at me. You need to know you're not alone. You need to know I won't let anything bad happen to you."

"My name is Sarah, Sarah O...O...Owens." Sarah sobbed, collapsing against Em. "Oh, please, let me go home."

Em held Sarah against her chest. "Darling, you are home. Char's granddaughter. I've been waiting for you."

"Waiting for me?" she gasped.

"Yes, waiting for you. Now it's time for you to read your grandmother's letter."

Em walked to the oak desk, so beautifully decorated with flowers by an eight-year-old Maggie. "I've kept the letter right here, in this drawer. Waiting, hoping for Sarah Owens to find her way home."

Em sat next to Sarah, holding the letter so that they could both read it.

Darling:

I've told you nearly all of my secrets. Most of them were small ones, about how I enjoy sneaking into the kitchen for a late night snack, or how I like to wake up early and watch you sleeping peacefully, always so grateful you were next to me.

What a life we have had. You shared your love and your family without restraint. I can't tell you how much that meant to me.

I've kept one big secret from you; I was too humiliated to speak it, to make it real. I've been so ashamed to admit the complexity of my relationship with Lawrence. I hope you can forgive me for this final secret.

When Jonathan was born, that very same year, I discovered that Lawrence also had a child, a daughter. I begged him to let me be part of her life, in some small way. I'm so ashamed of the way I groveled. I tried, oh how I tried to see her. I sent letters, cards, gifts, all of which were returned.

Now I'm asking you to do something for me. Do you remember when you began to write The Girls? You wanted each of us to pick a name for our character in the book. I picked the name Sarah, my mother's name, and as I found out later, my granddaughter's name as well.

The only link left to my family is the house at One Peppertree Lane. I'm asking you to live there with the hope that someday Sarah will come looking for her beginnings. She won't find me, but she can find you. You are the one who knows me best, who can share your memories of me—of us—with her. I know it's a lot to ask, to stay in this house on the slim chance that Sarah will want to discover her family.

If she finds you, tell her I loved her and tried to write to her and send her little gifts. I've made a financial arrangement with Lawrence; he will receive a generous monthly settlement if he sends Sarah away to the school of my choice. I know of a wonderful school built on the value of truth. It's a bit on the old-fashioned side and off the beaten path. She may bridle at the restrictions, but it will protect her.

I am so concerned for her welfare if she remains with Lawrence. I am afraid her legacy will be one of anger and hostility.

This secret is now yours to hold.

Forever,

    Char

Treat said, "I haven't thought of myself as Sarah for so many years. I was eight when I was sent to Chapman's. Miss Lily and Miss Violet cared for me, saved my life."

"May I call you Sarah?"

"I like the name, Em.

"Em, I'm sorry I told you, you know to..."

"To 'fuck off'? It's not the first time I've heard that, and I hope it's not the last. It makes me feel like a vital part of the world, not like some doddering old biddy with one foot in the grave. There's so much of Char in you; she would have been delighted. Do you know when I was certain you were Sarah?"

Sarah, sniffling, shook her head.

"When I described the way we had dressed Char for her funeral and you laughed—it was Char's laughter. It was as if she were sitting in the room with me. No one laughed the way she did. It started out like rain gently pelting a windowpane and crescendoed into sleet in a winter storm—raucous, contagious, demanding attention. And your eyes, they crinkle around the corner when you smile, just the way hers did. But hers glowed with a passion, a *joie de vivre*. Yours have been sad so much of the time. I was happy to see them lighting up with anger. You know the best part of an intimate relationship, Sarah?"

Sarah shook her head. "I don't have intimate relationships."

"I think you're in one now, with me. What has passed between us has been like the pillow talk Char and I shared. Holding each other and talking about everything...just everything. I loved that part of us. We learned so much about each other and ourselves. Those things that were so painful as children became understood."

Sarah remembered Jack's birthday dinner, when his wish was to lie in bed with her and hold her while they talked. She had been given so much at Chapman's—ways to survive in the wilderness, in New York City. But there was a missing piece: She couldn't seem to connect to people.

Sarah shook her head. "I don't know what to believe or feel. I was sent to Chapman's after my mommy...my mother left us. I was to spend a week with my father, during the summer. Miss Lily and Miss Violet drove me home. I was so excited, and I thought...I thought I could take my dolly to Chapman's. You see, the other girls all had their dolls or stuffed animals."

Sarah wiped her tears away. "When we walked into the apartment...he was living in filth. Just sitting in a chair. Miss Lily took me downstairs and when Miss Violet joined us, she held me and told me my daddy was sick. When I was little, I knew my daddy was sick. All I knew was he took medicine to make him better. I never saw him again.

"When we returned to Chapman's Miss Violet took me aside and explained in great detail about my daddy's illness." Sarah looked up at Em, her eyes filled with tears, opened wide. "Em, he was bi-polar. That's why, as a child, I saw him as different daddies, and I never knew which one would show up. When he died, I was the only one at his funeral. No friends, no one to mourn for him; not even me."

"I'm sorry. I wasn't aware he had died."

"Three months ago. He spent his last years in his apartment, a recluse. I went there after the funeral. Moldy food scattered around, filthy clothes. I was tempted to turn around and leave everything to be thrown away, but I had to know. Was there some evidence to help me understand, to lead me to the truth? Chapman's motto was *Seek the Truth.*"

"That's why your grandmother sent you there. In spite of her secrets, the truth was so important to Char."

"I found some papers in his desk. My birth certificate, the note from my mother, a few letters from his mother—no envelopes, no return address, and a couple of photos of a woman holding a baby. I was certain they must have been of my father and grandmother."

"Sarah, do you know why your mother left?"

Treat looked at Em, their eyes locking. Em thought of her dream about the children with the large, painfully sad eyes. Now Sarah's eyes were those eyes, staring at her. She only hoped that she could find her way to help Char's granddaughter, Sarah.

"She couldn't take the pressure. The note said she would come back for me when she was settled. But, she never came back."

"So many losses for you."

"Please, Em, don't be sympathetic right now. I can't go there." She muffled her cries and caught her breath until the tears stopped.

Em thought, *This is what she must have done all these years to avoid the pain.*

Sarah took a deep breath and spoke as if she were discussing the weather. "I decided not to dwell on the past...to let it go. Then, I began to think about the course on *The Girls*. I felt compelled to reread them, and the character, Sarah, seemed to match what little I knew about my grandmother. My father told me about the outfits she would put together. It seemed to be his one fond memory of her. You put all of that in *Number Seven*."

Em nodded. "*Number Seven* was published after Char's death. I revealed more about her in that novel. I was hoping, somehow, it would lead you here, to me."

"It did. I fought to get this interview. I thought it was probably just a coincidence, but then you mentioned her name." Sarah sighed, looked at her watch, and stood up. "If I hurry I might be able to make my flight."

"Sarah, it was the thread of life you were responding to. Don't make this a wasted trip. You were led here for a reason. I don't want you leaving this way, unfinished."

"It's finished for me. This is hurting too much. I have to go home, to Chapman's. Don't you understand? I don't connect with people. My only solace is in *my* world, my isolation."

Em patted the couch and spoke gently. "Sit next to me. If you couldn't connect, you wouldn't be in so much pain. When you got so angry with me, I felt the connection...didn't you?" She held her arms out. "I promise to let you go."

Em wrapped her arms loosely around Sarah. The sobs began, at first delicate, as if they were foreign to her, then, as Em gathered her

346

closer, the way she used to hold Maggie and Chris when they were infants, they became stronger, yielding to years of pain.

Em found herself humming a soothing lullaby she had heard Char hum over the years. Sarah melded into her until the sobs lessened and then stopped. "I have some things for you," Em said. "Would you like to see them?"

"Yes, please...Em, will you sit next to me?"

Em kissed her on the cheek. "I'll be right next to you every step of the way."

Em walked over to the desk and opened the bottom drawer. "Birthday cards, holiday cards, letters—all marked *Return to Sender.*"

Sarah held the package of cards and letters. She hunched over, small sobs shaking her body. "She really cared?"

"She loved you more than you'll ever know. I think you'll know everything about her from these. And I can always fill in the blanks."

"I've felt so alone all these years. All the other girls had families, homes to return to."

Em whispered, "You have family—oh my, what a family!—so many to love you. The house—Char wanted you to have it. I've been the caretaker, only the caretaker. That's why I refer to it as Char's house. It belongs to you now. Sarah, I think it would be a good idea for you to call your editor and tell him you won't be returning quite yet."

Sarah gasped, "I'll lose my job!"

"No you won't. You'll tell him you've got an exclusive on *The Girls: Number Eight.*"

"*Number Eight?*"

"Nonfiction this time. I want to write the truth about the Girls, what life was like for lesbians, for all women in the early days. I'll need a researcher and someone to handle public relations. Sarah, we are going to bust this last closet wide open. I think you'll be perfect for the job. And, if you're up to it, tomorrow you can meet the Girls. You do have six grandmothers, you know."

Sarah tilted her head and smiled. "Can we have a Girls meeting at midnight?"

Em laughed. "How does four o'clock sound? It'll be midnight somewhere in the world."

Epilogue

S enator Iris Bentonfield took a limousine from her apartment in Washington, DC, to Dulles Airport, boarded the private jet, and settled in for her flight to Los Angeles. It was midnight in DC, but 9:00 p.m. in Los Angeles. She remembered when the flight had taken five hours, modern technology had reduced it to three, and she would be able to celebrate the new day in both cities.

The plane had been designed with a suite that included a bedroom, office, and bathroom. The flight attendant brought her dinner: salad with champagne vinegar and olive oil dressing, poached salmon, baked potato, and broccoli. Somewhere over Kansas, dessert was served, consisting of fresh strawberries, madeleine cookies, and coffee with cream and sugar on the side.

Iris sighed. Christ, she was tired. The bill had passed, now they would have to face angry mobs and court battles. She would rest for a few minutes, shower, and change before they landed in Los Angeles.

There was a part of Iris that was kept hidden—from the Girls, from her lovers over the years, and even from herself. That was the Iris Fields who lived inside, no matter how the exterior was changed: a child raised by a prostitute, who lived in a trailer park on a dusty road and had one friend, Mr. Newly. Sometimes it was all she could do to maintain the confident façade, to act like the champion of the underdog—when she so often felt like the underdog herself.

The alarm buzzed and Iris, still half-asleep, fumbled for the off button. She felt groggy, hung over, and now she had to deal with a crick in her neck from dozing sitting up. She sat at the chair in front of the dressing table, and reaching up, removed the medium-brown wig before placing it carefully on the wig stand. With a sense of relief she ran her hand through her gray crew cut. Iris thought of the sacrifices she had made over the years, but none annoyed her as much as wearing the same style wig and red suits. Her suits and hairstyle helped to make her a national trademark, and with it came the power Senator Iris Bentonfield needed to get the Freedom to Marry Act passed.

She followed with a lightweight lotion to remove her makeup. Now an androgynous face stared back. *Not a bad one,* she thought, and not the product of the umpteen plastic surgeries everyone guessed she had had. Her one concession to vanity had been a facelift when she was sixty. She undressed, wanting to wash off the invisible dirt from the past twelve years as a senator, and turned the water on in the shower, making it as hot as she could tolerate.

She dressed, this time wearing a plain black T-shirt and jeans. Rubbing hair gel between her hands, she coaxed her hair into short spikes. *Now,* she thought, *this is the* real *Iris.* The plane would be landing soon. She held Em's e-mail in her hand. She chuckled at Em's resistance to using texting, but that was Em. She relished the two short words that filled her heart with hope: *Mission accomplished.*

The "real" Iris Fields walked completely unnoticed through the terminal to the cabstand. It was a quick drive from LAX to One Peppertree Lane. The remote control opened the gate and her key unlatched the front door. She closed the door quietly and went to the spare bedroom in the back of the house—a simple room furnished with a queen-size bed, a chest of drawers, two nightstands with lamps, and a desk. It was used infrequently, only when she came to town.

Iris broke into a grin when she saw Em sleeping soundly on her back, wearing her silver silk pajamas with crimson buttons. Boots was sound asleep on top of the blankets, firmly cradled between Em's feet. *My cat and my mouse,* she thought lovingly.

The pajamas were Iris's Christmas gift to Em, a Christmas they celebrated together at her house in Malibu. A full moon lit up the deck, and as the night gave way to dawn, they could hear the tide beginning to rise, crashing over and over against the massive boulders protecting the oceanfront house from the rising sea. They had stayed warm by huddling beneath blankets, drinking champagne, and talking until the sun began to rise. It was the way they had celebrated Christmas for fifteen years.

Em had opened her gift, a box wrapped in Santa Claus paper. Iris had been worried she wouldn't understand their significance.

She did.

Em hugged the pajamas. "They're my high school colors," Em had cooed. "Oh, Iris, you don't miss a trick. I didn't get to wear my cap and gown, but I can wear these whenever I want."

"Yeah. Until I tear them off you," Iris had said.

Em began to cry, and Iris held her tightly until the sobs became softer and then stopped.

Iris finally understood what Mr. Newly meant on that day so many years ago, when she was barely eighteen and getting ready to leave Slatterville.

You're starting a new life. Life has many beginnings, but only one ending. Iris, I want you to promise me one thing. What you did with Mr. Slattery—don't do it again, not for money. Next time do it for love.

She had had many affairs over the years, some with men and some with women; none were about love until Em.

In his sleep Boots kneaded the covers, his whiskers twitching, soft mews escaping. Iris wondered what he might be dreaming of. Probably not a mouse—more likely a tidbit of smoked salmon, his weekend treat. Spoiled little rascal. She loved him, too.

Em turned over on her side, dislodging Boots from his sleep nook and his dream. He jumped gracefully off the bed, greeted Iris by rubbing against her leg, and then slinked off quietly in search of some midnight feline adventure.

Em was muttering in her sleep—imperceptible words, not unlike Boots's meows. Her body began to twitch and then lay still. Iris smiled to herself. *My cat and my mouse—dreamers alike.*

Em stood in the stern of the long wooden boat, surrounded by glaciers and blue-toned icebergs, but she felt no cold. In the bow a hooded ferryman, his muscles bulging, stabbed a long pole into the fjord's frigid waters to propel the boat toward a small village built along the shore. Forlorn figures—insubstantial as smoke, their features gauzy, indistinct—sat unmoving on six rows of wooden benches that ran the length of the boat. She stared in awe of the stark seascape as a peaceful feeling embraced her. *I've never felt this free,* she thought. *And nothing hurts. All the aches and pains from being seventy-four are gone.*

The boat moved steadily across the fjord. When she turned her face, she saw Char standing next to her. Char was wearing the embroidered chambray shirt, filled with colorful flowers and rainbows. Em thought, *I was so naive. I didn't even know what the rainbows meant.*

They didn't touch, but she felt Char's love wrapping around her, protecting her from the cold.

The boat landed at the village filled with thatched-roof cottages, and she and Char disembarked.

"No one else is getting off," she said to Char.

"They have another destination."

"Char, are you telling me there is a hell?"

"No, darling, not in the way you think. They're not quite ready for the village. They have a few things to learn. Don't worry, Em. They won't be hurt; it's more like school."

They strolled through the seaside; it reminded Em of Gepetto's village in *Pinocchio*. "We're not in Disneyland, are we?"

Char laughed. Oh God, how Em had missed her laugh.

Suddenly, the right lens of Em's glasses fell out. Upset, she turned to Char. "What do I do? You know I can't see without my glasses."

"No one here can fix your glasses—you have to return. The boat is waiting for you."

"I don't want to go back," Em pleaded. "I want to stay here with you."

"Em, you can't stay here. Someone is waiting for you on the other side. I only came to thank you for taking care of Sarah."

"Are you upset because Iris and I..."

Char laughed the laugh that Em loved so much. "A testimony to love is to be able to love again." She was quiet a moment, then smiled beatifically at Em. "I had a tête-à-tête with God."

Em was amazed. "You spoke to God?"

"Oh yes, we're allowed to do that here."

"What did God say?"

"'To love once is a blessing. To love twice is a miracle.' Now go. Em, your miracle is waiting for you. You need to be with Iris, and to get your glasses fixed. You have so much left to see."

Iris sat on the edge of the bed, barely touching Em as she stroked her head. Then, as Em opened her eyes, she leaned over, brushing her lips across her forehead, her cheeks, taking her time to stop and gaze until their lips finally touched.

Iris said, "You were dreaming."

Em spoke sleepily, "I'm so glad you're here." She reached for Iris, wrapping her arms around her. "I had the weirdest dream."

"Move over, dearest. Let me hold you while you tell me your dream."

"You don't mind?"

"Not if I can have my way with you afterward."

"Maybe the dream can wait a while. I want to feel all of you next to me, now...not later."

"My little mouse." She brought Em closer, unbuttoning her top, her hands gently moving down Em's body.

Em sighed and reached up to take off Iris's T-shirt. "No bra," she whispered.

"No bottoms," Iris whispered back.

"I wanted to make it easier for you."

"Me, too."

Em moved tightly against Iris, her head resting against her breasts, their arms and legs interlaced. "Did you sleep on the plane?"

"Like a baby. How's Sarah?"

"I read her *Goodnight Moon* and stayed with her until she cried herself to sleep."

Iris nodded. "You do have a way with babies. It won't be too much for her to see me here in the morning?"

"She wants to meet all her grandmas. I want you here tonight, and I don't want us to be separated again." Em put a hand on Iris's cheek, stroking it lightly. "You're quite beautiful, Iris. I've always liked you best without your makeup and wigs."

"There's so much I want to tell you."

"Darling, can it wait—a little while longer? Right now, dearest, I want us to keep making love."

Three hours later, the lovers basked in the afterglow. Iris had thrown together a light brunch-in-bed for both of them.

"God, Em, I'd forgotten what it's like to hold you, to make love to you."

"Remember the first time...in your office?"

"How could I ever forget? I had no idea you were interested in me."

"It surprised me, too."

"I was working late that night on my first national campaign. I asked you to come over to review a letter and then our hands touched, and we looked at each other. You reached up."

"You reached down." Em laughed. "We couldn't get our clothes off fast enough. I was afraid the janitor would walk in."

"I locked the door. Did we ever get that letter out?"

"Not in time."

Iris took a small bite of toast and strawberry jam. "All this sneaking around for so many years. I've had time to think about your e-mail: *Mission accomplished.* Our lives have been a fifteen-year drama in the making. Catching a night here, stealing a weekend. Pretending I'm in Washington, and you're at a teacher's conference. Keeping our love a secret. For what?"

"We made that decision together, remember? You wanted to run for office, to try to get the Freedom to Marry Act passed. You said it was your dream, and we didn't want to give the enemy any ammunition. And I wanted to be here, at least some of the time, in case Sarah found us."

Iris gathered Em closer.

"When I looked at your e-mail, I thought: Finding Sarah is our last mission. I want to come clean to the Girls, to the world. I want everyone to know who we are, who I am: Iris Fields."

Her face bloomed in a wide smile, years seemed to fade from her face. "Dearest, I resigned from the Senate."

Em sat up, her expression a mixture of delight and concern. "You know how much I've hated keeping our secret from the Girls, from the kids...oh shit, Iris...from everyone."

"I don't want to die without letting everyone know about our love. And, I want us to get married. It's legal now. I know I should ask you properly, but is it okay if I don't get down on one knee? At this age, I'm not sure I could get back up."

"Okay, but this is my first official marriage proposal. Hit me with some pretty words, Iris."

Iris cleared her throat. Emily Elizabeth Scott, will you be my faithful life partner in times good and bad, joyful and sad? Will you love, honor, and cherish me, as I love, honor, and cherish you, and all your ideals and dreams? Will you be my comfort when I ail, my cushion when I fail? Will you promise to cry with me, laugh with me...stay with me...as long as our old bodies hold out against the storm of life? Will you be my forever lover, forsaking all others? In short, can you love plain old Iris Fields, the girl from the wrong side of the tracks?"

Em brushed her lips against Iris's. "I've always loved Iris Fields from the moment I met you. You were always there, hiding behind Iris Bentonfield."

"I'm done hiding. Em, what do you think of a White House wedding?"

"You're kidding, I hope."

"Nope. Talked to Julia, she's on board. She wants to make a statement to the world."

Em was silent for a moment. She could never get over Iris being on a first-name basis with the president of the United States. The idea of a White House wedding further overwhelmed her.

"I don't know, Iris. You know how shy I am."

Iris chuckled. "Not always, and you walked right into that one. I was thinking something simple...maybe in the Rose Garden. Just the six of us—and the kids, of course."

"And reporters?"

"No more than one or two, I promise."

"A triple wedding?"

"Why not? The Girls have done everything else together."

"Can I wear a wedding gown?"

"Darling, you can wear anything or nothing at all."

"That would be *quite* a sight." Em chuckled, but became serious. "We've kept Char's secret for twenty years. I know the Girls will forgive us about that one. But keeping your wigs and us a secret...that might be unforgiveable."

Iris drew her closer. "I'm betting on the Girls. Em, I'd like to take you back to where I started."

"To Slatterville?"

"Yeah. The town is gone, but the cemetery is still there. You know I bought that property years ago to make sure it was taken care of. It's like an oasis in the middle of a desert.

"I want you by my side when I put flowers on Mr. Newly's grave and my mother's, too. I want to thank Mr. Newly, and I want to tell my mother I've forgiven her. It's not too late, is it? To start fresh, the two of us?"

"No, it's never too late. Iris, about our wedding... Would you wear a white tuxedo?"

"Of course—for you darling, anything."

"Should we have flower girls and ring bearers?"

Iris laughed. "Em, are you making a list? You can't plan a wedding when you haven't given me an answer. It's against cupid's rules."

"I thought you knew my answer."

"I need to hear it."

"Oh, Iris, I do love you and I want to marry you. The answer to your question is yes."

This day in May was like no other day. It wasn't the mild weather that made it special or because the White House Rose Garden was resplendent with blooming tulips, hyacinth and fritillaria—and the roses! The gardeners scratched their heads in wonderment; the roses had opened their buds earlier than usual. President Julia Moorhead was convinced it was because the Girls were getting married!

The Girls were honoring Char by marrying under a traditional Jewish canopy, or *chuppah*— a blue velvet covering suspended on four poles. Family members showed their love and support by gathering around the poles: Sarah, Jonathan, and Charlene, Chris and Hillary, Maggie and David, and Max's nieces and nephews.

The remaining guests were seated on white chairs: four women representing Dykes on Bikes, the mechanics from Max's Garage, a smattering of Congressional representatives, and a special guest for Em. Max had used her superlative detective skills to find Izzy. Izzy sat in the first row, surrounded by her husband, children, and grandchildren. Iris kept her word to Em—there was only one reporter and one TV crew from CNN.

Em got the wedding she had always dreamed of. A string quartet played the Girls' favorite music: "I Only Have Eyes for You," "Dream (When You're Feeling Blue)," "Embraceable You," and "I Wished on the Moon"—music that had accompanied them on their journey of more than forty years.

The wedding procession began with President Julia Moorhead. As officiate, she took her place under the chuppah. Six of Max's great-nieces and nephews followed; they were the flower princes and princesses and ring bearers.

The music changed to the traditional wedding march: Richard Wagner's "Bridal Chorus."

As was the custom of the Girls, they had drawn straws to determine the order of the procession.

Bobbie and Frankie began the procession of brides. They were decked out in new motorcycle leather pants and sequined jackets provided by Dykes on Bikes. They held hands as if there was no tomorrow and didn't bicker once.

Max and Les followed, wearing matching ivory tuxes: Max's with pants, Les's with a long skirt.

Em finally got her white wedding gown, not the one she had dreamed of when she was seventeen, but an ankle-length, white satin wedding gown. Iris wore a custom-made white tux trimmed in satin to match Em's dress.

As they waited to walk down the aisle Em leaned over and whispered to Iris, "Have you noticed Sarah and Jonathan? They're eyeing each other."

Iris whispered back, "Em, I've been watching. They're into a major flirt."

"Do you think...oh, Iris, I would be so happy," said Em as she squeezed Iris's hand.

Iris leaned over to kiss Em. "Yes, I think. Now, it's our turn to walk down the aisle."

Iris and Em walked down the aisle, Em holding her bridal bouquet, a spray of white cymbidium orchids, exactly as she had dreamed of fifty-seven years ago.

President Julia Moorhead addressed the Girls, six women who had lived a lifetime with one overriding wish. Today, it would come true.

"Ladies, it is my great honor to perform your wedding. A few words first. Do you know I had to get a license to perform this ceremony?"

Everyone tittered.

President Moorhead continued, "There are some things the president of the United States can't do. But, as just plain Julia Moorhead, I am honored to grant you the same rights as every other citizen in our great country."

Julia wiped her eyes. "This is a very emotional moment for me. I remember growing up and watching you fight with great dignity for what should have been your right at birth. Now, it is."

Citizen Julia Moorhead began: "Dearly beloveds, we are gathered here today to celebrate one of life's greatest moments, and to give recognition to the worth and beauty of love..."

Em's thoughts drifted back to the night she had dreamed about being with Char. Char had said, "To love once is a blessing. To love twice is a miracle. Now go. Em, your miracle is waiting for you." When she woke from that dream, Iris was there, with a look of love that spoke louder than any words.

For a moment she thought she felt a familiar light caress on her shoulder. She looked...no one was there. *Could it have been?*

Her gaze now returned to Iris—her miracle and the beginning of a new life.

Acknowledgments

A book—either fiction or non-fiction—cannot come to life without those who support the author. To everyone who has helped bring *The Girls* to life, I offer my thanks and deepest appreciation.

I feel fortunate to have Proofed to Perfection [www.proofedto perfection.com] as my editors. Pamela Guerrieri and Kevin Cook continue to guide me toward a greater depth of writing.

Donna Casey [www.digitaldonna.com] created the cover for *The Girls*. She is amazing. A cover docs speak more than a thousand words.

Maureen Cutajar [www.gopublished.com] added her professional and insightful touch by formatting and designing the interior of *The Girls*.

To my family for their unfaltering support as I continue to do the dance called *My Life*.

To the girls from Hamilton High School, the mighty *Athenians Class of W'54*, who continue to gather regularly for luncheons.

To my Facebook friends and groups for their encouragement, insight and laughter.

To Meli Lussier, who so perfectly captured the essence of *The Girls* in her poem *Bashert*, my deepest gratitude and everlasting love.

About the Author

Sunny Alexander is from Los Angeles, and was born into a time when men and women followed their proscribed social roles. In her own case, she married at an early age in the 1950s. Impacted by the social revolution of the 1960s and '70s, Sunny Alexander returned to school and became a licensed marriage and family therapist. Fascinated by the power of dreams, she continued her education and received her doctorate in psychoanalysis.

Now, semi-retired from her private practice, she devotes her spare time to writing novels dealing with social issues.

The Girls was born from her passionate belief in equality, and in her dream that, one day soon, the right to marry will include everyone living in the United States of America.

She is currently writing the sequel to *Flowers from Iraq: The Storyteller and the Healer,* to be entitled *God Laughs.*

Sunny Alexander can be contacted through her website: www.sunnyalexander.com

Reading Guide
Questions and Discussion for *The Girls*

Please be aware that this discussion guide may contain spoilers!

1. The Prologue tells the story of Harry and Ethel Scott, and Sam and Marion Grant, who grew up during the Great Depression and then experienced the trauma of World War II. How do you think their experiences changed them and ultimately impacted Emily and Mitchell?

2. The first chapter begins with the Senate passage of the Freedom to Marry Act. What are your thoughts about this milestone becoming a reality?

3. There were three main themes expressed in *The Girls*:

    a. We are all on a journey through life. There are forks in the road and we make choices that can lead us to our destiny. Which character's journey resonated the most with you?

    b. The meaning of life and death. When faced with her own passing, Char reflects upon the meaning of life and death. Was this thought provoking for you?

    c. Em's definition around the concept of closets. *Being gay is not the only closet. So many closets in life, as she had discovered over the years.* Why do you think we create these closets?

    d. Did you discover any other themes with *The Girls*?

4. At the end, Emily was able to forgive Mitchell for abusing her. Were you able to have any empathy for Mitchell?

5. *The Girls* are seven individuals who, at times, melded into one psyche. What did you think about the Girls moving from their positive point of view on life to planning a murder?

6. Was there any one character that stood out for you? If so, why?

7. How did you view the interaction between Treat/Sarah and Em?

Made in the USA
Columbia, SC
15 July 2018